RULE OF EVIDENCE

JAG IN SPACE

RULE OF EVIDENCE

JACK CAMPBELL

WRITING AS JOHN G. HEMRY

TITAN BOOKS

JAG IN SPACE: RULE OF EVIDENCE
Print edition ISBN: 9780857689429
E-book edition ISBN: 9780857689610

Published by Titan Books
A division of Titan Publishing Group Ltd
144 Southwark St, London SE1 0UP

First edition: March 2012
10 9 8 7 6 5 4 3 2 1

This is a work of fiction. Names, characters, places and incidents either are the products of the author's imagination or are used fictitiously, and any resemblance to actual persons, living or dead, business establishments, events, or locales is entirely coincidental. The publisher does not have any control over and does not assume any responsibility for author or third-party websites or their content.

The right of John G. Hemry to be identified as the author of this work has been asserted by him in accordance with the Copyright, Designs and Patents Act of 1988.

Visit our website: **www.titanbooks.com**

What did you think of this book? We love to hear from our readers. Please email us at: readerfeedback@titanemail.com, or write to us at the above address.

To receive advance information, news, competitions, and exclusive offers online, please sign up for the Titan newsletter on our website: **www.titanbooks.com**

A CIP catalogue record for this title is available from the British Library.

Printed and bound in Great Britain by CPI Group UK Ltd.

To the Reverend Dr. Clayton O. Hughes,
a man who asked for no rewards
but only for the ability to serve others.
The embodiment of love and kindness,
it's easy to believe he is now among those
greeting and offering the Grand Tour
to new arrivals in Heaven.

For S,
as always.

"Evidence, including documents or physical evidence, which is under the control of the government and which is relevant to the investigation... shall be produced if reasonably available."

RULE 405(G)(1)(B)

RULES FOR COURTS-MARTIAL
MANUAL FOR COURTS-MARTIAL, UNITED STATES

1

"Every time I look at an intelligence report, it seems we're edging closer to war." Lieutenant Junior Grade Paul Sinclair leaned back and away from the Combat Information Center officer's console, gazing somberly at the intelligence report displayed there.

"I thought young US Navy officers like yourself looked forward to combat, Mr. Sinclair." Chief Imari grinned from where she sat at her own console.

Paul twisted one side of his mouth in a half-smile. "Not me, chief. I'll do it if and when I have to, but I won't be looking forward to it."

Imari nodded. "It's not a pretty business, sir. Not like the games we play on these." She waved at the consoles cluttering Combat. "Realistic combat simulations, hell. I tell you, sir, no simulation of combat is realistic unless you're sweating like a pig and scared to death while you're running it."

"Thanks for cheering me up, chief. But you know as well as I do that the simulations can only duplicate the physics of fighting in space. I depend on you to keep our happy sailors sweating and scared."

Imari grinned again. "Only if they screw up, sir."

Paul glanced toward one of the bulkheads, thinking of the endless dark which lay beyond the outer hull of the USS *Michaelson*. "There's a huge volume of space in the solar system, chief. But the South Asian Alliance keeps demanding what it calls its 'fair share' of that space. What the hell is 'fair' for them or anybody else?"

"Beats me, sir. The US Navy's never been big on 'fair,' so I don't know much about it. We're not the only one's the SASALs are pushing against, though."

Paul nodded, looking back at the intelligence report. "No, we're not. The SASAL pressure to expand back on Earth is pushing the Europeans toward us. It looks like we'll even have some joint maneuvers soon. That'd be different, operating with foreign warships in space. Have you ever worked with any, chief?"

Chief Imari shrugged. "Just a couple, a few years ago. Some kind of Brotherhood of Humanity in Space crap to show everyone we were all happy campers up here together." She paused, screwing up her face in thought. "Let's see. There was a South African ship, and a Japanese, and a Brit. I don't remember any of 'em doing anything stupid."

Paul smiled. That last statement qualified as praise from Chief Imari. "Back on Earth the Royal Navy has a good reputation."

"Oh, they're real good, sir. Never get in a drinking contest with 'em, though. Not if you're smart. They'll drink you three sheets to the wind and then convince you to play one of their crazy Brit games like naked zero-gravity rugby."

Paul felt his eyebrows rising. "Naked zero-gravity rugby?"

"Trust me, sir, it ain't as fun as it sounds. I hurt for a couple of weeks afterwards, and I was one of the lucky ones."

"I'll remember that, chief." Paul reached over and closed out the intelligence report. *Will we end up shooting at someone in earnest before this is all over?* It'd been a year and a half since the *Michaelson*'s former commanding officer had mistakenly ordered the destruction of a SASAL research ship, and Paul had never been able to shake the memory of the bodies he'd seen onboard the wreck afterward. *Maybe we'll have to destroy another ship, or maybe we'll take damage.* He looked around Combat, a compartment he thought of as his after several months as Combat Information Center officer, and imagined it riddled with holes from enemy lasers and particle beams, open to the vacuum of space, the bodies of his sailors drifting slack in their harnesses.

Chief Imari followed Paul's gaze, and as if reading his thoughts smiled reassuringly. "Don't you worry, Mr. Sinclair. If it comes to that, we'll kick butt. Ain't nobody gonna take down the *Mike*."

Paul grinned. "Not with the crew we've got." Then he laughed. "That sounds like something from a bad movie."

The chief cocked an eyebrow at him. "Sir, I sorta know what you mean. But it's important to say it and mean it. Or sound like you mean it, anyway. When the crew hears it, they believe in themselves a little more. Yeah, it's corny and macho and all sorts of other stuff, but you've got to tell the crew you believe in them. They want to hear it."

Paul nodded slowly. "It helps them believe in themselves?"

"I guess you could say that. It's part of being an officer, Mr. Sinclair. The crew looks to you for that kind of stuff."

Paul nodded again. *Now, that's a funny responsibility. I'm younger than most of the sailors in my division, and a whole lot less experienced in almost every way, but they look to me for guidance. For me to say I think they can kick butt when*

11

needed. Funny. But I'm sure Chief Imari knows what she's talking about. That's funny, too. I'm looking to her for some guidance while she's looking to me for other guidance. "I'll remember that, chief. For what it's worth, I do have a lot of confidence in the crew, and in the division. I'll make sure I express that every once in a while."

Imari grinned at him. "Don't go overboard, sir. Just a little. Otherwise it'll make it harder for me to tell 'em how screwed up they are."

"Got it." Paul checked the time. "As far as preparing for combat goes, it probably wouldn't hurt if I managed to show up for religious services every once in a while."

"Can't hurt and it might help, sir. You never know."

"Later, chief." Paul walked out of Combat, threading through the narrow hatch with the ease of long practice. He checked the time again, then shrugged. He'd spent too much time reviewing the intelligence summaries. No sense in trying to make Sunday morning worship services now. Instead, he started to head for the small compartment grandly labeled the officers' wardroom, but halted after a couple of steps and went down another passageway.

Being tied up at Franklin Naval Station always felt different than being underway. Part of it was the constant sensation of gravity imposed by Franklin's majestic rotation. But a bigger part, to Paul, was the nights and weekends when most of the crew went off the ship. Underway, it seemed the narrow passages and low overheads of the *Michaelson* were always crowded with sailors trying to dodge each other and all the wiring, equipment and controls almost covering every bulkhead and overhead. In port, on a slow Sunday morning, the *Michaelson* felt almost deserted by comparison.

Paul went through the ship, compartment after compartment, able after more than a year and a half onboard to almost subconsciously evaluate the status of everything he saw from the knife edges of the airtight hatches to the inspection labels on the emergency survival suit lockers. Near the bow, where the hull tapered to a blunt cone, he absentmindedly tapped a spot on the forwardmost bulkhead where the metal had been worn smooth by countless fingers following the same ritual.

When Paul reached the hatch leading into Forward Engineering, he paused, listening for a moment, then walked steadily in and through the compartment, trying to focus on important details even though his ears kept straining for any untoward sounds until he was done and back out the hatch. *That blasted compartment still spooks me. It shouldn't, but it does. And there's no way I'm admitting that to anybody.*

Then back and forth, working aft, until he reached the "end of the world," the last bulkhead, and repeated the tap he'd given at the forwardmost bulkhead. *Why do we do that, anyway? Funny ritual or superstition or whatever. It's like we're checking to make sure the last thing between us and empty space is really there. Or reassuring ourselves that those last barriers aren't ready to implode. Well, whatever the reason, like Chief Imari says, it can't hurt.*

A bit worn from the tour of the *Michaelson*, Paul finally made his way to the officers' wardroom. Inside the small compartment with the grand name, Lieutenant Sindh sat at the table sipping a drink labeled "chai—decaf—non-dairy—official issue—zero g." She looked up as Paul entered, waving a small greeting. "You look a little tired."

"Just took a tour of the ship." As he headed for the coffee, Paul flipped a half-salute toward Lieutenant Sindh. "I have the pleasure to report to the command duty officer that the ship is all secure, ma'am."

Sindh solemnly returned the salute. "Thank you, Mr. Sinclair. Paul, you don't have to check every compartment on the ship multiple times every duty day." Paul busied himself with the coffee to avoid answering. "It happened once. It wasn't your fault. I appreciate your thoroughness, but also fear you're driven by guilt you shouldn't carry."

Paul shrugged, still not looking her way. *That's easy for her to say. She wasn't on duty when that fire started. She wasn't on duty when Chief Asher died. And she didn't get implicated as part of the cause in the initial investigation.* The fact that the investigation's conclusions had been reached by his girlfriend's father still rankled even though those conclusions had been subsequently disproved. However, a friend like Sonya Sindh deserved some consideration for her concern. "It's okay. Really."

"There's much you've never shared about how that incident affected you, Paul. I'm a lay minister. We can talk."

Paul grinned at her. "Not my religion, Sonya. But thanks, anyway. For what it's worth, I've talked it over with Jen."

"Ah. That's worth something." Sindh smiled. "But both you and the inexhaustible Lieutenant Jen Shen are very close to the problem. A third party's advice might be of help."

"I've also talked it over with Commander Herdez a few times."

Sindh's eyebrows shot up. "Our former Executive Officer From Hell as trauma counselor? I assume our old XO recommended hard work at least twenty hours every day as the best means to recover from your experience?"

This time, Paul laughed. "I think she actually recommended at least *twenty-two* hours a day of hard work. Minimum."

Sindh's smile widened. "It's good to hear she's not slacking off while on shore duty. Everyone else should suffer as we did. Have you seen this?" she asked, indicating her data pad's screen.

Paul came closer to peer at the information. "Orders for someone?" He read through the standard format, looking for the key pieces of information. *Lieutenant Sonya Sindh... when directed detach from USS* Michaelson *(CLE(S)-3), proceed to Joint Forces Training Command, Norfolk, Virginia... upon arrival report Commanding Officer for duty.* "Oh. You're leaving."

"In about a month. Aren't you happy for me?"

Paul settled into the nearest chair, pushing aside the straps officers used to fasten themselves into their seats while the *Michaelson* was underway and no longer benefiting from Franklin's induced gravity. "I am. But you're a friend and a good officer, so I hate to see you go."

She smiled. "If you really thought of me as a friend you'd be thrilled I was heading for nice, relaxing shore duty. Earthside shore duty! Blue sky! Atmosphere! Constant gravity!"

"Insects. Bad weather. Pollen."

"Real food."

"That's a big one. Okay, I'm happy for you. But, you know, it's hard to see people leave the ship. We're kind of a—"

"Please don't say 'family.'" It was Sindh's turn to shrug. "Officers come, officers go. That's the Navy. We're on our third captain since you reported aboard, and our second executive officer."

"Yeah, but I don't work directly with the CO and XO like I do with you or the other junior officers."

"Look at it this way. Someday our fellow junior officer and dear friend Sam Yarrow will also leave. Isn't that nice?"

Paul laughed. "I don't know what I'll do when I don't have to worry about Smilin' Sam sliding a knife into my back."

"I'm sure you'll find plenty of things to fill your time," Sindh observed dryly.

Another laugh. "Oh, yeah. And if I don't, I'm sure Garcia will help."

Sindh took another drink, then made a face. "I'll also be able to get real chai again Earthside, instead of whatever this stuff is that they feed us. I wonder what real coffee will taste like after years of Navy coffee? But I digress. Paul, the job of a department head is to keep junior officers gainfully employed. Commander Garcia just happens to be a little bit incendiary in his approach to that."

"Incendiary? Hell, Sonya, there's been times I was sure he was going to strangle me for making him look bad because I'd screwed something up. And that's just when I screw up in my primary job as CIC officer. Garcia hates my collateral duty with a passion."

"Duty?" Sindh looked up questioningly. "You have more than one collateral duty."

"Yeah, but the one that torques Garcia off is the legal officer job. You know that. He hates the time I have to spend on it and he hates that I go directly to the captain or XO for stuff related to ship legal matters."

"If you'd manage to stay away from courts-martial for a few months at a stretch it wouldn't be such a burden and Garcia wouldn't be so sensitive about it." Sindh grinned again.

Paul smiled back. "It's been six months since the last court-martial. I'm not planning on getting involved in any more."

"You didn't *plan* on getting involved in the first two. Or did you? I ought to ask Jen. She'll know the truth. And, speaking of Jen, is she coming over tonight?"

Paul's smile turned rueful. "No. Jen's got duty, too. The *Maury*'s gone to three sections, so Jen's got duty every third day."

"Three sections? That's not pleasant. What happened?"

"They're trying to get the *Sorry Maury* working after that yard period. The modifications to engineering are driving Jen nuts. She's working overtime because of them."

"Paul, we're space warfare officers. We always work overtime." Sindh let out a sigh. "I was hoping Jen could bring some carry-out onboard so we wouldn't have to eat wardroom food tonight. Not that carry-out on the station is that great, but it's better than rations."

"Nope. I guess we're stuck with Navy cuisine."

Lieutenant Sindh paused in thought, then tapped her data unit. "Chief Imari. Do you have a meal run planned? I expected as much. Please contact Mr. Sinclair and myself prior to the run so we can place orders as well. Thank you." She settled back with a satisfied smile. "When in doubt, always check with the chiefs. They may've already solved your problem."

Paul rose and bowed toward her. "Thank you, master. I still have much to learn."

Sindh smiled and made a brief bow back. "Much more than you realize, Grasshopper."

About twelve hours later, Paul rolled out of his bunk, taking care to keep his body low so he wouldn't hit any of the pipes and ducting positioned just above his sleeping area. Yawning as he pulled on his uniform, Paul gave the digits on his watch a sour look. *Half an hour until midnight, and I'm getting up to spend four hours standing watch. The glamorous life of a naval officer.* Checking his appearance to make sure he looked fit to stand watch, Paul stumbled to the quarterdeck.

Petty Officer First Class Fontanelli was rubbing his eyes as Paul came up. "Sir, I don't mind telling you that you're a sight for sore eyes."

"Yeah. But you get to rest yours now and I don't. What's up?"

Fontanelli ran through the status of the ship, telling Paul nothing he didn't already know, advised that Captain Hayes and the ship's current executive officer, Commander Kwan, had both returned to the ship after taps, and closed his turnover with a warning to Paul that there'd been Franklin Station personnel conducting unannounced security checks of quarterdeck watches. Paul listened through it all, then straightened and raised his right hand, touching his brow in a casual salute. "Okay. I got it."

The petty officer returned the gesture. "I stand relieved." Fontanelli hoisted the heavy, old-fashioned brass telescope called a long glass which signified his status as officer of the deck inport and passed it to Paul. "Have fun, sir."

"Thanks." Paul put down the long glass and leaned on the watch desk as the petty officer of the watch finished turning over with his relief.

"Mr. Sinclair, I have the watch." The third class petty officer saluted Paul with the same kind of weary salute Paul had used earlier. "Any special instructions, sir?"

"Yeah, if I start to fall asleep, kick me."

The petty officer grinned. "Yes, sir. It'll be a pleasure."

About four long and essentially uneventful hours later, the hatch onto the quarterdeck opened and Chief Imari stepped out, yawning. "Have a fun mid-watch, sir?"

"They're always fun, chief."

"Oh, yes, sir. Anything happen?"

"Nope."

"Of course, if something did happen, we'd be a lot unhappier than we are with nothing happening," Chief Imari observed.

Paul snorted and nodded. "Yeah, 'cause anything that happens at

O-dark-thirty is bound to be bad." He briefed the chief just as he'd been briefed four hours before, exchanged salutes as Chief Imari relieved him, then walked slowly back to his stateroom and peered at the time. Zero four hundred. Two hours until reveille, when he and the rest of the crew would have to officially wake up, and when the lighting on the *Michaelson* and Franklin Station would brighten for the artificial day. Paul shrugged out of his uniform and pulled himself up into his bunk, ducking and rolling as he did so to avoid hitting the obstacles on the overhead.

It seemed only moments later that the piercing sound of a bosun's pipe wailed through the ship, followed by the announcement made every morning. "Reveille, reveille. All hands turn to and trice up."

One of Paul's four roommates in the starboard ensign locker staggered up and hit the stateroom lights. Three groans from those still in their bunks answered the brightness. Paul kept his eyes closed for a moment, trying to extend his sleep a few precious seconds longer. *Trice up. Why do they keep telling the crew to trice up? That's what you do with hammocks. The crew doesn't sleep in hammocks. Crews haven't slept in hammocks for who knows how long. Centuries? But if they ever sleep in them again, they'll know now is when they're supposed to trice those suckers up.*

"Hey, Paul!"

Paul kept his eyes closed. "Yeah, Sam." Lieutenant Junior Grade Yarrow, nicknamed Smilin' Sam by his fellow junior officers in recognition of his untrustworthy nature and false front of camaraderie, sounded unhappy, a fact which bothered Paul not at all given the many times Yarrow had caused problems for Paul.

"Did the guys in my division who had duty yesterday get their spaces cleaned up like I told them?"

"I don't know, Sam. Why don't you ask *them*?"

"You had duty! You should know."

"Sam, my duty responsibilities don't include supervising your division's internal tasking."

"Lousy attitude, Sinclair. Thanks for nothing." The hatch opened, then slammed shut.

Paul sighed, finally opened his eyes and rolled out of his bunk again, landing on the deck and groping for his uniform once more.

Ensign Jack Abacha stared after Yarrow, then at Paul.

Paul shook his head. "Don't worry about it, Jack. Once you've been screwed over by Sam as much as the rest of us have, you won't worry in the slightest about hurting his feelings." Abacha nodded, his uncertainty obvious. *Was it only eighteen months ago that I reported aboard the* Merry Mike *and was exactly like Jack Abacha? Overwhelmed and stunned by everything, wondering what I'd gotten myself into. Hell, I still haven't figured out what I've gotten myself into.* "Really, Jack. It's okay. Don't let Sam dump any of his work on you. He'll try to lay a guilt trip on you, but don't fall for it. Sam'll still try to take credit for whatever you did right and blame you for anything he does wrong."

"Okay. Thanks." Abacha hesitated. "Do I have to tell him off like that?"

Paul gave the new ensign an encouraging smile. *He only reported aboard two days ago. Two days after I joined the ship I still couldn't find my way around.* "Naw. When you realize he's trying to do it, tell him that you're too busy to talk and run off. He won't like it, but we're all usually too busy to talk, so Sam won't be able to tell if you're blowing him off." *Carl Meadows used to give me that kind of advice before he was transferred off the ship. I wonder how Carl's doing in his tour at the Pentagon?*

Zero seven hundred. Paul walked into Combat, where the rest of the officers from the Operations Department had already gathered for officers' call. Commander Garcia looked up from his data unit and scowled at Paul. *Oh, great. Now what'd I do?*

"Nice to see you made it, Sinclair."

"Sorry, sir. The XO—"

"I didn't ask for an excuse."

Paul took up position near the other officers. Ensign Taylor, the electronic materials officer, gave Paul a sardonic wink. Taylor was a mustang, an officer who'd worked her way up through the enlisted ranks to officer status, and as a result knew her job and the Navy so well she could run rings around much more senior officers. Kris Denaldo, like Paul a lieutenant junior grade and now serving as the *Michaelson*'s communications officer, glanced toward Garcia and rolled her eyes meaningfully. Paul nodded to both of them. *And so another Monday in the glamorous Space Navy begins. How come in the movies Captain Hardy Stud of the* Starship Spurious *never has Mondays?*

Garcia glowered at the three officers. Paul and Kris looked back with carefully neutral expressions, while Taylor returned a respectful but unmistakably not-intimidated gaze. "There's been a schedule change. Instead of spending the next two weeks in restricted availability to catch up on equipment maintenance, we have one week. The week after that, we're going out on as-yet-unspecified operations."

Paul barely managed to keep his exasperation from showing. Kris made notes on her data pad and shook her head.

Taylor raised both her hands heavenward. "Sir, just how am I supposed to get two weeks of work out of one week? We've got gear that's overdue for upkeep now."

Garcia focused directly on Taylor and intensified his glower. "You prioritize and you work as hard as you have to. These ops next week are high-priority and high-interest. That's all I can say right now, but saying we can't get underway for them is *not* an option."

Taylor shrugged as if unaware of Garcia's expression. "We'll be ready to get underway, but everything's not gonna get done. I'll shoot you my prioritized list and if there's anything that hasta be moved up on it, you tell me, sir."

"Fine."

Paul surreptitiously glanced from Garcia to Ensign Taylor. Odds were nobody but Taylor really knew for sure how important each item on that list was, and odds were Garcia knew that. *Unfortunately, Garcia does know a lot about all the items on* my *division's work list.*

"Do either of you two have any comments?" Garcia eyed Paul and Kris, but both had learned enough by now not to say a word. "There's an all-officers meeting in the wardroom at ten hundred."

"Sir?" Kris Denaldo looked like she'd instantly regretted blurting out the word.

"What?"

"Uh, sir, about a third of the wardroom is sealed off today while they work on gear on the other side of one of the bulkheads."

"So?"

"It'll be very hard to squeeze all of us into the remaining space, sir."

"What's the matter, Denaldo? Putting on weight?" Garcia grinned humorlessly. "The meeting's in the wardroom. Period."

Denaldo flushed but kept her voice level. "Yes, sir."

"Sinclair."

Paul braced himself mentally, shifting his stance slightly as if he were preparing for actual physical attack. "Yes, sir."

"Where's that operational events summary? It was due yesterday."

"I'll have it to you before the meeting in the wardroom, sir."

"It was due *yesterday*."

Paul nodded, even though he felt like snarling back at Garcia. "Yes, sir." An excuse wouldn't do any good. In fact, it'd be certain to just make Garcia madder. Not trying to make excuses was one thing the Naval Academy had taught him that had proven important in the fleet.

Garcia wasn't calmed by Paul's reply. "The XO already asked me where it was *this morning*."

"Yes, sir."

"Is anything else going to be late, Mr. Sinclair?"

"No, sir."

"It better not be. Get to work. I won't tolerate any excuses for not having every important piece of equipment on this ship ready to go before we get underway next week." Garcia spun on one foot, moving away with his habitually angry stomp.

After Garcia had cleared Combat, Paul glanced over at Taylor. "Akesha, is there any piece of equipment on this ship that isn't important?"

Taylor pretended to consider Paul's question. "Can't think of any. But I'm sure as hell going to talk to the snipes in engineering about making sure that little dingus that heats up the coffee containers in the wardroom is working. As far as I'm concerned, that's the most important thing on this ship. See you kids later."

Denaldo stared after Taylor's retreating back. "God help the Supply Department if this ship ever runs out of coffee."

Paul shook his head, laughing. "No worry. Commander Sykes wouldn't survive without coffee, either, so no way he's going to let us get underway without enough caffeine to float a cruiser back on Earth."

"Yeah."

"You okay, Kris?"

"I'm pissed off. It's Monday. I'm working for an ass. How are you?"

"The same. And I had the mid-watch last night."

"You win."

Five minutes later Paul stood before the enlisted sailors in his division, Chief Imari taking notes from Paul's words just as he'd earlier taken notes from Garcia's. *Not very efficient, I guess. But redundancy beats efficiency when lives depend on it. Might as well get the worst over with first.* "Ladies and gentlemen, we'll be getting underway in one week." He paused to let it sink in. "Our orders are to get all necessary maintenance carried out before then."

A chorus of groans erupted. "There goes the whole damn weekend," someone in the back said.

Chief Imari sighed. "Okay, sir."

The voice in the back came again. "It ain't all gonna get done!"

Imari turned slightly. "Fastow, see me after morning quarters." The grumbling from the other sailors faded away. She faced Paul again. "What else, sir?"

Paul cleared his throat, grateful that the chief had backed him up. "We haven't been told what we'll be doing when we get underway, but that it's something high-priority."

"We going to war?" another voice asked, this time in a tone that was hushed instead of angry.

"I don't know." Paul looked at the faces before him. All of them looked back with varying expressions, some worried, some curious, some eager as if they were heading for a softball game. "I've got a meeting at ten hundred. I'll let the chief know if I find out anything I can tell you." He caught a brief flash of disapproval on Imari's face.

A few minutes later Paul wrapped up his instructions for the day. "That's it. Chief, can I see you for a minute?"

"Sure, sir." Imari gave the sailors a hard look. "You all be waiting here when I get back."

Paul led the way out into the passageway. "Chief, I noticed you seemed a little unhappy in there at one point."

Imari screwed up her face. "Yes, sir. Uh, telling the division about that meeting of yours at ten hundred. I wouldn't have done that, Mr. Sinclair. Now the guys are gonna be expecting to hear something this morning. They're gonna be pestering me about it, and they're gonna be thinking and talking about what you might tell them instead of concentrating on their work, and we've got a lot of work to do and not much time to do it in. If you do hear something and can't tell them, they're gonna be even more wound up."

Well, hell. Paul felt himself getting angry at the chief and forced himself to backtrack. *And she's right about all of it. Dammit.* "Sorry, chief. That didn't occur to me."

"You don't have to apologize to me, Mr. Sinclair. But you asked and I told you."

"And I appreciate that, chief."

Chief Imari hesitated. "Sir, you do know all that work *ain't* gonna get done."

"We need to try, chief."

"Yes, sir. But it's either do it all half-assed or do a bit more than half of it right."

Paul closed his eyes while he thought. *Let's see. If I report to Garcia that maybe half of the planned maintenance hasn't been done, he's going to go into screamer mode on me. I don't want that. But if I say I got it all done and some of the "fixed" stuff doesn't work when we need it while we're on these high-priority ops, then Garcia, the XO and the captain will all be after my hide. Maybe nothing'd break, though. Then I'd be in the clear and my sailors would have time to fix everything right. Yeah, right. When would I be sure they could do that? And if something doesn't work that I said had been fixed... people remember stuff like that.*

Oh, great. I'm thinking of this all in terms of covering my butt. Hey, LTJG Sinclair, you jerk, maybe it oughta be about getting the job done? So what should I... hell, I ought to do what Taylor said she'd do. He opened his eyes. "Chief, put together a priority list for me. What we intend doing in what order given that we know we're getting underway in a week." *Do I send a copy of the list to Garcia? He'll be sure to raise hell and rearrange the list just for the sake of asserting authority. But if he signs off on that list, he'll have to admit it to the captain. I think. At least I'll have proof I told Garcia about it all.*

Imari nodded. "Okay, sir. I'll have it to you as soon as I can."

"Thanks, chief." Paul spent the next two hours sweating over the operational events summary. He knew from painful experience that every officer superior to him in the chain of command was certain to remember any event he might neglect to include, but he also was required to only include "significant" events in the summary. *No matter what I put in, Garcia or the XO is going to say I didn't put in something significant or did put in something insignificant. Okay. Fine.* Paul punched the command to send the report to his department head. *If I'm going to lose no matter what, why waste any more time on it? It's as good as I can make it.*

Paul glanced at the time. Enough remained before ten hundred for him to get into the wardroom and suck down some coffee to help stay awake through the meeting. Hopefully the subject would be interesting, but even interesting subjects could be sleep-inducing when presented in a dull way in small, warm compartments.

"Commander Sykes." Paul greeted the supply officer, who was seated in his usual place, drinking coffee.

"Good morning, young Sinclair. Bright and early this morning, I see."

Paul shook his head. "Just early, Suppo. It's already been a long day."

"Ah." Sykes leaned back a little more and took a slow drink. "The travails of line officers. I feel for you. Truly."

"Yeah." Paul grinned as he got his own coffee. He'd learned from experience that Sykes only pretended to be lazing about the wardroom, and only pretended to revel in his status as a limited-duty officer without the command and combat responsibilities of line officers like Paul. *At least, I think he's only pretending to revel in it.* "Any idea what the meeting's about, Suppo?"

"How would I be aware of the meeting's subject?"

Paul sat down. "Because you know everything important that goes on so you never get caught unable to meet the ship's supply needs."

Sykes looked horrified. "You've discovered my secret. Now, of course, you must die. Sorry about that."

"How are you going to do it? Are you going to serve some more of that Syrian beef stew for dinner?"

"The captain's forbidden me to serve any more of that particular item, you insolent young pup. However, I do know where I can get some artificial shark steaks."

Paul swallowed and gave Sykes a curious look. "Artificial shark steaks?"

"Yes. The real article, the sharks that is, are rare enough that

27

what steaks actually exist are far too expensive for the Navy to serve its wretched masses, so instead we have the joy of receiving artificial shark. Made from pure vat-cultured protein and assorted artificial flavors which I am assured produce a result at least superficially similar to the real article. In taste, at least. I understand the toughness of the artificial shark steaks is legendary."

"You make it sound so yummy." Paul only partially faked a shudder. "I abjectly apologize, Commander Sykes, sir. Your secret is safe with me. Now, do you have an idea what this meeting is about?"

Sykes grinned. "Matters dark and devious. I can say no more."

Kris Denaldo entered. "I'm going to try to get a corner to wedge myself into before everyone else tries to pack in here." She glared at Paul. "And if I hear any comments from you like I did from Garcia..."

"Kris, I'm not that rude. Or stupid."

"I hope not." She grabbed something to drink and chose a corner, bracing herself in the angle where two bulkheads met.

Ensign Taylor came in next and sat next to Commander Sykes without any regard for the technically more senior junior officers. "Hey, Paul, Chief Imari got with me about that priority list of yours." Taylor grinned. "Where'd you get a good idea like that?"

"I've learned to follow the example of mustang ensigns. You learn things that way."

"Uh-oh. Do that while I'm on liberty and you'll learn a few things you probably never imagined."

Paul felt his face warming and knew he was blushing from the way Taylor laughed. Fortunately, more officers started arriving and diverted Paul from having to come up with a response to Taylor's gibe.

As Kris Denaldo had predicted, the number of officers quickly exceeded the capacity of the wardroom. The *Michaelson*'s wardroom never felt like a large space, even when only a few officers were present. With one-third of the compartment blocked off and every officer on the *Michaelson* crammed in, Paul wondered whether claustrophobia or lack of oxygen posed the greatest hazard. The department heads pushed their way in last, followed by the ship's executive officer, Commander Kwan. Kwan glowered at the small space remaining by the hatch. "Move back and make more room up here!"

The grumbling from the junior officers was just low enough that Kwan couldn't make out the words. Ensign Taylor called out loudly, "Okay, people. Suck it up! Non-mustang ensigns onto the table!" The junior officers loudly exhaled and tried to push closer together as the ensigns climbed onto the table.

Paul found himself wedged next to the table, his head almost touching the thigh of Ensign Gabriel. Gabriel looked down and grinned at him. *I'm glad she's enjoying this. Too bad it's not Jen up there. No. I better not even start thinking about that.*

"Attention on deck!"

At the XO's command, the officers straightened to attention as Captain Hayes entered the compartment, grinned lopsidedly at the crowded conditions, and took his seat at the only chair left unoccupied. "Carry on. Ops, let's get this done."

Commander Garcia, standing near the large display screen mounted on one bulkhead, pushed one arm upward past the nearest bodies so he could point to the information which flashed into existence there. "The rumors you all may've been hearing are correct. When we get underway next Monday we'll be conducting a multi-national maneuvering exercise involving two US warships, the *Michaelson* and the *Maury,* and three foreign warships. They'll be a British ship, the *Lord Nelson*, a Franco-German ship, the *Alsace*, and a Russian Federation ship, the *Pyotr Veleki*." Garcia stumbled on the pronunciation of the Russian craft, glared at no one in particular, and stabbed one finger toward the name. "The *Peter the Great*. The *Michaelson* will be the flagship."

Captain Hayes raised one hand. "Correction. The *Michaelson* will be on-scene coordinator. There is no flagship. The foreign warships will *not* be under our command."

Paul strained to hear as the other officers around him murmured in reaction to the captain's statement. *We could conduct this same briefing with everyone in their own staterooms linked into a virtual conference and we'd all be able to hear everything and see everything and be halfway comfortable so we could concentrate on it. But, no. We all have to pack in here and suffocate and wonder who the hell didn't get a chance to shower lately. Because this is the Navy and this is how John Paul Jones held meetings.*

Lieutenant Kilgary, the main propulsion assistant, tried to shove her own arm up, but failing at that just yelled out her question. "Then who will be in command, sir?"

"Nobody." Another surge of murmurs. Captain Hayes gave the assembled officers a stern look. "This is diplomacy, ladies and gentlemen. Our allies—" Hayes broke off as Commander Garcia cleared his throat loudly. "Correction, our fellow 'participants' in the exercise want to send a message to the SASALs, but not too strong a message, and none of them want to make it look like they're placing their space combatant forces under US command or control. We're all going to waltz around in the same general area to let the SASALs know we could work together if we really wanted to. That's it. Just a friendly get-together."

Muffled but derisive snorts sounded throughout the wardroom. Commander Kwan glared around as if he had a chance of identifying individual offenders. "Belay that."

Garcia's glare matched that of the XO. "Every maneuver by the warships involved will be according to the preplanned exercise time line. Standard maneuvering interval between ships will be two hundred kilometers. Closest point of approach between ships is to be no less than one hundred kilometers at all times. Ship collision avoidance systems will be programmed to warn of collision if any CPA goes below fifty kilometers."

Paul would've shrugged if he'd had the space for it. With the individual spacecraft traveling at speeds measured in kilometers per second, fifty kilometers seemed a reasonable distance to really start sweating.

"Sir." Lieutenant Junior Grade Yarrow indicated the display screen. "With a standard interval of two hundred kilometers, the formation will be spread across a thousand kilometers."

"Hey, he's learned to add," a barely audible voice whispered.

Yarrow flushed, then flushed a deeper shade as Garcia focused his glare upon him. "We're only to be strung out in a line when the exercise starts. Review the plan, Mr. Yarrow." On the screen behind Garcia, representations of various formations popped into view as another round of murmurs sprung up.

Paul stared at the geometric shapes of the formations the warships were to assume. One resembled a pentagon with a warship at each corner, another seemed to be a sphere with the ships spaced evenly around it, and yet another a forward-tilted oblong shape.

Captain Hayes raised his hand again. "Okay, people. I know. It looks goofy. Let's face it, fleet maneuvers haven't been the norm up here. Ship combats are one-on-one and assuming neat formations like this would just make it a lot easier for someone to detect us and target us. But this isn't about effective war-fighting tactics. It's about sending a message. Professional space officers like ourselves will know this stuff is nonsense. But politicians and the general public will be impressed. That's the bottom line. It's going to be a little odd working with foreign spacecraft like this. It's a big solar system and it just hasn't happened much because no one really wanted it. Now they do."

Commander Sykes, until now silent somewhere in the back, spoke out clearly. "Sort of."

Hayes grinned as laughter erupted. "Right, Suppo. Sort of. Let's put on a good show, keep it safe, and let the SASALs know screwing around with us up here would be a bad idea."

More murmurs, this time of agreement. Paul saw Sonya Sindh and they locked eyes for a moment, sharing an unspoken understanding. *She remembers the last time the SASALs screwed with the* Michaelson. *She was officer of the deck when Captain Wakeman gave orders to fire on that unarmed SASAL ship that he thought was attacking us. This exercising together stuff to send a message might work, if everybody involved deals with it rationally. But we're all human, so nothing's certain.*

Captain Hayes pried the hatch open to leave. Commander Kwan bellowed out "attention on deck" again in a voice well suited to a parade ground but which echoed painfully inside the small compartment. Paul and the other officers once again did their best to straighten to attention as the captain left. Instead of releasing them from attention immediately, Kwan favored the group with a long, stern look. "Remember what the captain said. We'll be operating with foreign warships. I want the *Michaelson* to be the most impressive ship out there. Carry on." Kwan struggled out the hatch as well.

With two fewer bodies in the compartment Paul found he could breath easier. Most of the department heads, talking softly among themselves, headed out next, then the other officers began following. Paul took a moment to stretch in place before moving, then looked to where the ensigns, the most junior officers on the ship, were still standing on the table. "Dismissed," he echoed Kwan with exaggerated sternness.

"Yes, sir, Lieutenant *Junior Grade* Sinclair," Ensign Gabriel piped back. "This would've been a lot easier in zero gravity. We could've hung off the overhead and left room to breath."

"*Easy*, Ensign Gabriel? You want things *easy*?"

Commander Sykes dropped gratefully into his usual chair and made a shooing motion with one hand. "Thank you for chastising Ms. Gabriel, Paul, and saving me the trouble. Now, all of you line officers run off and do your line things. You shouldn't be hanging around the wardroom during working hours."

Lieutenant Denaldo grinned. "Yeah. What do you guys think you are, supply officers?" Sykes managed to look wounded. "But Suppo's right. We better get out of here before one of our department heads pops back in, sees us and decides we're all underemployed."

2

Paul checked over the list of completed maintenance items morosely. *Not enough. Garcia's going to bite my head off. Again.* "Chief, what're the odds any of the stuff we didn't get done is going to hurt our performance during this underway period?"

Imari shrugged. "Sir, the really critical stuff is done. Anything else goes, it'll give us some trouble, but we'll be able to work around it."

"Thanks, chief."

"Are you going to be in Combat when we get underway, sir?"

"Yeah. For once." Paul felt he'd drawn more than his share of getting underway watches. Observing the process from Combat wouldn't be stress-free, but at least he wouldn't be giving maneuvering orders to the *Michaelson*. "*Maury*'s getting underway first this morning."

"Yes, sir."

And you already knew that as well as I did, didn't you, chief? Maybe I ought to tell you something you don't already know. "The XO's acting pretty edgy about this exercise, chief. He really wants us to look good, so assume he's going to be prowling the ship monitoring everything."

Chief Imari didn't quite contain her reaction. "Yes, sir. No problem. I'll make sure the guys look good whenever the XO pops in."

"Even Seaman Fastow?" Paul couldn't help asking.

Imari's grin was slightly pained. "Even her. I may have to kill her and prop her dead body so she looks like she's doing something right, but I'll manage it."

Paul grinned back. "Don't let the Sheriff hear you talking about that."

"Ah, sir, Master-at-Arms Sharpe would understand. He's been watching Fastow."

Paul's grin faded and was replaced by a questioning look. "Really. Anything in particular?"

"You'd have to ask the Sheriff, sir. But I don't know of anything."

"Thanks, chief. I'll be back in here in about an hour." Paul dropped his tentative plan to review the exercise timeline once again, and instead went looking for Petty Officer First Class Ivan Sharpe. He found him standing near the mess decks, watching the crew file past as they grabbed their breakfasts.

Sharpe touched his brow with one finger in an informal salute. "Mornin', Mr. Sinclair."

"Morning, Sheriff. Got a minute?"

"For my favorite ship's legal officer? Of course, sir."

"I'm the only ship's legal officer." Paul led Sharpe away from the other sailors before speaking again. "I hear you've been watching Seaman Fastow."

Sharpe rolled his eyes. "Me, sir? Perish the thought."

"Come on. She's in my division. I know all too well that she's had an attitude problem since she reported aboard a couple of months back. Is there something else going on with her?"

The master-at-arms rubbed his chin and looked back at Paul. "Nothing for certain, sir. I've just got a feeling there's something else. Fastow's got trouble written all over her."

"Let me know if you find out anything specific."

Sharpe grinned. "Why, sir, I thought you were dedicated to motivating your sailors and helping them maximize their potential."

Paul gave the Sheriff a sour look. "Fastow doesn't seem to want to be motivated. Right now the only thing she's maximizing is the amount of supervision she requires."

"Yes, sir. If I can bust the little lady, I'll make sure you know it."

"Thanks, Sheriff. Anything else going on?"

Sharpe looked around thoughtfully. "Not that I can think of. Things've been pretty quiet lately."

"The XO's all wrapped up in making sure this exercise with the foreign ships goes perfect."

"Everyone needs a hobby, sir."

Paul just grinned, shook his head and walked back toward Combat. *Might as well get there early. I can watch the* Maury *get underway. Jen's ship. I wonder how many more times we'll have to watch the other's ship leave?*

His sailors were already at their watch stations, too. Chief Imari nodded a greeting to Paul then went back to discussing something with one of the petty officers. Paul went from station to station, speaking briefly to each sailor, getting some personal idea of how they felt and were doing, and letting them know he was personally interested in them. *Little stuff. But it makes a difference.*

His rounds made, Paul sat down at his own console, logged in, and centered the display on the *Maury.* The *Michaelson*'s own sensors couldn't see the *Maury* with a big chunk of Franklin Station in the way, but remote feeds from Franklin's own sensor net provided a clear picture. Like the *Michaelson*, the *Maury* resembled a slightly elongated football, all smooth surfaces and gentle curves designed to minimize reflections that would help someone spot the ship in space. With her visual bypass system shut down, the *Maury*'s hull was a dull gray that seemed to soak up light.

Once the system of fiber optic cameras and visual screens covering the hull was activated, the *Maury* would seem to vanish as the cameras picked up whatever they saw, routed it 180 degrees around the hull, and displayed it on the other side. Effectively, the *Maury* would bend light around herself, making her very hard to see. *But this time out* Maury's *not going to turn on her visual bypass system and neither are we. The whole point of this little exercise is to ensure that lots of people see what we're doing. Besides, hiding from the other ships that're going to be maneuvering close around us at high speed doesn't strike me as a very good idea.* He wondered at what point in his time in space he'd begun to think of distances of fifty or a hundred kilometers as "close."

As the time approached for the *Maury* to get underway, Paul could see the magnetic lines holding her tightly to Franklin being taken in. Precisely at the scheduled time, the last line left contact with Franklin and *Maury*'s symbol changed to indicate she was a freely maneuvering object.

With the last tie to Franklin gone, and her maneuvering thrusters providing gentle nudges, the *Maury* seem to drift up and away from Franklin. On Paul's display, symbols flashed on and off as the *Maury* fired thrusters or communicated with the station. Vector arrows displaying the *Maury*'s current projected path shifted constantly as the ship maneuvered away from Franklin. Finally, clear of the station and with bow and stern both pointed in the right directions, *Maury* lit off her main drive. A new vector arrow sprang to life on the display, rapidly growing as it matched the increase in the *Maury*'s speed and angling up and away as the ship settled onto her course to the operating area.

A piercing whistle sounded over the *Michaelson*'s general announcing system as the bosun mate of the watch on the bridge sounded his alert. "All hands stand by to get underway. All departments make readiness for getting underway reports to the officer of the deck on the bridge."

Paul glanced over at Chief Imari, who gave him a thumbs-up. He reached over and triggered the button which gave him communications with Commander Garcia. "OS Division ready to get underway, sir."

A brief grunt answered Paul. He flipped a thumbs-up back to the chief to let her know he'd passed on the information. *We could call each other on the intercom, but this is faster and simpler. Sometimes the tech gets in the way.*

"Captain's in Combat!"

Paul jerked his head around at the announcement, fumbling with the quick-release buckle on his straps so he could stand to attention. But Captain Hayes was already gesturing Paul and his sailors to remain seated. "Carry on. Stay strapped in." Hayes walked over to Paul and peered at his display. "Everything ready, Paul?"

"Yes, sir."

"I want us to show these foreign ships how it's done."

"Damn straight, sir. My guys'll show them."

Captain Hayes grinned. "I never doubted it." Then he headed on out the hatch.

"Captain's left Combat," Chief Imari called out, unnecessarily this time since every sailor had their eyes on Hayes as he cleared the hatch. Imari gave Paul another thumbs up.

Paul nodded back. *Tell them you believe in them. Right, chief. Just like Hayes just let me know he believes in me.* He keyed another internal communications circuit, this one to the bridge. "Bridge, this is Combat. The captain just left Combat, probably headed your way."

"Thanks for the heads-up, Combat," a voice answered almost absently.

Paul didn't take the tone amiss. He knew there were a lot of other things going on for the bridge watch to worry about, and that they were grateful to know the captain would likely be there soon. Lieutenant Kilgary and Lieutenant Junior Grade Sam Yarrow were standing watch as the officer of the deck and the junior officer of the deck. *The captain'll probably tell Kilgary to take the ship out today. Not that Smilin' Sam has any major faults as a shiphandler, but Kilgary has more experience and Sam tends to slam the ship around instead of using finesse. We don't want anything to make us look less capable than the foreign ships watching us get underway.*

Another whistle of the bosun's pipe. "All hands prepare to get underway. Standby for maneuvering."

Paul checked the straps holding him tightly into his own chair, then looked around to make sure all his sailors were also double checking themselves. If he'd wanted to, he could've activated a circuit that let him watch and hear everything on the bridge, but Paul already knew what orders would be said, and always hated the idea of someone else watching him on watch so he rarely did it to anyone else.

A warning came on his display, showing the *Michaelson's* quarterdeck was being sealed. Lines providing power, water and other necessary supplies from the station to the ship were likewise sealed, then retracted away from the ship. Then the magnetic grapnels tying the

Michaelson to Franklin began releasing, smoothly reeling back into the ship. Paul felt forces nudging at his body as the *Michaelson* left the constant rotation-inspired feeling of gravity which Franklin provided. As the ship drifted away from the station, Paul's stomach and inner ears began insisting he was falling. He gulped, fighting off the nausea. *We haven't been inport that long. You'd think I'd still have my space-legs.*

The last line holding the ship to the station came free. "Underway. Shift colors," the bosun announced. Sudden, gentle lurches pushed Paul against his straps as the *Michaelson*'s maneuvering thrusters fired. He watched the image of Franklin falling down and away as the ship accelerated farther from the station. More thruster firings nudged Paul in different directions as the *Michaelson*'s bow was brought around to the right heading. *Gentle and smooth. That's got to be Colleen Kilgary driving the ship. Sam Yarrow'd be giving us all bruises by now.*

A moment later the main drive kicked in. Paul sank deep into his seat as the almost nonexistent feeling of gravity was replaced by acceleration strong enough that he felt over twice his normal weight. His stomach complained again, protesting the changes in up and down.

Paul moved his hand carefully against the force of the acceleration, using controls to shift his display presentation to show the *Michaelson*'s new path through space. Symbols glowed to mark other spacecraft, each with vector arrows arching away to show their speed and direction of travel relative to the *Michaelson*. A pale line came into view, marking the vector the *Michaelson* sought, slowly converging on the actual course of the ship. The actual course and intended course lines merged as the main drive cut off.

Another stomach lurch as sustained heavy acceleration was replaced by freefall. Paul gritted his teeth. *I'm used to this. Just give it a little while to adjust again.* To distract himself, he scrolled out his display to where the symbol marking the *Maury* hung ahead of the *Michaelson.* With both ships moving along the same path at the same speed, the relative position of the *Maury* wouldn't change until the ships fired thrusters or main drives again. And they wouldn't do that for several hours, when they were approaching the area where the foreign ships awaited the Americans.

"Secure from maneuvering status. All hands are free to move about."

Paul shook his head, causing his inner ears to wobble a little more. For some reason, that helped his body adjust to zero gravity faster. He unstrapped, floating free of the chair, and using the handholds positioned everywhere began pulling himself toward the hatch out of combat. "Good job, everybody."

Over the year and a half since reporting aboard the ship he'd learned to pull himself through the narrow confines of the *Michaelson's* passageways, gliding through hatches while avoiding all the wires, cables and equipment which often seemed to have been diabolically positioned to slam or snag human arms, legs or heads. Sailors passed him, waiting for Paul to go through a hatch first because of his status as an officer, though Paul himself had to hug the side of a passageway and wait for the chief engineer, Commander Destin, as she came by. Destin, who always seemed to be carrying a virtual cloud of depression in her wake, brushed past Paul without a word. Paul spared one brief glance at Destin before continuing on his way. *Still no love lost there. I sure hope Captain Hayes doesn't decide I should transfer into the Engineering Department.*

Two hours later, Paul pulled himself onto the bridge for his own watch as junior officer of the deck. Kris Denaldo, who'd been standing the watch, pretended to make a prayer of thanks. "Hey, I'm not late."

"No," she agreed. "It's just soooo boring." Denaldo pointed to the maneuvering display, where the symbols representing the other ships seemed to hang unchanging against the immense emptiness of space. "We're going somewhere fast but you wouldn't know it. It's still six hours until we maneuver for the rendezvous with the furriners. Until then, we just bore a hole in nothing on our way there. Nobody and nothing else is near us."

Paul nodded, scanning the displays. Watches tended to be either way too dull or way too exciting. Once they joined up with the foreign ships, they'd probably all be exciting for a while, but they had a lot of space to cover before then. "Who's this on a slightly converging track with us?"

Kris pointed to the symbol. "The *Mahan*'s out here, too. Heading for the same general area."

"What?" Paul stared at the symbol. "They're adding in another ship? This late in the game? I haven't seen—"

"Relax, relax. We got briefed on it during our watch. The *Mahan* got tapped as an observer ship."

"What's the *Mahan* going to see that anyone watching from Earth's surface couldn't?"

"Nothing. But they loaded some VIPs onboard her. American and foreign. They get to 'be here' during the exercise."

"Whoopee." Paul settled into the chair, adjusting the straps to suit his larger body.

Kris Denaldo gave him a curious look. "Why's the *Mahan* got you spooked?"

"I'm not spooked."

"You're not happy."

"You know who the captain of the *Mahan* is!"

She frowned, then her expression cleared. "Oh, yeah. Jen's dad."

Jen's dad. Captain Kay Shen. A man who'd made it clear that he didn't think Paul measured up to what his daughter deserved, and who'd warned that he'd be watching Paul. *And now here he is, literally watching my ship. Oh, joy.*

Denaldo smiled at Paul's expression. "Captain Shen's not that bad, is he?"

Paul stared at her with exaggerated disbelief. "Do you know those illustrations for science fiction stuff where some big, dark character is looming over and menacing an entire galaxy? That's how I think of Jen's father. He's out there, always watching."

Kris laughed. "Paul, I met him once. He seemed okay."

"You weren't dating his daughter."

"That's true. Jen and I don't swing that way." Kris paused as if thinking. "Still, Jen *is* awful cute."

"And she's mine. Just in case you're not joking."

"*Yours?* Jen's like a cat, Paul, just in case you haven't figured that out yet. She might choose to hang around with you, but you'll never *own* her."

Yeah. Which is one of the things I like about her. But it leaves me to worry that someday she'll find some other tomcat that she likes better than me. Not that I have to worry about her father liking that other tomcat better than he does me. I think. "Point taken. Still, Captain Kay Shen is one very hard-assed individual. And I know he's keeping as close an eye as he can on everything I do."

"I thought Commander Herdez was keeping an eye on you to see if you were maintaining her standards."

"She is. Both of them are."

"Ugh. Better you than me." Denaldo ran down the rest of the information Paul needed to know. The turnover briefing didn't take too long, since Paul was familiar with upcoming events and because in this large area of space labeled "local" he and the other officers on the ship had become familiar with space traffic patterns, objects in fixed orbits and navigational aids. "Any questions?"

"Nah." Paul rendered a casual salute to her. "I got it."

She returned the salute, part of the formal ritual the watch followed. "I stand relieved." Raising her voice, Denaldo called out, "This is Lieutenant Denaldo. Lieutenant Sinclair has the conn."

"This is Lieutenant Sinclair. I have the conn." Paul listened as the other watch standers acknowledged the transfer of responsibility.

Lieutenant Sindh had been his more senior watch standing partner as officer of the deck for some months now. He'd regret losing her steady presence on the bridge, too. They passed the hours of the watch playing Foreign Navy Jeopardy, which could be entertaining enough to dissipate boredom while also professional enough not to get them in trouble if a more senior officer overheard them.

Paul was saying, "I'll take Russian Federation minor combatants for four hundred," when their reliefs arrived. Sam Yarrow gave Paul an annoyed look, ignoring Ensign Abacha who'd come onto the bridge right behind him. *Poor Jack Abacha. Standing under-instruction watches with Sam Yarrow. I wouldn't want to be in his shoes.* After turning over with Yarrow, Paul took a moment to talk quietly to Abacha. "Don't worry. Just hang loose and keep your eyes and ears open. You've got Sam Yarrow here, you've got a good officer of the deck watching both of you, and the enlisted are watching all the officers. Nobody'll let you mess up too bad."

Abacha nodded with the rapid head jerks that betrayed nervousness.

"I don't want to mess up at all."

"Of course not. But you will. That's what being an ensign is about. It won't be the end of the world as long as you learn from your mistakes."

"Thanks."

"Any questions?"

"Uh..." Abacha looked around. "Just one thing that's kinda driving me crazy."

"What's that?"

"You went to the Naval Academy, too, so you'll understand. This ship's name is the *Michaelson* and her sister ships have names like *Mahan* and *Maury*. Just like the academic buildings at the Academy. So why is *Michaelson* spelled with an 'a'? The guy who first measured the speed of light was named Michelson. No 'a.'"

Paul grinned. "I wondered that, too. The *Mike*'s not named after the scientist Michelson. She's named after Admiral 'Genghis' Conner Michaelson, the father of the Space Navy."

"Oh. That makes sense, but it still doesn't fit with the names of the rest of the ships in the class."

"Yeah. Rumor has it the *Merry Mike* was supposed to be named after the scientist, but the spelling error was discovered after the *Michaelson* name had been widely publicized, so since they couldn't change the name at that point without admitting they'd screwed up, they just changed the guy the ship was being named after. But that might just be a good rumor."

"Oh, okay." Jack Abacha grinned. "We meant to do it that way, right?"

"Right. Remember you've got some maneuvering in about two hours. Watch and learn."

"Yes, sir."

"And make sure you're tied down tightly to something before the maneuvering begins."

"Yes, sir!"

Paul spent the actual rendezvous inside Combat again, watching as the American and foreign ships fired thrusters and drives to bring themselves into a rough grouping. Tomorrow morning, the game of forming geometric shapes would begin. Paul opened the distance on his display, frowning as he spotted one large object heading in the general direction of the group. "Anybody know who this is?"

One of the watchstanders answered up. "SASAL combatant, Mr. Sinclair. The system IDs him as the *Tamerlane*."

"Thanks." Paul called up information on the *Tamerlane* from the combat systems database. The ship seemed roughly equivalent to the *Michaelson* in terms of size and armament. He checked the contact again. The South Asian Alliance ship wasn't using any methods to avoid detection, and proceeding at a leisurely pace through a neutral transit lane. *No big deal, then. They'll be plenty near enough to see us playing ring-around-the-rosie with the other ships, though, so I guess that's a good thing.*

Paul reached for the intercom to call the bridge, then hesitated. *Should I bother them with this? That SASAL ship won't come anywhere near us on his present heading, and the bridge already has plenty to worry about. Maybe—*

The bosun's pipe shrilled over the announcing system. "Lieutenant Junior Grade Sinclair, contact the bridge."

Uh oh. He finally tapped the intercom switch. "This is Lieutenant Sinclair."

Instead of the officer of the deck, he heard the voice of Captain

Hayes replying. "Mr. Sinclair, why weren't I and the bridge watch informed there was a SASAL warship in the vicinity?"

Crap. Five more lousy seconds and I could've made the call to the bridge before I got called. Crap, crap, crap. "Sir, the Combat watch and I were evaluating—"

"I don't want to find out by accident again that there's something like a SASAL warship nearby, Mr. Sinclair!"

Paul took a moment to be grateful he wasn't being chewed out face to face. *Not that I should be happy about that, because it means the captain's so ticked off he's ripping me up in public. What now? Say that SASAL ship isn't really "nearby"? Try to explain again that I was just about to call the bridge? He doesn't want an explanation. I screwed up. Just get it over with.* "Yes, sir. It won't happen again, sir."

"It'd better not." The click of the communications circuit cutting off sounded unnaturally loud to Paul.

He leaned back from his console and took a deep breath. His own Combat watch standers were concentrating on their displays, trying to pretend they hadn't heard or noticed anything. Paul took another slow breath to ensure his voice was under control. "Who's monitoring the long-range situation?"

Petty Officer Third Class Divalo raised his hand. "Me, sir."

"I should've been notified about that SASAL ship, Divalo."

"Yes, sir. I, uh..."

"That's in the standing watch instructions, right?"

"Yes, sir."

Paul felt anger flooding him and fought it down. *Don't scream at him. Divalo's a pretty good sailor. He just screwed up this time. And I'm responsible when he does.* He glanced over at where Divalo was hunched in front of his display, his face grim. *He's unhappy already. Make sure he remembers the lesson and not me screaming at him.* "Next time keep me informed, Petty Officer Divalo. When in doubt, let me know. That way neither one of us will get chewed out."

"Yes, sir. I will, sir. I'm sorry, sir."

"Let's just make sure we don't surprise the captain again. He doesn't like that."

Divalo smiled nervously at the understatement. "No, sir. Don't worry, sir."

"I won't." *The hell I won't. But Divalo's not a habitual screw-up. He deserves a second chance.* "I want you to work up some possible positions for that SASAL ship at the time the exercise is scheduled to begin. I especially want to know how close he could be if he headed directly this way at speed. I also want to know how far away he'll be if he continues along that transit lane. Then give me a picture of the area of space he could be in if he does something in between those two extremes. Understand?"

Divalo nodded several times, his face intent with concentration. "Aye, aye, sir. I'll have it to you real quick, Mr. Sinclair."

"Run it by Chief Imari first so she'll know what's going on, too." *I'm glad I thought of that. Hey, I could've failed to inform the chain of command above and below me at the same time.* "Make sure it looks clean because we'll be forwarding the picture to the captain."

"Aye, aye, sir."

Paul unstrapped and pulled himself out of Combat. Halfway to the wardroom, he passed Randy Diego. "Paul? Commander Garcia's looking for you."

"Did he say what about?"

"No. But he didn't look happy."

Wonderful. Now Garcia probably wants to chew me out for not telling him or the captain about the SASAL ship. Might as well get it over with. "Thanks, Randy." Paul went looking for Garcia.

"So," Lieutenant Sindh murmured, "how's your butt this morning?"

"Tender," Paul muttered back as he settled into the junior officer of the deck's chair and tugged at the straps. "After Garcia finished ripping into me he passed me off to the XO so Kwan could take some bites out of me. At least Hayes seems in a better mood today."

"That's because you warned him last night this might happen." Sindh indicated the maneuvering display, where the SASAL warship loomed far closer than it should've been if it had stayed inside the traffic lane. "I guess the South Asians want a real close look at our show."

"Yeah. I checked out the *Tamerlane*'s position in Combat before coming to the bridge. If he wants to, he could be right on top of us when we start our little multinational ballet."

"You sure?" Sindh ran some quick calculations herself. "That's not good. It's going to be hairy enough dancing around those foreign ships without worrying about that SASAL goon hanging around."

"At least we've got—"

Paul was interrupted by the bosun mate of the watch yelling out, "Captain's on the bridge!"

Hayes went straight to his chair on one side of the bridge and strapped in before looking toward Paul and Sonya Sindh. "Looks like you were right about the son of a gun, Paul. Good work."

"Thank you, sir." *Alright. I'm "Paul" again instead of Mr. Sinclair.*

"What if this guy tries to mess with our exercise? Do we use standard rules of engagement for foreign encounters?"

Sindh flicked a glance at Paul, who gave her a surreptitous thumbs-up back. "No, sir. Fleet's issued specific guidance for SASAL encounters during this period."

Hayes grinned. "Do you know them?"

"Yes, sir." *Studied the hell out of them last night after Kwan and Garcia finished reading me the riot act. No way I was going to be caught flat-footed again this soon.* "They're more restrictive than the usual rules of engagement."

"Damn. Well, hopefully he'll keep his distance and we won't need them." Commander Kwan entered the bridge and strapped into his own chair. "Hey, XO, we got company."

Kwan nodded, then gave Paul a glare. "Yes, sir."

"Okay, Sonya, Paul, let's get this show on the road."

The XO heard Hayes' tone and reference to Paul by his first name, gave Paul another less-hostile look, then focused on the displays near his chair. "Who's running Combat with Sinclair up here?"

Paul answered immediately. "Commander Garcia, sir."

Kwan nodded. "Good."

I'm glad you think so. My sailors aren't too happy about it.

They spent the next hour conducting communications checks with the foreign ships. The Brits sounded calm to the point of being relaxed, the Franco-German ship kept trying to pretend no one onboard spoke English, and the Russian Federation ship seemed so jovial that Captain Hayes wondered aloud if they'd been sampling their vodka rations already this morning.

Finally, the ships began their first planned maneuver. Paul found himself unusually nervous as the bosun sounded out his warning. "All hands prepare for extended maneuvering period beginning in five minutes. Secure all objects and materials. Undertake no task that cannot be completed prior to maneuvering."

Precisely five minutes later the *Michaelson*'s thrusters fired, shoving everyone onboard to one side. Paul and Sonya watched as the *Michaelson*'s maneuvering systems handled the job automatically, swinging the ship onto a new heading before the main drive cut in and slammed the crew back against their restraints. The stars spun on the visual display in front of Paul, where bright symbols superimposed on the blackness of space told him the positions of the *Maury* and the three foreign warships. On the maneuvering displays, the vectors of the five ships began pushing them into the shape of a huge pentagon with sides two hundred kilometers long.

"Bridge, this is Combat. The SASAL ship is up to something."

Every head on the bridge jerked over to check out the vector on the SASAL ship. It had lengthened and shifted, marking maneuvering and main drive firing by the *Tamerlane*. Captain Hayes, his face stressed by the force of the *Michaelson*'s acceleration, slapped his communications controls. "I want to know what he's doing the instant we have a reasonable estimate."

"Yes, sir. Preliminary system estimates put him heading this way."

Hayes glared toward Paul. "What can we do, Paul?"

"The rules of engagement say we should warn them off using all available means."

"Comms, get on the air to the *Tamerlane* and tell them to get the hell out of here. Feel free to be that blunt. Send it simultaneously using lasers on visual frequencies. Paul, what if he doesn't respond?"

Paul grimaced, knowing the captain wouldn't like what Paul was about to say. "Avoid confrontation, sir."

"What?"

"Avoid confrontation, sir. That's verbatim. If the SASALs don't veer off, we have to avoid them."

"Damn. Combat, what the hell is he doing now?"

"He appears to be angling to cut across our bow, sir."

"I can see that, Combat! I want his CPA!"

Paul fought down a burst of anger. *If I'd been down in Combat I'd have made sure my guys provided the closest point of approach for the captain. Garcia just got my sailors yelled at because he wanted to answer the captain right away.*

"Bridge, this is Combat. If we continue on our current course, CPA to the SASAL ship will be somewhere between forty and sixty kilometers."

Hayes' face reddened as he watched the SASAL ship continue onward. "I assume there's been no reply to our communications?"

"No, sir. None."

"Mr. Sinclair, I'd sure like to know whether or not that SASAL captain is also under orders to avoid confrontations!"

Paul, unable to think of any reply, simply nodded. "Yes, sir." Lieutenant Sindh somehow managed to make a gesture of long-suffering toward Paul without actually making it. Paul felt his frustration shifting to a similar sardonic acceptance of fate. A captain's many powers included the right to ask unreasonable questions and get ticked off if you didn't know the answers.

Captain Hayes drummed his fingers on his chair arm for several seconds. "Hell. Prepare to alter our current maneuver to avoid that ship. I want to open his CPA to one hundred kilometers."

"Aye, aye, sir," Paul and Sonya Sindh responded simultaneously, then both began calculating the necessary changes.

"Combat, notify all ships in the formation of our intended course change and tell them, uh, that is 'request' that they prepare to resume the exercise once the SASAL ship has finished ramming through here."

"Aye, aye, sir."

"Officer of the deck, do you have the evasive maneuver calculated?"

"Yes, sir," Sindh answered calmly.

"Execute it. Get us clear of that idiot."

Sindh pushed the engage button and the *Michaelson*'s thrusters fired again, pitching her over to the side and altering her course through space away from the place where the SASAL ship would come closest to her.

An alarm sounded. "Bridge, this is Combat. The SASAL ship has his active fire control systems locked onto us."

Captain Hayes' face grew even redder. "I've had just about enough of this."

Paul stared at the symbol representing the SASAL ship. *What are they thinking? Locking their fire control systems onto us is about the most provocative thing they can do. Surely they don't want us to shoot. They're just thumbing their noses at us, trying to show they won't be intimidated.*

"Mr. Sinclair," Hayes ground out. "Are there any loopholes in those rules of engagement? Do I have *any* discretion on responding to what that ship is doing?"

Paul shook his head carefully against the force of the *Michaelson*'s maneuvers. "No, sir. We aren't allowed to take any action except to avoid confrontation."

"Great. Let me tell you, Mr. Sinclair, I would dearly love to confront those guys right now."

Me, too. "Yes, sir."

"Captain?" Commander Garcia called from Combat, sounding aggrieved. "Our evasive maneuver combined with evasive maneuvers by *Maury* and *Alsace* are completely throwing off the formation. It'll take us hours to get everybody back into position to restart."

Commander Kwan shook his head. "It's almost like they planned it that way."

Captain Hayes glared at his display as he answered. "That ship certainly seemed to know where it had to be and when it had to be there to mess with us. We shared our exercise plans with the Euros and the Russians. What are the odds they didn't leak?"

Paul noticed new symbols spring to life on his display and frowned down at it. "Captain? HMS *Lord Nelson* is maneuvering again."

"Why?" Hayes frowned at his own screen. "They were well clear of the SASAL ship's track through our formation. Where's the *Nelson* going?"

"We can't tell yet, sir."

"As if I don't have enough trouble with unfriendly foreigners, now I have to worry about what the so-called friendly foreigners are doing." Hayes angrily punched a communications button. "HMS *Lord Nelson*, this is the exercise movement coordinator onboard USS *Michaelson*. Request advise the purpose of your maneuvers."

The Euro ship's reply, in a calm, lightly British-accented woman's voice, came after a pause. "This is HMS *Lord Nelson*. Roger. Wait one. Out."

"Wait one?" Commander Kwan questioned. "Don't they know what they're doing?"

Captain Hayes frowned again. "Of course they do. That's the Royal Navy over there, and that was the *Nelson*'s captain who answered us. What the hell is she up to?"

Paul heard a brief attention chirp from his display and glanced back at it. "The *Lord Nelson*'s firing thrusters and main drive again, sir." He watched as the arc of the British ship's projected path through space altered shape, quickly bending into a trajectory which crossed another projected path, then firmed as the warship steadied onto course. As the *Nelson* cut her drives to settle onto her new trajectory, a red symbol flashed to life on Paul's screen where the two paths came together. "Captain?" Paul tried to keep his voice from cracking. "HMS *Lord Nelson*'s settled onto a collision course with the SASAL ship."

"*What?*!" Hayes bent over his screen, as if being closer to it would resolve more detail.

"Bridge, this is Combat. The *Nelson*'s on a collision course with the *Tamerlane.*"

Lieutenant Sindh tapped in a request for the *Michaelson*'s systems to recheck and confirm their calculations. "Estimate confirmed, sir. *Nelson*'s positioned herself so her trajectory will intercept that of the SASAL ship."

"Why the *hell*...? HMS *Lord Nelson*, this is the exercise maneuvering coordinator. Interrogative your intentions."

The *Lord Nelson*'s captain responded immediately this time, her voice unruffled. "This is HMS *Lord Nelson*. I regret to report a possible problem with my maneuvering systems."

Captain Hayes stared at his display for a moment before replying. "Captain Vitali, you are on a collision course with the SASAL ship."

"Yes, we have noticed that."

"What is the exact nature of your maneuvering system problem?"

"We're still looking into it."

"Captain Vitali, you need to maneuver your ship again. You're on a very hazardous trajectory."

"The situation is a bit awkward, isn't it?"

Captain Hayes seemed lost for words for a moment before replying.

"Do you anticipate correcting this 'problem' with your maneuvering systems in the very near future?"

"It's very hard to say."

Hayes took a deep breath. "Captain Vitali, as exercise movement coordinator I very respectfully request that you immediately maneuver so as to avoid collision with the SASAL ship."

"What's that?"

"I believe you heard my request."

"Oh, rot. The signal's breaking up. We appear to've developed a communications problem as well. I must have a talk with my officers about these system problems. This is HMS *Lord Nelson*. Nothing heard. Out."

Kwan was staring at his display, his jaw loose. "I can't believe she's doing this."

Captain Hayes' face had reddened to a deep shade approaching purple. "Damn crazy Brits."

Paul leaned toward Sindh so he could speak in a whisper. "What're they doing?"

Sindh glanced toward Captain Hayes before replying in the same low tone. "The Brits? They're going head-to-head with the SASALs."

"They deliberately put themselves on a collision course with that other ship so the SASALs will have to maneuver to avoid them?"

"Right. They're playing chicken, and they've one-upped the SASALs."

"You don't play that kind of game with warships. That's insane."

"Well, yes. But the Brits aren't really insane. Just very sure of their inherent superiority over every other form of human life. So it's more of a calm certainty that the other person'll blink first."

"What if the other person *doesn't* blink first?"

Lieutenant Sindh shook her head. "Then you end up with what the Brits would no doubt refer to as a 'regrettable turn of events.'"

Captain Hayes glared around the bridge. "Combat, do you still have a data link active with the *Nelson*?"

Garcia's voice held weary resignation. "They're telling us they can't read our link."

"So they can transmit but not receive?"

"Yes, sir. That's what they're saying."

"Oh, for—" Hayes bit off the rest of his comment, his fingers drumming on the arm of his chair as he glowered at his display. "They're pulling that stupid 'blind eye' trick. Just because they're named after Nelson doesn't mean they have to pretend that they *are* Nelson!"

Paul took a moment to recall the captain's reference. *Oh, yeah. Copenhagen. The British commander sent up a signal ordering Nelson to withdraw and Nelson put his telescope to his blind eye, looked toward the signal and said he couldn't see anything. Then he went on to win the battle.* Paul studied the display again, watching the red symbol marking the probable collision point blinking with increasing urgency. *They won't move, will they? Sindh's right. The Brits won't back down.*

"Captain?" Lieutenant Sindh asked. "Should I alert our rescue teams to be prepared for action?"

Hayes snorted, pointing at the screen. "Look at the closing rate between those ships, lieutenant. If they hit at those speeds there won't be anything to rescue but dust particles."

Paul stared at the display, transfixed by the sight of two massive warships deliberately racing directly toward each other at tremendous velocities. Above the symbol indicating each ship, two time markers scrolled rapidly downward. The first marker, indicating time to collision, was less important at the moment than the second, which displayed the time remaining for one of the ships to maneuver to avoid the other. If either tried to take evasive action after that point, it'd be too late for the ships' drives to alter their paths through space quickly enough, and momentum would carry the ships into collision regardless. Even a glancing blow at those speeds and with that mass would be devastating to both ships.

The *Michaelson*'s maneuvering system spoke clearly across the now otherwise silent bridge, its composed voice at odds with the urgency of the message. "HMS *Lord Nelson* and SASAL warship *Tamerlane* will collide unless at least one maneuvers within five minutes of my mark... Mark. Recommend advise both ships to undertake coordinated maneuvers to avoid collision."

Captain Hayes answered the *Michaelson*'s system without looking away from his display. "We already thought of that."

Kwan leaned toward the captain. "Maybe if we fired ahead of the SASAL ship, it'd be scared and—"

"No can do, XO. That'd definitely be a confrontation. I'm not free to do that."

"Can we fire just in front of the *Nelson*, then?"

Sindh answered this time. "No, sir. The firing angle is too oblique given our relative positions."

"Four minutes remaining before collision between HMS *Lord Nelson* and SASAL warship *Tamerlane* becomes inevitable," the *Michaelson*'s maneuvering systems reminded them.

Captain Hayes triggered his communications again. "HMS *Lord Nelson*, this is the exercise movement coordinator on the USS *Michaelson*. For God's sake maneuver to avoid collision."

The *Nelson*'s captain sounded as unruffled as ever. "I'm afraid that's quite impossible."

"I notice you can receive my transmissions again."

"What's that? Say again, please."

Hayes closed his eyes briefly.

"Three minutes remaining before collision between HMS *Lord Nelson* and SASAL warship *Tamerlane* becomes inevitable."

Captain Hayes looked around the bridge. "I'd appreciate any suggestions anyone might have."

The red collision point symbol on Paul's display had grown larger, now pulsing continuously, and the time markers had also become much bigger and impossible to miss or ignore as they spun down toward zero.

"Two minutes remaining before collision between HMS *Lord Nelson* and SASAL warship *Tamerlane* becomes inevitable."

Paul caught Lieutenant Sindh's eye. Sindh shook her head. Paul looked back at his display.

"One minute re—"

Paul had to double check, then spoke with exaggerated care, his voice sounding louder than usual on the silent bridge. "We have thruster firings and aspect change on the SASAL ship." No one answered, but all bent closer to their displays as if willing the other ship to move. "We have main drive firing on the SASAL ship." Paul glanced at the time marker. Ten seconds from the point at which collision would be inevitable. The projected path of the SASAL ship began curving upward with agonizing slowness. The *Nelson*, still unwilling to maneuver, held her course and speed even though she could've taken her own action to further lessen the chance of collision.

The moment of closest point of approach came and went in a blur a tiny fraction of a second long. "How close were they?" Captain Hayes asked in a soft voice.

Sindh studied her display before replying. "Our system estimates CPA at about 800 meters, captain." Then, in an undertone only Paul could hear, she muttered, "There can't be a single pair of dry underwear on either one of those ships right now."

Hayes shook his head. "Mad dogs and Englishmen." He punched his communications again. "HMS *Lord Nelson*, request the status of your maneuvering systems."

"This is HMS *Lord Nelson*." Captain Vitali's reply sounded cheerful. "Our maneuvering systems are fully operational."

Captain Hayes rubbed his forehead as he replied. "It appears your communications systems are fully functional again as well."

"Why, yes, they are. Brilliant. HMS *Lord Nelson* is ready to proceed with the maneuvering exercise."

"Do you anticipate any *further* system failures in the near future, Captain Vitali?"

"Oh, no. Not at all. We're fully prepared for the next shed-yuled event."

Paul glanced at Lieutenant Sindh. "'Shed-yuled'?"

"Scheduled."

Captain Hayes was watching the SASAL ship's track arching away from the combined formation. It would take it a long, long time to slow down, reverse course and cause them any more trouble even if the SASALs intended doing so. "Captain Vitali of HMS *Lord Nelson*, this is Captain Hayes of USS *Michaelson*. You owe me a drink."

"You're a man after my own heart, captain. Your ship or mine? Oh, wait, I suppose it'll have to be my ship, won't it? You US Navy types being dry and all."

"I'm afraid so." Hayes laughed at Captain Vitali's reference to the US Navy not being allowed to serve alcohol onboard its ships except under exceptional circumstances. "All ships, this is the exercise movement coordinator. We will restart the exercise time line as soon as all ships can resume relative starting positions. Request you advise me of estimated times until you can regain positions."

Over the next few hours the five ships wrestled themselves back into starting positions. The SASAL ship didn't try returning, instead heading back toward the transit lane while the *Michaelson* filed a report that would be used to issue a diplomatic protest to the South Asian Alliance over reckless actions by its warship.

By the time Paul's watch ended, the ships had managed to reform the huge pentagon and were preparing to form what the crew had begun referring to as the "flat football" formation. Over the next twenty-four hours they formed the "empty ball" as well as the "big O" and the "more or less line-ahead" formations. Paul was in Combat when the last formation was completed, and a ragged cheer went up from the watchstanders.

The foreign ships took their separate departures, the *Nelson*'s captain reminding Captain Hayes he had a drink waiting and inviting the rest of the *Michaelson*'s officers as well, the Franco-German ship once again ignoring any messages sent in English, and the Russian ship demanding to know how well each of the ships had performed even though Hayes repeatedly assured them there'd been no evaluation or ranking process conducted.

"Exercise completed," Captain Hayes announced to the *Michaelson*'s crew. "Good job, everybody. You did yourselves and the US Navy proud. Now, let's go home."

That brought another cheer, even more enthusiastic.

3

"Got a minute, Mr. Sinclair?"

Paul looked up from his stateroom desk at Sheriff Sharpe. "What's up?"

"One of your and my favorite sailors, sir." Sharpe extended a small medicinal sample package toward Paul.

Paul took it and peered inside where a couple of objects resembling poppy seeds were floating in the container. "What is it?"

"Joy-Buzz dots. Found inside the locker of one Seaman Fastow."

"Joy-Buzz." Paul eyed the objects again with distaste. The drug wasn't physically dangerous to someone using it, but it seriously impaired judgment and was banned on ships as a result. "Just these two?"

"Yes, sir. Request authorization to acquire Seaman Fastow's butt and run her down to sickbay for a drug test."

"Permission granted. Let me know what the results are."

Sharpe grinned. "Of course, sir."

"There's a captain's mast scheduled for just before we get back to Franklin."

"Yes, sir. I believe Ms. Fastow is going to participate in that little evolution."

Captain's mast had its origins in ancient navies, where a ship's captain would render justice quite literally in front of the mast on the ship. Spaceships like the *Michaelson* had no actual masts, of course, but the non-judicial legal proceedings represented by captain's mast had been enshrined in the law governing military legal affairs known as the Uniform Code of Military Justice.

Paul braced himself against one side of the compartment where captain's mast would be held. As the collateral duty legal officer, he was required to be present for every captain's mast. Floating next to him was Senior Chief Kowalski, the senior enlisted crewmember. Standing at the hatch was Master-at-Arms Sharpe. "Attention on deck!" Sharpe called out.

Captain Hayes pulled himself into the compartment, nodded to Paul and the senior chief, then took up position near a podium fastened to the deck. He pulled out his data pad, placed it on the podium, called up the first case record, then gestured to Sharpe. "Let's go. First case."

Sharpe leaned out into the passageway. "Seaman Fastow. Front and center."

Fastow entered, her eyes darting about nervously. Sharpe pointed her to a position directly in front of the captain. Behind her came Chief Imari, who also nodded to Paul.

Hayes read over the information on his data unit, then looked sharply at Fastow. "Seaman Fastow, you are charged with violating the Uniform Code of Military Justice Article 112(a), Wrongful Possession of Controlled Substances." Hayes glanced at Sharpe. "What was it?"

Sharpe cleared his throat. "Joy-Buzz dots, sir."

The captain focused back on Fastow. "What do you have to say?"

Fastow licked her lips before replying. "Captain, Sharpe there went rummaging through my locker—"

"Seaman Fastow, Petty Officer Sharpe conducted a search of an area onboard this ship. Onboard *my* ship."

"But, he didn't have any warrant—"

"Mr. Sinclair?"

Paul looked steadily at Fastow. "Lockers, desks and all other areas onboard the ship are government property, not personal areas. There's no right of privacy for them and no warrant is required for them to be searched."

Hayes narrowed his eyes at Fastow. "That's the law. Now, what about this stuff found in your locker?"

Fastow's eyes looked to the side, then back at the captain. "Sir, I don't know how it got there."

"You're claiming it's not yours?"

"No, sir. I mean, yes, sir. It's not mine. I don't know how it got in my locker."

Hayes glanced at Sharpe again. "Was a drug test run?"

"Yes, sir." Sharpe couldn't hide a flash of disappointment. "Negative results."

"Hmmm. How long does Joy-Buzz stay in the system?"

"About seventy-two hours after use, sir."

"I see." Hayes speared Fastow with a demanding look. "You claim those drugs weren't yours."

"That's right, sir. They're just those little specks."

"Where did they come from, then?"

"I... I don't know, sir. Maybe when I was on liberty last

somebody spilled some on my clothes."

Hayes kept a hard look on Fastow but she didn't flinch. Finally, he looked over at Paul. "You're Seaman Fastow's division officer. What kind of sailor is she?"

Paul kept his own face unyielding. "Marginal, captain. Fastow requires a great deal of supervision."

"Have you seen any signs of drug usage by her?"

Paul thought, looking over at Chief Imari, who reluctantly shook her head. "Sir, I cannot say I have."

Hayes nodded slowly, his eyes still fixed on Fastow. "It seems I may have to give you the benefit of the doubt. But I don't want to, because your chief and your division officer both tell me you haven't been doing well. When things like this happen, Seaman Fastow, you want them to be telling me you're a good sailor. Otherwise, I'll be inclined to think you deserve to be hammered. Do you understand me?"

"Uh, yes, sir."

"Because of some doubt as to your guilt in this matter, I will go lightly this time. But if it happens again, and your performance remains bad, then I won't regard it as a coincidence, and I will nail you to that bulkhead. Do you understand?"

"Yes, sir."

"Fifteen days' restriction to the ship. Reduction in rate to seaman apprentice, suspended for six months." Hayes leveled a forefinger at Fastow. "Any more nonsense and you'll only be a seaman apprentice again for about two seconds, because I'll use that next captain's mast to bust you down to seaman recruit. Get your act together, Seaman Fastow."

"Yes, sir."

"Dismissed."

Fastow saluted and left. Paul couldn't tell whether she was relieved or frightened, but he passed another nod to Chief Imari as she followed Fastow out of the compartment.

Captain Hayes shook his head and then looked around the compartment. "I want a close eye kept on her."

"Yes, sir," Paul and Sharpe answered together.

"Who's next?"

"Seaman Jacob, sir."

Jacob pulled himself inside the compartment as his name was called. The lanky seaman had sweat droplets visible on his forehead as he stopped before the captain and came to rigid attention. Lieutenant Kilgary and Chief Petty Officer Meyer came in as well, taking up positions along the bulkhead opposite Paul. Captain Hayes gave Jacob a long look before consulting his data pad. "Seaman Jacob, it says here you are charged with violations of the Uniform Code Article 86, Absent Without Official Leave, and Article 87, Missing Movement. What do you have to say?"

Jacob licked his lips and took a deep breath before answering. "Sir, captain, I, uh, yes, I didn't get back from leave on time. But it wasn't my fault, sir. No, sir. I never woulda done it on purpose."

Hayes glanced at Lieutenant Kilgary and Chief Meyer, who were maintaining poker faces. "Then how did it happen, Seaman Jacob?"

"Well, sir, it all started 'cause I took leave Earthside to get married."

"Then I guess congratulations are in order."

"No, sir. No, I, uh, when I got back home, it turned out Justy was marryin' some other guy."

"Justy?"

"My girl, sir. Or at least she was my girl when I left for the Navy. I was pretty sure we had 'an understandin''."

Hayes took another look around the compartment before focusing back on Jacob. "You knew she was getting married, but thought she was marrying you."

"That's right, captain."

"You got an invitation to this wedding?"

"Yes, sir! But I guess since Justy and I had that understandin' I alluded to I just figured it must be *our* wedding and didn't read the thing too close."

Paul managed to avoid smiling only by an heroic effort. Opposite him, Lieutenant Kilgary was clearly biting the inside of her cheek to avoid smiling herself.

Captain Hayes looked down at his data pad for a moment, hiding his expression, then back up at Jacob. "You arrived at the wedding and found out it wasn't *your* wedding."

"Yes, sir, captain, and I got sorta ticked off, if you know what I mean. Justy and I had some words. But it wasn't nothin' violent. Not at first. No, sir. I didn't want to hurt anybody, just like I told the judge—"

"The *judge*? What judge?"

"The one what heard my case on the assault charges and he agreed with me that maybe me being in jail was a bit much—"

"You were in jail?"

"I said I'd been arrested, didn't I, captain?" Hayes shook his head solemnly. "Oh. Well, yeah. I mean, yes, sir. And that Frank guy threw the first punch—"

"Frank?"

"He's the one what was marrying my girl, sir."

"I see. I don't think she's 'your girl' anymore, Jacob."

"Uh, I guess not, captain."

"So, you got into a fight."

"Yes, sir. And I was winnin' 'til Justy kicked me in the ankle and that Frank swung some big punch bowl at my head and then I didn't know nothin' more 'til I woke up in the hospital—"

"The hospital?"

Paul couldn't prevent an involuntary spasm of his lips as he fought down a laugh. Lieutenant Kilgary and the two chiefs in the compartment faked brief coughing spells, while Captain Hayes somehow maintained a serious countenance.

"Yes, sir. That's where the sheriff arrested me." Jacob jerked and glanced over toward Sharpe. "Not our sheriff, sir. The one back home."

Hayes leaned forward, resting his arms on the podium even though the gesture was unnecessary in zero gravity. "So, after you went to someone else's wedding you thought was yours and got into a fight with the bride and groom and got sent to the hospital and got arrested and sent to jail, then you saw this judge."

"Yes, sir." Jacob nodded quickly. "And the judge, he agreed that life had treated me pretty damn, uh, pardon me, sir, pretty darn unfair and that maybe I just oughta go back to my ship."

"Well, Seaman Jacob, based on your story so far I have to admit I'd have been inclined to get you out of my town as soon as possible, too. So that's why you were late getting back from leave?"

"No, sir."

Paul clenched his teeth as hard as he could to stifle a laugh, even as he heard a strangled sound from Senior Chief Kowalski.

Captain Hayes ducked his head again, then looked up sternly. "All of that didn't make you late getting back from leave?"

"No, sir. Not directly, sir. You see, I'd taken enough leave for a little honeymoon, but now I didn't need that much time 'cause Justy and I wasn't goin' on a honeymoon." Jacob's face looked troubled. "Well, I guess Justy was."

"But not with you."

"No, sir. Not with me. Anyway, I cashed in my ticket back to base so I could pay my fine."

"The judge fined you?"

"Yes, captain. I didn't mention that? He was gonna make it more money than that but when he found out that was all I had he was willing to settle for it as long as I left."

Out of Jacob's sight, Sheriff Sharpe seemed to be fighting off convulsions. Captain Hayes nodded, his expression exaggeratedly intent. "How'd you get back to base, then, Jacob?"

"That's what I been tryin' to explain, captain! One o' Justy's cousins offered me a ride out of town, and damned, uh, darned if he didn't dump me in the middle of nowhere. I started walkin', 'cause I didn't want to be late getting back, but this guy stopped to give me a ride. Then the cops started givin' me a hard time—"

"Cops? What cops?"

"The ones that stopped the guy givin' me the ride, sir. They found all this stuff in the back o' the car and started waving guns around and pushing me onto the ground and searching me all over and I gotta say, captain, that Master-at-Arms Sharpe there he does searches just like that, too, sometimes and it ain't pleasant at all."

Jacob stopped, looking earnestly at Captain Hayes, who stared back. "Okay, Jacob. The car you hitched a ride in turned out to be carrying drugs. Is that right?"

"Yes, sir."

"You got arrested, again, along with the guy who'd picked you up."

"Yes, sir. And when they found some o' that stuff on my clothes—"

"How'd some of the drugs get on your clothes?"

Jacob flushed and looked toward the deck. "Uh, the guy who picked me up, she wasn't actually a guy. And she was pretty nice and I was kinda... well, I'd been expecting to be with Justy on our honeymoon so I was sorta ramped up, you know."

Captain Hayes stopped to rub his temples. "You got arrested for running drugs."

"Yes, sir. And that was on a Friday afternoon and what with the weekend and runnin' lab tests on me to prove I didn't have none of the stuff *in* me and straightenin' stuff out and all, it was the middle of next week before they let me go."

"Why didn't they tell the Navy you'd been arrested? That way we'd have known where you were."

"Sir, I didn't want to embarrass the Navy by admittin' I was a sailor!"

"Thank you for thinking of that, Jacob."

"You're welcome, sir." Jacob smiled briefly but quickly turned gloomy. "They found out, anyway. Then there was this, that and some other stuff, and the upshot was the cops there gave me a ride back to the base."

"That was nice of them."

"Well, yes, captain, but they said the judge—this was a different judge, sir."

"I understand."

"She kinda ordered them to take me back."

"Did she also kinda order you to go with them?"

"Yes, sir. But by the time I got back, I'd missed my ride back to Franklin. The transportation people were pretty unhappy with me, captain, even when I tried to explain what'd happened."

"Really?"

"It's true, sir! They made me wait for an openin' to get back here and that took another coupla days and that's why I was late, sir."

Captain Hayes massaged his forehead again. "If I understand properly, Seaman Jacob, the Missing Movement charge pertains to being late for your ride back to Franklin, while the Absent Without Leave charge is because missing your ride meant you didn't get back to the ship before your leave expired."

"Uh, yes, sir. In a nutshell, sir."

"Seaman Jacob, have you learned anything from this?"

Jacob nodded sadly. "Have I learned anything? Sir, it'd take me a while to tell you everythin' I learned. Why—"

Hayes held up his hands. "That's all right. Lieutenant Kilgary, what kind of a sailor is Seaman Jacob?"

Kilgary cleared her throat but her voice still had a slightly strangled quality as she spoke. "Seaman Jacob is a decent performer, sir. This is the first time we've had trouble with him."

"Very well." Hayes focused on Jacob again. "I'm going to go easy on you Jacob, but next time you go on leave you might take a friend along to help with the decision-making. Understand?"

"Yes, sir."

"Thirty days' restriction. One-half one month's pay forfeit, suspended for six months. Dismissed."

Seaman Jacob grinned with gratitude, saluted, and pulled himself from the compartment. Silence reigned for a moment, until Sharpe closed the hatch again, then Senior Chief Kowalski finally erupted in laughter, followed by Lieutenant Kilgary, Paul, Chief Meyer and Sharpe.

Captain Hayes gave Senior Chief Kowalski a wounded look. "Senior chief, why the hell'd you do that to me?"

"Sir, to be perfectly honest, sir, the XO and I knew there wasn't no way we could describe that story to you. We felt you deserved the full experience, sir."

"I'm not sure what I did to deserve the full experience. Lieutenant Kilgary, does that guy ever go near anything important?"

Kilgary stopped laughing and tried to respond in a serious tone. "Jacob is actually a very good mechanic, captain. He's a wonder with machinery."

"You're kidding."

Chief Meyer shook his head. "No, sir, captain. Jacob can fix damn near anything, even stuff we're not supposed to be able to fix. He's one great mechanic. Absolutely clueless about everything else in the universe, though."

"You don't say. Chief, try to give him plenty of work so he stays on the ship instead of wandering around bumping into police and nice drug-running female 'guys.' Are there any other cases?"

Sharpe shook his head. "No, sir."

Senior Chief Kowalski grinned. "The crew knew we were only going to be out for a few days, sir. Even the trouble-makers didn't want to risk being on restriction when we got back to Franklin."

"Good." Hayes headed toward the hatch, but paused his movement, hanging before the entry, to raise one arm and swing his extended finger across the whole group like he was aiming a weapon. "And don't you people *ever* do something like this to me again. I'm going down to sickbay to make sure I didn't get a hernia from trying not to laugh."

"Attention on deck!" Sharpe called out. After Hayes had left,

Kowalski and Meyer started laughing again.

Paul waved to Sharpe as he left. Sharpe shrugged in response. "Better luck next time, Mr. Sinclair."

"Maybe this'll scare Fastow straight."

Sharpe didn't hide his skepticism. "I'll believe it when I see it, sir."

"I've always admired your faith in human nature, Sheriff."

"I'm a cop. If you want faith in human nature, call a chaplain."

Franklin station loomed not far away, looking like a hollow discus, its rotation seeming leisurely from this distance. Paul glanced over at Lieutenant Sindh. "I hear your relief will be waiting for us on the pier."

Sindh smiled. "So I understand."

"This might be the last time you bring the *Merry Mike* into Franklin."

"Ah, the grief overwhelms me." Her smiled widened. "Bosun mate of the watch, notify all hands to prepare for entering port. Paul please notify the captain and the XO that we're ready for final approach on Franklin." Her fingers ran over the controls in front of her. "Lots of traffic out here, as usual, but it's all keeping clear of our approach lane."

"Captain's on the bridge!"

Hayes settled into his chair and fastened the straps. "Going to take her in, Sonya?"

"Yes, sir."

"Try not to scratch the paint." Hayes grinned, looking over as Garcia and Kwan pulled themselves onto the bridge. The three senior officers huddled, Hayes' smile fading into annoyance.

Paul leaned toward Sindh. "That doesn't look good."

"No. But we can't worry about that now, Paul. Pay attention to the maneuvering situation."

"Right. Sorry."

The *Michaelson* eased in toward Franklin at an angle, her thrusters firing to match the station's rotation. On the maneuvering displays, curved lines showed exactly where the ship was and where she should be. Sindh ordered the thrusters fired each time the *Michaelson* drifted off the right vector, almost seeming to know when to fire the thrusters before the ship's automated maneuvering systems did. "Send across line six."

"Send across line six, aye," the bosun mate of the watch echoed, transmitting the order.

A line shot out of the *Michaelson*'s hull, aimed right for the contact plate waiting at her berth. The magnetic grapnel hit and sealed itself to the station. The bosun sounded his pipe. "Moored! Shift colors!"

More lines went across, fixing the *Michaelson*'s mass to Franklin station, then very gently bringing the ship in toward her berth. The ship settled in firmly as Paul tried to readjust to a feeling of constant gravity again.

"Quarterdeck access seals are extending," Paul announced. It was all very superfluous, but he'd quickly learned that saying things over and over again, and announcing things anyone could see on the displays, made certain everybody knew what they needed to know. "Seals matched. Pressurizing. Ready for quarterdeck opening."

"Very well," Lieutenant Sindh replied. "Open quarterdeck hatch and match the brow to Franklin."

"Open quarterdeck, aye. Quarterdeck hatch opening. Brow matching. Quarterdeck reports they are ready to assume the watch."

Sindh looked over at the captain, who nodded. "Very well. Transfer the watch to the quarterdeck. Secure the bridge watch."

"The quarterdeck has the watch. Securing the bridge watch, aye."

Hayes unstrapped and stood up, slightly unsteady himself on his feet. "Good job, lieutenant. But you might get another chance to do this after all." He headed out.

"Captain's left the bridge!"

Paul unstrapped and stretched. "What do you suppose the captain meant by that?"

Sindh shrugged. "Apparently we may be going out again in the near future."

"Sorry about that."

"I'm still short, Paul. They can keep us in space every day until I'm scheduled to depart the ship as long as I get to leave that day! Just be glad we don't have duty tonight."

"I am. I just hope Jen doesn't have duty, either."

"Good luck."

Paul was just leaving the bridge when Kris Denaldo appeared in the passageway and held up her data pad. "Got a brief transmission in comms on the back channel."

Paul read "P—Fogarty's—J." Jen wanted to meet him tonight at the bar where the officers usually hung out. "Thanks, Kris."

"Thanks, he says. Me, I've got duty. I pass romantic messages for people even though I'm stuck on the ship tonight while certain other officers go gallivanting off to suck face with certain other officers."

"Not that you envy Jen and me or anything."

"Not at all. Come back one second late from liberty and I'll make sure your butt's hung out to dry." She paused. "I think I'm joking. You probably shouldn't test it, though."

"Understood. Can I bring you back anything in the morning?"

"Not unless it's a male willing to devote his life to satisfying my every desire." Kris paused again. "A halfway decent-looking male. Of the human species."

"You shouldn't be so picky."

"I know. I should just settle for whatever comes along like Jen did."

"Hey!"

"Kidding! Kidding! You two have fun tonight. Just don't tell me about it in the morning."

"Thanks, Kris." Of course, he couldn't just waltz off of the ship. Not until the ship's workday ended, and not until liberty call went down. *I could ask Garcia for early liberty... nah. Who am I kidding? And I couldn't take off early anyway while my sailors have to stay aboard and work. But I don't feel like really working at the moment, not right after coming off watch.* He headed for the wardroom, thinking of coffee and maybe conversation.

Lieutenant Mike Bristol, the assistant supply officer, was there along with another officer Paul didn't recognize. "Hey, Paul. Any word on when liberty's going down?"

"You tell me. Supply always knocks off work the earliest."

Bristol grinned. "That's just a rumor we encourage to ensure a steady stream of new recruits. Have you met Lieutenant Isakov?"

"No." He extended his hand. "Paul Sinclair. CIC officer."

Her shake was firm enough. "Val Isakov. I'm Lieutenant Sindh's relief."

"Oh. She'll be very happy to see you."

"I bet." Isakov smiled, a very quick quirk of her lips, then focused back on Mike Bristol. "Right now I need to get check-in done."

"Sure." Paul got some coffee and left. *Not the friendliest soul, but I've had my share of bad days, too.*

Colleen Kilgary was outside her stateroom and flagged Paul down. "Hey, you seeing Jen tonight?"

"I'm planning on it."

"Good. The *Maury* had that SEERS thingee installed during their last overhaul. Can you ask Jen how it's working out? We're supposed to get it, too."

"SEERS?"

"Ship's Engineering something something System. Some sort of unified power management gizmo."

"Uh, okay."

Paul entered his stateroom in the aptly nicknamed ensign locker and sat down at his desk. Sam Yarrow, the only other occupant at the moment, glanced over at him. "Garcia's looking for you."

Garcia's always looking for me. Garcia won't know what to do with his life when he can't look for me anymore. "What about?"

"Ask him yourself."

"Thanks, Sam." Paul tried to sound sincere, knowing that kind of reaction always threw Yarrow off. He stood up again and headed for Combat. Even if Garcia wasn't in Combat, Paul could catch up on paperwork at his console there.

Fogarty's tried to look like a comfortable neighborhood pub. The fact that it was located inside an orbiting naval facility made the illusion a bit hard to sustain, but the bar's wood-grain painted steel bulkheads were close enough to the real thing to be a welcome oasis for sailors tired of staring at gray steel bulkheads. Paul took a seat at one of the small tables just outside of the door, watching humanity stream past in one of the wide main "streets" on the station while he waited for Jen to show up.

"Hey, sailor, looking for a good time?"

Paul shook his head without looking behind where the voice had come from. "Nah. I've got a serious girlfriend. I'm not allowed to have a good time anymore." He felt a rap against the back of his head. "Ouch."

Lieutenant Junior Grade Jen Shen walked around and took the other seat, shaking her head. "Why do I put up with you, Paul Sinclair?"

"I've often wondered that myself. I guess I'm just really lucky."

"Maybe I just feel sorry for you."

"I can live with that."

She grinned. "How'd you like operating with the *Maury*?"

"Nerve-wracking, to tell the truth. All those big ships so close." He smiled at her. "But at least whenever things got boring I could imagine you were on watch at the same time I was."

"Boy, are you desperate."

"Hey, I like watching you."

"Watching my ship isn't exactly the same thing."

Paul smiled wider. "You're right. The *Maury*'s stern can't compare to yours."

She laughed. "Are you saying my bow isn't better, too?"

"Not at all. But I'm a stern man."

"Whatever spins your gears." She leaned forward. "I want to hug you."

"We're in uniform."

"And in public." Jen gestured with both arms. "Consider yourself hugged."

"Any chance of considering myself kissed?"

"Maybe later. Did you see the *Mahan* out there?"

"Yeah."

Her expression changed to exasperation at Paul's tone of voice. "Pardon me for being happy my father could see me operating my ship. That's pretty rare."

"It'd be pretty rare under any circumstances." Paul smiled ruefully. "Okay. Have you talked to your father?"

"Not really. I got a brief message from him. He thought the exercise went off okay."

"He must've really been impressed."

She stuck her tongue out at him. "He thought the *Michaelson* did okay, too."

"Really?"

"Really. What're your plans for tonight?"

"Well, let's see. I don't have duty on my ship. You don't have duty on your ship. We haven't seen each other for over two weeks. I don't know. What about you?"

"I was thinking about finding some sailor and shacking up for the night."

"Oh, well, I'm free."

"I guess you'll do, then." Jen grinned again. "Keep romancing me like this and I may have to marry you some day, Mr. Sinclair."

His heart literally seemed to skip a few beats. "Does that mean...?"

"Not yet."

"It's been over six months since I asked you to marry me."

Jen put her hands over her ears. "Oh, pressure! Pressure! Somebody get me a survival suit!" She lowered the hands and smiled fondly at Paul. "I'll know when I know, Paul."

He nodded, smiling back to mask his feelings. *I already know. I've known for a long time. But telling Jen I feel put off by her not being sure yet wouldn't make her any more likely to come to a decision. Kris was right. Jen's like a cat. If you push her, she pushes back instead of yielding. If that's what I want I have to live with it.* "Dinner?"

"Real food? You certainly know how to make me feel loved."

About an hour later, fed with passable versions of real food from one of the private restaurants licensed on Franklin to make life there a bit more bearable, they checked into a rent-a-shack. Paul edged inside the small room, just big enough to hold a bed, a tiny toilet, and an entertainment display. "Tight quarters, as usual."

Jen rolled onto the bed. "You never complained about having to be close to me before."

"I'm not complaining now." He lay down as well, just resting for a moment. "This is one exhausting life, Jen."

"Tell me about it. You work in one of those easy-going Operations Department divisions. I'm a snipe, laboring in the bowels of engineering for days on end without rest."

"I've worked in Combat for days on end without rest."

"I've worked for weeks without rest."

"Months."

"Years."

They both laughed. Paul looked over at her, wondering again at whatever luck had brought them together. *Well, it wasn't exactly luck. The Navy brought us together when it assigned us to the same ship. But if Jen hadn't been transferred off the* Michaelson *we never could've had any kind of relationship but friends, and I like this a whole lot better.*

Jen propped herself on one elbow and looked back at him. "A dollar for your thoughts."

"Same as usual."

"I should've saved my dollar."

"Truth to tell, I was thinking how the Navy brought us together."

"And then separates us again as often as possible, if not more often." She lay back, staring up at the low ceiling of the rent-a-shack. "I heard a rumor we're heading out again real soon."

"Me, too."

"Both ships again?"

"Looks like it. But that's all I've heard."

"Another attempt to impress the SASALs, no doubt." She exhaled heavily. "Sometimes I just feel like kicking their butts out of space and getting it over with."

"It wouldn't be easy or pretty, Jen."

She rolled her head to glare at him. "Do you think I don't know that?"

"Sorry." *She was on the* Michaelson, *too, when we blew away that unarmed SASAL research ship. And she's still got more time in space than me.* "I hate to think of you facing combat. Not because I doubt how well you'll handle it, but, you know... "

Jen looked away. "I know. There's luck, good and bad. There's a lot of things. If shooting starts, either you or I might not come home for the victory parades."

"Or both of us."

"Yeah." She looked at him again. "In some ways, that'd be easier for me."

"Me, too. There's only one Jen out there."

"I bet. There's probably some rule against creating another one of me."

"You and Herdez."

"Do not mention her and me in the same breath!"

"Yes, ma'am." *Even if you have a lot more in common with our old XO than you'll ever admit.* "I don't know. I knew the risks I was signing on to face. I just never really thought about having to worry about my One and Only facing the same risks."

Jen snorted a brief laugh. "I never thought I *wouldn't* have to worry about that. Paul, both your parents were Navy. Why didn't you think you might get involved with another officer?"

"I don't know. Really. Maybe because by the time I was a teenager Mom was retired and Dad followed soon after. But now here we are and maybe next time we go out the SASALs will do something even more outrageous and someone on our side will shoot and this time it won't be an isolated incident that everyone just wants to sweep under the rug."

"Maybe. We're doing our jobs as best we can. We'll keep our ships and our shipmates and ourselves intact if we possibly can, no matter what. If we can't, well, hell, we're both doing this job because we believe it's important. Right?"

"Right."

"So carpe diem and all that stuff." Jen yawned. "Are we going to talk political events and philosophy all night or do you want to get naked?"

"Uh, well..."

"Oh, please. Stop trying to pretend you have to think about it."

"I like your mind, too."

"As much as you like my stern?"

"Uh..."

"Men."

"Would you rather I was a woman?"

She reached for him as she answered. "No way."

4

"The SASALs weren't impressed enough by our little display."
Commander Garcia almost snarled the words. "We're going out
again."

"Second time's the charm," Taylor murmured.

Garcia ignored her. "No nonsense with foreign ships this time.
We're going out with *Maury*. We'll head for the border of the region
of space claimed by the South Asians, and when we get nice and
close we'll deactivate our anti-detection devices."

Taylor snorted. Denaldo raised her eyebrows. Paul nodded. *So this
time we're going to try to scare the SASALs by sneaking up on them and then going
"boo."* "Just us and the *Maury*, sir?"

"That's right. And here's the fun part." Garcia bared his teeth.
"They want us within ten kilometers of each other when we reveal
ourselves. Going on the same vector right along the border at high
speed."

"How the hell are we going to coordinate that when we can't see
the *Maury* any better than the SASALs can?"

"Because we're good, Mr. Sinclair. And because our fine communications officer Ms. Denaldo is going to figure out a way to pass information between the ships without giving ourselves away."

Kris spread her hands, looking dazed. "Sir, we can use visual signaling vectored only toward where the *Maury*'s supposed to be, but if both ships are moving at high speed she might not see the signals in time to react even if she is where we think she is."

"Then figure out a way they *will* see them in time to react. Feel free to consult with Ensign Taylor on the matter." Garcia grinned again without any trace of real humor, his expression reminding Paul of a hungry bear. "This is a chance to look good. I expect you all to look good. Is that clear?"

So you can look good, right, boss? Garcia's got orders coming up before long, too, and pulling this off might help him get real good ones. Paul glanced at Denaldo's face, now tight with repressed annoyance, and then addressed Garcia. "Sir, just how close are we supposed to be to the border?"

"Twenty kilometers."

Paul barely kept his jaw from dropping. "At high speed? That's no margin of error at all."

"We don't need a margin of error, Sinclair. Now stop complaining about the orders and start getting ready to execute them." Garcia checked his data pad, then glared at them again. "Oh, yeah. We're getting underway for this the day after tomorrow. Make sure your divisions are ready."

Ensign Taylor leaned against the nearest console. "I guess there's no sense in worrying about getting that back-logged maintenance taken care of."

Garcia focused on her. "Are there any equipment problems that I'm not aware of?"

"No, sir. Just all the stuff you *are* aware of. But that's okay. I'll tell my boys and girls to break out the chewing gum and duct tape again and hopefully everything important will hold together until we get back home."

For once, Garcia's grin held some real humor in it. "It'd better. Now, get to work. Denaldo, I want a workup on your communications plan before noon."

After Garcia left, Kris Denaldo looked at Taylor. "I sure hope you know a way to do this."

Taylor nodded. "Matter of fact, I do."

"You're kidding!"

"Nope. Ever hear of moon bounce communications?" Denaldo glanced at Paul and then they both shook their heads. "Didn't think so. It was pre-communications satellite stuff. Very primitive. To get a radio signal sent over a real long distance on Earth, one station'd send the signal straight at the moon. The signal'd bounce off the moon, and get picked up by the receiver back on Earth."

"That'd take a lot of power. And how did they aim the signal?"

"It did, and they didn't aim it. As long as the sending and the receiving station both had the moon up, they could bounce signals back and forth. But if we're just sending signals through vacuum we wouldn't need much power. And the spread from a reflected signal makes it real hard to trace back the angle to the sending station. Here's what you propose, Kris. Low-power, high-frequency signals."

"HF? That's Stone Age communications. You can't get any decent amount of information into an HF signal."

"What do you want to send 'em, movies? HF will spread real nice and nobody's going to be monitoring those frequencies for military communications. Just set up a simple code with *Maury* that'll let you pass basic location, course and speed data. Then every once in a while you guys bounce a signal at each other. You'll be transmitting away from SASAL space to bounce the signal off the moon, and by the time the reflected signal gets back to where we are it'll have spread out so much nobody'll be able to get a decent fix on the place it originated from even if they can work out the reflection angle."

Denaldo rubbed her chin, her expression showing she was thinking intently. "I can't see why it wouldn't work."

"Kris, you got Senior Chief Kowalski working for you. 'Ski was probably around when they were doing that moon bounce stuff."

"I don't think he's quite *that* old."

Taylor grinned. "Nah, but tell him I said so. 'Ski won't have any trouble setting up a system like that for us and the *Maury* to use."

"Thanks, Akesha."

"No prob. You need any brilliant plans, Paul? I got a two-for-the-price-of-one deal going this morning."

"I don't think so."

"Guess again."

Paul watched the older and much more experienced but technically more junior officer warily. "What?"

"The systems will provide proximity alert warnings when we get too close to something, like say that boundary of SASAL-claimed space, right?"

"Right."

"But we're already going to be within twenty klicks of that boundary."

"I... oh, hell. That's inside the parameters, isn't it?"

"Yup. You'll get continuous alerts. Drive you crazy and the captain won't like it. What do you do?"

"I have a funny feeling you know what to do already."

"Hey! You're right, college boy! Use the docking maneuvering system to set the alert distance."

"But that system won't work at transit speeds—"

"It will if you manually override the speed settings and input a simple fraction of our real speed. Then you just multiple any warning times by the appropriate factor."

Paul shook his head in amazement. "Wow. That'll work?"

"Of course it'll work."

"It's amazing what I can learn from you."

The former-enlisted officer gave Paul an exaggerated leer. "That's nothing. Boy, I could teach you things that'd make that girl of yours *real* happy. Though since we're assigned to the same ship that Wouldn't Be Appropriate," she intoned, emphasizing the capitals. "Your girl might wonder where you learned all that stuff, too. Then again, she might be so happy she wouldn't care." Taylor laughed, then rubbed her hands together. "Now, let's go tell our sailors the good news about getting underway again in two days and watch morale head for the nearest event horizon."

Kris Denaldo grinned at Paul as Taylor left. "She likes teasing you about sex because whenever she does you look like some ten-year-old boy who got caught sneaking peeks at a dirty vid."

"I do not!"

"Well, excuse me! Being so innocent and all myself I don't know enough to be embarrassed." Her smile faded and she looked out the hatch. "Fun time's over. Like Akesha said, let's go tell our troops the good news."

The rest of the day turned into a frantic swirl of activity as Paul huddled with Chief Imari to make sure everything important would be working well enough within two days, tried to plow through due-yesterday paperwork that had already been postponed to deal with other operational matters, and handled a sudden personnel emergency with Petty Officer Daniels when they got word both her parents had died in an accident back on Earth. The last thing he wanted to have to worry about at that moment was dealing with arranging emergency transport for her back to Earth for the funeral, but Paul also knew he didn't have any choice. Luckily, Commander Sykes had connections with the Transport Office and was able to get an unknowing officer bumped off the next shuttle home to make room for Daniels.

Sometime late in the day Paul realized he'd already worked into the early evening hours. He put in a hasty call to Jen, who peered blearily back him from the phone display. "Hi."

"Hi."

"Bad day. You know why."

"Yeah. Same here."

"Bye."

"Bye."

And then there was one day left.

"Bring in all lines." If Sonya Sindh was disappointed about taking the *Michaelson* out again, she didn't show any sign of it. "Bosun. Shift colors."

The familiar wavering whistle sounded as the bosun of the watch blew his pipe over the ship's general announcing system. "Underway. Shift colors."

They were heading out before the *Maury*, this time, which left Paul no leisure to watch Jen's ship. He focused all his attention on

Lieutenant Sindh, acutely aware that her place on the watch team would soon be taken by Lieutenant Val Isakov. Isakov herself was strapped into an observer position near the back of the bridge, hopefully learning by watching. Paul stole a glance back that way, seeing Isakov looking around with an expression he might've described as either calm or unimpressed. *She's supposed to be experienced. Qualified as an officer of the deck on the* Isherwood. So Sonya Sindh had told him, anyway, since Isakov herself seemed totally uninterested in talking to Paul about anything. *Not that I'm looking to be buddy-buddy with every officer I stand watches with. But I'm not looking forward to losing a great officer like Sonya, who I know I can depend upon, and getting an unknown quantity in return, supposedly qualified or not.*

The pressure of the main drive and lateral forces of the thrusters finally died down, leaving Paul's stomach doing the usual flip-flops, though at least this time the period they'd spent under Franklin's sensation of constant gravity had been so short that readjusting to zero gravity shouldn't be too hard. Captain Hayes, looking a little haggard himself from all the work of the last few days, unstrapped. "Nice job."

"Captain's left the bridge!"

Sindh smiled at Paul. "Perhaps *this* was the last time I'll take the *Merry Mike* out."

He looked at the hatch where Captain Hayes had departed. "The captain's not feeling too hot. He usually says more than that."

"Yes. We need to tread a little lightly. Val." Sindh turned to look at her relief. "Any questions?"

Isakov smiled and shook her head. "Nope. Same class of ship, same layout, and it looks like she handles like the *Ish-fish* did."

"Paul's familiar with the ship, too. He can help with anything you need up here, since he'll be qualifying as an independent officer of the deck himself before long."

Isakov shifted her look to Paul for just a moment. "That's nice."

Sindh unstrapped. "Why don't we swap places so you can get a first-hand feel for the watch station and get used to working with Paul."

The women switched seats. Isakov remained cool, but not off-putting, as she worked with Paul. He found himself feeling better about the imminent change in his watch team. *Okay. If we can work together, that's all I need.*

The watch relief went off easily, with nothing to do until they reached their positions near the border of SASAL-claimed space. Sam Yarrow scowled as Paul explained the moon-bounce messages which would provide brief, coded updates on the *Maury*. "What a lousy way of doing business. Prehistoric. Why don't we just toss out flares?"

"Taylor thought of it," Paul added, knowing Yarrow and she didn't get along.

"Figures," Smilin' Sam mumbled. "Okay. I got it."

"I stand relieved. On the bridge, this is Lieutenant Sinclair. Lieutenant Yarrow has the conn."

"This is Lieutenant Yarrow. I have the conn." Sam leaned a little closer to Paul as he strapped in. "What's she like?"

"Who?"

"The new lieutenant. Who else?"

Paul thought about his reply. Anything he said which could even be remotely twisted to cause trouble would be dangerous to say to Yarrow, who had a nasty habit of repeating suitably embellished accounts of such conversations to his superiors. "She seems fine."

"Not bad looking, is she?"

"I hadn't noticed."

"What, not your type?"

Paul just shook his head and left the bridge. His stomach had decided that, even though nauseous from zero gravity, it still wanted more food than he'd wolfed down in the last couple of days.

Lunch in the wardroom was unusually quiet, with the junior officers worn out from the recent press of work. Commander Sykes shook his head with mock sorrow. "They don't make them like they used to. In my day you could work junior officers for, oh, weeks at a stretch before they started wearing out on you."

Kris Denaldo gave him an arch look. "Suppo, in your day they had to use junior officers to spell the rowers in the galleys."

Sykes nodded, still affecting sadness. "Ah, yes. The good old days of the wine-dark sea. I still have the calluses on my hands from the oars."

"A supply officer with calluses on his hands? That'll be the day."

Everyone laughed, while Sykes made a production out of bringing out his data pad and making some notes. He glanced up and saw he had their attention. "I'm just making some notes on what to serve the junior officers for dinner."

"Not those fake shark steaks, I hope," Paul noted.

"Sadly, no. There was a problem with the manufacturing facility, and we were advised to return all the steaks as they were unfit for human consumption."

Mike Bristol, the assistant supply officer, nodded. "Not that that's ever bothered us before, but this time they were *officially* unfit for human consumption."

Colleen Kilgary eyed the odd-looking meal before her. "One shudders to contemplate what it'd take to get something officially declared unfit to serve us, considering what we get most days."

As he nodded in agreement, Paul remembered an uncompleted task, so he followed Kilgary out of the wardroom when the meal was over. "Hey, Coll, I hadn't had a chance to tell you. I asked Jen about the new engineering stuff on the *Maury*. SARS?"

"SEERS. What's she think of it?"

"She said they can't tell, yet. Too much stuff in engineering still didn't work quite right after that yard period. Their chief engineer's not letting SEERS do much so far, because the *Maury*'s snipes are spending their time trying to manhandle it all back into shape."

Kilgary grinned. "Tweak. In the high-tech, ultra-modern Space Navy we tweak things in engineering. We may use a sledge hammer to do it, but we tweak."

Paul laughed. "Okay. I've seen the electricians tweak a few things by hitting them, so I guess it makes sense for snipes to work the same way. Jen said they'll probably let SEERS handle things this time out because they think they've got the engineering systems about where they should be."

"Well, thanks for asking. I didn't expect she'd have too much to tell me at this point."

"What's the thing do, anyway?"

"Run things." Kilgary rolled her eyes. "The systems on this ship are incredibly complex and because it's pretty much a closed environment anything one sub-system does affects all the other sub-systems. If you let a metal brain try to handle too much of it, it ends up mismanaging power loads because it gets caught in feedback loops."

"You mean it reduces power somewhere, which means it has to do something else somewhere else."

"Which makes it have to go back to the first place and maybe increase power again. Then it reduces more, then it increases more, and soon enough circuit breakers start popping. When a metal head starts over-reacting at the speed of light problems develop real fast. Human brains can spot the patterns developing somehow and even things out. But it's a real pain in the neck to deal with, especially in a critical power situation like combat. It'll be nice to have a metal head capable of handling that part of the job."

Paul grinned. "Maybe we won't need engineers, anymore."

"Suits me. I can change over to one of those easy jobs in the Operations Department."

"Now you sound like Jen."

"We just both happen to know what we're talking about. Speaking of female officers, how'd Val Isakov do on watch just now?"

"She seemed okay. Confident. Why?"

Kilgary shrugged. "New officer. I'm just curious."

"Well, she's got the whole ball of wax on the mid-watch. Along with me."

"Lucky guy," Kilgary murmured, then left before Paul could ask what she meant.

The bad part about being on watch on the bridge from midnight to four in the morning was that you weren't sleeping. The good part, the only good part in Paul's opinion, was that just about everybody else was sleeping. The watches tended to be quiet. No senior officers bulling in to raise hell, no scheduled events to add stress, just you and the other watch standers. The bridge, itself darkened not from necessity but to keep human body rhythms happy, sometimes felt to Paul like a cocoon of life traveling independently through the nothingness, the glowing display screens and instrument panels providing nearby artificial counterparts to the cold, distant light of innumerable stars shown on the visual displays.

Paul yawned, then grimaced and grabbed a quick gulp of coffee from the container clipped to his belt. Quiet and dark could be too nice. Too conducive to falling asleep, anyway, and the last thing anybody wanted to do was fall asleep on watch. Or, as Carl Meadows used to advise him, "Falling asleep on watch is like falling off a cliff. It feels fine for a while, until you hit the bottom. Or in the case of sleeping on watch, until somebody finds you sleeping. Then you'll wish you *had* fallen off a cliff instead."

"Paul."

He looked over at Lieutenant Isakov. "Yes, ma'am?"

She laughed. "Ma'am?"

"You didn't tell me I could call you anything else."

"Oh. Right. So, I'm Val. I've got a question for you."

Paul couldn't be certain of her expression in the dim lighting. "What's that?"

Isakov tapped her control console with two fingers for a moment before speaking again. "I wonder... it looks like war, don't you think?"

"Maybe. I hope not."

"I've never been in combat."

"Neither have I."

"But you did lead that damage control team. I've heard about it. Pretty nasty fire, right?"

Paul took a deep breath as the memory flooded back. "Yeah. Forward Engineering was an inferno. We couldn't see a thing because of the smoke." He felt his heart speeding up and tried to calm himself. *That happened six months ago. But Chief Asher died in it and Scott Silver got court-martialed because of it. Because I helped chase down the evidence that Silver had been doing a lousy job and might've ordered Chief Asher to do something that started the fire. I wonder if anybody's told*

Isakov about all that? "It was pretty intense."

Isakov leaned toward Paul slightly, pitching her voice lower even though the enlisted watchstanders were deep in their own quiet conversation. "Then you know. What it's like to face that kind of danger."

"I... guess so."

"It must have been very exciting."

Paul shook his head. "No. I was too scared to be excited."

"Scared?" Isakov laughed again, in a way which bothered Paul. "Scared?"

"Yes. I had a lot of things to worry about." He wondered if he sounded defensive, and wondered why he cared.

She leaned closer. "So you don't believe in taking risks?"

"When I need to."

A little closer. He thought he could feel her breath on his face. "Some risks are worth choosing. Just for fun. Don't you think?"

Paul shook his head. "No."

Isakov grinned and leaned away again. "That's not very heroic of you," she noted with another laugh.

Not sure what Isakov was up to, he decided he should blow it off. "I'm not a hero."

She called up the captain's standing orders on her display and made a show of reading them. Paul spent a few more moments wondering what it had all been about, then mentally shrugged and concentrated again on staying awake.

A week later, after standing a lot more watches with Isakov, he still hadn't figured her out. She knew her job, and sometimes talked about her time on the *Isherwood*, or the *Ish-fish* as the ship was nicknamed in the fleet, in a friendly fashion. Other times she treated Paul like they'd just met, and she hadn't been impressed by the experience.

But he had plenty of other things to worry about on this particular watch besides whatever ticked inside Isakov's head.

The *Maury* had left Franklin nearly a full day after the *Michaelson*, cutting a slightly tighter and faster course toward their rendezvous point. Thanks to the moon-bounce updates on *Maury*'s course and speed they'd been able to localize her much better than if they'd just been depending on passive detection of what signs of the other ship's presence leaked past her various means of hiding in space. Paul checked the datum outlined on the *Michaelson*'s maneuvering displays again.

Commander Garcia swung onto the bridge and scowled equally at Paul and the displays. "Damn stupid idea," he grumbled, then pointed at the estimated position and vector for the *Maury*. "If we were just going to do a firing run, fine. That's great. It'd let us get close enough to precisely fix her and rip her guts out. But we're supposed to be on matching vectors and close to each other. Stupid."

Paul watched Garcia, trying to hide his curiosity. Garcia had a lot of experience, but rarely shared it with the officers in his division, and if he did, usually managed to put them down in the process. Now he was actually explaining something. *I guess that shows how nervous he is. That doesn't exactly calm me down.*

"If we don't hit each other, this'll look really good," Garcia finished, turning to go. Then he glared at Paul. "No collisions, Sinclair."

Isakov stared after Garcia after he'd left the bridge. "Was he kidding? Telling you not to run into any other ships like it was some kind of special instruction?"

"He wasn't kidding."

"I'm glad he's *your* department head."

Paul sweated through the watch, scanning his displays as the *Maury* and *Michaelson* converged on the point where they'd join up. No big deal, except both would be as invisible as modern technology could make them, and both would be traveling through space at velocities measured in kilometers per second and both were large enough that their masses carried plenty of momentum which wouldn't turn on any figurative dimes. As each ship drew closer to each other, the small signs of their presence became easier for the other to detect. A final moon-bounce update on *Maury*'s course and speed vector arrived, but it had taken so long to travel to the moon and back that it didn't provide much reassurance.

The estimated position of the *Maury* kept wavering on the *Michaelson*'s displays as probabilities shifted. Instead of the single, bright point Paul wanted to see, the estimate resembled a big, fuzzy ball. The *Maury should* be closer to the center of the ball, but it *might* be somewhere on the outer edge.

An hour before Paul's watch ended, the collision alarm sounded, jolting already frayed nerves and generating a volley of curses. "Shut that thing down," Captain Hayes snapped.

Paul slapped some controls, cutting off the computer-generated voice of the *Michaelson*'s maneuvering systems in mid-warning. "It's some of the probability vectors the *Maury* might be on, captain. They're falling inside the five-kilometer limit we put into the collision warning system."

"Five kilometers." Hayes shook his head. "This idea must've looked great to some genius back on Earth. You ever hear of a guy named Wellington, Paul?"

"The Duke of Wellington, sir?"

"Yeah. Him. Before Waterloo he went around inspecting his

troops, who were a pretty scruffy bunch, and then said 'I don't know what effect they'll have on the enemy, but by God they scare me.' That's what this maneuver reminds me of. I don't know what effect it'll have on the SASALs, but it's sure scaring me."

"Yes, sir. Maybe they'll try to duplicate it."

Hayes grinned. "That'd serve them right. XO?"

Commander Kwan, watching the final approach from his own seat on the other side of the bridge from the captain, turned at the hail. "Yes, sir?"

"Let's have this watch team relieved half an hour early. That'll give the new people plenty of time to get comfortable with the situation."

"We could just keep this watch team on until both ships have revealed themselves, captain."

Paul glanced at Isakov. One of the odder things about being on watch was when the CO and XO talked back and forth over your heads as if you weren't there.

Hayes shook his head. "No. I want Paul down in Combat so he can analyze things from there if we need to react fast. And," he looked directly at the watch team, "no disrespect, Val, but you're not as familiar with this ship as the other officers of the deck."

Commander Kwan pursed his mouth. "Should we just bring the ship to general quarters? That might be prudent in any event."

Paul watched Hayes consider the question, then shake his head yet again. "No. But I do want maximum airtight integrity set. Let's start doing that now."

Great, Paul thought. *One more thing to worry about during this watch.* The bosun sounded the alert over the ship's general announcing system, then as reports came in from different parts of the ship declaring their status Paul tabulated them and confirmed the reports against the remote read-outs on the bridge. The ship as a whole was always airtight, of course, but maximum airtight integrity meant sealing every internal hatch and nonessential opening inside the ship. That way, if anything punched through the ship's hull, the fewest possible compartments would lose air. *Of course, if the* Maury *herself comes through our hull a few closed hatches aren't going to help much.*

Sam Yarrow naturally wasn't thrilled to have to come on watch early, but he couldn't gripe too loudly with both the CO and XO on the bridge. He did manage to drag out the relieving process as long as possible just to aggravate Paul.

Yarrow studied the maneuvering displays again as he strapped into his seat. "Too bad nothing's near us."

"The *Maury*'s pretty close, Sam."

"So? It would've been nice to spring out on some fat, dumb and happy SASAL ship that thought it was alone out here. The two of us suddenly there, right on top of the guy. That'd impress them."

"I'm worried enough with just the *Maury* out here."

"What's the matter, Sinclair? No guts, no glory."

I'd prefer to keep my guts inside my body, Sam, glory or not. But Paul didn't say it out loud, not with Lieutenant Isakov still within earshot, and not after the mocking comments she'd made about his not being a hero.

Combat had more than the usual complement of watch standers hanging around. Paul's own sailors were obviously curious or concerned, as well. "How's it look, chief?"

Chief Imari made a face as she studied her own display. "Not as clear as I wished it'd look, sir."

"Yeah. For what it's worth, we're going to be ready to jump out of the way."

"Let's hope we have time to jump if we have to do it."

Paul nodded, then strapped in at his console. He rarely made use of the *Michaelson*'s internal video system, since he didn't like to think he was being watched when on duty himself, but now he wanted to have a heads-up to what the captain was thinking. Paul activated a window in his display to show video from the bridge and routed the audio from the bridge to his headphones. It'd be a distraction, but in this case he figured one worth the need to monitor the captain's intentions.

Time appeared to crawl after that. Combat seemed unusually quiet, without much of the usual conversation and wise-cracking among the sailors. When Paul glanced up he could see everyone intent on their displays.

At thirty minutes prior to the time when both ships were to reveal themselves, hopefully in close formation and going the same way at the same speed, a time counter popped into existence on the displays and began scrolling downward. Paul tried not to look at it, since the time counter made the minutes seem to drag even longer, like an old-fashioned clock in a classroom that never seemed to move if watched too closely.

Five minutes. Paul took another look around Combat. Everyone seemed ready for anything. The fuzzy ball that represented the *Maury*'s estimated position had thankfully shrunk considerably, but enough uncertainty remained to keep everyone on edge and the *Michaelson*'s maneuvering systems in a constant tizzy about the threat of collision. On the bridge, no one was talking, either, every eye and full attention focused on the maneuvering displays. *If something is seriously off, though, it won't matter. I know that. We'd have maybe a couple of seconds to react, which wouldn't be fast enough even if we could move the* Merry

Mike's mass instantaneously. But if even one second makes a difference, we'll be ready.

Chief Imari's voice sounded in his headphones. "What do you want to bet they're sweating just as bad on the *Maury*, Mr. Sinclair?"

"I wouldn't doubt it, chief." He wondered where Jen was. If the *Maury*'s crew was reacting like the *Michaelson*'s, then surely Jen and the other engineering officers were at their duty stations, ready for whatever might happen. It felt odd to be able to see her in his mind's eye, to know pretty much how Jen and her surroundings would look at this moment, even though he had no way of seeing her in reality.

Paul stole another look at the bridge. Ensign Jack Abacha, still standing watches under instruction, was looking around with ill-concealed enthusiasm. *Where ignorance is bliss. He's probably the only one on board not experienced enough to know how dangerous this is.*

The time counter scrolled down toward zero. On the window in Paul's display where video from the bridge was displayed, he saw Captain Hayes hold up one hand with his fingers crossed. Over his headphone he heard the captain's forced joviality: "Here's hoping."

5

There wasn't any noticeable change onboard as the time counter hit zero. The ship's systems responded as programmed and the *Michaelson* became highly visible to the universe. The visual bypass system shut off, making her once again easy to spot by the naked eye. Active scanning systems activated, sending out clear signals of the ship's presence as well as pinpointing her location.

The biggest change was the sudden looming presence of the *Maury*. The fuzzy ball wasn't there anymore. Now, her own anti-detection mechanisms deactivated, the *Maury* was there, another ship clearly pacing them at a distance of precisely eight point nine kilometers. Not exactly matching vectors, but close enough that there wasn't any threat of collision in the immediate future. A ragged cheer went up on the *Michaelson*'s bridge.

"Good job!" Captain Hayes exulted. "Congratulations, everybody. That ought to impress anyone who's planning to mess around with us."

Paul realized he was smiling widely. He turned to Chief Imari, raised one hand and exchanged a long-distance high-five with the chief. *Crisis over. Let's see if anybody we can see reacts to us.* Opening the range scale, he looked far outward to monitor the nearest SASAL ships, which were fairly deep within their claimed area of space at the moment.

He was still messing with range settings when the high-pitched stutter of the collision alarm shattered the euphoria on the *Michaelson*. Paul stared at his display as the *Michaelson*'s systems added verbal warnings. "Multiple objects on collision courses. Recommend immediate engagement of all objects on collision courses." A debris field had suddenly appeared, spreading out at high speed from the *Maury*. It only took Paul a moment to realize the debris was too close and moving too fast for the *Michaelson* to hope to evade it.

The general quarters alarm sounded, overriding the collision alarm, its repeated bongs reverberating through the ship and spurring everyone in the crew into immediate, trained responses. "General quarters! General quarters! All personnel to battle stations. Seal all airtight bulkheads. All personnel don survival suits and brace for multiple impacts."

A babble of voices sprung into life on the comm circuits, then Captain Hayes' voice overrode the rest. "Silence on the circuit! Combat, can you identify any of that debris? Are there any sailors in there?"

Paul looked toward Chief Imari, who quickly scanned her own displays even as she shook her head. "Sir, there's not enough time, and there's too much junk messing up our picture." Her face twitched. "Besides, sir, if any sailor hits us at the speed that stuff is moving, even a survival suit wouldn't save 'em."

"Yeah. Thanks, chief." Paul's brain was working on automatic, responding to all the training and experience he'd had so far. Emotions hadn't come into play, yet, and Paul didn't particularly want any emotions warring with the advice he knew he had to give. "Captain, this is Combat. No ID of individual debris items possible within time constraints. Assess chance of survival of any personnel on collision course with us as nil."

The briefest pause followed. "Understand. All combat systems, engage any object on collision course with this ship."

Paul tapped his communications circuit. "Chief, make sure we're double-checking combat systems' choices of highest-priority targets." Sometimes the computers would fixate on the wrong object or objects, blazing away at them while more dangerous things were left unengaged. On Paul's visual display, nothing could be seen but a twinkling of bright objects and a glowing cloud obscuring the view of the dim shape of the USS *Maury*. The *Michaelson*'s lasers and particle beams firing at the oncoming debris hurled shots invisible to the naked eye as they tried to divert the objects, blow them to dust, or at least shatter them into smaller fragments traveling at lower relative velocity to the *Michaelson*. Paul knew the weapons were firing from the subsonic hums that marked discharges of energy, from the occasional dimming of lights on non-critical circuits as weapons recharged, and from the symbols on his other displays, where objects headed for the *Michaelson* were vanishing or fragmenting. As Paul watched, a symbol representing a large object broke into a half-dozen smaller pieces, most of them heading off at angles to their original path. He wondered what the object had been, which small part of the *Maury* it had once represented.

Paul finished sealing his survival suit, then hurriedly checked his personnel. "Is everyone in Combat suited up?"

Chief Imari gave a thumbs-up. "Yes, sir. Any idea what the hell happened, sir?"

"I don't know, chief. I haven't heard anything."

"At least the *Maury*'s still there. Part of her, anyway."

Paul hadn't thought about that, caught up in responding to the immediate crisis. Hadn't thought about where the debris had come from, hadn't thought about what its sudden appearance implied. *An explosion on the* Maury. *Has to be. A big one, from all that debris.* He focused back on the symbol for the *Maury*. Her navigational beacon had stopped operating. Instead, the *Maury* had been tagged with a blinking red warning that the ship's emergency distress beacon had lit off. The *Maury*'s course had altered as well, shoved off to the side by some blow to her. *How big was that explosion? Where was it on the* Maury? *Jen. Please be all right.*

Debris began impacting on the *Michaelson*'s hull, mostly tiny particles but still traveling fast enough to damage even the extremely tough materials in the outer and inner hulls. Warnings flashed on Paul's display as sensors were destroyed by impacts, their functions immediately and automatically shifted to whichever other sensor could try to cover the same area. Paul imagined he could feel the *Michaelson* quiver from all the tiny impacts, though he shouldn't have actually been able to notice.

"Lost some water cells," Chief Imari reported.

Paul nodded. He saw the warnings appear, as small clouds of water vapor puffed out from the *Michaelson*. The water-filled inner hull was designed in part to do exactly that, absorb the heat and other energy of anything hitting the ship. Something big enough to rupture those cells had made it through the defensive barrage of the *Michaelson*'s weapons.

The glowing cloud around the *Maury* expanded rapidly, dimming as it did so. "We've got gases headed for us, too," Chief Imari noted. "By the time it gets here it shouldn't be dense enough to hurt us, though."

Paul checked his own data, where the *Michaelson's* systems had already automatically analyzed the composition of the cloud. *Vaporized water from the Maury's inner hull. Oxygen and other gases from shattered compartments. Various chemical vapors. Trace elements. Carbon. Carbon? Oh, no.* One likely source of that carbon had to be human bodies, blown into ashes by the explosion.

The *Michaelson* trembled as the wave of gases reached her then swept on past. Without those gases blocking the view, the *Maury* could be seen much better.

"Jesus Christ," somebody muttered, sounding more like a prayer than profanity.

The *Maury's* mid-section looked as if something huge had taken bites out of it. Paul increased the magnification on his visual display. The bites became holes with ragged edges, where something had blasted through the *Maury's* inner and outer hulls. Paul could vaguely make out the areas surrounding the holes, where structural members and internal materials were ripped and twisted. *It's like looking at a human with his guts torn open. Exactly where'd the damage hit the worst?* The *Maury* was the *Michaelson's* sister ship, so she had the same general layout. *Most of the forward section looks intact. Maybe half the ship. There's a section right at the stern that doesn't look beat up too badly. What would've been located in the parts of the Maury that've been torn up? That'd be... no. Please, no.*

A voice over the command circuit confirmed Paul's conclusion and his fears. "Captain, it looks like at least one of *Maury's* engineering compartments blew." Commander Destin, the *Michaelson's* chief engineer, sounded as if she couldn't quite believe it. "Probably both."

Captain Hayes' voice over the same circuit carried more than a hint of shock. "Blew up? An engineering compartment? How could that happen?"

"I don't know, sir. It'd require an awful lot of equipment and software to fail simultaneously, and a lot of people to miss warning signs. But those holes are where the *Maury's* engineering compartments are."

Captain Hayes' voice sounded flat and emotionless. "Where they were, you mean."

"Yes, sir. From what we can tell, *Maury's* lost all power. I recommend we get as many people as we can over there to assist."

"Do we have any communications with the *Maury*?"

"No, captain," Commander Garcia came on line, his answer blunt. "I'm in comms. We're picking up nothing but the emergency beacon's automated distress call. There's no telling what effect the shock from that explosion and its fragmentation effects had inside the *Maury's* hull."

"Very well. How many damage control teams can the gig hold?"

Commander Destin answered again. "Normally, two, captain."

"I don't want normally. How many maximum?"

"Uh, three, sir. If they're packed in tight. Very tight."

"Get three teams over there pronto. I'll see how close to the *Maury* we can maneuver the *Michaelson*."

Paul listened to the conversation, feeling as if it were some sort of audio-book, dealing with fictional events which couldn't have happened here and now. *Something I should be doing.* "Chief, I want a recommendation for the captain on how close to the *Maury* we can get."

Chief Imari looked back at Paul, her face questioning behind the survival suit's face shield. "Considering what, sir?"

"Debris. And possible secondary explosions."

"If you're concerned about secondaries, sir, this is as close as we should get."

"We're concerned about helping the *Maury*, chief!"

"Yes, sir. We'll scope out the debris and work up a recommendation disregarding the threat from secondary explosions."

"Good. Thanks." There. He'd done something. Not much. But something. Paul looked back at the image of the *Maury*, wondering why his mind kept insisting the picture couldn't be real.

He was jerked out of his detachment by a sharp voice. "Sinclair!"

Commander Garcia calling, his anger as usual easily apparent, but this time certainly not aimed at Paul. For all Garcia's faults, Paul knew he cared about the lives of sailors.

"Yes, sir."

"Get down to the gig. They want you to command one of the damage control parties."

"Me, sir?"

"Yes, you! Your chief can run Combat and you're one of the only officers on board with actual experience leading a damage control team. Now stop asking stupid questions and get your butt down there!"

"Aye, aye, sir." Paul switched back to Combat's internal communications. "Chief, I've been tapped to go over to the *Maury*. You've got Combat. Get that recommendation to Commander Garcia as soon as possible so he can pass it to the captain."

"Yes, sir. Good luck, sir."

Paul exited Combat as fast as he could, thinking as he went that he needed luck a lot less than the crew of the *Maury* did. Partway to the gig, the maneuvering alarm sounded and Paul managed to snap onto a tie-down just before the *Michaelson* lurched and swung in response to her thrusters. *Getting closer to the* Maury. *Probably not all that close. There's got to be lots of junk still floating around her. And lots of stuff that could still explode, like Chief Imari said.* Paul felt another inner chill. *Did* Maury's *fuel vent from all the ruptured tanks and lines? What happens to us if it blows while we're there?* He tried to remember if the cloud of gases had included vaporized fuel, how dense a free-floating cloud of fuel would have to be to ignite, but his mind wouldn't focus on the calculations.

The push of the thrusters halted, followed by an "all-clear" announcement. Paul unhooked and hastened the rest of the way to the gig.

The area around the gig was a mess. Too many sailors, bulkier than usual thanks to their survival suits, along with portable damage control equipment of every description crowded into the space near the gig. Paul pushed through until he was close to the gig, where Lieutenant Kilgary and Commander Destin were organizing the rescue effort. "Lieutenant Sinclair, reporting in."

Destin nodded absently. Colleen Kilgary gave Paul a quick look, all business. "Paul, you'll be in charge of Damage Control Team Two."

"DC Team Two. Roger."

"I'll be in charge of DC Team One and the overall effort. Have you seen Sonya?"

"No, I—"

Lieutenant Sindh pushed up next to Paul. "Here. I assume I have command of DC Team Three?"

Kilgary nodded rapidly. "Right. Commander Destin and I are

going to supervise loading everybody and everything into the gig. Try to sort out your people."

Sindh nodded back. "I'll move my team toward the aft bulkhead."

Paul checked his suit display, where a list of names had appeared, then activated the communications circuit designated for his team. "All personnel in DC Team Two, this is Lieutenant Sinclair. I want you up against the forward bulkhead." Sailors began moving as Paul's and the other damage control teams started sorting themselves out, the tightly packed crowd breaking into those moving forward, those moving aft, and those trying to reach the center. More quickly than Paul would've expected, the three groups formed up in their designated positions. *No horseplay or delaying. Everybody knows the guys on the* Maury *need us.*

Chief Meyer sketched a quick salute. "Team Two ready, sir."

"Thanks, chief." *Meyer's from engineering. Lieutenant Kilgary's division. He ought to be real nice to have along.*

"Any idea what things are like over there, sir?"

"Bad." The sailors in Team Two shifted uneasily at Paul's single-word reply. "I just got a quick visual look, but *Maury* looked real torn up from just aft of amidships."

Meyer nodded slowly. "Engineering spaces."

Paul felt the hollow space in his gut again. *Jen.* "Yes."

"How torn up, sir?"

"I don't know, chief. We'll know when we get there."

"Yes, sir." Paul watched Chief Meyer stare toward the gig. *Engineering's a fairly insular community. Odds are Meyer knows a lot of people in* Maury's *Engineering Department. How many of them are still alive?* He shied away from the question, wishing he could somehow banish it from his mind.

Team One shuffled forward as Commander Destin and Lieutenant Kilgary directed them to positions in the gig. Paul brought his own team up behind them, waiting until Kilgary pointed his way. "Your turn. Make sure your people pack in tight."

"Aye, aye. Team Two, I want everyone up close and personal in that gig."

A muttering of acknowledgements followed, along with a few cracks. "Sir, can I have a window seat?" "Sir, can I get up close and personal with Petty Officer Velos?"

Velos craned her head to look at whoever had spoken. "In your dreams, Gino."

Chief Meyer glared at the sailors. "Zip it. I don't want nothing else said that ain't mission-essential. Understand?" He faced Paul and shrugged. "They're nervous, Mr. Sinclair."

"I understand, chief. Just between you and me, so am I."

"I guess that makes it unanimous, sir."

The inside of the gig had never felt expansive to Paul anyway. With thirty-some sailors in survival suits and all the damage control gear they could carry being shoved inside, it felt like a king-sized can of sardines. Paul let Chief Meyer go first, then followed the last of his team in and pushed up against those already in place. Whoever Petty Officer Velos' admirer happened to be, he was probably pretty disappointed at the moment, since the survival suits let you feel nothing but the bare outlines of the shapes you were up against and in the press of bodies any motion with arms or legs was out of the question.

Lieutenant Kilgary came last, shaking her head. "We're breaking a few safety regulations doing this, people, but there's no doubt the *Maury* needs us and needs us fast. *Nobody panic*." She wedged herself in and cycled the gig's hatch shut.

Paul immediately understood Kilgary's last instruction. With the hatch closed, the gig's packed interior felt dangerously claustrophobic. Somehow the lighting also felt dim, perhaps because some of the internal lights were covered by sailors or equipment, which only contributed to the feeling of being crowded into too small a space. But no one panicked, at least not openly, as a series of bumps, jars and lurches marked the gig's lifting from its cradle. An unbearably long period, perhaps a minute, passed before the gig's main drive lit off. The sailors near the rear groaned as the mass of their companions pressed against them. "Take it easy!" Lieutenant Sindh called out. She was back there with her sailors, feeling everything they felt, and her presence kept any of them from being overwhelmed by the mental and physical pressure.

Paul chafed at the unfamiliar sensation of literally being in the dark. As an officer, he was used to being able to see situations. *But, then, I probably don't want to see the* Maury *until I have to. How bad is the damage? How many of her crew died?* That question again, the one he couldn't avoid thinking about.

"On final approach to the *Maury*," the gig's conning officer announced over the officers' command circuit. "Do you still want me directly amidships, Lieutenant Kilgary?"

"Affirmative." Kilgary's voice was almost that of a stranger, cold and controlled. "As close as you can get us."

"It's pretty ugly out there, lieutenant. Lots of junk drifting loose."

"Don't risk the gig. We can jump to the *Maury*."

Paul felt grateful he was surrounded too tightly by sailors to be able to shiver. The survival suits had a limited self-maneuvering capability and he'd jumped through space as part of his training.

But he remembered the endless dark all around, the sense of falling forever with nothing to grab onto, the feeling that if he missed his objective he'd just keep falling and falling until his suit's power and air gave out.

The gig lurched a few more times. Paul felt torn between dread at leaving the gig and a growing sense of urgency. *Let's get going, dammit!*

A moment later, the gig's conning officer called again. "That's as close as I want to risk it, Lieutenant Kilgary. I've got the gig's main hatch lined up with the *Maury*."

"Roger. I'm popping the hatch now." The hatch surface receded, then Lieutenant Kilgary pushed herself out, holding on to the inside with one hand while she looked around. "Mary, mother of God. Paul, Sonya, it's worse than I thought. The *Maury*'s amidships is totally devastated. Both main engineering compartments definitely blew."

"Can you see survivors?" Lieutenant Sindh asked.

"No. I don't expect to, either. Not in this area." Paul heard a hiss as Kilgary drew in a breath. "It looks to me like everyone in engineering must have been wiped out."

I didn't hear it. I didn't hear it. I don't know what's happened to Jen. I won't know for a while. Just do my job. Think about that. Only that. There are people depending on me.

"I'm going to take Team One in deep amidships, try to assess internal damage and find out if anything or anybody's left. Paul, Team Two goes forward. Sonya, Team Three goes aft. It looks to me like the survival bulkheads held, so we want to strengthen and seal them. Find weak points and get them reinforced. Plug holes. You know the drill."

Paul and Lieutenant Sindh answered up simultaneously. "Aye, aye, ma'am." Lieutenant Kilgary wasn't Colleen to them right now, she was the officer in charge.

"Look for airtight boundaries. Anyone in the forward or after sections will be trying to maintain the integrity of those compartments. If you find a working internal airlock, send someone through to make contact. We have to know what shape the *Maury*'s remaining crew is in. Any questions? Okay, I'm launching. I want everybody to follow, one by one. Keep your spacing."

Kilgary lined herself up on something Paul couldn't see, braced herself, then pushed off. The gig bobbled slightly in reaction, then the first sailor in Team One was at the hatch, raising fingers one by one as he counted to five before pushing off in turn. As more sailors left, the gig's maneuvering thrusters began firing in quick bursts, compensating for the reactions created by the sailors shoving off against the hatch.

Paul shuffled forward, getting only glimpses of the *Maury* until he reached the hatch. Once he got his first clear view, Paul gasped, staring at the damage. His first impression, that something had taken bites out of the *Maury*, was replaced by an image of monsters inside the *Maury* who'd burst out, shattering everything around them. Where the engineering compartments should've been there were instead a couple of irregular areas in which everything had been blasted outward and away. Surrounding those cleared areas were sections where the blasts had torn and smashed their way along the lines of least resistance, leaving a tangle of wreckage in their wake. The masses of wreckage gave way to either open space or disappeared in the shadows created by the still-intact portions of the *Maury*.

The last member of Team One leaped across the gap, his shape dwindling rapidly toward an area where Lieutenant Kilgary had gathered the rest of her team. Paul aimed for a point closer toward the *Maury*'s bow, where he could see the remains of a compartment that seemed to offer a decent landing area. *Okay. You've done this. Remember the drill. Line up your body. Both feet set firm. Push off evenly with both legs so you don't go off to one side. Don't push too hard because you'll reach your objective at that same speed. Keep your eyes on your landing spot. Ready. Go.* He aimed and jumped, pushing off just as he'd learned during his training, not putting too much force into the effort, trying not to think about the infinite emptiness he'd just hurled himself into.

There wasn't anything under him, or above him, or to either side. Just the endless dark, lit with trillions of sparks of light. If Paul looked in those directions, he felt as if he might have been motionless, unable to judge his own movement against the incredibly distant stars. Part of his mind marveled at that. Both the *Maury* and the *Michaelson*'s gig were traveling through space at speed measured in kilometers per second, yet Paul felt none of that since he was moving at the same speed and there was no air resistance, gravity or friction to slow him relative to the ships. He felt tempted to look back toward the gig, but remembered the warning not to take his eyes off his target. More than one jumper had slammed painfully into a target they'd forgotten to watch. But as he did look directly at the target, Paul felt like he was falling onto it. It took a determined effort to focus on the fact that his body wasn't accelerating under gravity's pull as it would in a fall, but was moving at a steady pace even though his Earth-bound experience kept insisting that couldn't be happening.

Despite his concentration on his target, the ruined compartment on the *Maury* grew in size with shocking speed as Paul got close. Paul swung his feet forward and took the impact with flexed legs. He could almost hear an instructor grunting out a reluctant "not bad" as he grabbed hold of the nearest object, in this case a section of electrical conduit swinging free on one end. The friction pads built into the survival suit gloves held firmly on to the conduit's smooth surface. Paul tested his stability, then looked up just as the first sailor on his team came flying into the compartment only about a meter from him. *Blast it. I should've remembered to get clear of the landing spot.* Paul swung off to one side, motioning the sailor to clear the area as well.

More sailors came sailing into the ruined compartment, landing with varying degrees of force and grace. Last came Chief Meyer, grunting as he landed. "Where to, sir?"

Paul looked around, trying to judge where best to go. "Our orders are to proceed to the survival bulkhead forward of the damage. Let's move toward the *Maury*'s bow."

"Yes, sir. Spread out or stay together?"

Tough question. Spreading out would let them learn more, faster. But also separate them in an environment rendered unknowable by the damage the *Maury* had sustained. "Together. There's no telling what's blocked up ahead. I'd rather not have some of the team cut off from the rest of us."

They moved through the compartments, roughly along the line where the *Maury*'s outer hull had been. Segments of the inner hull, unmistakable with their hollow, honeycomb shapes, still clung to structural members or were bent back by the force of the blast. Wires and fiber optic cables drifted across his path, while clouds of fragmented insulation and other materials floated amid the wreckage. A large piece of warped metal that might have once been a control console in engineering had been wedged across their path, requiring the team to traverse some of the rougher areas. Paul reached for a pale, white object for his next hold, then stopped in mid-reach. *It's an arm.* The limb, naked against space, protruded from a crushed compartment. *Is somebody still attached? I can't find out now. Not that I want to find out at all.* He reached elsewhere. "Watch out for human remains." Somehow, Paul's voice didn't shake.

"Sir? Mr. Sinclair?"

"Yeah, chief."

Meyer pointed inside the *Maury*. "I'm pretty sure we need to head inside, now."

Paul checked his position, trying to remember exactly where the next survival bulkhead would be located. Once seen, the survival bulkheads were impossible to mistake, with their extra armoring and damage control equipment. But from outside the *Maury*, with her hull torn ragged and internal compartment arrangements jumbled, Paul couldn't get be sure of the distance remaining. "How sure is pretty sure, chief?"

"Real sure, sir."

"Okay. Let's go." Paul led the team deeper into the *Maury*, wending past obstacles and wriggling through some tight spots. He reached a relatively clear passageway and followed it forward, his team following. *Funny. When I led that damage control team into a fire on the* Michaelson, *there wasn't time to think. And I couldn't see a thing because of the smoke and all. Now there's too much time to think and way more to see than I want to see.*

The survival bulkhead was easy to recognize when they reached it, both because of the scarred armor still protecting it, and the three bodies floating near the sealed hatch leading forward. Paul wanted to hang back, wanted to let someone else go close, but knew he had no right to demand that of anyone. Steeling himself and trying to tighten his throat against any urge to throw up, he pulled himself forward to the hatch. One of the sailors had somehow survived the blast for long enough to grab a survival suit which remained clenched within one of her frozen hands. The other two had apparently died in the explosion, judging from the injuries visible on them. "Chief." Paul felt his voice squeaking, swallowed, and spoke again. "Chief Meyer. Detail someone to secure these remains. We want to make sure nothing happens to them."

"Yes, sir."

Paul examined the bulkhead, trying to ignore the feeling that the *Maury*'s dead sailors were watching him accusingly. *It's not my fault. Whatever happened here isn't my fault. I'm trying to save your shipmates.* "Chief, it looks to me like the survival bulkhead is damaged but holding. There seems to be atmosphere on the other side, but the airlock here looks too damaged to use. What's your assessment?"

Meyer made a careful examination himself before answering. "I concur, sir."

"Okay, then, let's break the team into sections, two sailors per section. I want them to work to all sides from here, checking for damage to the survival bulkhead, pressure on the other side, and any working airlocks leading forward. Everybody is to exercise caution. Understood? Report in every... five minutes."

"Every five minutes, aye."

Chief Meyer quickly divided up the team. Paul found himself paired with Petty Officer Velos. Despite the circumstances, he found himself trying to remember what she looked like underneath the survival suit, then felt a wave of self-anger. *How can that thought even cross your mind?* He knew the thought was born of anxiety, a desperate need for distraction, but he still felt sick over it.

More wreckage blocked paths along normal routes, but openings were available where there shouldn't have been openings. "Sir?" Petty Officer Velos pulled herself down near deck level. "There's a hole here."

A hole. In a survival bulkhead. Whatever had made that hole had to have been traveling very fast. Paul grabbed a nearby tie-down and pulled himself next to Velos, then frowned as he checked the damage. "It's been patched. From the inside." *Somebody's still alive in there. Thank heavens for that, at least.*

"Yes, sir. I bet it could still use some reinforcing from this side."

"Good idea. Go ahead." Paul swung away as Velos pulled out some materials from her backpack and went to work. "Chief? Any luck?"

Chief Meyer's response sounded faint due to the interference of the transmission from the wreckage. "No joy, sir. A few teams report finding holes in the bulkhead. They're patching any that haven't been already taken care of."

"Roger, chief. Your transmission's weak. How do you read me?"

"Weak but readable, sir."

"Same." Paul looked around, finally spotting a compartment number. "I've just about reached the inner hull going this way. We'll be heading back your way in a few minutes."

"Aye, aye, sir."

As Paul had predicted, he and Petty Officer Velos ran into a dead-end at the inner hull only a few meters farther on. Paul thumped the inner hull sections nearby, trying to determine if they remained intact and still held water inside them. When that method failed, he checked his suit's radiation readings. *Radiation is being blocked. Water must still be in there. Good.*

The return journey went quicker, since they knew the way. Chief

Meyer and half the damage control team were already there when Paul arrived. "Sir? Lieutenant Kilgary wanted to talk to you soon as you got back."

"Thanks, chief." A quick circuit switch. "Lieutenant Kilgary, this is Lieutenant Sinclair."

"Paul. This is Colleen. What's your team found up forward?"

"It's a mess, but progressively better as we got farther forward. Number two survival bulkhead held. We patched some holes in it, and found other holes had been patched from the inside."

"From the inside? Great. Any communications with the *Maury*'s crew?"

"No, ma'am. None of the internal airlocks we found were judged safe to use."

"I was afraid of that. The damage near the engineering compartments is unbelievable. I've got my team and Lieutenant Sindh's team bracing the remaining structure so the *Maury* doesn't rip herself apart. I need two things from you. First, I want your team to check your area again, but this time for structural stability. Tell Chief Meyer to look for places that need to be reinforced. Second, can you find the forward external airlock on the *Maury* if you move along the outside of the hull?"

Paul pondered the question for a moment. He knew exactly where to reach that airlock from the inside, but the outside of the *Maury* provided few clues to your location when you were crawling along it. *Still, if I orient myself using the parts of the Maury's insides that have been exposed, I should be able to find it.* "Yes. I think so."

"There's still no communications with the *Maury*. We need to know what's going on inside her. Leave Chief Meyer in charge of your team and get to that airlock. Bring along a portable power unit so you can open it up. Find out what the survivors need, and make sure they know not to try to power up anything, especially any maneuvering systems."

"Aye, aye, ma'am." It wasn't until then that Paul realized he'd volunteered to crawl along the outside of a crippled spacecraft. *Okay. I can do this. Just keep my eyes on the* Maury's *hull. The friction pads on my hands and feet should hold me to her.* "Chief Meyer, this is Mr. Sinclair. I've been ordered to find the *Maury's* forward external airlock. You've got the team until I get back." He quickly passed on Kilgary's instructions.

"Aye, aye, sir. If we spot anything, do we try to fix it?"

Paul hesitated. "Try to report it to Lieutenant Kilgary. If you can't, use your judgment. Err on the side of keeping this ship together."

"Aye, aye, sir."

"I'll need a portable power unit with enough juice to cycle that airlock."

"No problem, sir."

No problem. Paul kept repeating that phrase to himself as he moved along the damaged portions of the *Maury*, peering into compartments ripped open to space so he could tell where he was relative to the airlock. Clouds of debris floated and spun through the wrecked areas, some of the larger pieces identifiable as the remnants of equipment or personal items, and occasionally one that was probably a remnant of one of the crew. *That's... one of the passageways through officers' country. I guess all the staterooms got taken out, too. I sure hope no one was in their bunk when it happened. Or maybe that would've been a mercy. Okay, that means the airlock should be about... that way.*

He paused, watching a rectangular piece of paper twisting through the airless ruin of the officers' staterooms. The paper's front came into view as it rotated, revealing it to be a photograph of a smiling woman, the seashore at her back a weird contrast to the deadness of space. *Girlfriend? Mother? Wife? Sister? Whichever, I hope your someone gets safely home to you. Or that they never knew what hit them.* The memory of the dead sailor at the survival bulkhead haunted him. She'd lived long enough to get the suit, feeling the cold and the emptiness as the compartments around her decompressed, knowing at some point that she'd never make it into that suit before she died.

The torn portions of the hull came to an end. Paul let go his last grip on the wreckage and began moving across the outer hull. Like all warships, the *Maury*'s hull had been kept smooth to minimize the chances of being spotted. Corners and edges caught things like light and radio waves, creating visible signatures for unfriendly eyes searching space. Right now, feeling a bit like a fly crawling over a sheet of glass, Paul wished someone had figured out how to install hand grips on a ship's outer hull anyway.

His friction pads gripped well, but the circular motions required to lift each pad before moving a hand or a foot began to fatigue his arms and legs rapidly. *How much farther?* The hull presented an almost featureless expanse on all sides. *If I miss it, how will I know which way to go looking for it?*

His arms and legs were aching now, but Paul stubbornly kept moving, trying to keep his eyes focused on the *Maury*'s hull for the small features which would reveal the presence of the airlock from up close. It occurred to Paul that he was probably being watched from the *Michaelson*, as if he were a bug on the expanse of the *Maury*'s hull. "USS *Michaelson*, this is Lieutenant Sinclair."

"*Michaelson*, aye."

"I've been ordered to reach the *Maury*'s forward external airlock.

Can you give me an idea how close I am?"

"Wait one."

Paul kept moving as he waited, wondering how long it would take to urge his screaming muscles back into motion if he stopped.

"Lieutenant Sinclair, we estimate you are within three meters of the airlock and slightly above it."

"I understand I am within three meters, slightly above." Paul moved over some more, angling downward now. One foot slid against something the friction pad wouldn't hold on. *That's the airlock rim. Got you.* A little farther over and down. His hands crossed the slick rim, then Paul saw the location of the external power plug. "I am at the airlock. Plugging in my portable power unit, now."

"Lieutenant Sinclair."

Paul recognized the voice even through the rasp of the communications circuit. "Yes, captain."

"Try to find the captain of the *Maury* if you can."

"Aye, aye, sir." Paul cautiously tried to attach his portable power unit, but the jack kept wobbling away from the plug, until Paul cursed and rammed it home. Using his suit's systems, he activated the airlock, waiting impatiently as it cycled, then as the hatch inched open. Swinging inside, Paul felt his limbs trembling with exhaustion and relief. *At least I'm not hanging on the edge of nothing anymore.*

The inner door swung open more smoothly. Paul pulled himself inside the *Maury*, looking either way down the passageway. *No one here. Anyone left is surely involved in damage control or repair. Air's okay in here. Pressure's a little low, though. I need to get to the* Maury's *bridge.* He knew the way, though as always traveling through one of the *Michaelson's* sister ships felt odd, as if he were simultaneously in a familiar and an unfamiliar place.

Paul checked the bridge hatch, finding it sealed. Paul released the hatch, opening it to swing inside.

The *Maury*'s bridge was crowded, something which brought Paul great relief after the eerie feeling of abandonment in the passageways he'd gone through. In the dim illumination of the emergency lights, sailors were working on equipment while officers huddled together. In their focus on their immediate tasks, in a compartment full of personnel in survival suits, no one seemed to notice Paul. He made his way over to the captain's chair, and found her seated there with a data pad on which a diagram of the *Maury* could be seen, watching the activity around her with an intent and agonized expression.

"Ma'am? I'm Lieutenant Sinclair, from the *Michaelson*."

Heads snapped around. The *Maury*'s captain gave Paul a brief nod of greeting. "Captain Halis. How'd you get here, Mr. Sinclair?"

"The *Michaelson*'s sent over three damage control teams, ma'am. I came in through the forward external airlock to establish contact with you."

A commander, probably the *Maury*'s executive officer, pointed brusquely toward the data pad held by the captain. "What's the damage look like from outside? We can't tell, and we've been focused on trying to maintain airtight boundaries in the forward part of the ship. All of our systems are off-line. Even a lot of the emergency gear. We took a helluva shock."

"Yes, sir." Paul noticed for the first time that the commander had one arm in a splint bound tightly to his body to keep it from drifting. He probably wasn't the only member of the *Maury*'s crew with broken bones or other internal and external injuries. Paul came forward a little more and pointed at the diagram of the *Maury*. "There's massive damage here and here."

Captain Halis stared grimly at where Paul had pointed. "The engineering compartments."

"Yes, ma'am. Damage spreads outward from them. We're still trying to assess damage, but so far there don't appear to be any airtight spaces left between the number two and number four survival bulkheads."

The commander tried to rub his forehead, his survival suit glove sliding over the surface of his face shield, his eyes glazed. "No wonder we can't talk to anybody back there."

"What about my engineering personnel?" Captain Halis demanded. "Massive damage, you said. What does that translate to in terms of my people?"

Paul felt a sudden tightening of his throat, but forced the words out. "Lieutenant Kilgary, our officer in charge, estimates... very serious casualties in engineering."

Captain Halis closed her eyes as if unable to accept the news. "Any idea what very serious means, lieutenant? Were those Lieutenant Kilgary's exact words?"

"No, ma'am. She..." The tightness grew, reaching down into the hollow space in Paul's guts. "She said she thought they'd been wiped out."

"Dear God." Captain Halis covered her eyes with one hand for a moment. "Dear God." She slowly lowered the hand and looked back at Paul. "Tell your lieutenant—" Her eyes finally focused on Paul's face. "Sinclair. From the *Michaelson*. You're Lieutenant Shen's sierra oscar, aren't you?"

Paul nodded mutely. The use of the Navy phonetic alphabet to spell out the initials for "significant other" had for some time struck him as an amusing in-joke. But not now.

Captain Halis raised one arm and gripped Paul's shoulder so hard he could easily feel the pressure through his survival suit. "Sorry," she whispered. "So very sorry." Then the arm fell and she was captain of a stricken ship once more. "What else can you tell me?"

Paul forced himself to concentrate only on his job. "Lieutenant Kilgary has our damage control teams trying to reinforce your ship's internal structure. It's badly ripped up. She asked that you be certain not to light off any maneuvering system, or anything else without coordinating with us."

The executive officer's jaw worked. "You think we could tear the *Maury* apart?"

"Sir, she's... really hurt bad, sir."

The commander grimaced, but Captain Halis merely nodded. "Bad doesn't mean hopeless. We'll save her. Don't worry, we won't try to get any navigational or maneuvering systems going. Why is your lieutenant concerned about other systems?"

"There's so many loose and broken wires out there, ma'am. It'd—"

Captain Halis held up one hand, palm out. "I understand. We need to establish reliable communications with people outside this ship. I need you to make your way back outside. Can you serve as a comm relay in the airlock?"

"We've got better than that, ma'am." A hollow-eyed petty officer with a large bruise visible on his left temple offered Paul some pieces of equipment. "Emergency relays. Plug one in to the jack inside the airlock and the other to the jack on the outside. It's a manual bypass. They should let us talk to the world again."

The task gave Paul the excuse he needed to try to shove away any more thoughts of Jen. "Will do. Any special message, captain?"

"If the relays don't work, tell your captain we need portable power units in here, as well as some air recyclers. Let your officer in charge of your assistance teams, you said Lieutenant Kilgary, correct? Let her know we're still trying to seal the number two survival bulkhead. Any further assistance from her side would be appreciated."

"Aye, aye, ma'am. You need portable power and air recyclers, and our continued assistance sealing the number two survival bulkhead." Paul came to attention, saluted, and then moved as quickly as he could back the way he came. He kept his mind focused on Captain Halis's message and the job he had to do. Once back at the airlock, he only had to look a moment to find the necessary jack for the first relay. Plugging it in firmly, Paul cycled the airlock, then slid outside and plugged in the second relay. "On the *Michaelson*, this is Lieutenant Sinclair. Do you copy?"

"We copy."

"The *Maury*'s captain says they need portable power units and air recyclers. I've installed some relays. You should be able to talk to the *Maury*'s bridge now."

"Roger." A pause, then the voice came again. "We have comms with the *Maury*'s bridge. Thanks, lieutenant."

"I'm returning to my team now." Paul began moving carefully across the still-too-smooth surface of the *Maury*'s outer hull, hoping his friction pads would hold, trying not to think beyond the next hand- or foothold. Finally reaching the edge of the damaged area again, Paul found his progress progressively easier, as tears and bends in the hull provided firm holds. His hand slipped on one attempted hold, though. Startled and angry, Paul tried to grab that point again, felt his hand slipping once more, then while reaching back for a third try noticed the survival-suited palm of his hand. There was something on it, now. Something black, with bits of paler material in it.

That's... oh, no. Paul fought down nausea, staring at the hull surface directly before his eyes. *Someone. What's left of someone. Pieces of someone. The blood's black. No oxygen to make it red. Dried out, all the moisture sucked into space, but the powder left makes the surface slick.* He looked around, desperately seeking something to wipe his palm on. Paul finally rubbed his hand quickly several times over the nearest protruding metal edge. He didn't look at the palm again, not wanting to know if his rough cleaning efforts had left a lot of material on his glove.

Swinging in past the ragged edge where the *Maury*'s hull had been blown open, Paul scanned the wreckage for signs of his team. Dark patches moved here and there amid the wreckage. Lighter objects could be seen among the dark, some of them still recognizable as bodies or large pieces of bodies. *Jen? I can't look. I—* He swallowed convulsively. "Chief Meyer."

"Here. Lieutenant Sinclair?"

"Right. I'm just aft of the number two survival bulkhead." Paul looked around, trying to see his surroundings without seeing the torn remnants of *Maury*'s crew among them. A bright object appeared on his display. *There's his beacon.* "I see you, chief. I'm on my way."

"Yes, sir."

"Lieutenant Kilgary? This is Lieutenant Sinclair."

There was a pause before she answered. "Here. Did you get to the bridge of the *Maury*, Paul?"

"Yes, ma'am." It felt a little odd to still be using formality with Colleen, but Paul needed to concentrate on professional rituals to keep darker thoughts at bay. "Captain Halis rogered up on not powering up anything. I helped establish comms from the *Maury* to the *Michaelson*, so they're talking now. Captain Halis says they're still trying to seal the forward survival bulkhead, and would like our assistance there."

He could hear Lieutenant Kilgary's heavy sigh over the circuit. "I need about twice as many people as I've got here. Okay. Chief Meyer tells me there's relatively less structural damage in your area. Take your people away from what I had them doing and start them going over that bulkhead again and sealing any problem areas."

"Aye, aye, ma'am."

"How's Captain Halis doing, Paul?"

"She's..." *How to say it?* "Very unhappy but on top of everything."

"I understand. How are you doing?"

"A little tired—"

"That's not what I mean. I know what the damage here implies for you personally. Can you still remain focused on your job?"

"Of course I can!" Paul put force into his reply, as if that could somehow fill the hollowness inside him.

"I wouldn't think less of you if it were otherwise. Okay, get your people moving. We've got less than an hour left before we need to get back to the gig."

Startled, Paul checked his own suit's readings. *The rebreather's okay so far, but it's not guaranteeing anything past another couple of hours. Power level's not great, either. Colleen's right. We need to allow a decent safety margin for getting back to the* Michaelson. "Chief Meyer, we've got new orders."

The maze of wreckage made it easier to forget other issues as Paul worked his way back to the forward survival bulkhead. Then he immersed himself in overseeing his damage control team, personally checking for ruptures or weak spots in the bulkhead whenever a free moment offered itself. At some point, he heard Kilgary warning everyone that the gig was delivering two more damage control teams and everyone should watch for sailors landing around them.

"That's it." It took a moment for Paul to recognize Kilgary's voice this time, hoarse with physical and emotional strain. "Paul, Sonya, get your teams back to the outer hull for pickup by the gig. It's coming in a little closer this time and it'll have a retrieval net spread around the airlock."

"Aye, aye. Chief Meyer, it's time to go." Out and back again, Paul both looking for and dreading seeing the frozen arm that'd been near their arrival point. But he didn't see it again, and soon enough his team was back near where they'd arrived on the *Maury*. He could see the gig floating where it awaited them, looking far too small against the emptiness around it. But he could also see the glowing lines which outlined the retrieval net, a large mesh surface spread out for ten meters around the airlock to catch anyone who aimed badly. As he watched, some of the glowing lines vibrated as a sailor from one of the other damage control teams landed in the net.

"That's all of my team," Kilgary advised. "Paul, take yours over next. Sonya, your team boards last this time."

"Aye, aye. Chief, you go first. I'll send the rest after you and follow last."

"Aye, aye, sir. Me first, you last." Chief Meyer's voice didn't seem to have changed, but then it had been emotionless and controlled since they got their first good look at the *Maury*. Paul watched the chief launch himself out, heading like a slow-moving bullet for the target center represented by the hatch on the gig. Meyer landed and pulled himself to one side, waving for someone else to follow.

Paul sent them off at the usual five-count intervals, concentrating on that task. When the last sailor was clear, he aimed himself and jumped.

Now, sailing between the *Maury* and gig, there was nothing to think about. Despite his training, Paul twisted his head to look back at the *Maury*. Up close, it had sometimes been easy to forget how widespread the devastation was, how insignificant the chance of survival had been for anyone caught in that blast. From here, and with all he'd seen inside the ship, it couldn't be mistaken or ignored. *Admit it to yourself. Jen's gone.*

Packed in tight on the gig again, Paul no longer had anything at all to divert his attention. No looming hazardous mission, no constant work with his hands and mind, no oversight of his team's work. All he could do was sit in the dimmed interior of the gig, feeling the survival suits around him press in from all sides, feeling the hollowness in him, and wondering if he'd ever feel anything but empty again.

Bumps and lurches announced their arrival back at the *Michaelson*. A wait followed, only minutes long but seeming an eternity for those inside the gig, as the gig's dock was pressurized. Finally, the hatch cracked open and sailors began pulling themselves out of the gig. Lieutenant Kilgary hung at the gig hatch, waving the sailors onward. "Everyone clear the gig area. Get into another compartment and get out of your suits. No bunching up. No ass-dragging. Keep moving."

Paul's turn came. He moved automatically, swinging out of the hatch, then feeling a hand on his arm. He looked to see Lieutenant Kilgary motioning him to the side. "How are you doing?"

"I..."

"That's what I thought." Kilgary had already pulled off her suit's helmet and now she assisted Paul in getting his helmet off. Her own eyes were haunted by fatigue and sorrow. "I don't want to risk you wandering around in this state oblivious to your own danger readings."

"I'm not that bad off."

"Can you hear your own voice? You held up great out there, Paul. I'd have never known you had such a personal stake in this. But now that pressure's off and you're feeling it."

Paul hung against the nearest bulkhead, staring at nothing. "I guess I am. Are you sure...?"

Kilgary's face sagged. "Damage to the after survival bulkhead hadn't been patched. We couldn't get in there, back into the less damaged sections aft of that bulkhead, but that says something."

"Yeah." A last very slender hope gone. "I guess—"

The comm panel in the compartment blared an attention signal. "Is Lieutenant Sinclair still down there?"

The sailor nearest the panel glanced at Paul, then pushed the transmit button. "Yes, sir. He's listening."

"We've received a Personal For message for him from the captain of the *Maury*."

Paul blinked in confusion, then felt the emptiness growing inside once more. *They found her. That must be it. Found what's left of her. I don't want...* But, as if of their own accord, his legs pushed him toward the comm panel and his arm raised so his hand could push the transmit key. He stared stupidly at the panel for a moment, the hollowness spreading to his brain, before he remembered to talk. "What is it? I mean... this is Lieutenant Sinclair."

"Personal for Lieutenant Sinclair from Captain Halis. Quote: Contact has been established with Lieutenant Shen and twenty-one enlisted who remain alive in the after section of the ship. Unquote."

Paul's vision hazed. As it cleared, he realized he was drifting limply against the bulkhead, one arm still raised toward the comm panel. Someone was yelling at him.

"Paul! Come on!" Hands grabbed Paul's arms and brought him

around to face Colleen Kilgary. "Don't lose it, Paul."

He tried to straighten his body, his arms and legs still feeling rubbery. "Jen—"

"I know. I heard. Somebody up there really loves you or her or the pair of you. Can you make it to your stateroom? How about sickbay?"

"I don't need sickbay." Paul looked around, blinking as if the lights in the compartment had just come on. Some of the enlisted from the damage control teams were grinning at him, not in derision at his weakness, but clearly in shared happiness at the news he'd received. "Thank you. Thanks all of you. I can make it now, Coll."

"Are you sure?"

"Yes. Yes, I can make it now." *In more ways than one. I can't believe it. Jen's alive? Not that I'm complaining, but how?*

6

He went back to the *Maury* six hours later, in charge of another team responsible for patching up what was left of the ship. He assumed Jen was somewhere in the forward part of the *Maury* by then, but didn't ask. He'd already grasped how incredibly lucky he'd been. Paul couldn't look anywhere on the *Maury* without being reminded that a lot of other people hadn't been lucky.

Back on the *Michaelson*, Paul staggered to the wardroom for coffee. Commander Sykes wasn't there, but Mike Bristol was on his way out, coffee in each hand. "Suppo's working nonstop to get anything the *Maury* needs out of our supply stocks," Bristol confided.

"He's going to ruin his reputation if he's not careful," Paul suggested as he slid into a chair.

"Strap yourself in, Paul. Since when does a line officer need a supply officer to tell him that?"

"Sorry." Paul fumbled with the straps and got them fastened just as Captain Hayes entered the wardroom. *Figures*. He tried to unfasten the straps so he could "stand" to attention, but Hayes waved him back.

"Carry on, Paul." Hayes grabbed some coffee himself, hanging for a moment near the dispenser. "You've been doing good work over there."

"Everybody has, sir."

"Yeah. Damn good job." Hayes took a big drink, his face weary. "We're bringing her back, you know."

"Sir?"

"Fleet's already decided. They're sending some tugs to take *Maury* in tow. That's why the damage control teams are concentrating on reinforcing her structure now. The bean counters probably want to just leave the wreck out here, but we'll bring her home." Hayes drained his coffee. "Captain Halis and a skeleton crew will ride the *Maury* back. She insisted. I would've done the same thing in her place. Helluva thing. The rest of the *Maury*'s survivors will be brought over here and we'll take them back to Franklin."

Paul nodded, not quite able to absorb all the information.

Hayes' eyes had gone distant. "The chief engineer on the *Maury* and I served together once. We were shipmates on the old *John Glenn*."

"I—I'm sorry, sir."

"We live in a small professional world, Paul. I hope you realize how lucky you are."

"I do, sir."

"Well." Captain Hayes looked at his empty coffee for a moment, then grabbed another. "Still a lot to do today." Paul watched him go, then sighed, unstrapped, and headed for Combat. Like the captain said, there was still a lot to do.

The *Michaelson* had been designed to have just enough room to carry her crew, with some means of emergency accommodations for a limited number of others in the event of emergency. She hadn't been designed to hold nearly as many extra personnel as were coming from the *Maury*. After using every available space, some of the sailors on the *Michaelson* still had to hot-bunk with survivors from the *Maury*, with two sailors sharing the same bunk, one sleeping while the other stood watch or worked. The only complaint Paul personally heard came from Seaman Fastow. Chief Imari had leaned close to Fastow, her face a devil's mask, and asked if Fastow would be happier if fewer members of the *Maury*'s crew had survived so she wouldn't have to be inconvenienced.

"Paul." He looked up at Kris Denaldo's hail. "Got a minute?"

"Is it important?"

"Very."

"Okay."

Kris led the way back to her stateroom, pausing a couple of meters from the hatch. "Old home week, Paul."

"What?"

She gestured. "Jen's in there."

"Jen? I thought they'd keep an engineer onboard the *Maury*."

"They don't need an engineer. It'll all be portable life support systems. Engineering doesn't exist on that ship anymore. And Jen, well, I'm no expert, but she's not doing well."

Paul stared at the hatch. "Shell-shocked?"

"Worse than that, I think. She's lost a lot of friends. Lucky she's still got you. But be careful with her. I can't believe even Iron Jen can shed this kind of thing without being really hurt inside."

"I understand."

"No, I don't think you do. Neither do I. Just do your best."

"Okay." Paul pulled himself slowly to the hatch, hesitated, then knocked on the rim. "Jen?" No answer. He looked inside. Jen was strapped into the seat she'd used when she'd been stationed on the *Michaelson*. Now it was Kris' desk, but Paul doubted Kris had told her that. Jen was staring at nothing, her face almost blank. "Jen?"

She turned her head and looked his way, her eyes coming into focus. "Paul."

"Is it okay if I come in?"

"Uh, sure. Keep the hatch open."

He almost smiled at the reminder. Even in shock, Jen remembered to maintain the Navy's standards for male and female officers together on a ship. "How are you?"

Jen looked back at him as if confused by the question.

"Okay. Really dumb question. I know. I'm... so very sorry."

"Thanks." She looked away, staring into the distance again.

"Is there anything I can do?"

She held out her arm. "Hit it."

"What?"

"Hit it."

Frowning, Paul made a fist and rapped her forearm gently. "Okay?"

"No. Harder."

He tried again, with more force. "Was that hard enough?"

"Yes." Jen retracted the arm and rubbed it. "I felt that. I shouldn't feel anything."

"Jen—"

"I should be dead. Along with the others."

"Jen—"

"The only reason I'm alive is because an after power coupling started acting up and Commander Juko, the *Maury*'s chief eng—" She bit off the word.

Paul watched helplessly. *She knows that Juko's dead, that everything about him now is past tense, but it's going to hurt every time you have to say it, won't it, Jen?*

Jen stared at Paul, her gaze more alive but slightly wild. "The chief engineer told me to check it out. I'd just cleared the aft survival bulkhead when the whole ship shook. The survival bulkhead *bent*. Those're armored, Paul. They're not supposed to bend."

"I know, Jen."

"I bounced off of some stuff, and when my head stopped spinning I realized it was dark except for the self-contained emergency lighting. I could feel a breeze. There were funny dark spots on the survival bulkhead. They were holes. We were decompressing."

"Jen—"

"I got into a suit. A couple of sailors showed up and got suited up as well. We started trying to reseal the survival bulkhead, but it was hopeless. Not enough of us, too many holes. Some other sailors started showing up in their suits, and tried to pop the forward hatch. No go. Frozen solid, probably warped by the blast. Found some more sailors. Not enough suits to go around. Some of the lockers got holed by fragments during the explosion, so the suits in them were torn up. Everybody started to panic. I screamed them into shape and herded them farther aft. We had to go back a ways until we found bulkheads which hadn't been penetrated by fragments. All the way to the end-of-the-world bulkhead. We sealed ourselves in while I tried to figure out what to do. Doctrine says wait for rescue. But we had no comms with anybody. No power. We didn't know how much was left of the ship forward of the explosion." She started trembling.

"Jen, for God's sake, you don't have to—"

"Everybody was looking at me. What do we do Ms. Shen? Can

you save us, Ms. Shen? Is anybody coming to rescue us, Ms. Shen? And I had to pretend I knew all the answers, because if I didn't they'd have all panicked and killed themselves doing something crazy. It seemed like forever, in the near dark with just the emergency lights. It started getting colder. The air felt like it was getting stale. Those of us with suits left them open to conserve power and the air recyclers. The rest just stared at us with helpless looks. None of them would ask one of us to give up our suits, but they knew without suits they'd die before long."

Paul couldn't repress a shiver of his own, imagining how it'd been inside that compartment.

Jen's eyes were fixed now on something Paul couldn't see. "I finally decided to go get help. Somehow. We couldn't afford to wait for rescue. We had twelve suits. Twenty-two people. I wanted to take Petty Officer Stokes with me. He was the steadiest guy I knew there. But he needed to stay and keep the others from losing it. I took someone else. We went forward, real careful. Kept finding vacuum on the other side of hatches. Every way we went. Finally found an internal airlock still able to function and went through. Real dark. Junk everywhere. Took a long time to get through it, reach an opening." Jen screwed her eyes shut. "*Gone*. Nothing but a huge hole where I'd left everyone else."

Paul said to hell with the regulations against displays of affection between officers and pulled himself down to hug her. "Jen, it's okay now."

"It's *not* okay. Dammit, it's *not* okay. It'll *never* be okay."

"You're right. You're right. I shouldn't have said that."

"All gone." Jen's eyes were open, but unfocused again. "Saw some people out there. Found out they were from the forward section. I guess your ship's teams had just left."

"We had to take the gig back to change out suits and personnel."

"Yeah." She sagged against him. "Why? Can you tell me why, Paul?"

Why what? Why did so many die? Why did you survive? Why this happened at all? Paul looked down at his hands, wondering what he could say, what answer he could possibly give. "Maybe sometimes there isn't any 'why.'" He didn't realize he'd spoken aloud until Jen answered, her voice wavering up and down with stress.

"That would actually be a bit easier to handle, you know, because it'd mean nobody'd picked and chosen who'd live and who'd die. Nobody else would've died so I could live. That's a comfort, you know?"

"Jen, I thought you'd died. I was sure of it. I... I thought..."

She finally looked at him, her eyes wide. "I thought I *would* die. I thought about you. I thought about never seeing you again."

"We're..." *What's the right word?* "Incredibly lucky, Jen."

"Yeah. Lucky. We were." Her face twisted as she looked away. "A lot of other people weren't. People who had loved ones, too. Chief Calhoun. His wife just had a kid. He couldn't wait to get back." Jen's face convulsed with rage. "Goddammit!" Her fist slammed repeatedly into the nearest locker surface. "God... God... God..." The blows finally stopped as Jen slumped. "Oh, God."

She finally turned herself toward him, collapsing into Paul's arms, her body wracked with sobs. Paul waited to feel the wet of tears on his shoulder, but none came. *Even now you won't cry, Jen?* He thought of what she'd said about Chief Calhoun and closed his own eyes. *The memories you're going to have. The memories you're going to live with for the rest of your life.*

Jen's sobs finally stilled. A long moment later, she pushed him away. "I'm sorry."

"For what? After what you've been through?"

"I'm an officer. I have to bear up under pressure."

"Bull. Jen, you did bear up under pressure. You saved at least some of those enlisted with you. Maybe all of them. Twenty-one people probably owe their lives to you. Now you're allowed to relax a little and let it out before it blows *you* up!"

Jen looked away, but her face didn't express disagreement, just an awful weariness. "It'll be a long time."

"Before you can think about it?"

"No. I'm thinking about it now. A long time before I can accept it. Maybe never." She looked back at Paul. "I'm not special, Paul. Why did I live?"

"You're special to me."

"And the universe cares about that?"

He reached out again and pulled her close, murmuring in Jen's ear. "I care about that. And if I can make the universe care, I will. Maybe you lived out of sheer chance. Maybe you lived so you could save those sailors. Maybe you lived because I needed you so very much. You did live. Don't throw away that blessing, Jen. I thought my world had ended."

"Ha." Her voice sounded distant. "You'd have gotten over me in no time. Then you'd have found some sweet little thing who thought you were heaven's gift to the universe."

"I'd much rather have a temperamental lieutenant who doesn't take any crap and who I know is a gift to *me*."

She shoved away far enough to look at him, a ghost of a smile finally touching her lips. "You have very poor judgment, Lieutenant

Sinclair." Jen hugged him close again. "But you're a gift, too."

A knock sounded on the hatch, then Kris Denaldo stuck her head inside. "I guess things are going well. Excuse me, but this is still my stateroom, too. Much as I hate to interrupt you two lovebirds, and by the way isn't all this hugging on a ship a violation of assorted regulations, but I need to get ready for the next watch." Her gaze shifted. "Jen! There's new dents in that locker!"

Jen smiled for real this time, though half-heartedly. "Sorry, Kris."

"Sorry! Is that all you can say? Tell it to the executive officer when he inspects this stateroom. I can't leave you alone for five minutes without you getting me into trouble again." Kris pointed at Paul. "As much as I'm sure you'd love to watch me change clothes, I prefer to have all the Y chromosomes on the other side of the hatch."

Paul pulled himself up. "Wondrous beauty though you be, Kris, I only want to see Jen, because my heart belongs to her."

"Oh, really? What about the rest of you? Do those parts belong to anyone?"

Jen pushed Paul toward the hatch. "You're going to make me ill with all your romantic nonsense, Mr. Sinclair. Go do your job for a while and let me rest. As for you, Ms. Denaldo, stop thinking about my boyfriend's parts."

Paul swung out of the hatch, but just before Kris closed it he saw Jen. Her face still drawn with pain, she was nonetheless trying to smile at him, and was silently mouthing the words "I love you."

"Now what?" Mike Bristol wondered. "I assume we're going straight back to Franklin?"

Lieutenant Sindh nodded. "Accommodations aren't the only thing stressed on this ship. The *Michaelson* isn't supposed to carry this many living, breathing people for any length of time."

"At least we've got enough food."

"If you call this food." Sindh squinted at her meal. "What is this supposed to be again?"

"Veal San Francisco," Bristol announced with an apologetic look.

Paul poked at his meal. "Looks more like Spam Francisco. Where's Suppo, anyway?"

"He's going to eat with the... uh... the..."

"Survivors."

"Yeah. From the *Maury*."

Paul no longer felt like joking or eating. "I wish we could do more for those guys."

Sindh smiled reassuringly at him. "We did what we could, and we still are. I've been working with them. Counseling sessions."

Paul nodded back. He knew Lieutenant Sindh was qualified as a lay minister and as a counselor, but not much beyond that. "Does it help?"

"I hope so. A great deal of it is still up to the individual." Her gaze lingered on Paul, communicating her concerns about Jen. "I'm just doing some emotional damage control here. The real work will be once they get back to Franklin and the experts can take over."

Randy Diego looked around. "Anybody know what this is going to do to schedules? I mean, we were spending a lot of time out as it was, and with *Maury* gone..." He flinched at a couple of hostile looks. "Hey, it's a legitimate thing to think about."

Even though Paul shared in the initial reaction to Randy's question, he felt a need to divert the anger it had brought. Randy Diego could be clueless, but he wasn't knowingly mean. "That is something we have to consider. I mean, I'm not thinking about more time underway as much as I am about getting work done on the ship. We've had to defer a lot of maintenance because of these short-fuse underway periods."

Kris Denaldo nodded as well. "And the hull got beat up by all that stuff that flew off the *Maury*. We need at least a minor overhaul period. Fleet staff need to decide whether they want a half-broke ship for the next few months or a fully working ship at the end of that time."

"Commander Destin said—" Gabriel suddenly paled and looked down at the table.

"Uh-oh," Kris remarked. "Breach of internal security procedures. All hands to emergency destruction stations. So, Dana, what'd Commander Destin say?"

Gabriel looked up, then back and forth as if seeking a way out, before grimacing in defeat. "She said maybe we'd, uh, could, uh, be lead platform for the, uh, certification on the, the..."

Lieutenant Sindh swallowed her bite of food. "Lead platform for certification of that new engineering device the *Maury* had? What was it?"

"Uh, SEERS."

"Yes. Is that what she said?"

Ensign Gabriel looked down again. "Yes."

Kris Denaldo's icy tone seemed to be within a few degrees of absolute zero. "She's looking forward to the chance to shine doing that, huh? Nice."

"I... I'm sure she didn't—"

"Yes, she did. Nice career boost for her if it happens. Bitch."

Sindh frowned at her. "Kris. That's inappropriate."

"But if—"

"She's still a superior officer. And we're in a professional environment."

Denaldo bit her lip, then nodded. "Sorry to everyone who heard that. But I'd really advise no one let Jen Shen know Destin feels that way."

Everyone else nodded, though Paul noticed Lieutenant Isakov seemed slightly amused. *What is it about that woman that annoys me?*

Randy Diego looked at Gabriel. "But won't Shen be working for Destin on the way back? I mean, she's an engineer and all."

Gabriel shook her head. "No."

"How come?"

"I don't know. Chief Meyer brought it up at a meeting and Destin made it clear Shen won't be working in engineering on the *Michaelson*. No reason given. It's just not going to happen."

Everyone looked at Paul, who fought down a surge of irritation. *Every time Jen gets mentioned everybody looks to me like I know everything that's going on in her head and her life. I don't know the life part and I don't think I'll ever know the head part.* "I don't know. I haven't heard anything about that."

"Jen's doing okay, isn't she?"

"As well as the other members of the *Maury*'s crew."

Bristol picked at his food for a moment. "Suppo said something to me. He said we should've left them on the *Maury*."

"What?"

"Yeah. Commander Sykes said if they'd stayed on the *Maury* they'd have had a lot to do. Standing watches and fixing stuff and keeping things working. But on here all they've got to do with their time is think about what happened. He says that's not good."

Sonya Sindh nodded. "Commander Sykes is, I believe, correct.

But the *Maury*'s not in any shape to sustain all those crew members all the way back to Franklin. We really didn't have any choice. But, speaking of the accident, has anyone heard if they have any idea what happened as of yet?"

Gabriel shook her head. "I was talking to Chief Meyer and Colleen. They say all we can tell right now is that the engineering spaces were destroyed by internal explosions."

"Explosions? Plural?"

"They think so. Very close together, though, so it seemed like one big explosion."

Mike Bristol shook his head in turn. "We'll find out for sure, right?"

"Well, Colleen wasn't sure of that. A lot of stuff was destroyed, including the engineering logs, and a lot of the, uh, fragments that might contain evidence were blown into space and dispersed so wide we'll never find them all."

Randy leaned forward. "Maybe it was a bomb." Everyone looked at him. "I mean it. The SASALs don't like us. Maybe they figured out how to get a bomb onboard the *Maury*."

"That's ridiculous," Kris Denaldo insisted.

"How do you know? Nobody else seems to know what caused the explosion. I'm not going to be the only one who thinks the SASALs might've had something to do with it."

Paul stared at the ensign. *He's right. Remember the* Maine. *Did the SASALs sabotage the* Maury *somehow? If they did, could we prove it? If they didn't, will that matter to those who want war?* He found himself torn inside. *I don't want to think those sailors on the* Maury *died because of an accident. Just by chance. But do I want their deaths to lead to war?* He became aware people were looking at him again. "What?"

"We were just wondering if Jen'd said anything about what she thought'd caused the explosion," Randy explained.

"No. And I haven't asked her and I won't ask her." Paul checked the time, eager for an excuse to leave. "I need to be in Combat. See you guys."

It was only partly a lie. It seemed Paul usually had to be in Combat, but he didn't have any specific requirement at the moment. He reached Combat, had a few words with the sailors from his division who were standing watch, then sat down at his console and stared at the screen. He wasn't sure how long he sat like that.

"Hi, sailor."

Paul looked up at Jen. "Hi. What brings you to Combat?"

She hooked herself through the tie-down on Paul's console so she could float nearby. "Boredom and a desire for decent company. That and I have no appetite and the rest of my wardroom is eating at the moment."

"You should eat, Jen."

"Yeah. Yeah. I'm eating enough. Do you need anyone to stand watch up here?"

"You?"

Jen seemed unable to decide between angry and amused. "I was standing watches in Combat while you were still staging panty raids in college, Mr. Sinclair."

"I didn't go to college. I went to the Naval Academy."

"Oh, yeah. Trade school. Don't avoid the question. Can I do some work up here?"

"Well, I'm sure—"

One of Paul's sailors called out "attention on deck" as Captain Hayes entered Combat. "Good afternoon, Paul. How're you doing, Ms. Shen?"

Jen smiled politely. "I'm fine, sir. Thank you for asking. My shipmates and I are very grateful for the hospitality the *Michaelson* has shown us." The reply sounded to Paul almost mechanical, as if she were reciting a script, but he didn't think anyone who didn't know Jen as well as he did would detect that.

"It's the very least we can do. Do you personally need anything?"

"Yes, sir. I need something to do. I'm a line officer, sir. I'm going crazy with all this free time."

Captain Hayes grinned. "That's not a complaint I'm used to hearing from junior officers. I may be able to do something about that. A ship can always use another officer, but I'll be frank. I've been advised to minimize the stress on you and your fellow officers from the *Maury*. Watch standing is out."

"Sir, right now I'd do paperwork and be glad for it."

"Can you concentrate on that sort of thing?"

Jen's smile grew strained. "It beats concentrating on other things. If you know what I mean, sir. I've served on the *Michaelson*. As auxiliaries officer, before I went to the *Maury*. I'm familiar with the ship."

"So I understand, Lieutenant Shen." Captain Hayes gave Jen a long, appraising look, as she gazed back at him. "I'll talk to our chief engineer about getting you some gainful employment, Ms. Shen."

Jen didn't bother trying to hide her reaction. "Thank you, sir. That really means a lot to me."

"I try to look out for my officers, Ms. Shen, and if you're unhappy then Paul here would be unhappy, too." Hayes winked at Paul, smiled, and left.

Jen kept her eyes on the hatch after the captain had left. "What's he like?"

"Hayes? Really good." Paul hesitated. "He served with the chief engineer on the *Maury*. They were on the *John Glenn* together."

Jen's face froze for a moment, then she smiled sadly. "Juko was a good boss, too. What about your chief engineer?"

"Commander Destin?"

"Yeah. What's Destin like?"

"She's an exile."

Jen laughed for just a moment. "Do you remember when I explained that stuff to you? Exiles and slackers and all? A few days after you joined the *Michaelson*?"

"Oh, yeah. I remember. You scared the hell out of me."

"Me personally or what I told you?"

"Both, I think."

She smiled briefly. "So Destin's an exile."

"And she doesn't like me, and something must've happened to her once that really hurt, because she's always walking around looking melancholy."

"Wonderful. But I'd be happy to settle for a boss like that if I can just get something to do. Let's see if your captain can wrangle some work for me from her."

Paul just nodded back, not wanting to share what Ensign Gabriel had told the other officers at lunch, and hoping Captain Hayes would change Destin's mind. *Once she's seen how well Jen works, even Destin will have to admit Jen's really good.*

After chatting a bit longer, Jen finally admitted to hunger, so Paul escorted her to the wardroom, then headed for his own stateroom. Paul's path took him by the executive officer's cabin. Just before he reached it, the hatch opened and Commander Destin swung out, her face flushed and her mouth tight. Commander Kwan followed, also looking unhappy. Seeing Paul in the passageway, Destin glowered at him for a long moment before turning and heading away. Kwan spotted Paul as well and gave him an annoyed look before going back into his stateroom.

Oh, great. Now what? Destin hasn't liked me since Silver's court-martial, but this seems pretty recent. Wait a minute. The captain said he'd talk to Destin about putting Jen to work. I guess he already did. Too bad I couldn't overhear that conversation. Destin must've just been venting to Kwan about it, and Kwan's not thrilled, either.

But it'd make Jen a little happier, and that made it worth it.

"Hey, Paul, have you seen this stuff?"

Paul looked over to Ensign Randy Diego, who had a news feed visible on his terminal. This close to Franklin, they could pick up the local data stream without much delay, and with the whole world knowing the *Michaelson* was bringing most of the *Maury*'s survivors home there was no reason Franklin shouldn't maintain a constant stream of communications to the ship. "No. What is it? Something about the *Maury*?"

"You might say it's about the *Maury*! They're blaming it on the SASALs. Just like I said they would!"

"What?" Paul punched buttons, hurriedly bringing the news feed up on his own display. *Remember the* Maury. *Just like I feared.* Paul switched news channels several times, finding the same stories being reported on each. He finally settled on a channel with several talking heads who seemed marginally more civil to each other than the average commentators.

An angry man held up his fist. "It's obvious the South Asian Alliance had to be behind this. There's no other explanation."

Another man held up both hands, palm out. "Now, George, it's a possibility. There's no evidence——"

"Evidence? Ships don't just blow up! You've seen the Navy's statements on this."

"The Navy says they don't know what could've caused such explosions. That's not the same as saying they know it was sabotage!"

"Sabotage, hell! Try act of war!"

Paul muted the sound, shaking his head. *Act of war? Somebody's trying to get us to start fighting a hot war with the SASALs because of what happened to the* Maury? *Well, Randy was right. Too bad. Unless the SASALs did do it. Then I want them to pay.*

Randy cleared his throat. "Paul? How could the SASALs blow up the *Maury* like that? Our engineers won't really talk about it. I mean, you can't exactly smuggle that much explosives onto a ship without someone noticing, right?"

Paul sighed. "I'd guess people are claiming they did smuggle a bomb on board because they don't understand how hard it'd be. Or that it was some other kind of sabotage. Messing with software or hardware so all the systems in engineering on the *Maury* blew."

"A virus? Could a virus do that?"

"They're not supposed to be able to do that. *Nothing's* supposed to be able to do that, from what I've heard. I'm not sure how we'd ever prove it anyway, with all that equipment blown to hell along with whatever software it carried."

"Do *you* think the SASALs did it?"

Paul hesitated, thinking through his answer. "I don't know they did, and I don't know they didn't. But I haven't seen anything to make me believe they did. And I can't believe the SASALs would risk war with us in order to take out the *Maury*."

"A lot of other people believe it. I saw some public opinion polls."

And what's true sometimes isn't nearly as important as what people believe to be true. There's been wars fought in the past because of that. But, dammit, if I'm going to fight a war I'd like there to be a solid reason for it. "Randy, a lot of people are being told that right now. Hopefully everyone'll have time to think things through before rushing off to avenge the *Maury*."

"I'd think if anybody'd want to get even with them, it'd be you!"

Paul stared back at Diego for a long moment, fighting down a wave of anger before he replied. "If they did it, I want them to pay for it. But I don't want to start a war because some people didn't want to wait until we got answers."

"But if Jen had—"

"*That's my business.* Not yours." *And I'm getting pretty tired of people trying to leverage my relationship with Jen.*

It was Randy's turn to stare, blinking at the uncharacteristic outburst from Paul. Then he flushed a bit, shrugged, and turned away. "Sure."

Paul gritted his teeth, concentrating on relaxing. "Sorry I blew up like that." He was out the hatch of the stateroom before Randy could reply.

Combat didn't seem to offer much refuge any more, and the wardroom was likely to have some of the officers from the *Maury* hanging out to kill time. Paul wandered through the ship, wishing they were docking at Franklin right now instead of the next morning.

"Mr. Sinclair?"

Paul looked up to see Senior Chief Kowalski regarding him, and realized he was right outside the chiefs' quarters. "Hi, senior chief."

"You doing okay, sir?"

"I think so, senior chief."

"May I ask how Ms. Shen is doing, sir?"

Paul smiled. He knew Senior Chief Kowalski had always respected Jen. "She's about as okay as she can be. I think. You know."

"I understand, sir. Helluva thing."

"She's glad she managed to get assigned some paperwork, but, uh..." *Oh, hell, I shouldn't discuss this with the senior chief.*

But Kowalski nodded. "She don't feel too welcome in engineering, right, sir?"

"How'd you know?"

"Sailors, sir. Superstition. Ms. Shen survived while the rest of the *Maury*'s Engineering Department got wiped out. There's people who worry about that."

Paul stared. "Like she's cursed or something?"

"No one's *saying* that, sir, and I sure as hell ain't saying it. But, it's there."

Maybe that's why Destin didn't want Jen working for her. "I don't believe it. She's not exactly unscathed by the experience, and now they want to slap some sort of scarlet letter on her to keep her out of the work she loves and knows best?"

Senior Chief Kowalski held his hands up in a calming gesture. "Sir, I wouldn't get all upset. It won't help. I'm just telling you so you'll maybe understand a bit better and help Ms. Shen through it. It'll pass. Ms. Shen's one fine officer. You know that. She'll do okay."

Paul nodded. "Thanks for caring, senior chief. I wish I could do more."

"Me, too, sir. For her and a lot of other people."

"Yeah."

It felt very odd, coming into port this time. No festivities, despite some joy at the *Michaelson*'s return. No one wanted to look like they were celebrating while the survivors of the *Maury* filed off the ship. "We'll be staying at temporary barracks near the shipyard section of the base," Jen told Paul. "When Captain Halis brings the *Maury* in, we'll be there to start putting her back together."

First aboard the *Michaelson* was the fleet commander. Bells bonged, bosun whistles wailed and sideboys snapped to attention as the admiral boarded to talk personally to the *Maury*'s survivors. Right after the admiral came what seemed like an army of others— chaplains and secular counselors to deal with trauma, Navy technical investigators to interview the survivors from the *Maury* and members of the *Michaelson*'s crew, shipyard workers to assess the state of the *Michaelson*, check her for exterior damage from the *Maury*'s debris field, and determine how much maintenance she'd need to be fully capable again.

Paul found himself in Kris Denaldo's stateroom again, this time not only with Jen but with a chaplain who extended her hand in greeting. "Mary Hughes. I'm here to talk with Ms. Shen, and it was suggested that you be present as well."

"Okay, Commander Hughes."

"Mary."

"Yes, ma'am. Uh... Mary."

They sat, close in the confines of the women's ensign locker, Jen sitting with the rigid correctness of an officer in a formal meeting with a superior. The chaplain leaned back a bit and smiled at her. "Ideally, this sort of thing should happen within a few days of the event. We couldn't do that this time for obvious reasons. I understand Paul was able to give you some comfort immediately afterward, at least."

Jen flicked a glance at Paul, who made an expression meant to convey "I didn't tell her that." Then she focused back on the chaplain. "Ma'am, immediately after the... event I was focused on saving the lives of the sailors trapped with me in the aft end of the ship. I didn't see Mr. Sinclair until some time after that."

"I'm sorry. I should've stated that differently. Could you please tell me what happened to you? I mean, just before and after the event."

"The explosion, you mean." Paul saw the muscles in Jen's jaw tighten for a moment. "I've already provided statements about that. I can get you copies."

"I'd prefer to hear it from you."

Jen blew out a breath in apparently barely controlled exasperation. "All right. I was ordered aft to check out a malfunctioning power coupling."

"Ordered by...?"

"The——" Jen paused to take another breath. "——chief engineer."

"Commander Juko?"

"Yes. He sent me aft, told me to see what I could figure out from looking at the thing directly because we kept getting odd fluctuations in the remote readings."

"Why'd he send you? Because he trusted you?"

"Yes." Jen smiled for the first time, though defiantly. "I'd just cleared the after survival bulkhead when... whatever happened happened. It blew a lot of holes in the bulkhead, too many to patch. I gathered what intact survival suits and survivors I could find, took them to an interior compartment to await rescue, and when conditions began to look critical I went looking for help."

The chaplain waited several seconds after Jen stopped talking. "That's all?"

"That's all."

"You must have been severely affected by the explosion, even before you knew how bad it had been."

"I was worried," Jen admitted. "But I didn't have time to dwell on it. I had a job to do. That's all I thought about."

"But later, sitting in that interior compartment, there was time to think then. Time to feel."

Jen shook her head, her face unyielding. "I was focused on keeping those sailors alive. That's all I thought about."

"What you had to do to save them?"

"That's right."

"You didn't think about yourself?"

"Only to the extent that I needed to stay calm and in charge."

The chaplain leaned back some more, eyeing Jen. "You had to stay calm. You couldn't relax, couldn't think about past events."

"That's right."

"Did you have any thoughts or emotions about the other personnel in engineering?"

Paul noticed Jen's cheek twitch and wondered if the chaplain had seen it, too. Jen took several breaths before answering. "I... hoped they were okay."

"You were worried about them."

"Of course I was!"

"But you couldn't do anything to help them." Jen's mouth opened for a moment, then closed. "Do you think perhaps you focused so intently on saving those sailors with you because that was something you *could* do?"

Jen finally looked fully over at Paul, her eyes wide, then back at the chaplain. "That was all I could do at the time," she agreed in a soft voice.

"All you could do. You wanted to do more?"

"Yes! Of course! But I couldn't even get out through the damned internal airlock! And when I wanted to find another route forward I had all those sailors looking to me for help. To me. I couldn't go forward until I did everything I could for them. I had to do that."

The chaplain nodded. "Yes. You did. You couldn't go to try to help the others in engineering because those sailors needed you."

"That's what I said. Ma'am."

"And you learned later that there never was anything you could've done. They were already dead." Jen flushed, though with anger or other emotion Paul couldn't tell. "You were able to save those sailors, though. You made the right decision."

Jen looked down, then back up as she suddenly grinned tightly. "Yes. Someone advised me I should try to focus on what I could and did do and not on what I couldn't have done."

Chaplain Hughes' eyebrows rose and she looked over at Paul. "You told her that?"

Paul nodded. "I received that same advice some time ago, after a fatality on my ship."

"It's good advice. You talked to a grief counselor?"

"No, ma'am. A supply officer."

"One with a more than adequate supply of wisdom, it appears! Jen, are you having difficulty working?"

She shrugged. "I haven't had much to work on."

"What you have been doing. Have you been able to do it?"

"Of course I have."

"You're completing tasks assigned to you?"

Jen glared at the chaplain. "I *always* complete tasks assigned to me."

"Do you dream about the explosion? About those events?"

"No."

"Nothing? No flashbacks?"

"*No.*"

Chaplain Hughes looked over at Paul, then back at Jen. "There's a time for strength and a time for confronting problems."

"I don't have any problems."

"I understand your father is commanding officer of the *Mahan*?"

"Yes."

"And the *Mahan* just departed on a long patrol. Your mother is...?"

"Dead."

"I'm sorry." The chaplain leaned forward. "Your father a commanding officer and your mother dead. You must be pretty tough."

Jen shrugged again. "I'm nothing special."

"You saved, let's see, twenty-one sailors in the aft section of the *Maury*. That sounds pretty special to me."

Jen sat silent for a moment. "Anyone else could've done the same."

"Maybe. But the fact that you did it counts." Jen didn't answer. "Listen, Jen, this is just a first preliminary session—"

"I don't *need* any more sessions."

"You'll get them, anyway. Courtesy of the US Navy."

"I *don't*—"

"Did I mention the sessions are mandatory? By order of the fleet commander?" Jen subsided, looking sulky. "It won't be that bad, Jen."

"I have other things to do, ma'am."

"Mary. Sadly, not enough other things. Maybe you won't need much help. But my job is to see if you do and help you through any rough patches."

Jen leaned forward, her face earnest. "I help myself. I mean that. I can't go running for a shoulder to cry on whenever things get tough. I have to be able to work through it myself."

"You can't be weak, in other words."

"I didn't say that."

"This isn't about being strong or weak, Jen. It's about being human. You've been subjected to tremendous stresses. If you were a piece of this ship and had been stressed, you might need to be reinforced. Not because you weren't strong, but because even the strongest can be overstressed. Do you see?"

Jen nodded with visible reluctance. "I honestly do not believe I need reinforcement."

"I believe you. Let me do my job, though." Hughes checked her watch. "Too many people to see and too little time. I'll schedule the follow-up sessions and make sure you're notified." She pointed to Paul. "Use him."

Jen couldn't help smiling. "I do."

"I didn't mean it that way. Though if it helps... no, just remember you've got someone to confide in, someone who won't think you're not strong if you need to talk." Hughes looked at Paul. "Right?" Paul nodded. "You've got my contact information, Jen. I'm always available, too. But I have to leave now. Paul, could I see you for a moment?"

He followed Commander Hughes out of the stateroom. She studied him for a long moment. "Paul, I think you understand Jen's in serious denial about the effect this has had on her."

"That's who she is, ma'am."

"Mary! You line officers... I can tell Jen's like that. She never admits weakness, does she? Well, you watch her and you contact me if you think I need to know something. At some point Jen's going to confront her feelings, and somebody'll need to be there for her."

"What feelings? Do you know?"

"Not for certain. In a case like this survivor's guilt is common. 'Why did I survive when others died?'"

"She said something like that. The first time I saw her after the accident."

"She did? Then she's at least admitted to that feeling. But there'll likely be more. Feeling she should've prevented it, done something, somehow. She's maintaining a protective shell of being professional and controlled because that's what she thinks the world wants to see, but there's got to be a lot of doubts inside."

"Yes, ma'am."

"Mary!" Chaplain Hughes walked off, shaking her head.

7

Carl Meadows didn't seem to have changed much as he grinned out from the display screen at Paul's desk. Paul hadn't expected a video letter from his old shipmate, but it'd been a pleasant surprise. "Greetings from the Pentagon, Paul. Long time no see. I miss you guys." Carl's smile faded. "Truth is, I sent this because I heard about the *Maury* and you guys. That must've been real tough. Thank God Jen made it okay. Just wanted you guys to know I'm still thinking about you."

Meadows ran one hand through his hair. "There's been a whole lot of running around in the Pentagon. Admirals and generals bouncing off the walls right and left. All those stars in motion at once reminds me of maneuvering the *Merry Mike*. Anyway, I get the real feeling they're trying to put a lid on all this. It's no secret that we're not really ready for a war in space with the SASALs, and I don't think they're really ready for a war with us. Nobody wants to start shooting at each other down here on Earth, either. We're seeing a lot of stuff about cooling things down, confidence-building measures and junk like that. There's going to be a lot of pressure on the investigators to figure out what happened to the *Maury* as fast as possible, and I gather all the military and political brass are keeping their fingers crossed that whatever it was didn't involve the South Asians."

Carl rambled on some more, with Paul enjoying listening to his friend again, then closed his letter with a list of people to say hi to on the *Michaelson.*

Colleen Kilgary stuck her head in his stateroom. "Did you hear?"

"Hear what?"

"Preliminary investigation results released."

Carl had been right. Given the damage to the *Maury*, that was a very quick announcement. "What did they say?"

"Bomb definitely ruled out. No residue of any kind that'd be consistent with that."

"That should calm the war talk a little."

"Also, external sabotage ruled out. The *Maury*'s safety interfaces would've kept any software or hardware problems from producing that kind of catastrophic failure of so many components in engineering."

"Wow." Paul stared at his now-blank display. "Are they saying what they think *did* happen?"

"Not yet. But I thought you'd like to tell Jen, just in case she hasn't heard."

"Thanks."

Colleen left and Randy Diego entered, dropping into the seat at his own desk. Paul waved in greeting. "Hey, Randy, did you hear what Colleen said? No bomb."

"Really? That's good."

Paul gave Randy a curious glance. "What's up? You seem distracted."

"No. No. Just, you know, busy."

"Sure." Paul bent back to his own work.

"Uh, okay if I ask you something, Paul?"

Paul glanced at Randy again, alerted by his hesitant tone. "What about?"

"Well, I mean, you and Jen, you're both on active duty and you're dating and all." Randy paused, looking into one corner of the stateroom while Paul waited. "I was just wondering how that's working out."

"It's working out fine, Randy. You know we don't see each other nearly as often as we'd like. My ship's out, or her ship's out, or we've got duty or have to work all night or something. You know how it goes. And of course there's the hazards of the job. I guess if my girlfriend worked as a stockbroker on Earth I wouldn't have to worry about that kind of thing. But since Jen was on the *Maury* I had some real heart-stopping moments." He found it easier to talk about, now. Now that the immediate fears of those awful hours had finally begun receding into memory like the remnants of a bad dream.

"Uh, yeah. But, what about... uh... I mean... you guys must've gotten interested in each other while you were both onboard the same ship, right? While you and Jen were both on the *Michaelson?*"

Paul frowned, not sure now where Randy was trying to go. "Not really. We were friends. We didn't do anything beyond that until Jen transferred to the *Maury.*" That wasn't strictly true, since they'd actually gotten very personal a few nights before Jen's transfer, but Paul knew the relationship had remained hidden until Jen had left the *Michaelson.* Hidden from everyone except the *Michaelson's* old XO, that is. But Commander Herdez had trusted their professionalism. *Randy, on the other hand, isn't a bad guy, but he's not the sharpest tool in the shed, either. No way Herdez would've cut him that slack.*

Randy nodded rapidly. "Yeah. Sure. But you got to know each other real well before that, right?"

Alarm bells finally sounded in Paul's mind. *Great. Randy's got the hots for one of the other officers.* "Not that well. In no way, shape or form. It's a bad idea, Randy. It's also against regulations. Keep it professional until she leaves the ship, Randy."

"I didn't say—"

"You don't have to. Look, maybe she feels the same interest you do. If she does, you can try dating *after* she leaves the ship. If she's not interested after she leaves the ship, then she's not interested now. Right?" Randy avoided Paul's eyes. "There's no way to hide a real romance inside the wardroom, Randy. Anybody'd be able to see you two making goopy eyes at each other." Jen's phrase, though Paul'd never been sure exactly what "goopy eyes" were.

"But—" Randy interrupted himself this time, still avoiding Paul's gaze.

Paul felt another suspicion arise. "How recent is this?"

"Who said it was recent? Who said anything's recent or anything's going on?"

"Has Isakov been flirting with you?"

Randy jerked his head around, then tried to pretend nonchalance. "A lieutenant? I wish."

"Randy, she's been teasing at me off and on. When she's not acting like I'm someone she's never seen before and doesn't want to talk to. I think it's some kind of weird power game she plays. Stay away from her."

"You know, just maybe there's some good-looking female officers out there who don't think you're the only game in town."

"This isn't about my ego, Randy. I don't want anything to do with Isakov outside of work. She's trouble."

"I wasn't born yesterday. I can take care of myself."

Famous last words. "Be careful. Think really hard and don't do anything the crew might find out about." His sailors didn't exactly love Randy from all Paul had heard, which wasn't necessarily a problem except they didn't respect him as much as they should, either. Randy had too great a tendency to insist he was right when he wasn't. If he handed the crew a way to get back at him... "Just think."

"Sure. Right. Fine. Sorry I brought it up." Randy Diego turned away, hunching forward toward his display, his back clearly communicating an end to the conversation. A few minutes later he stood and left the stateroom without a see-you-later.

Paul shook his head. *Maybe one of the other female officers can talk some sense into Randy. Why couldn't he get interested in Gabriel if he wants to mess around on the ship? Not that Gabriel's acted interested in him. She's got a load more common sense than Randy does.*

He tried to concentrate on his work again.

"Mr. Sinclair?"

Paul threw up his hands. "I give up. What's up, Sheriff?"

Sharpe looked puzzled. "Something wrong, sir?"

"Just the usual one-damned-thing-after-another. So, what's up?"

"Drug bust."

"Fastow, again?"

Sharpe shook his head. "Nope. She's either scared straight or lucky. This is some bright boys in Mr. Diego's division."

"Dealers or users?"

"Maybe both. I'm going to contact the local special agents to see if they can help run down where our boys are getting their stuff.

Commander Kwan told me to 'keep you informed' since you're the legal officer." Sharpe rendered a rigidly correct salute. "I hereby inform you, sir."

Paul casually returned the salute. "Thanks."

"My pleasure, sir. Anything to make your days brighter and more interesting."

"I've had a bit too much of that, lately. How are you at making them darker and duller?"

"Hi." Jen knocked on the hatch to Paul's stateroom. "Hello, Sheriff."

Sharpe inclined his head and touched his brow. "Nice to see you, ma'am."

"Likewise. What're you two plotting?"

"Mr. Sinclair was just complaining he hasn't had enough legal stuff to keep him busy lately."

Paul snorted derisively. "That tells you what a judge of character Sheriff Sharpe is. See you later, Sheriff."

Sharpe moved to leave, but Jen raised a hand to forestall him. "Can you hang around a minute? Something kind of funny happened that you might help me with."

Sharpe nodded. "Of course, ma'am."

"Have you worked with special agents much? The guys in the Naval Criminal Investigative Service?"

Sharpe frowned, but nodded again. "Yes, ma'am. Mr. Sinclair and I were just talking about that, as a matter of fact. I'm a cop, they're cops."

"I just had a long meeting with some of them. About the *Maury*."

"Your ship?" Sharpe eyed her. "They interviewed you about that?"

"They didn't call it an interview. They just said they wanted to

166

meet with me. But... it was weird." Paul noticed Sharpe's expression grow more intent as Jen continued. "First they made a lot of small talk. Then they finally gave me something to sign before we really talked about the *Maury*. They said it was all routine and no big deal. I told them I was an engineer and I didn't sign anything without reading it."

"What'd it say?"

She glanced from Paul to Sharpe. "The part I really focused on was where it talked about waiving my rights to counsel. I asked them what that was about and they said it was all routine. Then they started asking why I thought I needed a lawyer." Sharpe began frowning. "I don't like that kind of pressure. I gave them back their form and told them I wouldn't sign it. They didn't get upset, seemed not to care, but they started asking a bunch of questions."

"What kind of questions, ma'am?" Petty Officer Sharpe seemed more concerned every time Paul looked at him.

Jen shrugged, her expression aggravated. "Why I'd gone aft before the explosion. I told them I'd been ordered to do that. Then they asked who ordered me and I said the chief engineer. I told them it was all in the official statements I'd provided. Then they wanted to know if I had any witnesses to that. Witnesses! Of course not. Everyone who witnessed it is dead."

She shook her head. "They asked why I'd gone aft, and I told them about the power coupling acting up. They asked about records on that, and I pointed out they'd have been in the engineering logs which were destroyed by the accident."

Paul let his puzzlement show. "But all they'd have to do is examine the power coupling. That'd show what was wrong with it."

"No, it wouldn't." Jen bit her lip. "It showed... shows... what *is* wrong with it. After the shock of the explosions that ripped through the *Maury*. I never got to the coupling before that happened. I don't know if what's wrong now is what was wrong then."

Sharpe seemed to be chewing on the inside of his cheek. "Anything else, ma'am?"

"Just a lot of unconnected stuff. How was my relationship with my father, was work on the *Maury* really stressful, how things were going with my boyfriend." She glared at Sharpe. "Like I was going to talk about things like that with them! Then they asked if I had any ideas how someone could've caused an explosion like that if they'd wanted to—"

"Did you answer that one, ma'am?"

Jen frowned, then shook her head at Sharpe's question. "No. I just said it would've taken a tremendous number of overloads to cause that strong an explosion."

"And they asked you about your love life, ma'am?"

"Yes. I told you they did. And I told them it was none of their business."

Paul looked over at Sharpe. "Sheriff, why were they asking Ms. Shen questions like that? What are they driving at? You seem to know."

Sharpe licked his lips, his face uncertain for the first time Paul could remember. "Yes, sir, I know what they're driving at. At least, I know what I'd be driving at if I asked questions like that, and tried to get my subject to waive rights to a lawyer."

"What?"

"Sir, I'd like some time to look into it."

Jen leaned toward him. "Sharpe, you've got some idea. Tell me."

"Ma'am, I'd really rather—"

"Tell me. What's up with those guys?"

"They think you were involved in some way. In the explosion."

Jen's face twisted in confusion. "Involved? What—?" The confusion shifted, transforming into rage. "They think I *caused* it?"

"Maybe, ma'am." Sharpe took a step back, as if worried what Jen might do.

Paul shook his head, unable to believe what he'd heard. "Sheriff, why the hell would they believe that?"

Sharpe eyed Jen with concern as he spoke. "Meaning no disrespect to Ms. Shen, sir, and not implying *I* believe this is right, but what it sounds like is they think maybe someone caused the explosion, because if I've heard right they're ruling out other causes? So I'm guessing what they're thinking is that maybe somehow someone caused the explosion. Since Ms. Shen reached safety just before it blew, they're looking at her. From what Ms. Shen says they were asking her it looks like they're also trying to find a motive."

"Why would they reach that kind of conclusion? That's insane!" Paul felt anger flaring within him and fought it down, knowing he'd have to keep Jen from blowing her own top.

Sharpe bit his lip. "Some guesses, sir. If they can't find a mechanical or software reason for the explosion, they'll look for a human agent. Something must have caused it. If they think they've ruled out hardware, that means they'll look for a sailor. Someone who deliberately or accidentally screwed up. And anyone who escaped while everyone else bought it." He looked straight at Jen. "Ms. Shen, it does sound to me like they're investigating whether you did it."

Instead of erupting into further anger, Jen sat still, her red face growing pale. "Oh my God. Paul? How can they?"

Paul grabbed her shoulder. "They can't and they won't. Sheriff, can you talk any sense into those guys?"

"They won't be doing this on their own, sir. They'll be following the lead of someone higher up."

"It's ridiculous! No one who knows Ms. Shen could ever believe it."

Sharpe nodded. "Yes, sir. I agree with you, sir. Ms. Shen would've had to have gone totally insane to do something like that, and she sure looks to me like she's always looked. I'll talk to them. No guarantees, you understand. They don't work for me, and some special agents look on masters-at-arms like me as uniformed Deputy Dawgs. But I'll try. Even if they don't listen to me, I'm sure whatever they're finding out will show them they're barking up the wrong tree this time." He paused. "I'm real sorry, Ms. Shen. I know how this must feel to you. They're trying to do their jobs. They've got to check out all the angles. Sometimes cops just go off on the wrong tangent."

"Why would they pick this tangent?"

"Like I said, sir, they've looked at possible causes for the explosion and come up empty-handed so far. Now they're looking at other possible causes."

"This isn't a possible cause. It's impossible."

"I agree, sir. I'll talk to them." Sharpe paused on his way out of the hatch. "By the way, Ms. Shen, you did right not signing that paper. Don't sign anything else without a lawyer checking it."

Jen stared at him, looking like she had when Paul had first seen her after the explosion on the *Maury*. "I won't."

"Get them to shut this down, Sheriff. I can't believe they're doing this to her."

"I'll try, sir. No promises, but like I said, I'm sure when they've looked into it a bit they'll realize Ms. Shen couldn't have done something like that."

* * *

Fogarty's felt oddly subdued for a hail and farewell party. Lieutenant Sindh moved among the officers of the *Michaelson*'s wardroom, chatting politely. With Jen standing duty at the barracks where the *Maury*'s crew had been billeted, Paul sat alone in a corner and mostly watched. *Kris Denaldo's on duty on the ship, and I don't really feel like getting happy drunk with anybody else, and I don't feel like getting morose drunk at all. And Sonya, God bless her, isn't the partying type. I think she's only having this hail and farewell because it's traditional.*

Sindh stopped by. "I probably won't see you when I leave tomorrow, Paul. I need to get off the ship early to catch my shuttle, so I'll depart during morning quarters."

"I'm sorry to hear that. You deserve a proper send-off."

She laughed. "All the officers lined up at the quarterdeck saluting as I march grandly off to a bright, shiny new future? That's not really my speed, Paul."

He didn't know whether or not it was the drink he'd had, but Paul blurted out his thoughts. "You were always there for everyone else, Sonya. I'm glad I got to serve with you."

"And I with you." Sindh made a small smile. "There was a song, long ago. Part of it says 'hello, hello; good-bye, good-bye; that's all there is.' We meet, we go on. Say my fondest farewells to Jen."

"I will."

Sindh made to go, then looked down at Paul with a mischievous smile. "I expect to be invited to the wedding."

"If there is one, you'll be there."

Another smile, this time seeming reassuring, and she went on to talk with a gaggle of ensigns. Paul had another drink, watching her and thinking of the other officers who'd already come and gone since he'd joined the *Michaelson*. *I'm becoming a veteran of the crew. Why do I still feel inside like I'm the new guy?*

Someone plopped down next to him. Paul looked over, startled, at Val Isakov.

Isakov hoisted her own drink. "You look lonely."

She obviously favored outfits off-duty that showed off what she had to offer, which in Isakov's case was quite a bit. Paul felt a curious mix of attraction and repulsion as he looked back at her. "Not really."

"Are you dating your invisible friend?"

"No. Jen's on duty tonight."

"Ah, too bad. No one to warm your bunk." Isakov's hand snaked out under the table and she drew one finger across Paul's leg. "Must be hard."

His lower spine liked the sensation, but Paul's brain didn't. He twitched his leg away. "I'm happy."

"Did I say you weren't?" She laughed and took a drink. "Lighten up. It's a party."

"Sure."

Isakov leaned over, her breast pushing against Paul's arm, and held the position for a moment. "See you around," she whispered. Then she pulled away, laughed again, and walked over to another group of officers.

Paul stared after her. He put down his drink, stood up, found Sonya and said farewell again, then left and walked back to the *Michaelson*.

Kris Denaldo was sitting in the wardroom, eating popcorn and watching a movie on the big display. "Hey, early night."

"I didn't really feel like partying." Paul grabbed some coffee and sat down on the other side of the wardroom.

Denaldo eyed him. "I don't bite. At least, that's what I'm told.

And if I tried biting *you*, Jen'd come charging in here and throw me halfway to the Oort Cloud."

Paul grinned. "It's not you."

"Crazy Ivana?"

"You mean Isakov? How'd you know?"

"Just a guess." Kris shook her head. "Women know."

"Well, whatever the hell Isakov is up to, I don't want any part of it."

"Good boy. Truth to tell, I'm not sure myself, yet. But I wouldn't fix my brother up with her."

"And I'm going to be stuck working with her for more than a year. Great. I already miss Sonya."

"I missed Sonya before you did." Denaldo took another bite of popcorn and chewed for a moment. "Just keep Crazy Ivana at arm's length. Literally, if necessary. We'll invite Jen over for dinner some night so Isakov can see what she's messing with."

"I'm not sure that'd scare her off. Isakov keeps talking about loving excitement and stuff."

Kris grinned. "Messing with Jen's boyfriend would be way too much excitement for me to risk! How's Jen doing, by the way? I didn't get a chance to talk to her when she stopped by yesterday."

"Okay, I guess." Paul tossed his empty drink container into the recycling bin. "She's really haunted by what happened."

"I'm not surprised. I bet I'd be an emotional basket-case in her place."

"And she's having some funny problems with investigators. People looking into what happened to the *Maury*." Even with Kris, he didn't want to discuss the full details. It was just too outrageous, too sick to think Jen had played any role in what had happened to her ship.

"Really? Engineers?"

"No, uh, Navy cops, I guess you could say."

"Did you talk to that lawyer of yours about it?"

"Lawyer?" Paul looked at her with real puzzlement. "I have a lawyer?"

"Yeah, that hottie who helped nail Silver. What was her name?"

"Carr. Alex Carr. *Commander* Alex Carr. Why do you and Jen keep trying to imply there's something going on between her and me?"

Kris grinned. "Because Jen's a bit jealous and I'm trying to cause trouble."

"You and Isakov?"

"Whoa! Low blow. I'm not going to go Crazy Ivana on you. But, seriously, if there's something you don't understand about what the cops are asking Jen, why not ask Carr? Can't hurt."

"Good, idea, Kris. I'll skip lunch tomorrow and stop by her office." *Maybe a full-bore JAG commander can get those special agents to back off.*

Paul paused in front of the door with A. Carr, CDR, USN, JAGC stenciled on it. *After Silver's court-martial, Commander Carr said if I ever needed legal help, I should check with her. This sure seems to fit.* He knocked, annoyed at his own nervousness.

Alex Carr looked up as Paul entered. "Lieutenant Sinclair."

"Yes, ma'am. Commander, I need some advice and maybe some assistance." *Why does she seem reserved? Maybe I just caught her at a bad time.*

"Something on your ship?"

"Uh, no, ma'am. It's about the *Maury*, about—"

"I'm sorry."

"Thank you, ma'am, but—"

"No." Carr gestured decisively. "I'm sorry I can't help you. I can't even talk about it."

Paul stared at her, puzzled. "Ma'am, I just wanted you to know some NCIS agents have been talking to a friend of mine——"

"Lieutenant Shen." Carr looked away, the quick smiles Paul remembered as being characteristic of her completely absent now. "I know. Paul, I can't discuss it."

He felt a chill inside. "But... ma'am? What's going on?"

She covered her forehead and face with one hand, her elbow resting on the desk. "I can't discuss matters in litigation. I can't discuss cases I'm involved with."

Litigation? Cases? "I don't... Commander Carr, please."

She lowered the hand and looked straight at him. "You'll know within a few hours."

"I want to know now! Dammit, I'm as dedicated as any officer in the Navy and I've proven it! I went on the *Maury* and helped patch her together and got pieces of what was left of her crew on my *hands*! What's going on, commander?"

Commander Carr stood up, looking steadily at Paul. "A military magistrate has ordered the arrest and confinement of Lieutenant Junior Grade Shen on charges pertaining to the deaths of sixty-one crewmembers and extensive physical damage to the USS *Maury*. Happy, Mr. Sinclair?"

He knew his jaw had fallen open. He knew he was just staring back at her. But he couldn't say anything.

"Mr. Sinclair. Sit down."

He sat automatically, barely noticing the concern on her face.

"I'm *very* sorry. I'm already involved in the case. I can't discuss it with you."

Paul finally found his voice. "Ma'am, it's impossible."

"That'll be for the court to determine."

Court-martial? Jen? His shock was replaced by a burst of anger. "How can you do that to her?"

"I'm doing my job, Mr. Sinclair. It's not always personally pleasant. Evidence was gathered and presented. An Article 32 investigation was conducted. In secrecy, given the sensitivity of the matter. Conclusions were reached and a warrant for arrest issued."

"You're going to be the prosecutor?"

"Those are my orders."

His worst nightmare. He knew how good Carr was. He'd seen her do a great job nailing Scott Silver for his negligence. And now she'd be going after Jen. "Ma'am, can I very respectfully ask that you refuse to prosecute Jen?"

"On what grounds, Mr. Sinclair?"

"Personal involvement!"

"I don't know her. I barely met her once." Her fist thudded onto the surface of her desk. "I have my duty to carry out." Then she turned away. "Whether I like it or not. Those sailors who died deserve to have justice done."

"She didn't do it, ma'am. She *couldn't.* Not Jen."

"I'm sorry. I can't discuss anything else about it. Lieutenant Shen should have a military lawyer appointed soon. Whoever that is can talk to you about it."

"Commander, I can't believe there's evidence to support those charges!"

Carr spun around, her eyes flashing. "Paul, don't make me order you to shut up and get out of my office! You're a good officer and as far as I know a good human being. But I have a case to prosecute to the best of my ability. Lieutenant Shen's lawyer can talk to you about the evidence until you're both blue in the face. I can't."

Paul stood silent for a moment, then nodded. "Yes, ma'am."

"Paul, for Christ's sake——"

"Ma'am, you'll be fair. I know that."

Carr nodded back. "Yes."

"If she's innocent, you'll admit that. You won't try to convict if you see proof she didn't do it."

Another nod, slower this time. "I will fairly evaluate all evidence available in the case. I have no trouble promising you that."

But you'll also do your best to convict her, because that's your job.

Who do I turn to, now?

He hesitated outside of Carr's office. *What do I do? Jen. That's priority one.* He tried calling her at the barracks where the *Maury*'s crew were working, but a stunned voice informed him Lieutenant Shen had been taken away under arrest a half-hour earlier. He called the brig, but no one could or would tell him anything. He called Petty Officer Sharpe. "Sheriff, they've arrested Je——, Ms. Shen."

A moment of silence answered him. "Damn, sir."

"She was arrested, but the brig won't tell me anything."

"I'll get you something, sir. Give me a few minutes."

Paul waited impatiently for more than a few minutes, feeling a wild urge to charge off and do *something* but fighting it down. Sharpe finally called back. "Yes, sir. She's in the brig. Pre-trial confinement."

"Pre-trial? They're going to keep her there?"

"That's the judge's orders, sir. Confinement until trial."

"I swear I'm going to find out who did this and——"

"Sir, with all due respect, don't let your temper run away with this. It won't help, and it will hurt."

"I'll go——"

"The only visitor Ms. Shen is authorized right now is her lawyer."

Her lawyer. "Who is that?"

"My contact at the brig didn't know. The lawyer may not've been appointed, yet."

"So she just sits there? Alone?"

"Sir, I... yes, sir."

Paul stared at nothing for a long while, then remembered something and made another call. "Commander Hughes. I hope you can do something."

Two hours later Paul was sitting on one side of a video screen set to look like a window. On the "other side" sat Jen, still in uniform but with all her insignia and ribbons removed. She stared back at him with an uncomprehending expression. "Paul, what's happening?"

"They didn't tell you?"

"They told me. Charges. About the *Maury*. God. It's a nightmare. Wake me up, Paul. Please."

"I can't."

"I'm in a cell. Like I'm some kind of threat."

"I'm trying to get you out, but they haven't appointed a lawyer to represent you, yet."

"They said I can't see anybody. How'd you manage this?"

"Commander Hughes. She's giving you counseling, remember?"

"I—"

"She's your doctor, Jen. They have to let you see your doctor."

The message got through. Jen nodded rapidly. "When?"

"She's going through search procedures right now. She'll see you in person in a few minutes."

"Okay." Jen swallowed and sat straighter. "It's ridiculous. They'll see that and I'll be out of here."

"Yes." A red light blinked in one corner of Paul's "window." "I've got the thirty-second warning before they cut this off. Should I send your father a message?" Not that he'd necessarily get it for a long time with the *Mahan* out on patrol.

"No! We'll fix this and then tell him."

The blinking light sped up, indicating only seconds remained. "I love you. I'm with you."

"Tha—"

The screen blanked. Paul stood up and left the small visiting room. Outside the door, a master-at-arms stood at parade rest awaiting him. Paul looked at the sailor. *Every other time I've seen a master-at-arms I've thought of them as being on my side. One of the good guys. And now they're holding Jen in the brig. Like Commander Carr, they're just doing their jobs.* "Do you know Petty Officer Sharpe?"

The master-at-arms nodded. "Ivan Sharpe? Yes, sir."

"He works for me."

"Yes, sir. That doesn't matter, sir."

Paul met the master-at-arms's eyes. "Professional courtesy. He believes she's innocent."

"Yes, sir." Totally noncommittal.

Frustrated and angry, Paul realized he'd been off the *Michaelson* for hours. He headed back for the ship, wondering what to do. Talk to Sharpe. *Find out if Jen's got a lawyer assigned yet. Why did Alex Carr have to be assigned to prosecute her?*

Approaching the *Michaelson*'s quarterdeck, Paul rapidly saluted the national ensign aft, then Ensign Gabriel, the officer of the deck. "Request permission to come aboard." Gabriel watched after him, startled by his abruptness. Paul turned right off of the quarterdeck and ran straight into Commander Garcia, who glowered at him. "Where the hell have you been all afternoon, Sinclair?"

"Sir, I..." Paul told him.

Garcia's eyes narrowed, then he nodded. "You've got the rest of the day off. Put in for as much leave as you need." He turned away, then looked back with a glare. "Make sure Chief Imari knows everything she needs to know while you're wrapped up in this."

Stunned, Paul watched him go through a hatch and disappear. "Thank you, sir." *Life and death. Garcia's a pain the butt for lesser issues, but when it comes down to life and death he can be a decent human being.*

There was a message waiting for him in his stateroom. Paul didn't recognize the number and hurriedly dialed it, thinking it might be from Jen's newly appointed lawyer.

But when the screen cleared he immediately recognized the woman who answered, as well as the man who joined her. "Paul! Surprise!"

"Mom? Dad?" Paul couldn't think of anything else to say.

"Yes. We got a contract job up here on Franklin and thought we'd surprise you."

"That's, that's great."

"I know you're probably not ready for us and you probably have a lot of work every day, but we should have some opportunities to get together. Your father and I really want to tour your ship and see how it compares to the old relics we used to sail around in up here."

"Sure."

"And we're both really looking forward to finally meeting this girl of yours we've heard so much *and* so little about."

"Uh..." *Gee, Mom and Dad, my girlfriend's in pretrial confinement in the brig, awaiting court-martial on charges of killing over sixty of her fellow crewmembers and sabotaging her ship.*

I know you want to see the woman I haven't yet told you I want to marry, but the brig probably won't allow all of us to visit her.

I think I can safely wonder how things could possibly get any worse today.

8

Lieutenant Ahmed Bashir, United States Navy, Judge Advocate General's Corps, was a few years older than Paul, but looked far too young to be Jen's lawyer in Paul's eyes. He wanted somebody who looked like he or she had argued and won cases in every court and venue. But the best lawyer he knew had been assigned not to defend Jen, but to prosecute her. He could only hope Bashir could go toe-to-toe with Alex Carr and not get steamrollered. "When can you get Jen out of the brig?"

Bashir sighed. "I doubt I'll be able to do it all."

"Why not? Do they think she's going to run away on a space station?"

"It's not about that. It's about the safety of the station."

"What?"

"Look." Bashir leaned back and spread his hands helplessly. "This is how the government's looking at it. Lieutenant Shen is charged with sabotaging the equipment on the *Maury*, causing it to blow up and kill scores of sailors. If she's free on Franklin, she could presumably do the same thing here."

"That's so completely ridiculous."

"Maybe. But the government's convinced the military magistrate, so Lieutenant Shen is in the brig and in the brig she will almost certainly remain."

Paul slumped back. *Great. This guy isn't even going to fight for her.* "Have you even talked to her yet?"

Bashir picked up on Paul's tone of voice and attitude, leaning forward and pointing both forefingers at him. "Yes. I have. And I'm going to do everything I morally and legally can to get her acquitted of these charges. Clear?"

"Clear. What can I do?"

The Navy lawyer relaxed again, shaking his head. "I don't like this. I don't mind telling you. Secret Article 32 investigation. Secret findings. Secret hearings. I've demanded to see all the evidence they've compiled to justify those charges against Ms. Shen, but as far as I know right now it's all circumstantial."

"Won't that help us?" *When we tried Silver on circumstantial evidence, they didn't want to convict him of some charges because of the uncertainty of his guilt.*

"It should, but..." Bashir rubbed his face. "You try someone for one murder on circumstantial evidence, and everybody gives them the benefit of the doubt. Try them for six murders on circumstantial evidence and they assume they're guilty. Why? Because they've been charged with something extra bad."

"That doesn't make sense."

"Tell me about it. But that's the way it works. People figure if someone's charged with something so bad, there must be good reasons." Bashir slapped his desk. "Even if there aren't. Tell me about Jen Shen."

Paul spoke, at first hesitantly, then more quickly. Bashir listened closely, occasionally asking questions. "She sounds like a great officer."

"She is a great officer!"

"But they're trying her for some pretty horrendous crimes. Why?"

"I hoped you'd know."

Bashir thought, looking up at a corner of his office. "This is a big deal, of course. The *Maury* badly damaged. A lot of her crew dead. Lots of attention. A lot of people wanting to blame the South Asians even if that means we start shooting. The authorities have to find a cause, and I'm sure they don't want to find one involving the SASALs."

"Are you saying they're going to use Jen as a scapegoat?"

"Maybe. She seems like an odd choice, though. And they'll have to fill in some blanks if they hope to make that stick. I can't see Alex Carr playing along with that kind of thing, either." He looked closely at Paul. "You could be asked to testify against Lieutenant Shen, you know."

Paul's laughter sounded harsh even to him. "Let them. I'd back Jen one hundred percent."

Lieutenant Bashir rubbed the back of his neck with one hand and smiled halfheartedly. "I'm sure. Odds are the prosecution realizes that. Besides, they don't want to build sympathy for Lieutenant Shen, and putting her officer boyfriend up on the witness stand is likely to do just that. Still, those questions you said the agents were asking Lieutenant Shen. If they uncover any evidence which might make you look wronged, they might still do it."

"Evidence that I've been what?"

Bashir looked away for a moment, plainly uncomfortable. "Is there any of that?"

"Any of *what*?"

"Indications that since meeting you Lieutenant Shen has committed personal indiscretions, been involved in other relationships—"

"No!"

"Paul, I understand your emotions, but I need to be aware of anything which might impact on Lieutenant Shen's defense. I assure you nothing you tell me will ever—"

"There's nothing to tell you!"

"I won't be able to prepare to counter anything they find if I'm not already aware of it."

Paul fought to control his temper, feeling his face warming with anger. "Sir. There's nothing to be aware of."

Bashir looked down at his hands, speaking carefully. "Nobody's perfect. You know the Navy. Long separations. Close working relationships—"

"It hasn't happened. Jen would've told me. She's not perfect. But she's honest. She wouldn't lie to me."

"It wouldn't have to be an actual indiscretion, you realize, just something that looked like one. Anything which an outsider might interpret as, uh, infidelity towards you."

Relax. He's trying to help. "I swear I don't know of anything like that."

"Nothing that anyone might twist around?"

"No. I've never heard of anything."

"What about you?"

"What?!"

"Anything that might imply fooling around on your part? Something that would've made her jealous."

I don't believe this. I do not believe it. "No."

"Are you going to be available at any time during the trial?"

"I'll be there every day."

Bashir's eyebrows rose. "I thought you were assigned to a ship."

"I am. They just put her in restricted availability. She needs a lot of work inside and her hull took a lot of damage from debris from the *Maury*. Not structural stuff, but sensors and that kind of thing. The *Michaelson* won't be going anywhere for months, and my department head and commanding officer have both told me to take as much time off as I need."

"Well, good. I guess."

"I want to be able to see Jen. In person."

"I'm not sure—"

"Please."

Bashir rubbed his forehead. "Okay. I'll do everything I can. If you know anyone with any influence at the brig, it wouldn't hurt to ask them to help. And I'll have to make sure the government doesn't object."

"Commander Carr and I... have worked together before."

"Really?" Bashir's smile was rueful. "Then you know what a challenge defending Lieutenant Shen is going to be. I understand the government even tried to get a statement out of a chaplain who counseled Lieutenant Shen after she got back to Franklin."

"Commander Hughes?"

"Yeah. She told them to pound sand. My kind of chaplain."

"Mine, too."

"I'll let you know as soon as I've had a chance to look at the government's case. I want you to see everything as well, since you apparently know Lieutenant Shen better than anyone else." Bashir paused. "Except maybe her father. And his ship, I understand, won't be back from patrol until the court-martial's likely to be over. I wonder if he even knows what's happening?'"

"I don't know. Jen asked me not to send him anything, but he might hear from someone else. If the *Mahan* gets any mail or news updates."

"Well, nothing we can do about that." Bashir rose and extended his hand. "I won't say anything stupid like 'don't worry.' But people like to say I'm smarter than I look."

Paul grinned, feeling a bit better, and shook Bashir's hand. "You'll win this case."

"Against Alex Carr? That'll be a feather in my cap. I'll call you, Paul. Try to get some rest until then. You look pretty beat up."

I bet Jen looks worse. How can I rest with her alone in the brig? "Okay."

His parents took the news with outward calm. "Oh," was all Paul's mother said. His father said nothing at all and just tried not to let anything show in his expression.

Somehow, Lieutenant Bashir, Sheriff Sharpe and Chaplain Hughes were able to get the necessary strings pulled for a visit to the brig to actually see Jen in person. Jen had obviously done her best to look good, though given the limitations of her cell and her unadorned uniform that still left her appearing far from great, especially in the bare surroundings of the brig's secure visiting area. From the look in her eyes, Paul could tell Jen knew that she looked every inch a prisoner. But she stepped forward as if she were on the bridge of her own ship, managed a small smile and extended her hand to Paul's father. "Commander Sinclair. It's a pleasure to meet you."

To Paul's relief, his father took the offered hand. "Retired. I'm just plain Frank Sinclair, now." He gestured to Paul's mother. "And this is the other Commander Sinclair. Also retired."

Jen nodded and smiled again. "A pleasure, ma'am."

Paul's mother made a small smile as well. "I have to admit, Lieutenant Shen, I never imagined meeting you for the first time in this, uh, environment."

Jen's smile grew even more forced. "Believe me, it's not my idea. And please call me Jen."

"Alright... Jen. Please, let's sit down."

Jen sat in one of the plain metal chairs, which was bolted securely in place like every other object in the visiting room. Jen's movements were stiff, and she shot Paul a quick glance before looking back at his parents. "Thank you. How'd you get up to Franklin?"

Frank Sinclair shrugged. "A couple of retired commanders ought to know enough people to get them a space-available slot on a shuttle. But actually we're up here working for Con-Dyn on some system upgrades for the station."

"Paul tells me you've both been in space before."

"That's right. I rode one of Genghis Conner's research platforms. That's where I met Mrs. Sinclair. She was a ship driver like you two."

"That's what Paul said. What ships, ma'am?"

"The *Glenn* and the *Carpenter*." She smiled ruefully. "It was rough duty. They made me chief engineer on the *Carpenter*. I was always afraid I'd mess something up..." The smile vanished. "Oh, I'm... sorry."

Jen's polite smile froze. Silence fell, increasingly uncomfortable as the seconds ticked by. "I'm innocent of these charges. Totally innocent."

Paul nodded. "I already told them that."

"Too bad you won't be allowed to serve on the court-martial."

Paul tried to think what to say next. *Say anything. What would I say if we were just together like usual? Some joke, I guess.* "I tried to pack it with members of the *Michaelson's* wardroom, but I think they caught on to me."

Jen gave him a blank look, then smiled sardonically. "The lawyers? Of course they did. They all know you. I expect you're on a first-name basis with every lawyer on Franklin."

"Hardly."

Paul's father coughed. "Whistling past the graveyard, folks? It's a time-honored tradition in cases like this, but given the severity of the charges—"

Jen grimaced. "I'm sorry, sir. You're right. I'm under a lot of stress and I—"

"Have nothing to apologize for," Paul interjected.

"I can finish my own sentences, Paul Sinclair."

Paul looked at Jen, letting his surprise at her anger show, then nodded in agreement. *It's not like she doesn't have every right to be tense.* "Yes, you can."

Jen shook her head, her own gaze dropping. "I'm sorry, Paul. I... just started another sentence like that. But this is so hard. Commander Sinclair and, uh, Commander Sinclair, I've looked forward to this meeting, but like everything else in my life lately it hasn't gone as I expected. I'm very grateful for Paul's support. Oh, hell, I'm very grateful for Paul. No matter what happens."

Mrs. Sinclair eyed Jen. "What do you expect to happen?"

"Expect? I don't know what to expect, anymore. They've charged me with killing my shipmates! I couldn't ever do that, but the Navy's trying to prove I did do it. Now, I don't know what else to expect. Nothing makes sense."

"Surely you have witnesses—"

"My witnesses are *dead*, ma'am."

Mrs. Sinclair paused. "Paul says you've a great reputation."

Jen's smile seemed half-born of pain. "Oh, yes. A great reputation. That doesn't seem to have helped much."

Paul shook his head. "Jen's still in confinement because the government's arguing that she could sabotage Franklin like they say she did the Maury."

Paul's mother leaned close, looking directly into Jen's eyes. "But you're innocent."

Jen locked eyes with Paul's mother. "Yes, ma'am. I couldn't do what I've been charged with."

They held each other's gazes for a moment, then Paul's mother reached out and squeezed Jen's hand. "Yes. But I'm Julia, not 'ma'am.'"

A knock on the door and a master-at-arms appeared. "I'm afraid that's all the time you're permitted."

He wasn't supposed to touch her, but Paul leaned as close to Jen as he could without doing so. "I'm here. Always."

"Thanks," she whispered back. "God, why now?"

But the master-at-arms was coming forward, frowning, and Paul had to pull back without answering. Jen gave the petty officer a stern look, came to attention, pivoted on her heel, and marched out the door back toward her cell.

Paul and his parents walked back toward the temporary lodging area. His mother smiled brightly in a deliberately overdone display of cheeriness. "How about dinner?"

"Thanks, Mom, but I'm not all that hungry."

"You need something to eat."

"Mom—"

"That's an order, lieutenant." She grinned. "I love being able to say that to you."

Paul led them to one of the private restaurants, having no desire to take his parents to Fogarty's where he had so many memories of him and Jen together. He picked at the food his mother insisted he order, trying to answer questions with replies longer than a word or two, while everyone avoided talking about Jen.

His mother finally sighed and leaned back in her seat. "Well, she seems like a fine enough person. Under the circumstances."

"You didn't exactly meet her at her best." Paul thought again of Jen, putting up a brave front even while she wore a uniform stripped of insignia and decoration. *Would I have been able to carry myself as well as she did under those circumstances? I bet she's imagined meeting my parents a thousand times, and the difference between those dreams and the reality must've been heartbreaking. But she didn't show it.*

His mother gazed at Paul intently, as if reading his thoughts. "Your Jen is a very strong woman, isn't she?"

"Yes. That's just one of the things I love about her."

"And you're absolutely certain these charges are false?"

"Yes!"

Paul's father frowned. "They must have had good reasons for charging her. Those sort of charges aren't brought lightly."

His mother shook her head. "We don't know what motivated the charges."

"The Navy wouldn't—"

"Don't lecture me about the Navy, Frank! I spent just as many years in it as you did. As an institution, it's far from perfect. It can do some terrible things. And I know that's true even though I know there's a lot of good people in the Navy. I'm married to one and the mother of another."

"And the future mother-in-law of a third," Paul muttered. He looked up at the sudden silence. "I guess I said that out-loud."

His mother leaned forward with an exaggerated questioning expression. "You're engaged?"

"Not yet."

"I'm glad you haven't forgotten to mention that. Have you already asked her?"

"Yes."

"Then I assume she hasn't given you an answer?"

Paul felt as if he were being cross-examined by Commander Carr. "No. She wanted more time for us to get to know each other."

"That's nice. Otherwise you'd probably have gotten married and not brought it up until now."

"Mom—"

"I wanted to let you know we were coming. But not your father. Let's surprise Paul, he said."

Paul's father shrugged. "How was I supposed to know his girl would be in the brig? We weren't even sure what her last name was."

"That's true." His mother focused back on Paul. "Here you are getting ready to marry the girl and we hardly know a thing about her."

"I told you lots of things about Jen."

"Oh, yes. Let's see. She's a great officer. She's really nice looking. And she's a great officer."

"I've told you more than that. Haven't I?"

"Not really. You never mentioned that she's tough enough to put up a good front for us even though she's going through personal hell at the moment."

Paul let his sense of helplessness show. "She didn't do it. If I know anything at all, I know Jen couldn't have done what they're accusing her of."

"That's what the court-martial will decide, won't it?" his father remarked.

"I don't care what the court-martial decides! I already know!"

"Surely if she's as innocent as you say, she doesn't have to fear conviction."

Paul sighed and shook his head. "I wish I could be sure of that. But all the witnesses to what really happened on the *Maury* are dead. All the records and logs that might've explained the accident were destroyed. It may come down to Jen's word that she did nothing against the fact that something apparently inexplicable happened."

"Something she survived." Paul's father raised one palm to forestall another outburst from Paul. "I know. But that looks damning, right?" He glanced at Paul's mother. "Maybe David can help."

Paul frowned. *David. My big brother the hot-shot civilian lawyer. Who somehow always manages to shove that fact in my face. But I shouldn't let my feelings about his attitude rule out David's helping Jen. Can he really help, though?* "Does David know military law?"

His mother frowned in turn. "Not as far as I know. That could be a problem, couldn't it?"

"It could be. There's different rules, different procedures. Jen has a right to have David as her attorney if she wants him, but..."

"But it might not be all that smart." Paul's mother glanced at his father. "What do you think, Frank?"

"Oh, my opinion matters? Then, for what it's worth, I think Paul brought up a good point. Even though I suggested David, he'd be on unfamiliar ground. Plus he's one hundred percent civilian. You remember how you and I would've thought about a civilian lawyer back when we were on active duty."

"Yes, indeed. What about Jen's father? You told us he's a captain?"

"That's right. Commanding officer of the *Mahan*."

"The *Mahan*? She's not in port."

"No. Deep patrol. She won't be back for months."

"That's not good. What about her mother?"

"Dead. Years ago." Paul inhaled deeply. "I'm all she's got."

"Not quite. No son of mine is going to stand alone in a matter like this. Frank?"

His father sighed. "What if she's convicted, Paul? You seem to think that's a real possibility. Those charges will put her in confinement for a very long time."

"I can wait."

"So you say now. Look, I know how it feels to be in love. You can't imagine your love object has any flaws——"

Mrs. Sinclair smiled briefly. "I broke that illusion of your father's pretty quick."

"You certainly did. And I'm not saying your girl did what she's accused of doing. But, she could be convicted. Think of ten years down the line, her in Fort Leavenworth and you outside, waiting for another thirty or forty years to pass, if not more."

"You don't think I should stand by her."

"That's not what I'm saying. I'm saying maybe you do your best, but she's convicted and the appeals are rejected..."

Paul snorted a brief laugh, looking away for a moment. "Dad, I'm not under the slightest illusion that Jen is perfect. She's pushy, temperamental, stubborn, willful and rough-edged. She's also the best thing by far that's ever happened to me."

His father smiled for a moment. "Sounds a lot like your mother."

His mother gave his father a sharp look. "I beg your pardon?"

Paul couldn't help smiling briefly himself at the byplay. "After the *Maury*'s engineering spaces blew to hell I had to face what seemed to be the certainty that she'd died. I couldn't imagine what I'd do, how I'd ever find someone else who could fill the hole Jen'd left in me. Then I found out she'd survived. I know how it'd feel to lose her, because I thought I had. Do you think I'd ever let her go, now?"

"Not if you were worth a damn," his father replied.

"Yes," his mother agreed. "There may not be much we can do to help, but what we can do, we will."

Lieutenant Bashir offered Paul his data pad. "Here's the convening order for the court-martial. Do you know any of the members of the court?"

Paul took the device and read through it slowly. A general court-martial had been convened, the most serious. It made him wince internally even though he'd known Jen would be charged with offenses too serious for either of the less severe forms of court-martial, special or summary. Unlike the special or summary courts-martial, which had limitations on the punishments they could order, a general court-martial could assign any legal punishment, no matter how severe. It was reserved for only the worst offenses.

He read the list of personnel identified in the convening order. *Military Judge. Captain David V. McMasters. I'll have to ask Bashir about McMasters. President of the court-martial is Captain William Carney. Carney? That doesn't ring any bells. No, wait. Isakov mentioned that name. He was the commanding officer of the* Isherwood *at one point. I wish I knew more than that, but I'm really leery of asking Val Isakov anything. Then there's Commander Francesca Bolivar. Commander of the Fleet Intelligence Support Activity on Franklin. Doesn't look like she's ever served on ships. Lieutenant*

Commander Gavin Cloud. Just came up from Earth duty, awaiting assignment. It says he's open space warfare officer qualified, so he must have some experience, but it must predate my own arrival up here. He's been on Earth since before I got to the Michaelson.

Lieutenant Daniela Kalin. Off the Dahlgren. *And Lieutenant Karl Ishiki. Fleet staff. I don't know any of these people.*

Paul repeated his last thought out loud. Bashir nodded. "Not too surprising. You and Lieutenant Shen moved in the same crowd, right? They couldn't choose any members for the court who knew her well, so it follows you wouldn't know them. And they had to rule out people who'd served with Shen's father on the *Mahan* or elsewhere, too. But it was worth a try to see if you could tell me anything about any of them."

Paul indicated a couple of names. "Carney, Cloud and Kalin are all open space warfare officers."

"Is that good or bad?"

"Well..." Paul hesitated before replying. "It's a tough community. OSWOs can be really supportive, or they can eat you alive. You never know."

"I'll say that's likely to be bad, then."

"What about the judge? What's McMasters like?"

Bashir looked noncommittal. "He runs a tight courtroom. No nonsense. No games. He doesn't tend to favor either the prosecution or the defense. He leaves that part of things to the trial counsel and the defense counsel."

"That sounds good."

"Oh, yeah. It can be a lot worse. Now..." Bashir held up his data unit again. "Here's the list of evidence I've been provided by the prosecution."

Paul paged through the lists of documents. "This is almost all engineering stuff."

"Yeah." Bashir squinted at his display. "And I'm a lawyer. I don't know a blasted thing about any of it."

"Jen can explain it."

"Yeah." Bashir settled back, rubbing his eyes. "But that's part of the problem. Lieutenant Shen really knows this stuff."

"Why's that a problem?"

"I can only guess at the prosecution strategy, but based on this stuff and the very limited evidence available, I'd say they're going to argue that this couldn't have been an accident. If they rule out an accident, that points it right at Lieutenant Shen."

"Why? They have to prove she did it."

"No." Bashir leaned forward again, resting on his elbows. "They can't *prove* she did it. But they can try to prove that there's no other way it could've happened unless she did it."

Paul shook his head. "Jen's got to prove she didn't do it?"

"Essentially, yes. Not directly, that is. But we have to come up with alternate explanations for what happened."

"And?"

Bashir exhaled heavily. "Let me know if you think of any."

"But Jen—"

"Tells me she hasn't a clue. Can't even imagine a scenario."

"But there's got to be alternative explanations!"

"Like I said, I'm open for suggestions."

Paul hastened back to the *Michaelson*, finding Colleen Kilgary sitting in the wardroom. "I really need your help."

Colleen gave him a curious look. "You, or Jen?"

"Both." Paul explained the problem. "You're main propulsion

assistant on the *Michaelson*. You know this stuff a lot better than I do. So, what else could've done it?"

Kilgary sat back, staring at the overhead, and stayed that way for a long time before shaking her head. "Damned if I can think of anything."

"The systems can't be that perfect!"

"They're not! But you're not talking about *one* component failing. You're talking about everything going boom at pretty much the same time. It can't happen."

"It *did* happen."

"Yes." Kilgary bit her lip. "Paul, I just can't come up with something that would've done that. Not on the *Michaelson*."

"The *Maury* wasn't the *Michaelson*."

"True. There's always at least minor differences even between sister ships. And *Maury* had just gone through that overhaul. But if the accident happened because of something on the *Maury* that was different from the *Michaelson* it means I can't help you much. I know *this* ship."

Paul slumped and nodded. "Thanks, Colleen. I'd appreciate it if you'd ask Chief Meyer for his assessment, too."

"Uh, okay." Kilgary looked away, twisting her coffee container in her hands.

"What's the matter?"

"Noth— Oh, hell. Paul, when Jen got charged with doing that... people got strange."

"Strange?"

"You know." She stared at her hands. "Like... they don't..."

Paul felt like a lead weight was settling in his stomach. "They think she did it?"

"No! Uh, well, they're kind of... concerned."

"They think she did it."

Colleen looked up at him. "Sorry, Paul. Even I wondered for a second. But I know you. Better than I ever knew her. And I trust your judgment in this. But why'd they charge her with doing it? They must have a reason."

Paul heard his voice laughing bitterly. "The reason is that they don't have any other reasons. They can't explain it otherwise. So they're blaming Jen."

"Oh." Kilgary looked back down at her hands. "She ought to be able to beat it, then."

"Yeah." *She ought to be able to beat it. If she can prove she didn't do it. Is that what this case comes down to? People assuming Jen was charged for good reason and demanding she prove her own innocence? But how can she do that?* "Thanks for talking, Colleen. Please tell everyone that Jen is innocent."

"Sure. But like I said, that's about all I can do, because the *Michaelson* and the *Maury* have, uh, 'had' I guess, different engineering plant configurations."

"You said that you couldn't see any way it could happen."

"No. I said I couldn't see any way it could happen on the *Mike*. Based on what I know, I'd be looking at any differences between the *Mike* and *Maury* for whatever might've caused it."

Paul nodded. "How many differences could there be?"

"Lots. Mostly little stuff. But it all adds up. *Maury* had that SEERS thing installed."

"I should look into SEERS?"

Colleen shrugged. "I would."

"Have you heard anything about it?"

"Just what you told me Jen told you. That and the fact that it was approved for introduction into the fleet."

Paul nodded, knowing that neither fact gave any indication SEERS posed a danger to the *Maury*. Quite the contrary, in the case of it being approved for installation on the *Maury*. He knew Colleen knew that as well, but was being kind enough not to say it out loud. *It's a big difference, though. The biggest I know of. I need to look into it and hope it does some good. From what I know now, it won't. But I've got to try. I guess I need to go through Lieutenant Bashir to do that, though, and I can't do that until tomorrow. There's nothing else I can do tonight but worry.*

He was sitting alone in Combat, the lights turned down, when a knock sounded on the hatch rim. "Mr. Sinclair?"

"Here, Sheriff."

Sharpe came walking into Combat. "Catch."

Paul snagged the beverage container he saw flying toward him and glanced at the label. "Hey, this isn't the cheap, generic stuff. This is real."

Sharpe popped his own and took a drink. "Yes, sir. But the senior chief managed to snag a case and allowed certain individuals to score a tube or two."

Paul managed a smile. "I'm honored, Sheriff. To what do I owe this favor?"

Sharpe grimaced, leaning against a nearby watch console. "Sir, I think you know that. Sort of a very small attempt to cheer you up."

"Thanks." Paul took a drink himself. "It's good."

"How you doin', sir?"

"I've been better. A lot better."

"Ms. Shen?"

"She's... lot's of things. Baffled. Shocked. Outraged. Confused. Pick an emotion."

"I bet." Sharpe sighed. "Mr. Sinclair, my job means I do my best to bring people to justice. But that doesn't always make people happy."

"You don't think she's guilty, too, do you?"

"No, sir. I know Ms. Shen. Unless my ability to judge human nature is totally gone, she couldn't have done that. But..."

"Right now the entire Navy's trying to prove she's guilty, and I'm trying to prove she's innocent."

Sharpe actually smiled, his teeth looking unnaturally white in the darkened compartment. "You're not quite that alone, sir. But there ain't much I can do."

"I know. Can you do anything about how they're treating her in the brig?"

Another grimace. "They figure they got a mass murderer on their hands, sir."

"If they—"

"Sir." Sharpe held up a restraining hand. "I've guarded prisoners. There's all kinds of things you can do to a prisoner. Things that maybe ain't technically right but ain't technically wrong either. Little stuff. It doesn't leave any marks except on the inside of their brains. And ordering guards not to do that kind of stuff is like waving a red flag at a bull." He took another drink. "I always figured that was fair since the prisoners must've been guilty. Maybe I wasn't being so smart about it."

"Can't you tell the brig guards something? Anything?"

"I'll try, Mr. Sinclair. I've already talked to them before. But, to be perfectly honest with you, I don't see them listening this time any more than they did the last couple of times."

Paul drained his drink. "It's kind of like a nightmare, isn't it, Sheriff? Things just keep getting worse and nothing we try to do helps."

Sharpe nodded grimly. "That doesn't stop us from trying, sir."

"No. Nothing's going to stop me from trying. Thanks, Sheriff. Knowing you still believe in Jen, excuse me, Ms. Shen, means an awful lot."

"Sir, a good cop's gotta be tough, but he can't be blind. And he's gotta know who deserves his trust." Sharpe touched his brow. "Goodnight, Mr. Sinclair."

"'Night, Sheriff." Paul watched him leave the compartment. *A nightmare. But you never think you're in a nightmare when you are. It all seems perfectly real. And you wake up from nightmares sooner or later. You never hit the ground at the end of your fall. Unless you're dying, and then urban legend says you hit the ground and die in your dreams and in reality. How is this nightmare going to end?*

Preparations for the court-martial proceeded with all due haste. Paul found himself avoiding news sources. They all kept reporting the charges against Jen, going over her "crimes" again and again, showing highly amplified pictures of the battered *Maury* being towed gently back toward Franklin, showing high-ranking politicians trying to calm the storm of anger which had swept up against the South Asian Alliance and redirect it. At Jen, whose name the politicians never mentioned but which everyone knew.

Paul started getting a trickle of messages asking for interviews, then a flood. He deleted them all without reading, thankful that the news media couldn't get free run of Franklin to try to chase him down in person.

"What're they waiting for?" Kris Denaldo asked him one day as Paul was making a show of trying to work.

"They're waiting for the *Maury* to get back. They want some of her personnel at the court-martial."

"Why? I thought all the other engineers died."

"They did. It'll probably be about other stuff."

"Other stuff?"

"I don't know, Kris. I really don't know." Which was a lie. He knew. He just didn't want to talk about it at all, even to someone who knew Jen and he as well as Kris did. They wanted to ask the rest of the survivors of the *Maury* about Jen. About whether she'd been having an affair with anyone. About whether she hated anyone. About anything that might help build a case against her.

One night he went into Combat and called up a display with the estimated position of the *Mahan* on it. The estimated position didn't mean much. Captain Shen had authority to move his ship anywhere within a large volume of space. Keep the enemy guessing. Paul wondered if Captain Shen had heard what had happened to the *Maury*, and to his daughter. Jen still insisted he shouldn't send a message, though even if she allowed it there was no telling when the *Mahan* would reveal her location precisely enough to allow high-speed communications. Captain Shen might get back and discover everything that had happened, discover Jen convicted. Welcome back, captain. We hope you had a pleasant voyage, and we hope you weren't planning on your daughter meeting you at the dock. She's in a military jail cell back on Earth.

The *Maury* finally returned to Franklin with fanfare that almost matched the world's interest in the event. Various military and civilian VIPs had flown up to Franklin, their entourages requisitioning every spare resource on the station as well as quite a few resources that were already needed for other purposes. Every display screen on the station was set to watch the *Maury* as the battered warship was eased into the space-dock which dominated one section of Franklin. Paul, far from the crowds and the VIPs at the dock, stared like everyone else, appalled yet again by the damage he saw, amazed that his own memories of the devastation had somehow been dulled.

His eyes locked on to the after survival bulkhead. *Jen was back there when I thought she was dead. Then I thought she was okay. But she wasn't, not after losing every person she worked with in engineering. And not after getting charged with causing it to happen. Now Commander Hughes tells me Jen won't even see her anymore. Too worried about being labeled mentally unstable just because she's getting counseling. How's that for a Catch-22? If you need help, you can't seek it without people thinking you're full-scale nuts. But Hughes can't make Jen talk to her, and Jen won't listen to me on that score.*

Paul shifted his display to the dock itself. Standing in the large group awaiting the *Maury*, he knew, was at least one military lawyer waiting to personally interview Captain Halis after the senior officers and senior politicians had given their speeches and pinned a medal on the captain. *I wonder what Captain Halis thinks about all this? I'm sure she'd trade it all for half those dead sailors back. Or maybe even one of them. What'll Halis say to the lawyer? I know she's already listed as witness for the prosecution, but that doesn't tell me what the prosecution wants her to testify about. Events? Character? Background? I'll just have to wait for that answer. Won't be long now. Now that the *Maury*'s home.*

He looked back at the severely wounded warship again. The reinforcing members laid across the *Maury*'s gapping wounds stood out clearly. He'd helped with that. Not a lot of help, measured against everything it'd taken to get the *Maury* home, but something.

On the bridge, he knew, Captain Halis would be watching as well, while the tugs which had brought the *Maury* this far carefully handed her off the station. Riding a crippled ship unable to maneuver on her own, the captain would just be an observer, but still surely watching everything and looking out for her ship. *I can understand that. I hope I'd do the same. It must hurt, though, being towed back into port, with her ship ripped wide open.*

Paul wished he could see Captain Halis in person, plead for her help, but he suspected that might fall into the category of witness tampering. Though he doubted it'd have much effect in any case, even if he could fight through the crowds of VIPs and other well-wishers, because his very brief meeting with Captain Halis in the midst of tragedy had left Paul convinced that Jen's commanding officer would hold to whatever course she thought proper.

And there wasn't time, anyway. The court-martial would begin tomorrow. People needed to be assured as quickly as possible that the incident was being "handled." That the South Asians hadn't been involved, that justice was being done, that appropriate punishment would be meted out to the guilty. The only problem Paul had with any of that was his certainty that what people were being assured would happen wasn't the same thing he saw happening.

9

The courtroom selected for the trial was the same one in which Captain Wakeman had been court-martialed. Given the small number of courtrooms available on Franklin, that wasn't too surprising, but Paul thought it an unnerving coincidence. As far as he could remember, the layout hadn't changed. But the paint on the walls had been freshened, the entire room cleaned and scrubbed, ready for any media scrutiny. Cameras would record the entire trial, of course, as they did every trial. Because classified material might well be discussed, open media access wouldn't be allowed and the proceedings wouldn't be televised in real time. But once the trial was over, that record might be released, edited or whole, to satisfy the curiosity of those watching from a distance.

The judge's bench dominated the front of the courtroom, rising higher than any other table or seat. There were two doors in the back of the room. One, Paul knew, led to the judge's chambers. The other was the entrance to be used by the five officers who were the members of the court. The member's table, just a long standard-issue military table which had been glamorized by having a navy blue tablecloth draped over it, had five chairs behind it, the whole arrangement angled to face the judge's bench and the witness stand.

Actually facing the judge's bench on either side were two tables. Commander Carr already sat at the trial counsel's table, studying her data pad and ignoring the spectators. At the defense table, Lieutenant Bashir sat, his fingers drumming slowly on the table.

Paul sat directly behind the defense table, the only officer of his lowly rank that far forward in the courtroom. But Lieutenant Bashir had been able to reserve a seat for him there, where Paul tried to look straight ahead and ignore the curious looks he knew he was attracting.

A loud murmuring finally made Paul look around. Coming in the main door was Jen, walking with stern dignity that couldn't banish the image of the two masters-at-arms escorting her, a prisoner under guard. Even though the masters-at-arms tried to lead Jen toward the defense table, she moved to block them and take the lead herself, then stood at attention for a moment before sitting down next to Lieutenant Bashir. The masters-at-arms retreated back to the main entrance of the courtroom, where they went to parade rest and kept their eyes on Jen. Jen and Bashir exchanged some quiet words, then she turned enough to look at Paul and nod, her eyes revealing far more than her rigidly controlled expression.

As Paul smiled encouragingly back, he finally caught a glimpse of the band on her ankle which marked Jen's bonds. He'd seen such bands on prisoners, the violent, dangerous ones who might flee or attack their guards. Seeing it on Jen just emphasized how unreal the entire situation felt. *If I'm going to wake up from a bad dream, now would be a real good time.*

The court bailiff had walked to the center of the room, standing before the judge's bench. She looked around to ensure she had everyone's attention before speaking. "When the military judge enters, I will announce 'all rise' and everyone is to rise. The military judge will instruct everyone to be seated. When the judge directs me to summon the members of the court, everyone should rise once again. The military judge will once again instruct when you are to be seated. Are there any questions?"

The bailiff didn't bother waiting to see if there were any questions. She went to the judge's door, knocked gently, then stood back as the door opened. "All rise."

Paul sprang to attention along with everyone else. Captain McMasters walked up to his bench, settled himself, then looked at the trial counsel, the defense counsel and defendant, and all the spectators. Apparently reassured that all was in order, McMasters addressed the crowd. "This Article 39(a) session is called to order. You may be seated. Trial counsel?"

Commander Alex Carr stayed standing as everyone else sat. "The court-martial is convened by general court-martial convening order 0322, Commander, United States Space Forces, copies of which have been furnished to the military judge, counsel, and the accused. The charges have been properly referred to the court-martial for trial and were served on the accused on 22 March 2101. The accused and the following persons detailed to the court-martial are present: Captain McMasters, Captain Carney, Commander Carr, Commander Bolivar, Lieutenant Commander Cloud, Lieutenant Bashir, Lieutenant Kalin, Lieutenant Ishiki."

McMasters nodded and gestured to the bailiff. "Ask the members to enter."

This time the bailiff went to the other door in the back of the courtroom, knocking again and standing aside once more. "All rise," she ordered as Captain Carney led his four fellow officers into the courtroom. Carney took his seat in the center of the five chairs, the others sitting to his right and left in order of descending seniority. Paul studied the members of the court as well as his distance from them allowed.

Carney leaned back in his chair with a casual air of command and a demanding expression. Paul could imagine him in the same posture when junior officers reported to him, and almost hear Carney asking them, "What'd you screw up this time?" On Carney's immediate right, Commander Bolivar sat forward, her forearms resting on the table, her eyes searching the courtroom, her face wary. To Carney's immediate left, Lieutenant Commander Cloud seemed cautious as well. The two lieutenants, seated in the outside chairs on each side, were the only ones who actually looked nervous. Ishiki looked old enough that he probably had enlisted experience, while Kalin seemed almost as young as Jen.

"You may be seated," Judge McMasters instructed the spectators. As Paul and others sat, the judge nodded to Carr. "Proceed, trial counsel."

Carr spoke clearly but unemotionally. The exact words she was saying were familiar to Paul. Carr herself had probably memorized them. They were spelled out in the Manual For Courts-Martial, and had to be spoken at the beginning of every trial. "I have been detailed to this court-martial by order of the Fleet Judge Advocate General's Office. I am qualified and certified under Article 27(b) and sworn under Article 42(a). I have not acted in any manner which might tend to disqualify me in the court-martial."

Lieutenant Bashir stood up again. "I have been detailed to this court-martial by order of the Fleet Judge Advocate General's Office. I am qualified and certified under Article 27(b) and sworn under Article 42(a). I have not acted in any manner which might tend to disqualify me in the court-martial."

McMasters nodded once more, then motioned Jen to stand up. She did so, coming back to attention instead of just standing. "Lieutenant Junior Grade Shen, you have the right to be represented in this court-martial by Lieutenant Ahmed Bashir, your detailed defense counsel, or you may be represented by military counsel of your selection, if the counsel you request is reasonably available. If you are represented by military counsel of your own selection, you would lose the right to have Lieutenant Bashir, your detailed counsel, continue to help in your defense. Do you understand?"

Jen remained at attention. "Yes, sir."

"In addition, you have the right to be represented by civilian counsel, at no expense to the United States. Civilian counsel may represent you alone or along with your military counsel. Do you understand?"

"Yes, sir."

"Do you have any questions about your right to counsel?"

"No, sir."

"Who do you want to represent you?"

"I wish to be represented by my detailed defense counsel, Lieutenant Bashir, sir."

"Very well. Counsel for the parties have the necessary qualifications, and have been sworn. I have been detailed to this court by order of the Judge Advocate General's Office of the Commander, United States Space Forces."

Commander Carr stood up and walked to face both the judge and the table where the members of the court sat. "The general nature of the charges in this case allege deliberate sabotage against a warship of the United States Navy, the USS *Maury*, which resulted in the murders of sixty-one officer and enlisted personnel of the United States Navy and extensive damage to US military property. The charges were preferred by Commander, United States Naval Space Forces, and forwarded with recommendations as to disposition to Commander, United States Space Forces." Commander Carr faced Judge McMasters. "Your Honor, are you aware of any matter which may be a ground for challenge against you?"

"I'm aware of none."

"The government has no challenge for cause against the military judge."

Lieutenant Bashir stood yet again. "The defense has no challenge for cause against the military judge."

Judge McMasters leaned forward and looked at Jen. "Lieutenant Shen, do you understand that you have the right to be tried by a court-martial composed of members and that, if you are found guilty of any offense, those members would determine a sentence?"

"Yes, sir."

"Do you also understand that you may request in writing or orally here in the court-martial trial before me alone, and that if I approve such a request, there will be no members and I alone will decide whether you are guilty and, if I find you guilty, determine a sentence?"

"Yes, sir."

"Have you discussed these choices with your counsel?"

"Yes, sir, I have."

"By which type of court-martial do you choose to be tried?"

Lieutenant Shen still hadn't moved, maintaining rigid attention. "By members, sir."

"Very well. The accused will now be arraigned."

Commander Carr looked toward the defense table. "All parties and the military judge have been furnished a copy of the charges and specifications. Does the accused want them read?"

Jen moved for the first time, turning her head and nodding firmly to Lieutenant Bashir, who nodded back and addressed Commander Carr. "The accused wishes the charges to be read."

"Very well." Carr positioned her pad where she could easily read it. "Lieutenant Junior Grade Jenevieve Diana Shen, United States Navy, is charged with violations of the following articles of the Uniform Code of Military Justice."

"Article 107, False Official Statements. In that Lieutenant Junior Grade Jenevieve Diana Shen, United States Navy, did, on board USS *Maury* CLE(S)-4, on or about 5 March 2101, with an intent to deceive, make to officers investigating the damage which had been suffered by the USS *Maury*, an official statement, to wit her knowledge of events onboard USS *Maury*, CLE(S)-4, the afternoon of 21 February 2101, which statement was false in that it failed to correctly state Lieutenant Shen's actual knowledge of and role in those events, and was then known by said Lieutenant Junior Grade Shen to be false."

"Article 108, Military Property of the United States—sale, loss, damage, destruction or wrongful disposition. In that Lieutenant Junior Grade Jenevieve Diana Shen, United States Navy, did, onboard USS *Maury*, CLE(S)-4, on or about 21 February 2101, without proper authority, willfully damage and destroy by unknown means military property of the United States, to wit all equipment located within the engineering compartments onboard the USS *Maury* as well in surrounding compartments as enumerated below." Carr glanced up. "Does the defendant desire me to read through that enumeration?"

Paul saw Jen shake her head. He hadn't seen her expression change as the charges were read. *Trying to look as professional as possible. That's good. Isn't it? Or will it make her look unmoved by the tragedy instead?*

Commander Carr returned her gaze to the data pad. "Article 109, Property Other Than Military Property of the United States—Waste Spoilage or Destruction. In that Lieutenant Junior Grade Jenevieve Diana Shen, United States Navy, did, onboard USS *Maury*, CLE(S)-4, on or about 21 February 2101, willfully bring about the destruction of personal effects belonging to members of the crew of the USS *Maury* and then located within berthing compartments onboard the USS *Maury* which were substantially destroyed as a result of the destruction of equipment within the engineering compartments of the USS *Maury*.

"Article 110—Improper Hazarding of a Vessel. In that Lieutenant Junior Grade Jenevieve Diana Shen, United States Navy, did, on or about 21 February 2101, onboard USS *Maury*, CLE(S)-4, willfully and wrongfully hazard the said vessel by bringing about by unknown means the destruction of equipment within the engineering compartments of the USS *Maury*, thereby leading to extensive internal and external damage and creating conditions in which the total loss of the ship could have occurred.

"Article 118—Murder." Carr paused after the word, then went on speaking. "In that Lieutenant Junior Grade Jenevieve Diana Shen, United States Navy, did, on or about 21 February 2101, onboard

USS *Maury*, CLE(S)–4, with premeditation, deliberately murder sixty-one officer and enlisted personnel of the USS *Maury* by bringing about by unknown means the destruction of equipment within the engineering compartments of the USS *Maury*." She paused again and once more looked up. "Does the defendant wish the list of victims to be read?"

Paul could see Jen's jaw twitching, but she shook her head steadily once again.

"Article 124—Maiming. In that Lieutenant Junior Grade Jenevieve Diana Shen, United States Navy, did, on or about 21 February 2101, onboard USS *Maury*, CLE(S)-4, maim by concussion and fragmentation effects eight surviving members of the crew of the USS *Maury* by bringing about by unknown means the destruction of equipment within the engineering compartments of the USS *Maury*." Another pause. "Does the defendant wish—?"

Jen was already shaking her head.

"Article 131—Perjury. In that Lieutenant Junior Grade Jenevieve Diana Shen, United States Navy, did, on or about 12 March 2101, onboard Benjamin Franklin Naval Station, in a statement under penalty of perjury pursuant to section 1746 of title 28, United States Code, willfully and corruptly subscribe a false statement material to the matter of inquiry, to wit her knowledge of the cause of the destruction of equipment within the engineering compartments of the USS *Maury*, CLE(S)-4, and which statement she did not then believe to be true.

"The charges are signed by Commander, United States Naval Space Forces, a person subject to the code, as accuser; are properly sworn to before a commissioned officer of the armed forces authorized to administer oaths, and are properly referred to this court-martial for trial by Commander, United States Space Forces, the convening authority."

Paul had never before noticed how the charges against a defendant seemed to roll out like vast weights, each one seeming to press down upon the courtroom and oppress everyone within it. He looked at Jen, realizing the weight of the charges had actually fallen upon her, and wondered how she'd been able to maintain her composure.

Judge McMasters looked at Jen Shen again. "Lieutenant Junior Grade Shen, how do you plead? Before receiving your pleas, I advise you that any motions to dismiss any charge or grant other relief should be made at this time."

Jen seemed uncertain for a moment, first facing the judge, then turning to face the members. "I plead not guilty to all charges and specifications." To Paul, her voice sounded stilted, and he realized how much difficulty she was having controlling it. He wondered how it sounded to others who didn't know her as well as he did.

"Very well," Judge McMasters noted. "Do you have an opening statement, trial counsel?"

"I do, Your Honor." Commander Carr studied her data unit, then for just a moment looked up toward Jen. Paul couldn't tell if in that moment she'd also looked at him. Then Carr faced the members of the court and began speaking unemotionally. "The prosecution intends to prove that on 21 February of this year, Lieutenant Junior Grade Shen deliberately and with malice sabotaged the engineering systems of her ship, the USS *Maury*, not only bringing about extensive damage to her ship, but also executing the premeditated murder of sixty-one of her shipmates, including every other member of the Engineering Department on the USS *Maury*, after ensuring for her own safety. Lieutenant Junior Grade Shen then lied about her role in the sabotage and murder, complicating and impeding the initial and official investigations into the cause of the awful events of 21 February. Lieutenant Junior Grade Shen should be found guilty as to every charge and specification and brought to justice for the awful fate she visited upon her ship and the sailors who worked alongside her."

Commander Carr walked back to the trial counsel's table and sat down, resting her chin in her hands so her expression was half-hidden. Her eyes seemed hooded, though. Paul stared at her as an awful realization finally hit. *Premeditated murder. That's not just a life sentence. That's a death-penalty offense. And Jen's charged with* sixty-one *premeditated murders. Oh my God.*

Paul hadn't noticed Lieutenant Bashir standing and making his own way to the area before the judge's bench. Now Bashir addressed the members as well. "The defense contends that Lieutenant Shen did not commit the acts with which she is charged. The cause or causes of the damage and death on the USS *Maury* remain unknown, but that in no way justifies trying to pin the blame for that horrible event on an officer who has repeatedly demonstrated her humanity and devotion to duty. An officer who, in the wake of the accident on the USS *Maury*, saved the lives of twenty-one enlisted personnel who looked to her for leadership in conditions of utmost peril. An officer whose loyalty, skill and dedication to duty have never before been questioned. Lieutenant Shen should be found innocent of these charges, because she is innocent, and because there is no evidence she played any role in the accident or the deaths which we all regret."

Lieutenant Bashir returned to his seat. Paul tried to focus fully on the courtroom and not on his internal turmoil. The standard preliminaries for a court-martial were over and the actual trial fully beginning. The judge pointed his ceremonial gavel toward Commander Carr. "You may proceed, trial counsel."

"The United States calls as its first witness Rear Admiral Michael Hidalgo, United States Navy."

Rear Admiral Hidalgo marched to the witness stand, his uniform crisp, his manner confident. He watched closely as Commander Carr approached the witness stand and administered the oath. "Do you swear that the evidence you give in the case now in hearing shall be the truth, the whole truth, and nothing but the truth, so help you God?"

"I do."

"Are you Rear Admiral Michael Hidalgo, United States Navy, currently serving on the staff of the Commander, United States Navy Space Forces?"

"I am."

"Rear Admiral Hidalgo, what is your exact job title on the staff of the Commander, United States Navy Space Forces?"

"I'm the N4."

"What exactly does that mean?"

Hidalgo broke his gaze on Carr as he answered, looking around the courtroom. "That's the staff code for engineering. I'm the senior engineering representative in the fleet."

"As such, are you regarded as an expert on the engineering systems onboard US spacecraft?"

"I am."

"Are you familiar with the engineering systems on ships similar to the USS *Maury*?"

"Yes. Very familiar. I personally served as chief engineer on the USS *Dahlgren*, which is one of the *Maury*'s sister ships."

"Sister ship meaning of the same class and design?"

"That's right."

"Were you involved in the investigation of the damage suffered by the USS *Maury* on 21 February?"

The rear admiral nodded, his expression clouding slightly. "I was. Yes. I was appointed to head that investigation by Admiral Yesenski."

"Admiral Yesenski being the Commander, United States Navy Space Forces."

"Yes. Sorry."

Commander Carr smiled politely. "No need to apologize, Admiral Hidalgo. Can you summarize the results of that investigation?"

"Yes." Hidalgo nodded several times. "In summary, we found that the USS *Maury* had suffered serious damage as a result of multiple, near-simultaneous explosions caused by overloading and catastrophic failure of most of the equipment within her engineering spaces."

"Were you able to determine what caused that to happen, sir?"

Hidalgo looked unhappy. "No. Too much damage had been suffered and too much evidence either completely destroyed or unrecoverable in space."

"Were you able to rule out any causes?"

"Yes. Absolutely. There wasn't any sign of a bomb or other explosive device. No chemical residue or anything like that. We also ruled out an accident."

Carr looked intrigued. "You ruled out an accident?"

Rear Admiral Hidalgo nodded vigorously this time. "Yes. The investigation confirmed that such an accident is physically impossible due to the many safety factors incorporated into the *Maury*'s engineering systems."

Commander Carr waited a moment for Hidalgo's statement to

sink in, then gestured toward a diagram of the USS *Maury* which dominated the courtroom display screen. "Admiral Hidalgo, as the senior engineering representative on the staff of the Commander, United States Navy Space Forces, had you ever personally inspected the engineering systems of the USS *Maury*?"

"Of course I had. I've personally inspected the engineering systems of every ship in the space fleet. That's part of my responsibilities."

"When was the last time you examined the engineering systems of the USS *Maury* prior to the damage she suffered?"

Hidalgo looked toward Jen for the first time. "A couple of days before the *Maury* got underway. I wanted to review the status of some major modifications she'd undergone. I met her entire complement of engineering officers at that time and went over the engineering system in detail."

"Would you provide your assessment of the *Maury*'s engineering system at that time, two days prior to her getting underway?"

"Excellent. The *Maury*'d just come out of an extended yard period. Everything looked great."

"Did Commander Juko, the chief engineer of the *Maury*, express any concerns to you at that time regarding the engineering system on the *Maury*?"

Hidalgo looked toward Jen again, who gazed back almost defiantly. "No, he did not."

Commander Carr begin pacing slowly back and forth in front of the witness stand as she spoke. "No problems, Rear Admiral Hidalgo?"

"No."

"Sir, you've summarized the conclusions of the official investigation into the damage suffered by the USS *Maury*. Do you know of any reasons, based upon your own expertise and experience as well as your familiarity with ships like the *Maury*, that would cause you to personally disagree in any way with the investigation's conclusions that the damage was sustained as a result of nearly simultaneous catastrophic overloads of the *Maury*'s engineering equipment?"

Hidalgo shook his head. "I do not. That's the only thing that could explain what happened."

Commander Carr stopped pacing, standing directly in front of the witness again. "Rear Admiral Hidalgo, you also say it isn't possible for such a thing to happen by accident."

"It isn't."

"Would you explain, sir?"

"Yes." Hidalgo leaned forward slightly, one hand coming up to emphasize his points with an extended forefinger. "It can't happen. Not by accident. There's too many safety interlocks. Circuit breakers. Automated control mechanisms. Software safeguards. Emergency shutdown systems. All of those things working individually and in concert are designed to prevent exactly that sort of disaster. There simply isn't any way they could've all failed at the same time in such a catastrophic fashion. Not by accident."

Carr nodded, then held up her data pad. "With the court's permission, the trial counsel would like to enter the ship's engineering system manual for *Mahan*-Class Long-Endurance Cruisers into the record. It details every safety mechanism to which Rear Admiral Hidalgo has testified."

Judge McMasters nodded. "Enter the manual into the record."

Focusing on Rear Admiral Hidalgo once more, Carr took a step toward him. "Sir, you've testified based upon your expert knowledge that there is no possible way in which the engineering system of the USS *Maury* could've suffered accidental nearly simultaneously catastrophic failure of its components. How, then, would you explain what happened?"

Hidalgo licked his lips, looking at Jen for a third time and then looking away. "It had to have been done on purpose."

Carr once again paused for a long moment before speaking again, letting the phrase settle firmly into the minds of listeners. "On purpose. By sabotage, you mean?"

"If you want to call it that."

"Internal or external sabotage?"

"Internal. No question."

"A human agent on the *Maury*. Someone had to have done something to cause all those safety mechanisms to fail."

"Absolutely. They had to have done a lot of somethings! Override the software, mess with the physical safety interlocks like circuit breakers, cross-connect some things that aren't supposed to cross-connect. I don't know exactly how'd you do all that, but that's what'd have to happen."

"A lot of somethings, you said, sir. So a single act of carelessness, a single error, couldn't cause it."

"Absolutely not. You might lose a single piece of equipment that way, if everything else went wrong, but not damage on this scale."

Paul stared at Lieutenant Bashir, who was frowning down at the surface of the defense counsel's table. *Object, you idiot. You're letting them point the whole thing straight at Jen.* But Bashir said nothing.

"Rear Admiral Hidalgo, could you cause such a thing to happen?"

"Perhaps. I've never considered doing it, for obvious reasons, but I assume I could."

"Objection." Lieutenant Bashir finally stood, speaking clearly but without force. "Witness is making an assumption based not upon his expertise and experience but upon pure speculation."

Judge McMasters looked toward Carr, who spread her hands as if not comprehending the objection. "Your Honor, the witness is an expert on these systems. His informed judgment, whether based upon things he's actually done or things he has only considered in theory, is still expert."

Bashir shook his head. "Your Honor, I would argue that this speculation goes outside the witness's area of expert knowledge. By his own statement, he's never considered doing it. Perhaps the trial counsel could ask the witness if he would be willing to swear that he unquestionably *could* do such a thing?"

McMasters looked at Carr. Carr looked at Hidalgo. Hidalgo scrunched up his face in thought. "I... think so."

The judge looked directly at Hidalgo. "The question, admiral, is whether you would certify it definitely could be done by someone."

Hidalgo's mouth worked for a moment, then he nodded. "Yes. I would be willing to so certify."

"Then the objection is overruled. Continue your questioning of the witness, trial counsel."

Bashir sat down, his mouth a thin line.

Commander Carr faced Rear Admiral Hidalgo again. "You say it could only happen on purpose, sir. Would it be hard to do?"

Hidalgo nodded briskly. "Very hard."

"Complicated?"

"Absolutely. That's why I said it'd have to be an internal agent. Everything would have to be done just right. Or, just wrong, I guess I should say." Hidalgo started to smile, then looked guilty over making his joke.

"It would take an exceptionally competent and capable engineer to do such a thing?"

"Yes. Certainly. Someone who'd have to know that system cold."

"Would that someone also have to be well trusted?"

"I'm not sure..."

"Trusted. Able to go pretty much anywhere in engineering and not have what they were doing checked out."

"Objection." Lieutenant Bashir gestured toward Rear Admiral Hidalgo again. "Your Honor, what is the basis for the trial counsel's question? She's leading the witness."

McMasters frowned in thought, but looked over at the members' table as Captain Carney cleared his throat. "Judge, if I may, my personal opinion as someone who's held command is that knowing a system cold and being trusted are pretty much the same thing. One implies the other."

Lieutenant Bashir spoke with obvious care. "Your Honor, in this case, I would respectfully suggest that knowledge and character are two separate issues."

Carney frowned slightly despite Bashir's careful tone and phrasing.

Judge McMasters thought a moment longer, then shook his head. "No, I believe the argument presented by the captain is a sound one. These are two sides of the same coin. Objection overruled."

Bashir sat again. Paul couldn't read his disappointment from his expression, but he knew it had to be there. *Not only did he get overruled, but the senior officer among the members stuck his nose in and got it a bit bent out of joint. Great.*

"Thank you, Your Honor. Rear Admiral Hidalgo, should I repeat the question?"

"Uh, no. You asked if it would need someone who wouldn't be

watched or have what they did checked, right? Well, of course. They'd have to do a lot of stuff they weren't supposed to do and not get caught."

"Thank you, admiral." Commander Carr turned to face the defense table. "You've already testified that you met all of the engineering officers on the USS *Maury* prior to her last underway period. That included Lieutenant Junior Grade Shen?"

"Of course."

"What is your professional assessment of her as an engineer?" Bashir began to rise. "Based upon what you know," Carr added. Bashir frowned and sat down again.

This time, Hidalgo avoided looking toward Jen. "She seemed very capable."

"Did you, personally, see any reason to question her expertise as an engineering officer?"

"No."

"Would you say it was fair to describe Lieutenant Junior Grade Shen as being exceptionally competent and capable?"

"Objection." Lieutenant Bashir's word held more force this time. "The trial counsel is putting words in the witness's mouth, and asking him to make an in-depth evaluation of an officer he met only briefly."

"Sustained." McMasters pointed his gavel at Commander Carr. "Let the witness answer questions in his own words."

"Yes, Your Honor. Thank you, Rear Admiral Hidalgo. I have no further questions at this time."

Lieutenant Bashir, still standing from his last objection, walked up to the witness. "Rear Admiral Hidalgo, hadn't the USS *Maury* recently had extensive changes made to her engineering system?

Changes which rendered her engineering system unique?"

Hidalgo frowned. "Well... unique..."

"The Ship's Efficiency Engineering Regulator System. SEERS for short. It's brand new."

"That's true."

"How much experience do you have with SEERS-equipped engineering systems?"

"None! You said yourself, it's brand new. No one has experience with such systems in an operational environment."

Lieutenant Bashir frowned as if puzzled. "But, then, how can you be so certain of what that system would do under any and all circumstances? Isn't your expertise and experience with *different* engineering systems, sir?"

Hidalgo flushed slightly. "It's still basically the same. More so. SEERS was designed to reinforce and consolidate all those safety features. Everything I had to say about safety in an engineering system goes double for a ship with SEERS!"

Bashir paused. Even Paul could see he'd been thrown off by the force of Hidalgo's reply, but Bashir recovered quickly. "Admiral, you're a very experienced officer, but upon what experience do you base that assessment of ships equipped with SEERS?"

"On... on... tests prior to its acceptance into the fleet. We don't just plop equipment onto ships, lieutenant. SEERS was extensively tested. That's part of the design and acquisition process. Test it over and over again. Make sure it does what it's supposed to do and passes every test."

"But not in an 'operational environment.' Is that right, admiral?"

"Well, yes. The *Maury* was the first ship with SEERS. That was the operational integration phase. But I've seen the background material on the system, lieutenant! SEERS was certified to be ready for employment on warships. That may make it a bit unique but it doesn't make it one tiny bit less safe. Quite the contrary. There are people responsible for reviewing these things, for making sure something is ready for the fleet. They said SEERS was ready."

"Your Honor." Commander Carr had stood and was gesturing toward Lieutenant Bashir. "Counsel for the defense is apparently attempting to argue that the SEERS on the USS *Maury* somehow represented an unknown modification to safety measures on the *Maury*'s engineering systems. But the defense has introduced no evidence to substantiate that line of questioning. The trial counsel objects to any attempt by the defense to make unsubstantiated claims regarding the safety or reliability of equipment which has been certified as ready for employment on ships of the US Navy."

Judge McMasters nodded. "An excellent point, commander. Lieutenant Bashir, if you want to pursue this line of questioning, you need to provide something to indicate it's anything other than pure speculation on your part. Are you prepared to do so?"

"Your Honor, since the case against Lieutenant Shen rests on speculative modifications—"

"No, defense counsel. Do you have information substantiating your argument that SEERS could've altered the safety status of the *Maury*'s engineering systems?"

Lieutenant Bashir shook his head, his expression again grim. "No, Your Honor."

"Do you intend to call any expert witnesses to claim SEERS adversely affected the safety of the *Maury*'s engineering systems, or to otherwise counter Rear Admiral Hidalgo's statements?"

"No, Your Honor. Not at this time."

"Objection sustained."

Bashir consulted his data pad. "Rear Admiral Hidalgo, you testified previously that when you visited the USS *Maury* two days prior to her getting underway she had nothing wrong with her engineering system."

Hidalgo, who'd listened to Carr's objection and the judge's dressing-down of Bashir with a smile, smiled again. "That's right."

"But the *Maury* had numerous casualty reports on file regarding her engineering systems. Fleet staff was an addee on those casualty reports."

Hidalgo's smile vanished. "Well, yes, routine CASREPs."

"Routine?"

"The usual stuff. Nothing ever works one hundred percent right one hundred percent of the time."

"But you testified there were 'no problems.' Your exact words, sir."

Hidalgo flushed again, deeper this time. "No significant problems."

"Fleet reporting requirements state that only significant problems with systems are to be reported via CASREP. Isn't that right, sir?"

A long pause, then Hidalgo nodded. "That's what the instruction says."

"Then the *Maury*'s engineering system wasn't in perfect shape when she got underway."

"No. Of course not. No engineering system is ever in perfect shape. But—"

"Thank you, sir. When you met with the chief engineer of the USS *Maury*, did he indicate in any way to you that he lacked confidence in Lieutenant Shen?"

"Objection. Hearsay."

"Your Honor, I am asking Admiral Hidalgo what the *Maury*'s chief engineer said to *him*."

A nod from the judge. "Objection overruled. You know what constitutes hearsay, trial counsel."

Bashir directed his attention back to Hidalgo. "Sir?"

"What was the question?"

"Did the chief engineer of the USS *Maury* communicate to you, in any way, any kind of misgivings regarding Lieutenant Shen?"

Admiral Hidalgo finally looked at Jen again. "No. He did not."

"Thank you, sir. No further questions."

Commander Carr came forward once again. "If it please the court, I'd like to redirect. Rear Admiral Hidalgo, did any of these casualty reports just referenced regarding the engineering systems on the *Maury* generate safety concerns?"

"No! I was going to tell the lieutenant that!"

"Then the fact that the *Maury*'s engineering systems weren't in perfect condition didn't mean they were unsafe."

"Of course not. That ship never would've left the dock if she were unsafe."

"Then would you say those casualty reports have no bearing on the issues we've discussed?"

"That's right! I..." Hidalgo glared at Bashir. "I'd never let a ship leave this station in an unsafe condition!"

"Thank you, admiral."

Paul had to resist an urge to bury his face in his hands. Hidalgo's last statement was bound to play well with the members of the court. *Did Bashir screw this up or was there no way to get anything good for Jen out of this witness? I don't know. But it went badly for Jen.*

Judge McMasters gestured toward Captain Carney. "Do the

members of the court have any questions for this witness?"

Lieutenant Ishiki looked as if he might be preparing to speak, but Captain Carney looked at him and Ishiki subsided. Carney was shaking his head when Commander Bolton spoke up.

"Excuse me, captain. Admiral Hidalgo, I'm not an engineering expert. I do know there's always some degree of uncertainty in any engineering process. Some level of concern. As you yourself said, no engineering system is ever in perfect shape. But you say it's still possible to rule out any accidental cause for what happened to the *Maury*'s engineering system?"

Hidalgo nodded firmly. "Yes, commander. It's more than possible. It's the only possible conclusion. Every sub-system in engineering has safety interlocks, both physical and virtual. They all have been extensively tested to absolutely minimize any chance of the sort of overload that causes explosive failure. But, yes, that doesn't mean it's absolutely impossible for one piece of equipment to have that happen. But every piece of equipment? Every sub-system? Nearly simultaneously? The odds of that are so very, very tiny that only the word impossible fits."

Bolton nodded, looking impressed. "Thank you, admiral."

Carney took another look at the members. "Nothing else. Right?" It was much a command to the more junior members of the court as it was a question. "Fine. Thank you, sir."

Judge McMasters turned toward the witness stand. "Rear Admiral Hidalgo, you are temporarily excused. Please ensure you are present for the remainder of this court-martial in the event you need to be called again. As long as this trial continues, do not discuss your testimony or knowledge of the case with anyone except counsel. If anyone else tries to talk to you about the case, stop them and report the matter to one of the counsels."

"Absolutely." Rear Admiral Hidalgo stood and marched back down the aisle.

Paul watched him go, then focused back on Captain Carney. *He's obviously planning on running a tight ship. How much does he have the other officers on the court intimidated? Will he be able to keep them from asking anything Carney doesn't want them to ask?*

10

The next two witnesses for the prosecution, a civilian supervisor from Franklin's shipyard who'd overseen the *Maury*'s engineering systems work and the captain in charge of the Fleet Engineering Readiness Group, simply reinforced the points elicited from Rear Admiral Hidalgo. No, it couldn't have been an accident. Yes, someone had to cause it to happen. No, we don't know exactly how they did it, but it had to be sabotage.

"The United States calls as its next witness Captain Richard Hayes, United States Navy."

Paul had known his own commanding officer was going to be called to testify, but he still didn't enjoy watching Captain Hayes come down the center of the courtroom and take his place on the witness stand. Hayes scanned the room quickly after he'd sat, giving Paul a sharp, quick nod of recognition as Hayes' eyes swept over him.

Commander Carr faced the witness stand. "Captain Hayes, what is your current duty assignment?"

Hayes shifted position slightly in the witness chair as he answered. "I'm commanding officer of the USS *Michaelson*."

"Were you in command of the USS *Michaelson* on 21 February of this year?"

"I was. Yes."

"And was the USS *Michaelson* operating with the USS *Maury* at that time?"

"Yes. We were."

Commander Carr walked over to the courtroom display, where an image of an area of space had appeared, two long, curving tracks superimposed over the emptiness. "Captain Hayes, this is a representation of the area of space in which the *Michaelson* and the *Maury* were operating on 21 February." One of the curving tracks glowed brighter for a moment. "This was the path of the *Michaelson*." The other track glowed. "And this the track of the *Maury*."

Hayes studied the picture, then nodded. "That looks right."

"The two ships rendezvoused here." An small area where the two curving tracks swung close together shone a bit brighter. "Can you tell us in your own words what happened immediately thereafter, captain?"

"Nothing at first." Hayes tilted his chin toward the diagram. "As you see, the two ships came together. Then we both deactivated our anti-detection devices at the same time."

"You were on the bridge of the *Michaelson*?"

"Yes. It was a somewhat risky maneuver, coming so close to another ship at those speeds with the anti-detection devices fully operative. I was on the bridge, along with my executive officer."

"You said nothing happened 'at first.' What happened after that?"

Hayes looked as if he tasted something sour. "The *Maury*'s

image was suddenly obscured on our sensors. Full spectrum obscured. It took us all a minute to realize what it meant. But our combat and maneuvering systems immediately identified the hazard to us."

Carr looked concerned. "Hazard? To the *Michaelson?*"

"Yes." Hayes glanced toward Paul. "An explosion like that generates a lot of debris. The *Michaelson* was in the path of some of it. We had to worry about the damage it might do to us."

"You couldn't just evade it?"

"No time. We were too close to the *Maury* and with the stuff spreading out in all directions it would have taken too long to get us clear of it. I ordered my ship to engage large pieces of debris and we rode out the impact wave."

"Your own ship sustained some damage, sir?"

Hayes made a dismissive gesture. "Superficial damage. Outer hull mostly."

Commander Carr indicated the display again. "Just before the *Maury* suffered her damage, was the *Michaelson* monitoring conditions in the area, captain?"

Hayes nodded. "Sure. We do that all the time."

"What do you monitor?"

"Everything we can. Any objects, natural or artificial. Radiation levels across the spectrum. You name it."

"Did the *Michaelson* detect anything out of the ordinary prior to the *Maury* suffering damage?"

"Out of the ordinary?" Captain Hayes shook his head. "No."

"No unusual radiation levels in any part of the spectrum?"

"No."

"No hazardous objects near the *Michaelson* or the *Maury?*"

"No."

"Nothing that caused you concern for the safety of either your ship or the *Maury*?"

"No."

Carr came to stand before the witness stand again. "You detected no signs of any danger to your ship or the *Maury*. No external elements which could've accounted for what happened to the *Maury*."

Hayes shook his head again. "No, commander. Nothing like that."

"And no unusual or worrisome detections from the *Maury* herself?"

"No. She'd lit herself up, just like we had, but it was all normal equipment emissions."

"Then, captain, would you say as a commanding officer whose own ship was present in the same location as the *Maury* that whatever caused the damage to the *Maury* had to have originated inside the ship?"

Hayes pondered the question for a moment, then nodded slowly. "Yes. I'd have to say that."

"But there were also no warning signs from the *Maury*."

"That's right. It just happened."

Commander Carr lowered her voice slightly. "Captain, what was the reaction of your engineers when they discovered the *Maury*'s engineering compartments had been destroyed?"

"Shock." Hayes nodded firmly this time. "Disbelief."

"Did you ask them how such a thing could've happened?"

"Yes, I did."

"And what did they say?"

"They... said they couldn't imagine. Had no idea."

Carr nodded as well. "And then the *Michaelson* rendered aid to the *Maury*."

"Yes. I brought my ship in a little closer and started sending over damage control teams."

"Did those teams include any engineering personnel?"

"Yes. My main propulsion assistant and her leading chief petty officer."

"Did they see anything on the *Maury* which would've explained what happened?"

Hayes snorted. "They had other priorities, commander. Saving that ship and her crew."

"I understand, captain." Commander Carr lowered her head briefly as if in apology. "But they didn't report seeing anything which would explain the damage?"

"They said what the investigation later confirmed. It looked like just about everything in the engineering compartments blew at just about the same time."

"If I may summarize, Captain Hayes, your ship, there beside the *Maury*, saw no external cause for what happened to the *Maury*. Your personnel, first on the scene of the disaster, likewise saw nothing to indicate it was caused by anything but internal explosions."

"That's a fair summary. Yes."

"Thank you, captain. No further questions."

Lieutenant Bashir glanced back at Paul as he stood, then advanced deferentially on Captain Hayes. "Captain, are there things out in space which you can't detect?"

Hayes snorted again. "The details are classified, lieutenant, but of course that's true. I'd love to have a crystal ball. Any captain would."

"Things that pose threats to spacecraft?"

"Conceivably."

"What about internally? You testified your ship detected nothing unusual from the *Maury* immediately before the destruction of her engineering compartments. But isn't the *Maury*, like your own ship, designed to minimize the chances of radiation going out as well as going in?"

"Sure." Captain Hayes pointed toward the schematic of the *Maury* still on display. "Just that inner hull alone. It's filled with water cells. They help block radiation from reaching the crew. But they also block any emissions going out."

"Which would make it impossible for your own ship to have detected internal problems on the *Maury*?"

Carr was watching Bashir narrowly, but said nothing.

Hayes pondered the question, then gave another nod. "Essentially, yes. I mean, nothing's impossible. But it'd be very, very hard. Once something's strong enough to come through the hulls, well..." He grimaced and indicated the schematic again. "At that point you're in trouble."

"Thank you, captain."

Commander Carr stood again as Bashir returned to the defense table. "Captain Hayes, to the best of your knowledge, is your ship incapable of detecting any *threats* to it?"

"No. If it's that dangerous, as far as I know we'll see it coming."

"So the fact that your systems aren't 'perfect' doesn't mean they can't detect anything important enough to worry about?"

"Uh, you could say that. Yes."

"Were you in communication with the *Maury* immediately prior to her suffering damage?"

"Yes."

"Did anyone or anything on the *Maury* indicate to you internal problems which you wouldn't have picked up with your own sensors?"

Once again, Captain Hayes shook his head slowly. "No. Nothing like that."

Commander Carr sat again, and Judge McMasters pointed to Captain Carney.

Carney gave Captain Hayes an approving smile. "Captain, I hope it's not out of line for me to express my admiration for how well your ship rendered assistance to the *Maury* in her time of need."

Paul barely restrained showing annoyance. *I can't believe he's sucking up to Captain Hayes during the court-martial. Isn't there anything illegal or improper about that?* He looked at Lieutenant Bashir, who took no action and revealed nothing by his expression. *I guess not.*

Jen's faced remained rigidly unemotional, providing no clues to whatever she felt inside. Paul couldn't see her eyes, which would've told him something even if Jen had been trying to hide her feelings.

Captain Hayes nodded his head to acknowledge Carney's praise. "Thank you, captain. I'm proud of my crew."

"Didn't the defendant ride the *Michaelson* back to Franklin?"

Hayes nodded again. "Yes, she did."

"Any impressions of her from that ride?"

Bashir had tensed, as if ready to object, but he glanced toward Paul first. Paul tried to indicate it'd be a good idea to let Hayes speak, and apparently got that across, because Bashir relaxed again.

"Not many," Captain Hayes was saying. "We were all very busy. She was in shock, like the rest of *Maury*'s surviving crew, but she also asked me for any work I had to do." Hayes looked toward Jen for the first time. "I guess you could say that even in the aftermath of the disaster on the *Maury* she impressed me a bit."

"Did she do any work in engineering on your ship?" Carney pressed.

"Yes. Just paperwork, though she asked to do anything we needed help at."

"How'd she know the *Michaelson* well enough to make that offer?"

"She'd served on the *Michaelson*. Before I became CO."

"You didn't think it was odd that she volunteered to work so soon after such a tragedy?"

Hayes frowned, then shook his head. "No."

Carney made an expression Paul couldn't interpret, but before he could say anything else, Lieutenant Kalin spoke. "Sir, did any other members of the *Maury*'s crew volunteer to help out on the *Michaelson*?"

Carney shot her an annoyed glance, but Hayes was already nodding. "Quite a few. They wanted to repay our help. They wanted to earn their keep."

"Thank you, captain." Kalin acted as if unaware of Carney's disapproval.

Lieutenant Commander Cloud, perhaps taking advantage of Captain Carney being distracted, gestured for attention. "Captain Hayes, could you tell us, sir, as commanding officer of one of the *Maury*'s sister ships, what your assessment is of the odds that what happened to the *Maury* could've been the result of an accident?"

Hayes stayed silent for a few seconds, then, his mouth a thin line, shook his head. "From my own knowledge, from what my own engineers have told me, it doesn't appear possible for it to have been an accident."

"Then you agree that some form of deliberate sabotage is the only possible explanation?"

Once again, Captain Hayes took a few moments before answering. "No. I feel fairly confident I know one thing that *didn't* cause it. I am far less confident that means one particular thing *did* cause it."

"Thank you, captain."

Captain Carney cleared his throat. "Captain Hayes, do you know of anything else that could've caused what happened to the *Maury*? Any other specific cause that could explain the disaster?"

Hayes favored Carney with a flat expression Paul recognized. *He's not impressed by Carney. He knows Carney's trying to drive the discussion in just one direction.*

But Captain Hayes' answer was only one word. "No."

"Uh, thank you, captain."

Captain Hayes left, but deliberately offered a brief wave to Paul as he walked out of the courtroom.

Judge McMasters held up a hand to forestall Commander Carr. "Lunchtime, trial counsel. This court-martial is closed and will reconvene at 1300 in this same courtroom."

McMasters stood even as the bailiff bawled out, "All stand." After the judge left, the members of the court filed out through their door. As soon as that door closed, the ranks of spectators congealed into a crowd heading for the courtroom's main exit.

Paul waited, hoping Jen would turn and speak to him after she and Bashir finished an intense, quiet conversation. Finally, just as the masters-at-arms arrived, Jen looked his way and offered Paul a smile which wasn't either confident or genuine. But he smiled back as if reassured, wondering if his own mood was as transparent.

Lieutenant Bashir remained behind as the masters-at-arms escorted Jen to a holding cell near the courtroom where she'd get a fully nutritious and horribly bland meal. Paul took a couple of steps toward the lawyer. "Well?"

Bashir gave Paul a sidelong look. "I've had better mornings.

Thanks for not saying so directly."

"I still don't really understand why it's so hard. I mean, they haven't presented anything yet that links Jen to what happened to the *Maury*."

"It doesn't make sense, does it? But it's an uphill battle. Listen, your Jen Shen isn't helping me as much as she could. She's trying to look cool and professional, but that also looks cold. I know you won't have a chance to see her before tonight, but can you convince her to show more emotion?"

"I can try."

"Mind you," Bashir added dryly, "if she looks too emotional they'll decide that's bad, too."

"I guess we should've got a drama coach appointed in addition to a lawyer."

"It wouldn't have hurt." Bashir pointed to Paul's seat. "Make sure you're back here from lunch early. We've got the trial's prime witness coming up, and some high-and-mighty might try to grab that seat despite the sign."

Paul shook his head. "I'm not hungry. I'll stay there until the trial restarts."

"Suit yourself." Bashir went out, his face a mask.

Paul sat back down, looking around, and saw Commander Carr still seated at the trial counsel's table. *She always stayed a little later at Silver's court-martial, too.* Carr finally finished whatever she was working on and stood. Turning to go, she saw Paul and looked at him for a moment, then looked down and away as she left the courtroom. *Not happy. Cold comfort, but she's not enjoying this at all.*

The room emptied of the last occupants but Paul. The bailiff came through at one point, glanced at Paul with disinterest, then continued onward. After about half an hour, people began trickling back in. A captain came by at one point, frowning down at Paul in a why-are-you-in-that-chair way, but Paul just pointed to the placard on the back. "Reserved, sir." Apparently believing Paul must be place-holding the seat for a more senior officer, the captain moved off.

Almost last to reenter was Jen and her escorts. She took time to offer him another tight-lipped smile, then bent her head to talk to Lieutenant Bashir. Paul could see her shaking her head, but couldn't hear anything.

"All rise."

Once the judge and the members of the court had once more taken their places, McMasters used his gavel to once again indicate Commander Carr. "This court-martial is open. Proceed, trial counsel."

"Thank you, Your Honor. The United States calls as its next witness Captain Elizabeth Halis, United States Navy."

The courtroom, already quiet, seemed to fall even more silent as Captain Halis entered, walking steadily to the witness stand and taking the oath with a stubbornly unreadable expression. Commander Carr stood a little further back from her than she had other witnesses, as though granting Captain Halis an extra measure of respect. "Captain Halis, please state your current assignment."

Halis actually twitched one eyebrow as if amused. "I am currently serving as commanding officer of the USS *Maury*."

"And you were serving in that capacity on 21 February of this year?"

Halis stared evenly back at Carr. "I was."

"Previous testimony has established that on the afternoon of 21 February 2101, the USS *Maury*, your ship, was wracked by devastating internal explosions that destroyed her engineering compartments and killed sixty-one members of her crew. Prior to that happening, had you received any notification from your engineering personnel of concerns or problems in engineering?"

"There are always problems and concerns in engineering, commander." Halis's voice betrayed nothing of whatever she was feeling.

"Anything out of the ordinary, then? Anything that aroused particular concern?"

"No. Not that aroused particular concern. As for out of the ordinary, I received a report about noon from Commander Juko that the engineering system was continuing to display what he called 'teething troubles' in the wake of our yard period and modifications."

"'Teething troubles'? Nothing Commander Juko or you regarded as too serious, then?"

"No. I would not have taken my ship out of Franklin if either I or Commander Juko had safety concerns regarding the ship."

"Then you received no warning whatsoever prior to the destruction of the *Maury*'s engineering systems?"

Captain Halis bent her head in thought, then shook it. "No."

"No alarms sounded. No warnings delivered. Just sudden destruction."

Halis closed her eyes for a moment. "Yes."

"Did Commander Juko tell you he had sent Lieutenant Junior Grade Shen to another part of the ship?"

Halis' jaw worked for a moment before she replied. "No. He did not. But that was not necessarily a matter he would've brought to my attention."

Commander Carr took a step closer but remained in a respectful pose. "Let me clarify that issue if I may, captain. One of the engineering officers left the engineering compartments allegedly to personally investigate a piece of equipment. Had you received any reports of engineering equipment in the after portion of the ship malfunctioning in a fashion that would apparently require an officer's attention?"

Another pause. "No."

"Commander Juko did not inform you of any unusual concerns regarding the after power coupling on the USS *Maury*?"

"No. He did not."

"How long had you been Commander Juko's commanding officer?"

"Commander Juko served as my chief engineer for seven months."

"In that time, is it your opinion that he kept you, as commanding officer, well informed of engineering issues?"

"Yes."

"Did you ever feel that Commander Juko had failed to inform you of any significant problems?"

"No."

"Ma'am, did you ever personally discover that Commander Juko had actually failed to inform you of any significant engineering problems?"

"No."

Commander Carr turned and took a few steps to one side so that Captain Halis was now looking toward both her and the members of the court. "After the explosions, when you discovered that Lieutenant Junior Grade Shen was still alive in the after part of the ship, what was your first thought?"

Halis' eyes moved away from Carr and settled on Jen. "Relief. One officer and twenty-one enlisted personnel I'd thought dead were in fact alive."

"Were you surprised to learn Lieutenant Junior Grade Shen had been in the after part of the ship when the engineering compartments exploded?"

Halis visibly bit her lip. "Yes. I was." She looked back at Jen. "Pleasantly surprised."

"Did you wonder why she'd been there? Safe from the destruction visited upon the other members of her department?"

"Objection!" Bashir looked as heated as Paul had seen him. "Your Honor, the trial counsel's last sentence is inflammatory, leading and improper. She is attempting to prejudice the witness and the members of the court against the defendant by implying misconduct *which has not been proven.*"

Commander Carr stared stolidly back at Lieutenant Bashir. "Your Honor, my job as trial counsel is to prove misconduct over the course of this proceeding. I am doing so."

McMasters shook his head. "That went over the line, commander. Objection sustained. The last sentence spoken by the trial counsel is to be stricken from the record and disregarded by the members of the court."

Bashir sat down, no signs of celebration evident even though his objection had been sustained. Paul looked at the members of the court and realized why. *No matter what the judge says, the members of the court heard that and they'll remember it. As if Captain Carney needed that extra dig at Jen to make up his mind. But the others might still be swayed by statements like that. I sure wish Alex Carr was defending Jen instead of prosecuting her.*

Commander Carr bent her head in brief acknowledgment of the judge's rebuke. "Yes, Your Honor. I will restate the question prior to that statement. Captain Halis, when you discovered Lieutenant Junior Grade Shen had been in the after portion of the ship, did you wonder why she'd been there?"

Halis slowly nodded. "Yes. Only for a fraction of a second. I had other things to worry about."

"I understand, captain. But you did wonder?"

"Yes."

"Because you knew of no reason why she'd have been there instead of at her duty station in engineering?"

Captain Halis stared stolidly ahead for a moment before answering. "Yes."

"If I may summarize your testimony, then, Captain Halis, you had no indications prior to the destruction of engineering on the USS *Maury* of any problems, and had received no notification of any problems specifically in the after part of the ship which required special attention. Is that an accurate summation?"

The captain chewed her lip for a moment before answering. "Yes."

Commander Carr indicated her data unit. "I have here the performance reports prepared by Commander Juko and signed by you regarding Lieutenant Junior Grade Shen. They're very impressive."

Paul was certain a trace of wariness had appeared in Halis' eyes as she nodded. "Lieutenant Shen is an impressive officer."

Carr nodded. "In fact, one of the performance reports you signed states that Lieutenant Junior Grade Shen is quote an exceptionally capable and competent engineering officer unquote. The performance reports also state quote I believe there is no engineering task which I could set to Lieutenant Junior Grade Shen which she would be incapable of mastering unquote."

Paul tried not to wince. *I remember that wording. That's what Carr got Rear Admiral Hidalgo to say would be needed to sabotage a ship's engineering systems.* He could see the side of Jen's face as she watched Captain Halis. *What are you thinking, Jen? That being good at your job isn't supposed to be a bad thing?*

Captain Halis, unaware of Rear Admiral Hidalgo's earlier testimony, nodded. "I can't recall off-hand the exact wording, but that sounds like the sort of assessment I would've made of Lieutenant Shen, yes."

Commander Carr leaned a little closer. "You believe, based on your judgment as her commanding officer, that Lieutenant Junior Grade Shen could do anything in engineering which she set her mind to."

"Objection." Lieutenant Bashir waved both his hands, palms down, at chest level. "The trial counsel is seeking to lead the witness, to put words in her mouth, and to reformulate the witness's statements in a prejudicial fashion."

Carr spread her own hands out. "Your Honor, I am merely attempting to accurately summarize Captain Halis' own assessments."

Judge McMasters shook his head. "Let Captain Halis summarize her assessments, commander. Objection sustained."

"I have no more questions at this time, Your Honor."

Paul watched Commander Carr return to her seat. *Damn. They're turning Jen's skills as an officer against her. Just like when they put her in pre-trial confinement. How do you fight charges that claim you're so good you can do anything? It's not like Jen can plausibly argue that she's incompetent.*

Lieutenant Bashir approached the witness stand with even more deference than Commander Carr had. "Captain Halis, these 'teething troubles' you mentioned with the engineering systems. Did they concern you or Commander Juko at all, ma'am?"

"Yes, obviously, or he never would've mentioned them to me."

"So they weren't regarded as imminently unsafe, but were a concern?"

"Yes. That's correct."

"Captain Halis, the court has been told that the engineering systems on your ship were designed so that near-simultaneous catastrophic failures were impossible. But your ship had received extensive engineering modifications recently. Did Commander Juko indicate to you that these engineering modifications had caused any unusual problems?"

Paul could see Commander Carr watching Captain Halis intently as the captain pondered her answer.

Finally, Halis nodded. "Yes. Commander Juko specifically told me the SEERS was giving him some headaches."

"That's what he said, ma'am?"

"Yes. He said it was giving him headaches. I remember that exactly because he told it to me on at least two occasions."

"Did he specify the nature of these 'headaches'?"

"No. Lots of little things. That's all he said."

"Did Commander Juko routinely inform you of his orders to the other officers in engineering?"

Captain Halis shook her head firmly. "No. Of course not."

"If he sent an officer to carry out some task, he wouldn't inform you?"

"No. I don't micromanage my junior officers, lieutenant."

"Thank you, Captain Halis. So is it fair to say that there's absolutely nothing unusual or uncharacteristic about Lieutenant Shen having been ordered to go aft and you not being specifically informed of that tasking?"

"Objection." Commander Carr gestured toward the defense table. "It has not been established that Lieutenant Junior Grade Shen in fact received such an order."

Bashir looked toward McMasters and read the judge's answer before it could be spoken. "I will rephrase my question, Your Honor. Captain Halis, is it fair to say there would be nothing unusual or uncharacteristic if Lieutenant Shen had received such an order and you had not been specifically informed?"

Halis nodded. "That is absolutely correct, lieutenant. It would've been unusual if I *had* been specifically informed."

Lieutenant Bashir turned slightly and pointed at Jen. "Captain, do you have any reason to believe Lieutenant Shen deliberately caused your ship's engineering equipment to fail catastrophically?"

"No. I do not."

"Do you believe Lieutenant Shen would purposely plot and execute the murder of her shipmates?"

"No. I do not."

"Do you know of any reason she would do such a thing?"

"No. I do not."

"Thank you, Captain Halis."

Commander Carr stood again but remained at the trial counsel's table. "Captain Halis, did Commander Juko ever tell you that the 'teething troubles' with engineering in the wake of the yard period constituted any kind of threat to the ship?"

Halis, her expression now openly grim, shook her head. "No."

"Do you have confidence that Commander Juko would've told you of any specific concerns regarding the safety of his equipment?"

"Yes, I do."

"Ma'am, would your chief engineer, Commander Juko, have

characterized any problems he believed serious enough to lead to loss of life and damage to the USS *Maury* as 'a lot of little things'?"

Halis glanced at Jen, then shook her head. "No."

"In your opinion and based upon your experience with Commander Juko, would he have informed you of any equipment problems in the after portion of the ship which he regarded as unusually dangerous?"

"Yes." Captain Halis' face worked for a moment. "Commander Juko was a good man."

Commander Carr nodded several times, slowly. "Yes, Captain Halis. Captain, I believe it's fair to assume you were well acquainted with all your officers?"

"I know, or knew, them, yes."

"But not intimately. Would you say you knew all their personal secrets?"

"Of course not."

"Would you say you knew every factor that motivated every officer under your command?"

Halis laughed briefly. "I'm not God, commander. The Navy may seem to give me that degree of power over my ship and crew, but I can't read minds." Commander Carr nodded, turning away before speaking again. "Then you couldn't say you knew the reasons for every action of your officers, everything that might cause them to take an action."

"*No*," Captain Halis replied. "But that doesn't mean I'm incapable of judging the sorts of actions they will take. And the sorts of actions they would *not* take."

Carr nodded again. "Thank you, again, captain." She returned to the trial counsel's table.

Captain Carney leaned forward, placing his elbows on the table before him. "Captain Halis, you and your ship have been through hell. So let's cut to the bottom line, please. Do you think Lieutenant Junior Grade Shen was responsible for what happened to your ship?"

Halis shook her head firmly. "No. I do not."

"Do you have any other explanation for what happened to your ship? I mean, another specific explanation that might explain what happened?"

Captain Halis hesitated, then shook her head with visible reluctance. "No."

Captain Carney looked to either side. "Any other questions? No," he answered without pausing to see if the other members in fact had any. Carney focused back on Captain Halis. "May I express my personal condolences for the loss of so many of your crew, captain."

"Thank you, captain."

"One more question, Captain Halis. Is there anything you would've done differently, knowing what you know now?"

Captain Halis finally showed a flash of emotion, raw pain which quickly vanished again. "I have asked myself that very question many times, captain. I haven't thought of any answers."

"Would you let Lieutenant Junior Grade Shen serve under you again? In your Engineering Department?"

Paul held his breath. *That's two more questions, Captain Carney, but I bet no one calls you on it.* He looked at Jen, sitting rigid with her eyes fixed on Captain Halis, then back at Halis herself, who was obviously struggling with her answer.

Halis spoke slowly. "I... am responsible for the wellbeing of my ship and everyone on it."

"Captain Halis? Does that mean you would or would not accept

Lieutenant Junior Grade Shen in your Engineering Department again?"

Halis looked downward for a long moment, then back at Jen. "Yes. I would. She's given me no reason to feel otherwise."

Paul could see Jen's back quivering and knew how deeply Captain Halis' words were affecting her. *And me. Thanks, captain.*

Captain Carney nodded, smiling politely. "Thank you, Captain Halis. Your loyalty to your crewmembers is commendable."

What does that mean? Paul wondered. *Is he brushing off Captain Halis' response as just reflecting loyalty? Was this question a lose–lose for Jen?* He looked at Bashir's face and saw no joy there. *Yeah. You know, don't you? Carney, and maybe other members of the court, would've jumped on it if Halis had said "no". But they're blowing off a "yes" as not proving anything. Just a captain standing by her crew.*

Captain Halis stood and walked out, every eye following her until she'd left the courtroom.

11

The next two witnesses had less drama but posed less support for Jen.

The fleet surgeon from the military hospital on Franklin testified to the injuries suffered by the sailors Jen had been accused of maiming. The slide show on the display screen portrayed each injury, some the results of fragments striking bodies, some from blunter, massive objects hurled by the explosions and hitting soft humans in their path, one the result of a sailor whose hand stayed on a hatch rim too long when the *Maury*'s emergency mechanisms started sealing hatches. Bashir objected, futilely, to the parade of suffering.

Autopsy results and official findings were entered into the court record, establishing that as a result of the explosions sixty-one officers and enlisted personnel of the USS *Maury* had been declared dead in sufficient form and detail to satisfy all legal, medical and bureaucratic requirements. The names had to be read into the record at this point. Paul listened, trying to numb his emotions. *Strange. I've heard a lot of lists of names read. Class rosters and unit members and just going through a phone directory. But listening to this list, knowing they all died on the* Maury *like that, is so painful.* When he looked at Jen, she was clenching her hands together as tightly as she could and staring down blankly at the surface of the defense table.

Then came a Supply Corps officer, who provided mind-numbing detail on the property losses suffered by both the US government and by individual sailors as a result of the explosions on the *Maury*. Paul thought a convention of accountants would've been thrilled by the presentation, but an almost audible sigh of relief went through the courtroom when that witness had finished testifying.

Lieutenant Bashir rubbed his eyes wearily and leaned toward Jen. "There should only be one more," Paul heard him tell her.

"The United States calls as its next witness Lieutenant Edwin Taber, United States Navy."

Lieutenant Taber walked briskly to the witness stand. He didn't look toward Jen even though Paul knew Taber was part of the *Maury's* wardroom. Commander Carr stood a bit further back from Taber than she had even from Captain Halis, but in this case it didn't seem to be a matter of deference. "Lieutenant Taber, what is your current assignment?"

Taber kept his gaze locked on Carr as he answered. "I'm the weapons officer on the USS *Maury*."

"Do you know Lieutenant Junior Grade Shen?"

Taber still didn't look her way as he nodded. "Yes. We've served together for several months."

Commander Carr paused before speaking again, though Paul couldn't tell why. "What can you tell us of your personal observations regarding Lieutenant Junior Grade Shen's relations with her fellow officers?"

Taber's lips twitched in a spasmodic smile. "She was very friendly with Lieutenant Schmidt."

Paul saw Jen twitch involuntarily, then her eyes narrow as she stared at Taber.

"Lieutenant Schmidt?" Carr asked.

"Yes. Helen Schmidt. The, uh, former main propulsion assistant on the *Maury*."

"Lieutenant Schmidt died in the destruction of the engineering spaces?"

"Yes. Yes, ma'am."

"What do you mean by 'very friendly?'"

Taber's hands, held together in his lap, could be seen clenching and unclenching restlessly. "Uh, well, for example, one time I entered a compartment... I mean, I made to enter a compartment, and Lieutenant Schmidt and Lieutenant Shen told me to wait, and when I finally opened the hatch Lieutenant Shen was just finishing putting on her uniform and they both seemed to be, uh, breathing heavily."

Paul felt his face warming and knew he was flushing with anger. He could spot a similar reaction on Jen's face.

Commander Carr paused again. "You interpreted that as a sign of an intimate physical encounter between Lieutenant Schmidt and Lieutenant Junior Grade Shen?"

Lieutenant Bashir stood. "Objection, Your Honor. This is the crudest kind of character assassination."

Commander Carr didn't look toward Bashir as she answered. "Your Honor, it is unfortunately necessary to establish motive for the offenses which Lieutenant Junior Grade Shen is charged with committing. Improper physical relationships tell us about the emotional stability of those who engage in them, as well as a pattern of actions contrary to good order and discipline. They also indicate that working relationships had been poisoned with... unpredictable results."

Paul wanted to yell across the courtroom at her, but he knew that wouldn't do Jen any good and would get him ejected for the remainder of the trial. *I can tell you don't want to say this stuff, Commander Carr, but I wish to God you hadn't had to do this.* Carr's eyes strayed toward Paul and he read a message there. *And you wish to God you hadn't had to, either, don't you?*

Lieutenant Bashir was also shaking his head. "Your Honor, this testimony isn't evidence of anything. It's pure innuendo and unworthy of the trial counsel."

McMasters looked unhappy, but he shook his head, too. "No, lieutenant. It's too early to determine whether we're talking innuendo or meaningful observations. As long as the trial counsel continues to base the witness's testimony on his actual observations and personal knowledge, I must allow this line of questioning to continue. Objection overruled."

Commander Carr didn't look back toward Taber as she repeated her last question. "Lieutenant Taber, did you then believe you had witnessed the end of an inappropriate physical encounter between Lieutenant Schmidt and Lieutenant Junior Grade Shen?"

Taber glanced rapidly around, his eyes settling nowhere before resting back on Carr. "Yes. Yes, ma'am."

"Was that the only occasion when you witnessed physical encounters between them?"

"No. I'd see them touch each other sometimes."

"Did you ever confront them on such occasions and express your belief that their behavior was inappropriate?"

"Yes, ma'am. They... they laughed at me. Like it was some kind of joke."

Carr nodded, her gaze still averted from the witness stand. "And this behavior continued up until Lieutenant Schmidt's death?"

"I... I think so. But Lieutenant Schmidt got engaged just before we got underway, so maybe——"

Carr held up her palm. "No more questions."

McMasters looked toward Lieutenant Bashir with a grim smile. "I assume defense counsel has questions for the witness?"

Bashir, listening as Jen whispered to him with a fierce expression, nodded. "Yes, Your Honor." Paul heard him whisper back to Jen, "I've got it covered," as he stood up.

Lieutenant Bashir walked slowly and steadily toward the witness stand, coming close until he stood just before Lieutenant Taber, his face reflecting skeptical interest. "Let me recap what you just testified, lieutenant. You say on one occasion you approached a compartment occupied by Lieutenant Shen and Lieutenant Schmidt. You were asked to wait before entering the compartment. When you were allowed to enter, Lieutenant Shen appeared to be in the act of finishing dressing. Correct so far?"

Taber nodded briskly. "Yes."

Bashir leaned even closer to Taber. "This compartment. Wasn't it Lieutenant Shen's stateroom?"

"I... "

"Was it or wasn't it?"

"I don't recall exactly."

"That's an odd detail to forget, isn't it, lieutenant? When you remember so much else about the event so clearly?"

"Objection." Commander Carr didn't rise, didn't even look

toward the bench. "Defense counsel is harassing the witness."

"Sustained." Judge McMasters seemed just as unenthusiastic as Carr. "Just ask your questions, Lieutenant Bashir."

"Yes, Your Honor. Lieutenant Taber, you're under oath. Lying under oath is perjury. Now think again. Was the compartment in question Lieutenant Shen's stateroom?"

"I... okay. Yes."

"Then, if I may summarize again, your testimony indicates that Lieutenant Shen was getting dressed in her own stateroom."

"I—"

"Do you find anything unusual about being asked to wait while a female officer finishes dressing in her own stateroom?"

"Objection—"

"Overruled."

Bashir leaned in closer to Taber, who seemed increasingly nervous. "Lieutenant, did you ever ask Lieutenant Shen for a date?"

"Objection!"

McMasters frowned down at Bashir. "Does counsel for the defense have any grounds for asking that question?"

"Your Honor, I have in my possession sworn statements signed by two surviving officers from the USS *Maury* that Lieutenant Taber had asked both Lieutenant Shen and Lieutenant Schmidt for dates on separate occasions. According to the statements, he was turned down in both cases. I will be happy to offer both statements to be added to the record for the trial."

Paul looked over at Commander Carr, who was finally looking at Lieutenant Taber with an icy expression.

Judge McMasters also looked toward the trial counsel's table. "Commander Carr? Do you still wish to object?"

"No, Your Honor, though I reserve the right to bring up the issue again after I've reviewed the statements in question."

"Very well. Continue, Lieutenant Bashir."

"Thank you, Your Honor." Lieutenant Bashir focused back on Taber, who looked both nervous and unhappy. "Will you answer the question, lieutenant? Didn't you ask Lieutenant Shen for a date?"

"I might've."

"And Lieutenant Schmidt?"

"Maybe. I don't really remember."

Bashir leaned very close to Taber. "You're *still* under oath, lieutenant," he said softly.

Taber nodded once. "Okay. Yes. I guess I did. If I had to say, I'd say I did. So what?"

"I'll ask the questions, if you don't mind, lieutenant. When the hatch to Lieutenant Shen's stateroom opened, was there any physical contact apparent between her and Lieutenant Schmidt?"

"No, I said—"

"No hugging? No touching? No kissing?"

"No!"

"Lieutenant Schmidt was fully dressed?"

"Uh, yes."

"You testified you *thought* they were breathing heavily. Was either woman's hair in any disarray?"

"I... can't remember."

Bashir leaned very close. "Lieutenant, you've testified that a female officer was getting dressed in her own stateroom with the hatch closed, with another female officer present. Have you ever been in your own stateroom, getting dressed, with another male officer present?"

"Objection. Counsel for defense is harassing the witness."

"Overruled." McMasters shook his head. "It's a legitimate line of questioning for this witness."

"Your Honor, it implies—"

"I'll remind the trial counsel that she introduced such implications into the trial. Continue, Lieutenant Bashir."

"Thank you, Your Honor. Lieutenant Taber? How about it? Have you ever gotten dressed in your stateroom, the hatch closed, with another male officer present?"

Taber glared at Bashir. "I'm sure I have."

"Would you regard it as reasonable to assume you had a physical relationship with that other officer because of that fact?"

"No."

"These other occasions you testified to, when you say you saw Lieutenant Schmidt and Lieutenant Shen touching each other, what kind of touches? Where?"

"I really don't—"

"On the arm?"

"Yes."

"The hand?"

"Uh, yes."

"Shoulder?"

"Maybe. I don't—"

"Did you ever see them touching each other *inappropriately*? Touching each other on any part of their anatomy which was improper in public?"

"I... not directly."

"Not directly. I see." Lieutenant Bashir leaned back, still eyeing Lieutenant Taber. "Lieutenant, wouldn't you agree that any assumption that Lieutenant Shen and Lieutenant Schmidt had an inappropriate physical or emotional relationship based upon your testimony would be absurd, and that in fact your own assumptions are grounded in little more than anger at your own rejection by both women and your own sexual fantasies?"

"Objection!"

Before an obviously angry McMasters could speak, Lieutenant Bashir stepped back. "I withdraw the question, Your Honor. My apologies to the court."

McMasters didn't seem mollified by the apology. "Pull something like that again, Lieutenant Bashir, and you'll be held in contempt. The members of the court are directed to disregard counsel for the defense's last statement. Trial counsel, do you wish to redirect?"

Even from where he sat, Paul could see the contempt in Commander Carr's eyes as she looked at Taber. "No, Your Honor. The government is quite through with this witness."

But Captain Carney leaned forward, his elbows on the members' table, his face intent. "Lieutenant Taber, you started to say something about Lieutenant Schmidt getting engaged?"

Taber, visibly sweating, looked toward Carney and nodded rapidly. "Yes, sir. She got engaged right before we got underway for the ops with the *Michaelson*. To some guy stationed on Franklin."

"Some guy? A male officer?"

"Uh, no, sir. He's some kind of civilian contractor."

"Very interesting, Lieutenant Taber. Thank you. No other questions? Thank you, lieutenant."

Paul tried not to glare at Carney. The captain's thought process was transparent—that Jen and Lieutenant Schmidt had been pursuing some kind of affair, that Schmidt had broken it off to become engaged to a man, and Jen had been jealous. The stuff of bad movies. *Commander Carr couldn't stomach that. She cut off Taber before he could really bring it out. But Carney did it, anyway.*

Lieutenant Taber left, not looking to either side as he marched rapidly out of the courtroom. Commander Carr stood as soon as Taber had left. "The prosecution rests."

"Very well. Lieutenant Bashir, do you wish to make any motions?"

"No, Your Honor."

McMasters rapped sharply with his gavel. "This court-martial is closed. It will reconvene at 1000 tomorrow morning for the presentation of evidence by the defense. In this courtroom."

Once again everyone waited, standing while the judge and members of the court left through their respective doors. Jen stood at attention the entire time, moving only after the masters-at-arms came to stand beside her in order to escort her back to the brig. She also didn't look at anyone as she left the courtroom.

Paul waited while Lieutenant Bashir made some notes on his data pad. "I never thought Commander Carr would do something like that."

Bashir glanced at him. "Like what? That stuff at the end?"

"Yes. I mean, it's crap."

"Almost certainly. But the government had to find some motivation for what they allege Lieutenant Shen did."

"But they didn't prove anything! That little bastard Taber just described totally innocuous things and implied there was something improper about them."

"Right." Bashir shook his head. "Unfortunately, in this case all the government has to do is introduce a reasonable level of belief in the members' minds that something was going on. I warned Jen about this. I told her a military judge would be far less likely to be swayed by innuendo. But she insisted on being tried by members, because she was sure they'd stand with a fellow officer."

Paul sagged back into his seat. "But why would Commander Carr stoop to that kind of thing?"

"Because she's got a job to do, Paul." Bashir pointed toward the trial counsel's table. "She's in charge of prosecuting this case. Carr's in charge of bringing to justice someone she believes murdered sixty-one of her shipmates. I disagree, obviously. But that's why Commander Carr would do that."

Paul nodded, feeling numb. *Carr really believes Jen must be guilty, doesn't she? Carr wouldn't do this if she didn't believe that, didn't believe that she was legally right to introduce something like Taber's garbage. Even if I could tell Carr hated having to do it.*

"If it's any consolation," Bashir added, "she pulled her punches."

"What?"

"You heard me. Carr pulled her punches. She had to sow suspicion in the minds of the members of the court that Lieutenant Shen had engaged in improper relationships with other officers on the *Maury*. She did that. But if she'd really gone after the accusations it would've looked a lot more damning."

"How?"

"Oh, take that little sleaze Taber. The Alex Carr I know would've checked up more on him, found out if he had ulterior motives for his little fairy tale about Shen and Schmidt. She didn't. Consciously or subconsciously she left me an opening to discredit Taber. She also could've raised the issue of hearsay on those statements about his asking the ladies for dates. It wouldn't have held up because my sources personally witnessed the events, but still..."

Paul looked over to where Carr was reading something at the trial counsel's table. "She hasn't looked happy. Not like when she was trying to get Silver convicted."

"She's got a job to do, Paul. She's doing it. She thinks it's necessary. But, like you say, she's not loving it this time." Bashir sighed. "Unfortunately, even when she's not loving it, Alex Carr is one tough opponent."

"It doesn't help that Captain Carney's obviously made up his mind already."

"You've picked up on that, eh? No. It doesn't help. But he's allowed to do that. He's not allowed to order the other members of the court how to vote, but he can exercise his seniority as president of the members." Lieutenant Bashir looked toward the now-vacant table used by the members of the court, his jaw tight.

Paul just nodded, knowing what Bashir was probably thinking. Captain Carney had decided what decision he thought the Navy wanted, so Captain Carney was going to do what he could to make sure that decision was reached. That way, the Navy would hopefully be grateful to Captain Carney, and it never hurt to have the Navy grateful when the next promotion board came up. *I hope he's wrong. I hope the Navy as an institution isn't pushing for Jen's conviction regardless of whatever the truth might be. I can't believe it. I can't believe that some of the people involved in this, people like Alex Carr, would be part of that kind of thing. Like Mom said. There's a lot of good people in the Navy. People who surely wouldn't stand for that.*

"It'd be a lot simpler if it was a big conspiracy, wouldn't it?" Paul stated aloud.

Bashir gave him a skeptical look. "Why?"

"Something that big, somebody'd talk, right? Somebody would refuse to play along."

"I like to think so." Bashir shook his head. "But it doesn't feel like a grand conspiracy to me. The senior people I've seen pushing for this court-martial seem to think Lieutenant Shen's guilty. That's why they're pushing it." He laughed bitterly. "It'd be a lot simpler if they didn't believe it. Then you and I and Lieutenant Shen wouldn't be here." Bashir paused, then reached into his pocket and offered Paul a data coin. "You asked me to look into SEERS. This is everything the government provided."

Paul took the coin gingerly. "Everything the government provided? Nothing else?"

"There isn't supposed to be anything else, Paul. I asked for all material pertaining to SEERS. The government's obligated to provide that if I ask for it and it's reasonably available. When Commander Carr gave me this she said it's the whole ball of wax and she's looked at it all. If Alex Carr says it's everything, then it's everything, and if she says she's looked at it, then she's looked at it. Now here it is for you to look at. Development, testing, evaluation, the works. I've skimmed it and I don't know how they managed to pack so much stuff into one data coin."

"You've just skimmed it?"

Bashir raised one eyebrow at Paul. "Don't sound so shocked. I went through all the executive summaries, did global searches for certain words and phrases, and so on. I'll be frank. I didn't find anything that contradicted what Admiral Hidalgo said. But if you want to dig into it, be my guest. I'd really appreciate input from a line officer, especially one as motivated as you are."

"You'll get it." Paul put the coin away carefully. *Good thing I'm on leave. If this contains all the material Bashir says it does then I'll take a long time to go through it. And there's only so much time somebody like Colleen can give me for it because she's got her own job to do.* "Thank you, sir. I'm sorry I..."

"Thought I wasn't working hard enough for Ms. Shen? I'm doing all I can. Let me know if you find anything in there. As soon as you can."

Paul rushed back to the *Michaelson*, where Colleen Kilgary copied the coin and promised to look at it even as she couldn't help casting a despairing glance at the lengthy "to-do" list visible on her display. Sitting down in his own stateroom, Paul began scrolling through documents, trying not be overwhelmed by the sheer mass of material on the disc. Just the listing of document titles seemed to go on forever. *Now I know why Bashir just went to summaries and did word searches. There's months of work in here. Why can't he get the court-martial suspended until we have time to go through this in detail?* Even as he framed the question to himself, Paul saw the probable answer in his own search results. Every reference to "failure" or other likely keywords was in the context of avoidance or ensuring it couldn't happen. *Because we need to find some indication in this mass of charts, graphs, data and words that SEERS could've caused or contributed to what happened. And none of it's saying that.*

Paul kept going, nonetheless, until he realized he wasn't actually absorbing what he read anymore. His numbed brain just slid over the surface of endless pages, all of which seemed to say that SEERS was doing just fine, thank you very much. *Just my luck. The one system I want to be screwed up somehow or other, and it's the* only *system in the Navy that* isn't *screwed up somehow or other.* Something in the back of his head hesitated over that, but the thought dwindled away into nothing before he could grasp it. Paul shut off his display with a muttered curse. *I can't even think. I need a break. Sorry, Jen. Jen... Maybe they'd let me talk to her. Cheer her up a bit, and remotivate me. I can ask.*

* * *

The brig allowed him some time to visit Jen. That surprised Paul at first, until he mentioned it to Sharpe and the master-at-arms nodded knowingly. "They want you to soften her up, sir. Not deliberately. But maybe get her to blurt out something to you, maybe get her thinking about cutting a deal."

While he was waiting for Jen, Paul read the warning posted on the wall of the visitor's room. "All conversations and movements within this compartment are subject to audio and video monitoring at any and all times. Use of this compartment indicates acceptance of these conditions." *I hadn't really noticed that before. I wonder how many prisoners have said something here that they regretted?*

A master-at-arms escorted Jen into the room, checked the door Paul had entered by to ensure it was securely locked, then left through the other door. Jen sat down heavily in the chair opposite Paul. Paul cleared his throat cautiously. "Hi, Jen."

"Hi."

"I, uh..." *Want to cheer you up but hadn't really thought about how I'd do that beyond being here, which doesn't seem to be doing the trick.* "How—" *I'm going to ask how she's doing? What a stupid question.*

Jen looked away from him. "I can't decide whether to be angry or despairing."

"We'll beat this, Jen."

"*We* aren't facing anything. *I* am. Thanks in no small part to your favorite lawyer."

"Commander Carr's doing her job, Jen. It's not fair—"

"*Fair?*" Jen finally looked at him, glaring with anger. "If you're going to bring up fair then what am I doing here?"

"I... I just wanted..."

"It's very convenient, isn't it?"

"What? Convenient?"

"You know what I mean. That hot-shot babe gets me convicted, leaving Paul Sinclair free to fill the role of her part-time boy-toy."

Paul held up his hands in a calming gesture. "Jen, are you serious? You can't really believe—"

"How am I to know what to believe, Paul Sinclair?"

"I would never choose Commander Carr over you. Not for an instant."

"Then why are you defending her? Siding with her even while she drags my reputation through the mud?"

Paul looked down, unable to meet her gaze for a moment. *Look at it from her perspective. She's right.* "I'm sorry. I'm here, I'm at the trial, for you. Not for anyone else."

"Can you believe it? Bad enough I had to sit there while they recited all those names. Names of my friends and co-workers." Her face worked with emotion. "And what could I do? Cry? I couldn't do that. I'm an officer. I have to be strong."

"You're stronger than I believed possible, Jen. I mean that."

"I wish it helped. But I'm sure they're figuring out some way to use that against me. Just like they're using my professional skills against me. How can I defend myself against this? I'm supposed to be able to refute evidence. To strike back at hard facts. But there aren't any. There's just these ghosts, things I can't hit no matter how hard I swing. How do I prove I'm not guilty? Or am I crazy to even ask?"

"You're *not* guilty, Jen. And you're not insane, either."

Jen sank back into the chair, elbows on her knees and her head buried in her hands. "No hard targets to hit. That little son of a bitch Taber. I can't believe he made that stuff up."

"Lieutenant Bashir discredited him."

"No, he didn't! You saw the members!"

"Bashir proved Taber didn't know what he was talking about, that he'd distorted what he testified about, that he had ulterior motives. Jen, I'll tell Bashir that I'll go on the stand and testify for you. That I know you couldn't have had anything improper going on with Schmidt because you couldn't have done that. You're too honest."

Jen smiled sourly. "Honest. That's doubtless another crime on my part."

"Everyone knows Taber was wrong. Nobody'll believe him."

"That's wrong, Paul Sinclair. You know that's wrong. You know what everyone'll be thinking. Sailors. They leave their marriage vows and other commitments at the pier. They sail off and have affairs and patronize hookers, and it's always been that way and always will be that way. You know they'll think that. And even if you *and* Schmidt's guy go up there and swear teary-eyed that she and I were faithful to you two everyone'll just think 'those poor guys. Always the last to know. Don't they know what sailors are like?' You know that's what they'll think, Paul!"

Paul bit his lip as he met Jen's gaze. *Do I deny that? Knowing she's right? I can't see where pretending that I'm oblivious is going to make her feel any better.* "Yeah. I know that."

"How the *hell* do I prove I *didn't* have an affair with a dead woman? How do I *prove* that?"

"I don't know." Paul let his helpless feelings show. "This isn't how it's supposed to work."

"Oh, that makes me feel a lot better. Thanks for letting me know that."

"Jen, I'm doing everything I—"

"*Then why am I still here?*"

Paul stared at her, momentarily silent with shock at the way her anger had erupted. Anger obviously directed at him once again. *How do I answer a question like that? I don't know. Maybe that's the only answer that fits now.* "I don't know." Jen leaned forward so she could press her fingertips against her temples. Paul could see the flesh around her nails whitening from the force Jen was using. "I'm there every day, Jen."

She didn't look up. "For me or for her?"

"Her? Her who?"

"Commander Carr." Jen almost spat the name this time.

Paul felt his own anger flaring now. "Jen, for God's sake knock it off. I told you that's nonsense. You know full well—"

"I don't know *anything* anymore, Mr. Sinclair." She finally raised her head to look at him again, but Paul found his own eyes flinching away from the emotions mirrored in Jen's. "I'm fighting for my *life*. And I don't know *why*."

Paul's voice sounded rough to him. "I told you I don't know why either."

"Then you're not doing either of us much damn good, are you?"

He stared straight into her eyes, not believing what he'd heard. "What...? Jen, what're you doing?"

She looked down again, concealing her haunted eyes from Paul once more. "I don't know," she whispered. "Just go away."

"No!"

"Then shut up or something."

"Jen, this isn't like you."

"What do you know what I'm like? What do *I* know what I'm like? Maybe it's all a big illusion, maybe I've always been an awful screw-up, an accident waiting to happen. And I did something or didn't do something and a lot of people who trusted me died. How do I know *that* isn't true?"

"Because it's not!"

"*Then why am I here?*"

"I..."

"You're not helping me. You're not helping *you*. Give it up. Just go away and let me sail off to hell alone."

"I don't want to."

"And I don't care."

"Jen." Paul waited as minutes passed without Jen moving, then finally he stood up slowly. "Okay." *Shouldn't I say something else? What? I understand? How the hell could I understand? I don't even know what the hell's going on.* "I'll see you tomorrow." Jen didn't respond, so Paul left, feeling an emptiness inside only partially filled by his anger at her.

Franklin offered no refuges, no places to hole up alone with his anger. The rent-a-shacks were all tied up, used by people brought in to work on the *Maury* or assist in or provide press coverage of the court-martial. He didn't even dare wander about, knowing that he might run into some press crew looking for a chance to stick a camera in his face. He'd never wanted that, and certainly didn't want it while his anger with Jen was burning so bright. *All I've done for her. All I've tried to do. And she shoves me away. Great. Thanks. You're welcome. And go to hell, too.*

Fortunately, there was always the ship. The *Michaelson* sat securely at her berth, her quarterdeck quiet at this time of the evening. A startled Jack Abacha standing watch on the quarterdeck saluted Paul onboard.

Paul swung in the wardroom door in search of coffee, then tried to swing back out again immediately when he saw Commander Sykes seated at his usual place. Sykes, however, raised a commanding hand and gestured to a seat near him. Paul scowled, but obeyed. "Yes, sir?"

"Ah. 'Yes, sir.' What's the occasion for the formality, young Sinclair?"

"Suppo, I'm sorry, but I'm really not in the mood for a discussion."

"In this case, that may mean you require one." Sykes lost his habitual smile and eyed Paul. "You've been to see Jen Shen."

"Yes, sir."

"It didn't go well."

"Commander Sykes, sir, with all due respect—"

Sykes raised his hand again, cutting off Paul. "Not well at all. Would you be surprised to know I expected this? No, don't turn that unflattering shade of red. It's not really about you and her. It's about what she's trapped in."

Paul took a long, deep breath, trying to calm himself. *Sykes has given me a lot of good advice, and I know he really cares about Jen. I ought to listen to him.* "Suppo, I know what she's trapped in. But why would that make her..."

"Lash out at you? I assume that's what happened?"

"Yes, sir." Paul stared at Sykes. "Do you know what's going on? What?"

"I'm afraid it comes down to two things, Paul. One is what's happening to Jen, and the other is that you haven't fully appreciated the impact of those events upon her."

"Dammit, Suppo, I've been doing just about nothing *but* trying to appreciate what she must feel like!"

Sykes took a drink before replying. "Think about it from Jen's perspective, Paul."

"I've been doing that, Suppo. I understand how awful it must feel to be unjustly accused of such a crime."

"But you haven't fully grasped Jen's feelings." Sykes looked off into the distance for a moment before focusing back on Paul. "Jen's being accused of having done something horrible by people who, so far as she knows, have no reason to persecute her. The entire ponderous machinery of the Navy seems focused on proving she did this awful thing. Why? Why would they accuse her of such a thing? Why work so hard to prove her guilt? Jen wouldn't be human if she didn't fear deep inside that there might be a reason, that she might somehow in some way be guilty."

"Suppo—"

Sykes gestured for silence. "Wait. I'm not saying Jen's guilty. Not at all. I am saying she must in the dark hours of the night wonder why so many are convinced of her guilt. And she must wonder what about her causes them to be so convinced. Why did they charge her with these crimes? Why do they seek to convict her? Somewhere inside her, Jen surely fears there might be some basis for it all. Under such stress, under such accusations, even saints would question themselves. It's common after major traumas like what the *Maury* experienced. Feelings of inadequacy, of failure. Survivor guilt. You've heard of that? Wondering if you could've done *something* to change the outcome."

Paul stared silently at the supply officer for a long moment. "Like I felt after Chief Asher died."

Sykes nodded. "Exactly like that. Magnified sixty-one times. And magnified as well by the criminal charges against her."

"My God." Paul felt an icy knot inside. *After Jen's father finished that investigation into Asher's death he didn't directly blame me, but he laid enough guilt on me for maybe not preventing the fire that I've carried it around ever since. And Jen isn't just being blamed by implication, but directly.* "She's actually wondering if she's really, somehow, guilty. If she deserves what's happening to her."

"Either because of this crime or because of something else she's imagining she's done wrong and this is a cosmic way of balancing the scales. She'd never admit it, Paul. Not Jen. But I'm certain such fears haunt her. Only an insane person wouldn't question their innocence when so many seem intent on proving their guilt."

Paul closed his eyes for a moment, trying to recall the emotions he'd seen in Jen. *He's right. Sykes is saying some of the same things Jen did, but from a different perspective. Jen's scared. Not just scared of being convicted. She's scared of somehow being guilty.* "She's not."

Sykes nodded as if Paul had spoken aloud his entire train of thought. "No. I certainly don't believe so." He sighed and took another drink of coffee. "All we have to do is convince the world of that. And all you have to do as well is ensure Jen knows you remain certain of that, regardless of what else may happen."

"If she needs me to reassure her, then why'd she push me away?" Paul felt his anger rising again at the memory. "I wanted to help and she practically kicked me out the door."

"Jen isn't the sort to ask for help, even when being subjected to the kind of test she's now enduring."

Paul shook his head, looking down at the patterns in the floor. "So she treats me like hell and I'm supposed to ignore it? How can I retain my own self-respect if I let her rip me up? Okay, she's being tested, but if she reacts to it by attacking me, what am I supposed to think?"

"Perhaps, Mr. Sinclair, you should think about the possibility that

Jen's not the only one being tested."

Paul stared at the swirls in a small patch of the floor. *Is it also about me? Isn't that self-centered to even think? No. It's the opposite. It's about whether I'm good enough for her, whether I really believe in Jen, whether I'll really stick with her for better or worse. Even when she's being a psycho-bitch from hell for reasons beyond her control.* His anger faded and he looked up, meeting Commander Sykes' eyes. "You're right. If I don't stick with Jen, I'll be fulfilling her worst fears. I can't let that happen." *If I did... I'd never deserve anything good in my life again. What'd my dad say? "Not if you were worth a damn." He was right, too.*

Sykes waited until he knew Paul was listening again. "I think it's safe to say that right now Jen is believing she doesn't deserve you because of her own faults. Real and imagined. If you go away, it proves she's right about that, doesn't it?"

"Then for once I'm going to prove her wrong and refuse to let her say otherwise."

Sykes smiled. "Good lad. Mind you, if you end up marrying her this may be the last time you get to do that."

"If only I could answer her question, Suppo. Why? Why is this happening to Jen?"

"If we knew the answer to that, I suspect we'd also know how and why the deaths on the *Maury* actually occurred."

"You think the people trying Jen know the real truth?"

Sykes pursed his lips, then took another drink. "Do you believe the people trying Jen would be doing so if they knew she wasn't guilty?"

"No." He thought of Captain Carney. "Oh, some of them. But not all of them. Not even close."

"I'm afraid that may rule out a grand conspiracy. And I confess to having no other ideas, myself."

Paul nodded. "I can't fault you for that. No one's been able to come with other ideas, even Jen and her lawyer. Small wonder she's feeling despair. I just didn't... What am I going to do when you're gone, Suppo? I'm going to miss you."

"Nonsense. Once free of my critical oversight you young officers shall doubtless frolic in wild abandon."

"After the outstanding example you've provided us of minimizing movement during the day? I don't think so."

"Hmmm." Sykes gave Paul an arch look. "I'm not sure that's a compliment. But I'll nonetheless offer you some bonus advice. If you want Jen to feel supported, then support from someone she respects as a professional but thinks personally dislikes her would mean much, I think."

Paul frowned. "Who do you mean?"

Sykes took another drink and smiled. "She Who Must Be Obeyed."

"Commander Herdez?"

"Exactly."

"Does she know you call her that?" Paul asked, laughing despite everything.

"Let's say she tolerates the occasional use of the phrase. From me. I wouldn't recommend it for use by, say, lieutenants junior grade."

"Suppo, I'm not an ensign anymore. I wouldn't do something that stupid."

Sykes smiled again. "Young Mr. Sinclair, I have seen admirals do things which could be characterized as 'that stupid.' Go see Commander Herdez, first thing in the morning."

"Tomorrow's Saturday. They're going ahead with the court-martial but it's not a normal working day."

"Not for most, but as you're aware Commander Herdez is not

normal. You know she'll be in her office, and she'll be there early. Tell her of your worries and see how she responds."

"Yes, sir." Paul paused. "How much does she already know about all this, Suppo?"

"Already know? About what everyone else knows, I suppose."

"She's not getting any inside information?"

Sykes managed to look puzzled. "Inside information? From whom?"

"I can't imagine."

Colleen Kilgary intercepted Paul on his way to his stateroom. "Sorry I hadn't got back to you on that SEERS documentation, Paul."

Paul took in Colleen's haggard appearance and tried to smile reassuringly. "That's okay. It's not like you don't have a lot of other things to do."

"Yeah, but I know how important this is." She made a frustrated gesture. "I've been over it. A lot of it, anyway. I can't find anything concrete in all that garbage about significant problems with SEERS." Colleen stopped to yawn mightily. "Sorry. Anyhow, I did get this vague feeling something's missing."

Paul felt a surge of interest. "Really?"

"It's just vague. There's nothing solid there. Everything looks good. It's just this feeling that there ought to've been more problems with the thing. But it looks like SEERS hit its developmental time line in all the right ways. That's unusual, but not impossible."

Paul nodded to cover up his disappointment. "Nothing's really missing then, that you can tell."

Another extended yawn. "Nope. It's just a feeling that there ought to be some more problems documented on such a big project. You know, engineers have got to be skeptical. But Jen herself said they hadn't run into major problems with SEERS on the *Maury*, right?"

"But, missing..." Paul knew he was grasping at straws. "Could there be something that's being kept from Jen's defense?"

"By who?" Colleen frowned. "Or is it whom? I can never get that straight. Look at the people bringing the case against Jen. I've met Admiral Hidalgo a number of times. He's a bit pompous and certain that he knows everything there is to know, but why would he cover up problems with SEERS? Leaving out any human or professional considerations, it wouldn't help Hidalgo's career any if the engineering plants he was responsible for started blowing up right and left. Or Admiral Silver. Maybe he doesn't like *you*, and maybe his leadership style makes Stalin look like Santa Claus, but deliberately letting something into the fleet that'll tear apart ships?"

Paul nodded again, his head sagging. "I wish I could argue that point, but as far as I know you're right. They wouldn't do this if they had any indications SEERS was dangerous."

"And what you had sure seemed like everything on SEERS."

"The prosecution swears it is, and I honestly don't believe the trial counsel would lie about that."

Colleen spread her hands helplessly. "Then it couldn't have been an accident. That's my professional judgment."

"Damn."

"Paul, I'd lie if I thought it would help Jen. But even a lie has to have credibility. It has to match what people expect. I'm really, really sorry."

"Thanks, Colleen. You've done an awful lot, and I really appreciate it, and I'm sure Jen does, too." *Even though if she saw you right now she'd probably try to tear your head off like she did with me.*

Colleen's small answering smile looked as forced as it certainly was. She staggered off to her own stateroom. Paul reached his, grateful his roommates were either absent or already asleep, and pulled himself up into his bunk. His dreams were full of mazes, all ending in blank walls.

12

"Ma'am, I need your help." Paul glanced at the time. 0700. Three hours left before the court-martial resumed. As Sykes had predicted, Paul had found Herdez in her office.

Commander Herdez kept her own expression noncommittal. "What about, Mr. Sinclair?"

Paul licked his lips, aware he looked as nervous as he felt. Commander Herdez' office ashore looked much as her stateroom on the *Michaelson* had. A few personal mementoes, reminders of her earlier duty assignments, but otherwise sparse and professional. "Ms. Shen, ma'am."

Herdez let regret show. "I'm sorry, Mr. Sinclair."

"You know she couldn't have done it."

"Yes. I was, in fact, approached as a possible member of the court because of my experience on a ship similar to the *Maury*, but informed my superiors I could not render impartial judgment in the matter."

That alone would surprise Jen. She's sure Herdez has been gunning for her from the first minute they met.

"But," Herdez continued, "I'm afraid I know of no concrete information which would exonerate Ms. Shen. I cannot help with that."

"That's not what I'm asking for, ma'am. Lieutenant Shen is..." Paul struggled for the right words. "She's feeling abandoned." *And she'd scream bloody murder if she knew I'd told you that.*

"Not by you, surely."

"No, ma'am. I'm there as much as I possibly can be. But that doesn't seem to help her enough."

"That's understandable, Mr. Sinclair." Commander Herdez seemed slightly amused by Paul's reaction to her words, then sobered. "Your support is a given. It's assumed. Thus it means less to Ms. Shen than it probably should." She fell silent for a moment. "Just as sometimes my own support to the Navy is assumed."

Paul eyed her with amazement. It was the only time he'd heard anything approaching criticism of the Navy from Herdez. "Jen— I mean, Lieutenant Shen, needs more than I can give, ma'am. But she knows how professional you are. She really respects your judgment, even though... uh..."

"Even though Ms. Shen believes I hold her in low regard as an officer and as an individual?" Herdez asked dryly. "Yes. I'm aware of that. You want me to express support for her?"

"Yes, ma'am. Just a message would mean so much, I think."

"It will be more than a message, Mr. Sinclair. Whatever the cause of the *Maury*'s incident, my professional and personal judgment tells me Ms. Shen could not have been responsible. For whatever it is worth, I will ensure she knows that."

"Thank you, ma'am. Thank you." Paul made to rise, but Herdez waved him back to his seat.

"How are you doing on the *Michaelson*, Mr. Sinclair?"

As if you didn't know. I bet Commander Sykes sends you daily updates. "Pretty good, ma'am. There's still a great deal to learn, but I'm getting there."

"No open space warfare officer pin as of yet, though."

Paul hoped he wasn't flushing with embarrassment. "Not yet, ma'am. Within the next few months though, I think."

"Good. It still appears I will receive my own command when I leave this assignment. New construction perhaps. Would you be interested in serving on her?"

Oh, wow. New construction. A bright, shiny new ship with all the latest stuff on it. But— "When would that be, ma'am?"

"About a year and a half."

"I should be on shore duty, then, ma'am. In the middle of my tour of duty."

"It could be truncated, Mr. Sinclair."

Yeah. It could be. Instead of having some nice shore job for a couple of years I could go back to spaceship duty early. No way. But Herdez is asking me. What a compliment. Especially from an officer like her. What would Jen say? She'd be real unhappy. Wouldn't she? We don't know where we'll be serving next. Maybe it wouldn't matter, if one of us was stationed on Persephone and the other had duty on one of the submerged coastal platforms. Then we'd be separated a lot worse than if I was on ship duty again. I don't know. How can I know now?

Herdez nodded as if Paul had said something out loud. "I understand, Mr. Sinclair. It's hard to make a commitment at this point in time. Please keep it in mind, however. When does the court-martial convene?"

"Ten-hundred, ma'am."

"Ten-hundred?" Herdez let some exasperation show. By ten

hundred, Paul knew, she expected anyone to have put in half a day's work already. Even if it was a Saturday. "Pleasant working hours, indeed. I'm sure I can arrange something for Ms. Shen prior to that late hour of the day."

Paul rose again at the implied dismissal. "Thank you, ma'am."

From Herdez' office in the fleet staff complex, Paul moved as fast as he reasonably could to reach the courtroom. He was very early, of course, but preferred that to sitting somewhere else alone with his worries and fears.

Lieutenant Bashir arrived well after Paul but still fairly early. "Can't chat, Mr. Sinclair. I've got some preps."

"I understand. A lot of witnesses, I hope."

Bashir glanced at Paul. "Not exactly." Then he bent to his work, leaving Paul to ponder what Bashir's words might mean.

The room gradually filled. The ranks of high-level spectators seemed much thinner this morning. Paul looked around, not seeing nearly the same number of admirals and captains. *They've already seen what they wanted to see, the evidence against Jen. They're not interested in whatever she says in her defense. No. That's not entirely fair. The ones who're here are obviously interested, and I don't know how many yesterday were drawn by the chance to see and hear Captain Halis.*

A pause in sound told Paul that Jen had arrived. Once again she came up the aisle, her master-at-arms escorts moving in tandem. As she reached the front of the courtroom she saw Paul and he actually saw her stumble slightly in reaction. Then she had moved on to stand at the defense table.

Jen and Bashir conferred quietly for several minutes. Then she turned so she could just see Paul out of the corner of her eye. "I didn't think you'd be here," she murmured so softly he barely heard it.

He tried to answer at the same volume but still give his reply force. "I'll *always* be here, Jen."

Jen's jaw quivered, but she just nodded. Then someone came to stand at the seat next to Paul's and Jen's face went rigid again. He looked over, seeing Commander Herdez, who was gazing steadily at Jen. Herdez inclined her head slightly toward Jen in greeting, then sat with calm deliberation in the seat next to Paul, publicly and unmistakably placing herself in support of Lieutenant Shen.

"Ms. Shen," she murmured. "Do your best today. Your best is exceptional."

Jen's fixed expression altered a bit as she stared back at Herdez. Paul could see disbelief there. He spoke just loudly enough for Commander Herdez to hear. "Thank you, ma'am."

Herdez acknowledged his words with a small gesture.

Then the bailiff was at the front of the courtroom again, eyeing the spectators. She repeated her instructions for the benefit of those who might not have heard them the day before, then went to notify the judge. "All rise."

McMasters took a moment to look at the defense table, his expression impossible for Paul to read, then he gestured to Lieutenant Bashir. "Proceed."

"The defense calls as its first witness Lieutenant Harold Falco, United States Navy."

Paul watched Falco stride to the witness stand. Despite his relatively junior rank, he carried enough age on him to make it obvious he must have had extensive enlisted service before being commissioned. Falco sat and stared out across the courtroom, his manner almost defiant.

Lieutenant Bashir approached the witness. "Lieutenant Falco.

What is your current duty assignment?"

Falco shifted his seat as he answered. "Assistant plans supervisor, Franklin Naval Shipyard."

"What does that job entail?"

Lieutenant Falco shrugged. "A lot of things. But they all have to do with making sure jobs in the shipyard are well planned and well executed."

"Jobs on US Navy ships, you mean?"

"Usually, yes."

"Are you familiar with the contents of the investigation into the damage suffered by the USS *Maury* on 21 February of this year?"

"Yeah." Falco nodded brusquely. "That's required reading, in my line of work."

Bashir turned to face toward the members of the court-martial. "Before I go any further, Lieutenant Falco, would you describe your experience in the field of engineering?"

"Certainly. I enlisted as a space systems machinist mate. Served on one research platform and on the *Carpenter*. When I reached petty officer second class the Navy wanted fewer machinist mates and more space system electricians, so I passed all the tests and switched rates. Worked on system upgrades for the *Glenn*, the *Carpenter*, the *Grissom* and a lot of other old ships. Then Admiral Genghis Conner Michaelson asked for me to help set up Franklin. I was a chief petty officer by then. A couple years later I applied for a commission. Since then I've served on the *Mahan* and in the shipyard. Two back-to-back tours in the shipyard, actually, because they asked me to stay."

Paul tried not to look impressed. The resume Falco had recited covered much of the actual engineering involved in the history of the US naval space effort. He couldn't tell if the members of the court were also impressed, as all maintained poker faces.

Lieutenant Bashir nodded to acknowledge Falco's words. "Thank you. Now, as an extremely experienced engineer, do you agree with the conclusions of the investigation into the damage suffered by the USS *Maury* on 21 February?"

"No."

A rustle of interest followed Falco's very brief reply.

Bashir nodded again. "Why not, lieutenant?"

Falco leaned forward in his seat. "Because they made too many assumptions that stuff would work as designed. I'm here, every engineer in the space fleet is up here, because stuff doesn't always work as designed. Any engineer with an ounce of experience could tell you that."

Bashir walked slightly to one side, making Falco turn also so he faced the members of the court better. "You don't agree that an accidental cause for the *Maury*'s damage was impossible?"

"No. I don't. That's garbage. You can try to make stuff work perfect and you can try to make it sailor-proof and you can try to make it safe, but nothing is one-hundred-percent."

Bashir faced Falco squarely, speaking in a slightly louder voice to emphasize his next words. "Then, as probably the most experienced naval engineer in space, you do not believe sabotage is the only possible explanation for what happened to the *Maury*?"

"No, I don't."

"As an experienced engineer, who would you send to investigate a piece of equipment which was giving you problems?"

Falco grinned. "Whoever was best qualified to find out what I wanted to know. Maybe that's a new seaman. Or maybe that's my most senior engineer. It depends."

"Would you blame the only surviving officer for an accident based solely on the fact that she by chance survived?"

"Objection." Commander Carr gave Bashir a tired look. "Counsel for the defense is leading the witness and making prejudicial statements."

"Sustained." McMasters leveled his gavel at Bashir. "That's two, lieutenant. Make it three and you'll regret it."

"Yes, Your Honor. No more questions at this time."

Commander Carr approached Falco with a calm demeanor that worried Paul. *She seems too confident. What does she know about this guy?*

"Lieutenant Falco, when you said you switched ratings from machinist to electrician, isn't it true that you'd failed to advance three times running to machinist mate first class even though there was a shortage of such machinists?"

Falco's mouth twisted in a stubborn expression. "People weren't advancing in that rate. That happens sometimes."

"And when you said Admiral Michaelson asked 'for you', didn't you mean he assigned your entire unit to the construction of Franklin?"

"He knew I was part of the unit."

"Lieutenant Falco, you were commissioned as an ensign nine years ago. Normal promotion periods should have you a lieutenant commander by now. Can you explain why you haven't made rank?"

Lieutenant Bashir stood up. "Objection, Your Honor. The trial counsel is harassing the witness."

McMasters shook his head. "The trial counsel is asking legitimate questions, lieutenant. Overruled. Proceed, Commander Carr."

"Thank you, Your Honor." Carr turned back to Falco, who was now openly glowering at her. "Lieutenant?"

"I don't always rub people the right way, commander. I may not be the most diplomatic man in the Navy but by God I know my job!"

"Why were you asked to do back-to-back tours at the Franklin Naval Shipyard, Lieutenant Falco?"

"Because they needed me!"

Carr consulted her data pad. "Do you want me to quote from the recommendation of your superior, Lieutenant Falco?"

Falco flushed. "I told you I rub people the wrong way, sometimes. That b— excuse me, my superior didn't know her job and wanted me to stay so I could cover for her."

"Didn't she actually say, in a memo endorsed by each of your superiors, that you needed to be closely supervised and were best held in that position at Franklin until you could be forced to retire next year?" Falco just glared at Carr. "Lieutenant?"

"I don't know what that memo said. I don't know what my superiors said. None of them know half what they should know to do their jobs right!"

This time, Paul tried not to let his despair show. *Oh, great. Falco's a blustering braggart. His credibility just got shredded.* Paul looked toward Lieutenant Bashir, who had the expression of a gambler who had just failed to draw to an inside straight.

Commander Carr audibly sighed. "Lieutenant Falco, are you an expert on engineering systems on *Mahan*-Class warships?"

"I'm as expert as anybody!"

"Lieutenant Falco, you're under oath. What do you believe qualifies you as an expert on the engineering systems on *Mahan*-Class warships?"

Falco stabbed his forefinger at her, his entire face now red. "I know engineering! It's all the same. It doesn't change."

Carr waited for several seconds after Falco finished, as if waiting for him to continue. "That's all, lieutenant? General knowledge of engineering? That's make you a better expert on the engineering systems on the *Maury* than, say, Rear Admiral Hidalgo, the fleet engineering staff officer?"

Falco slumped back, his face still red. "Practical experience. Yes. Hell, yes. I've worked on all that stuff." He held up his hands. "I've got calluses from working on it! Not a bunch of college courses and theory and garbage, but on-the-deck working experience!"

"I see." Carr's tone carried a dismissive meaning that penetrated Falco's anger and made him glare even more angrily. Commander Carr eyed him a moment longer, then shook her head slowly. "I have no further questions for this witness."

Bashir shook his head. "No redirect."

Paul thought he could read Bashir's mind. *Just get that idiot off of the witness stand before he does more damage to the credibility of the defense case. Why'd Bashir choose him for a witness, anyway? Why not somebody else?* He felt a sick sensation in his stomach not unlike what happened when the main drives shut off. *Maybe there wasn't somebody else. Maybe Falco was all Bashir could find willing to testify that the investigation was wrong.*

Captain Carney had a smile on his face, but it wasn't a pleasant smile. "Lieutenant Falco, are you *always* right and your superiors *always* wrong?"

Falco sat up straight again. "It usually seems to work out that way, yes, sir."

Paul barely restrained himself from slapping his forehead. *You idiot. You didn't even recognize the sarcasm in Carney's question.*

Carney nodded. "I kind of thought you'd say that, lieutenant. Any more questions for Lieutenant Falco?" This time, at least, the rest of the officers on the court-martial didn't need to be intimidated. All shook their heads with varying expressions of amusement or annoyance. "Thank you, lieutenant."

Falco looked around as if unsure what to do now. The bailiff gestured him toward the main door of the courtroom and Falco walked out, his face and neck still red with anger.

Lieutenant Bashir stood again. "The defense calls as its next witness Mr. Victor Zimmer."

Zimmer wasn't really out of shape, but in a courtroom full of officers and enlisted personnel who were required to meet rigorous standards for weight and fitness, the civilian looked a bit chunky. Unlike the military witnesses, he didn't march up to the witness stand, but almost seemed to stroll. Paul remembered the suggestion about using his brother David as a lawyer for Jen. *He'd look like that, too. Out of place. As far as I know, David's a fine enough lawyer, but he'd be a fish out of water up here.*

"Mr. Zimmer." Bashir smiled encouragingly. "What is your current position?"

Zimmer ducked his head and smiled back as he answered. "Team supervisor, Franklin Naval Shipyard."

"Did you work on the USS *Maury* during her recent overhaul?"

"Yes, sir. I certainly did." Zimmer nodded firmly. "Shift on and shift off for months. There's not all that much to do up here but work, so we usually work shift on and shift off."

"Yes, Mr. Zimmer. What can you tell us about the work you observed during that time?"

"Oh, we had some problems. Yeah. Drugs. Booze from local stills. Sloppy work. You name it."

Paul wanted to believe Zimmer, but at the same time he found his testimony a little too good. *How could all that have been missed by the people overseeing the work on the* Maury? *And Jen never said anything to me about the work being exceptionally sloppy.* He looked at her, but Jen's face wasn't revealing anything.

Bashir leaned closer as he pressed Zimmer. "Miswiring?"

"Sure."

"Safety rules ignored?"

"All the time."

"Work not done according to specifications?"

"Yeah."

"Do you have any estimate as to what the combined effect of all this on the engineering systems of the *Maury* would be?"

Paul looked toward Carr, expecting her to object, but she simply watched Zimmer.

Zimmer shook his head with a sorrowful expression. "Bad. I mean, I don't know how bad. But it wouldn't work like it should. No, sirree."

Bashir paused, then nodded. "Thank you, Mr. Zimmer. No more questions."

Commander Carr once again rose as if tired, staying behind the trial counsel's table. "Mr. Zimmer, how much time have you spent actually working at Franklin Naval Shipyard?"

"Uh, lessee, came up in, uh, September, about."

"Six months?"

"Well, I didn't start for a few weeks 'cause of some paperwork issues—"

"Five months."

"About. Yes."

"What is your primary area of work?"

"Excuse me?"

Commander Carr bent her head for a moment, then looked at Zimmer again. "What do you work on at Franklin Naval Shipyard?"

"Ships!" Zimmer looked around at the reaction to his answer, then his face cleared. "Oh, you mean like, exactly, right? I'm a multi-system connectivity specialist."

Carr nodded. "That means you run cables through the ship, right, Mr. Zimmer? Fiber optic, electrical, and other cables?"

"Right."

"Did you file any reports on this miswiring and safety violations and other problems you say you observed?"

"Uh, well, now, I talked to some folks about it."

"Did you file any formal reports?"

"Uh, no."

"How do you explain the fact that the records on the *Maury*'s overhaul at the shipyard show the work on her passed quality assurance inspections at every stage?"

"I guess they missed some stuff."

"How do you explain the fact that the *Maury*'s crew did not complain of the conditions you say were easily visible?"

"I dunno."

Commander Carr looked down at her table and shook her head again. "No more questions."

McMasters gave Lieutenant Bashir a questioning look. Bashir shook his head. The judge turned toward the members. Captain Carney, smiling the same way he had with Lieutenant Falco, shook his head. "The witness is excused."

Bashir had his head bent as Jen whispered to him with a fierceness that could be easily seen. He shook his head. She whispered again, her face stern. Bashir nodded and stood. "Your

Honor, the defendant wishes to testify on her own behalf."

McMasters seemed nonplussed for a moment. "You're kind of rushing things, aren't you, lieutenant? If Lieutenant Shen wishes to make a sworn statement during that portion of the trial, she's free to do so."

"Your Honor, Lieutenant Shen wishes to testify as a sworn witness in her own defense."

The judge bent a stern look on Jen. "Lieutenant Shen, I'd normally be giving these instructions a bit later in the trial, but I'll give them now to ensure you understand your rights. You have the right to make a statement. Included in your right to present evidence are the rights you have to testify under oath, to make an unsworn statement, or to remain silent. If you testify, you may be cross-examined by the trial counsel or questioned by me and the members. If you decide to make an unsworn statement you may not be cross-examined by the trial counsel or questioned by me or the members. You may make an unsworn statement orally or in writing, personally, or through your counsel, or you may use a combination of these ways. If you decide to exercise your right to remain silent, that cannot be held against you in any way. Do you understand your rights?"

Jen stood to attention and nodded. "I understand, Your Honor."

"And you still wish to testify at this time under oath?"

"I do, Your Honor."

Judge McMasters made a bemused gesture. "Very well, Lieutenant Shen. You may proceed."

As Jen walked to the witness stand, her movements carefully controlled, Paul finally realized the implications of what was happening. *Those were the only two witnesses Bashir could turn up, and they were both really weak. He couldn't find any real experts to testify for Jen. He couldn't find technical evidence to exonerate her. So now it's all up to Jen to defend herself, to try to convince the members of the court what I already know is true, that all the experts are wrong.*

Jen reached the witness stand and turned to face the courtroom. She slowly raised her right hand for the bailiff to swear her in. "Do you, Lieutenant Junior Grade Jenevieve Diana Shen, swear to tell the truth, the whole truth, and nothing but the truth, so help you God?"

"I do." Jen sat, her back perfectly straight, her eyes scanning the courtroom before settling on the members of the court. Paul grimaced at her voice, so controlled and unemotional that it sounded almost robotic. *But what else can she do? How else can she speak that wouldn't also look bad? Emotional is bad. Unemotional is bad. She just has to be neither emotional or unemotional. One more trap for her in this court-martial.*

Lieutenant Bashir stood before her. "Lieutenant Shen, please describe in your words what happened onboard USS *Maury* on 21 February."

She took a deep breath. "The engineering system on USS *Maury* had been displaying minor but erratic problems since we had come out of overhaul. Commander Juko told Lieutenant Schmidt and me that he was getting increasingly frustrated trying to deal with the problems. While each problem was individually minor, Commander Juko told us that he was concerned they might indicate some underlying problem that could prove more serious."

Paul glanced over at Commander Carr, who was listening intently and taking notes, but not revealing any reaction.

Jen swallowed and took another breath. "On the afternoon in question, we had just deactivated our anti-detection systems. That caused some fluctuations in power loads. Most of them seemed to be dealt with, but the after power coupling kept saying it was overloading and then immediately saying it wasn't. Up, down. Up, down. We couldn't figure out what the problem was by remote readings. I suggested sending one of our petty officers to check out the coupling in person. Commander Juko instead ordered me to go check it. He told me he wanted to be sure we could figure out what the problem was."

Another pause, another breath. "I headed aft. I'd just cleared the after survival bulkhead when a tremendous shock shook the ship. I was hurled against the nearest bulkhead. When my head cleared, I could see the survival bulkhead had been badly damaged and the area I was in was decompressing. I accessed the nearest survival locker. Many of the suits had been damaged by fragments from the explosion, but I found an intact one. After donning it, I tried to open the hatch leading forward. It was jammed solid. Within moments of discovering this, enlisted personnel began entering the same area I was in, trying to find out what had happened and seeking safety. Since we couldn't patch the survival bulkhead with the means available to us, we salvaged as many intact survival suits as we could and headed farther aft in search of undamaged compartments."

Jen paused. "We initially followed instructions to wait for rescue, but without enough survival suits we determined that would result in the death of many of the personnel. So I took an enlisted crew member and proceeded forward again, attempting to make our way past the survival bulkhead in hopes of contacting the rest of the ship. When we finally found a route into the area where... where... the after engineering compartment had been, we encountered a few members of the crew conducting emergency repairs.

"At no time did I take any action which could have caused the destruction of the engineering compartments on my ship. I did nothing which could have led to the deaths of so many of my shipmates, many of whom... whom... were my friends. I don't know why anyone, let alone me, would have wanted to harm them. I do not know what caused the events of 21 February. I do know I had nothing to do with them."

Jen stopped speaking and abruptly looked straight at Lieutenant Bashir, unable to conceal her nervousness. Bashir smiled reassuringly. "Lieutenant Shen, when you said 'we' undertook various actions to ensure the safety and survival of the personnel in the after portion of the Maury, didn't you actually mean *you* did those things?"

"I was the senior line officer present, lieutenant. I had the responsibility to take command and order such actions as necessary given the situation in which we found ourselves."

"Then you saved them. By your quick and effective actions. You saved twenty-one sailors."

Jen swallowed again, then nodded. "I... did what I was supposed to do."

"What was your reaction when you learned the extent of what had happened to the USS *Maury*?"

She visibly paled at the question. "I..."

"I'm sorry, Lieutenant Shen. Is it fair to say you were grief-stricken?"

"Yes."

"Horrified?"

"Yes."

"What was your reaction when you learned you would be charged with causing those events?"

Jen's mouth worked for a moment before she answered. "Disbelief."

"Do you know of any reason why you in particular should be held responsible for what happened?"

"As God is my witness, no."

"I'll ask this directly, Lieutenant Shen. Did you do anything, either any act of commission or omission, on or before 21 February, which in any way could have contributed to the destruction of the engineering compartments on the USS *Maury*?"

"I did not. I am offering sworn testimony to emphasize that I have nothing to hide. I did not commit the crimes of which I am accused. I could not."

Lieutenant Bashir nodded, then faced Commander Carr with a challenging expression. "Your witness, ma'am."

Judge McMasters exhaled heavily, then looked toward Carr as well. "Does the trial counsel wish to cross-examine the defendant?"

Paul looked over at the trial counsel's table. Commander Carr had her head bent as she massaged her face with both hands. Lowering her hands and raising her head, Carr stood slowly, focused on Jen, and began walking toward her. Jen's eyes flicked toward Paul, her face betraying no emotion now.

Carr stopped before Jen and began speaking in a quiet but clear voice. "Lieutenant Shen, you've just testified to several things. You testified that Commander Juko, the chief engineer of the USS *Maury*, had stated concerns regarding the engineering system on the ship. Do you have any witnesses to this?"

"Lieutenant Schmidt, Ensign Guerrero, chief—"

"Any *living* witnesses, lieutenant?" Carr interrupted. "Anyone who can come to this stand or provide a statement supporting your testimony?"

Jen shook head, eyeing Carr defiantly. "No. They're all dead."

"Do you have any documentary evidence?"

"No. Everything was destroyed."

"You testified that the after power coupling was giving contradictory signals. Do you have any living witnesses to this?"

"No."

"No documentary evidence?"

"No."

"You testified that Commander Juko personally ordered you to go aft and investigate the power coupling. Are there any living witnesses who can corroborate this?"

"No."

"Any documentary evidence?"

"No."

Commander Carr looked downward, then back up. "What did you find at the after power coupling?"

"I never got to it."

"Are you aware that the investigation into the incident could find nothing wrong with the power coupling which was not clearly attributable to the shock of the explosions which the *Maury* suffered?"

Jen's eyes were wide now, but she kept her gaze steady. "I have been told that."

"Can you explain why the investigation found that there was nothing wrong with the power coupling when you claim to have been ordered to investigate problems with it?"

"No. Commander Juko told me to check it."

"We can't ask Commander Juko to confirm that, can we, Lieutenant Shen?"

Jen's jaw tightened spasmodically. After a few seconds she managed to answer. "No."

"How do you explain the fact that you reached safety from the explosions just moments before they destroyed the engineering compartments on the USS *Maury*?"

"I..." Jen stared at Paul for a moment.

I remember, Jen. You asked me "why". I couldn't tell you. How can anyone know the answer to that?

"I..." Jen swallowed again. "I don't know."

"You don't know?"

"I don't know why the explosions happened then and not five seconds earlier!"

Carr nodded, her own expression momentarily shifting in a way Paul couldn't decipher. "Thank you, Lieutenant Shen. Then you cannot offer any evidence to substantiate your account of events or any explanation as to how you happened to survive something which killed all of your co-workers?"

Paul almost flinched from the look in Jen's eyes as she stared at Commander Carr. *Now I really know what "if looks could kill" means.*

But Jen just shook her head. "Only my word as an officer."

"Thank you, Ms. Shen. What were your relationships with the other personnel in engineering on the *Maury*?"

"I... fine. Not perfect. Good working relationships."

"That's it? Nothing closer with anyone?"

"No!"

"Not with your superior, Commander Juko? Not with Lieutenant Schmidt?"

"*No!* That earlier testimony from Lieutenant Taber was bu— totally unsubstantiated."

Carr lowered her head again. From his angle, Paul could see her biting her lip, but when she raised her head Carr's face was composed. "Lieutenant Shen, have you ever had a physical relationship with another officer assigned to the same ship?"

Paul felt his throat tightening so much he couldn't breath. Jen's face had frozen. A long moment passed. Jen didn't look at him again, even for an instant. *She did have one. With me. Only after we both knew she was leaving the ship within a few days. But still, she had one. With me. And now she has to decide whether to lie about that. Under oath. But if she doesn't lie about it, it'll look bad.*

How did Carr find out? I never even hinted at it. Who else knew? Kris Denaldo wouldn't have— Paul's eyes jerked involuntarily over toward Commander Herdez. *Herdez knew. As our XO back then.*

Even though she didn't return Paul's stare, Herdez moved her head back and forth slightly in a single, firm denial.

"Objection!" Lieutenant Bashir was either angry or very convincingly faking it. "The trial counsel is introducing issues which were not part of the defendant's sworn statement."

Carr shook her head. "Your Honor, the defendant made statements as to her relationships with others on the *Maury*. This is an elaboration on that."

"Your Honor, there is—"

Bashir subsided as McMasters held up one hand. "I'm sorry, lieutenant. But Lieutenant Shen did address the issue when she described her relationships with her shipmates and when she made the very general statement that she knew of no reason why she'd want to harm her shipmates. That opens the matter for cross-examination by the trial counsel. Objection overruled. Proceed, Commander Carr."

"Lieutenant Shen?" Commander Carr leaned a little closer. "Did you understand the question? Do I need to repeat it?"

Jen closed her eyes for a moment, then opened them with every appearance of calm. "Yes, ma'am."

"And what is your answer?"

"Yes, ma'am."

Carr kept her eyes on Jen even though she seemed to be addressing the entire courtroom now. "You've had physical relationships in the past with officers assigned to the same ship."

"*No*, ma'am. I had *a* physical relationship with *an* officer during a period of six days in which we were still assigned to the same ship. That is the *only* time such a thing has ever occurred and it wouldn't have happened then if I hadn't been leaving the ship in the very immediate future."

"But, lieutenant, by your own admission, it is not something you'd *never* consider. Not something you'd *never* do. Can you disagree with what I'm saying?"

Jen looked as if she were choking but her voice was clear. "No, I cannot. But I swear I had no such relationship on the *Maury* with anyone."

Commander Carr watched Jen for a long moment, then turned away. "No further questions."

Lieutenant Bashir stood again. "Lieutenant Shen, let's get this out in the open. Did you have any personal reasons to dislike or even hate any members of the *Maury*'s crew, officer or enlisted?"

"Not that much, no."

"Did you want even any single one of them dead?"

"No. They were normal working relationships. I didn't *hate* anyone on the ship."

"Did you have any *reason* to want any of them dead?"

"No."

"Thank you, Lieutenant Shen."

Judge McMasters gestured toward the members of the court. "Captain Carney, do the members of the court wish to question Lieutenant Junior Grade Shen regarding her testimony?"

Captain Carney frowned and looked to either side. "I, um, what else can we ask?"

Lieutenant Kalin looked beseechingly toward Jen, ignoring Carney. "Lieutenant Shen, can you provide us with any alternate explanation for what happened to the USS *Maury*?"

Jen stared back, then shook her head. "No, ma'am."

"You were *there*. You can't provide any other possible cause?"

"I don't know of one, ma'am."

"Do you agree with the expert witnesses offered by the trial counsel that it should've been impossible for that engineering equipment to fail catastrophically by accident?"

"I... as far as I know that is correct, ma'am."

"You can't offer *any* alternative explanation?"

"I don't *know* of any specific alternative explanation. It had to have been an accident but I don't *know* how it happened."

"Lieutenant Shen, you're hanging yourself!"

McMasters frowned but before he could say anything Captain Carney had interrupted, speaking sternly. "Lieutenant Kalin, I understand your desire to fully question this witness, but we have a responsibility to avoid emotional outbursts."

Kalin ducked her head. "My apologies, sir."

"Anyone else? Anything?"

Commander Bolton leaned forward this time. "Lieutenant Shen, can you explain why you are here? In this courtroom, charged with these crimes?"

Jen shook her head slowly. "No, ma'am. I cannot explain it."

Bolton stared earnestly at Jen for a long moment, than sat back again. "Thank you, lieutenant."

Carney looked up and down the members' table again, then looked back at the judge, avoiding looking at Jen as he did so. "I guess that's it. I have no questions."

Jen stood up and walked back to the defense table, where she seated herself. Paul could see what perhaps no one else could, the way Jen's right leg was trembling with suppressed emotions.

McMasters watched her all the way back to the defense table, then looked at Lieutenant Bashir, who stood. "The defense rests."

"Very well. Commander Carr, is the trial counsel prepared for closing argument at this time?"

"Yes, Your Honor."

"Please proceed."

Commander Carr looked toward Jen, watching her steadily for a long moment, while Jen gazed back at her. Then Carr walked a couple of steps away from the trial counsel's table, facing the members as she spoke. "Your Honor, members of the court-martial, on 21 February 2101 the USS *Maury* suffered awful damage to her engineering compartments. Sixty-one members of her crew died outright. Eight more suffered injuries so serious they have required extensive reconstructive surgery. A ship of the United States Navy was so grievously stricken that there were fears the ship would be lost.

"You've heard the testimony of experts on the engineering systems of the USS *Maury*. It couldn't have been an accident. You've heard the testimony of the *Maury*'s captain. She received no warning of any safety problems from her chief engineer or from any of the automated systems designed to prevent such a tragedy. Long ago a famous dictum was set forth—when you've eliminated the impossible, whatever remains must be the truth. The *Maury*'s trauma, the deaths of so many of her crew, couldn't have been an accident, so they must have been caused by deliberate sabotage.

"Who could have sabotaged the ship? Again, the experts testified that it would have required an insider, a very capable engineer, someone familiar with the engineering systems on the *Maury*, someone trusted by the other engineers so she could secretly do what was needed to cause those systems to destroy themselves as well as the lives of those shipmates who'd placed their trust in her. Someone who somehow survived the devastation, who should've been at her own duty station and died with her shipmates, but survived, reaching safety just moments before disaster struck. You've been told that officer was ordered aft, but the equipment she was supposedly personally ordered to examine for problems has been determined to have been in perfect working order prior to the explosions on the *Maury*.

"There are no alibis that can be corroborated by any living witness, by any surviving records, by any memories of those on the *Maury* who survived. There are no other possible explanations for what happened to the USS *Maury* except deliberate sabotage. Sixty-one officers and enlisted personnel of the *Maury* were murdered. The ship was severely damaged. I ask you to bring to justice the only one who could possibly bear responsibility for those acts, and to find Lieutenant Junior Grade Shen guilty on all counts and specifications for the criminal offenses with which she is charged."

The courtroom stayed silent as Commander Carr stepped back to the trial counsel's table and took her seat.

Lieutenant Bashir stood, walking to a position in front of the judge's bench, facing the members of the court-martial. "Your

Honor, members of the court, a terrible tragedy took place. The USS *Maury* was badly damaged and many members of her crew died. But condemning one officer who survived that horrible event will only compound the tragedy.

"The trial counsel has spoken of facts and proof. But the facts are that proof of these charges doesn't exist. None of the expert witnesses could explain how Lieutenant Shen could've carried out her alleged sabotage. None of them could point to her and say, 'she did this and she did that and those actions caused this tragedy.' They couldn't do that because there is *absolutely no proof* Lieutenant Shen was in any way responsible what happened. On the contrary, her actions following the tragedy ensured the survival of twenty-one enlisted personnel in the after portion of the *Maury* who might otherwise have died."

"Lieutenant Shen's own captain testified that she believed Lieutenant Shen to be innocent. There's no evidence to the contrary, just supposition piled upon supposition. No evidence of her guilt. No evidence of a motive for such an act except some gossip from a single fellow officer. The entire case against Lieutenant Shen is circumstantial. You're being asked to convict her of these horrible crimes based solely on the suspicion that she *might* have *somehow* been involved even though no one can say *how* she might have carried out these crimes. This is no basis for convicting anyone of murder, let alone an officer with an unblemished record, an officer who has given her best to the Navy, an officer who has earned the trust and the praise of her captain. Lieutenant Shen is not guilty of these crimes she's been unjustly charged with, not responsible for what happened to the USS *Maury*. The government has failed to provide any real evidence of guilt. I ask you to find her not guilty as to all charges and specifications, because Lieutenant Shen *is not* guilty."

Lieutenant Bashir walked back to the defense counsel's table.

Judge McMasters looked around the silent courtroom. "It is Saturday. I don't know how long it will take the members to render a verdict, but the Judge Advocate General has directed that courts are not to be convened or conducted on Sundays except in the case of emergencies. Therefore, this court will now close, and reopen at ten-hundred on Monday."

13

As people began leaving the courtroom, Commander Carr hastily scribbled something on her data pad, then glanced over at Lieutenant Bashir. He frowned downward as he read the message, then spoke in a voice just loud enough for both Jen and Paul to hear. "The trial counsel wants me to know she asked the question about a relationship with another officer serving on Jen's ship purely on speculation. She had no information from anyone on whether such a relationship had actually existed."

Paul took a deep breath, trying to wash the lingering sense of numbness out of his body. "Did Carr have to tell you that?"

"No, she didn't. She has to ensure I have access to witnesses and evidence. She's not under any obligation to tell me this. She wanted you both to know that none of your confidants had betrayed you."

"Why did she have to ask that question?" Paul knew his voice sounded ragged, and struggled to get his voice under control. "For God's sake, why did she have to ask that question?"

Bashir looked away for a moment before answering. "Because

Commander Carr believes in what she's doing."

Jen said nothing, staring straight ahead. She didn't try to look at Paul as she was escorted out again. Commander Herdez gave Paul a grim nod of farewell and joined those leaving.

He stood waiting while the courtroom emptied, then spoke to Jen's lawyer again. "Lieutenant Bashir, there really wasn't anyone else, anything else, that'd support Jen?"

"No. Do you think I'd have used those two if there had been?" Bashir shook his head. "I shouldn't have used them anyway. They just made the defense look bad. I should've known Carr would do her homework on them."

"Are things as bad as I think they are?"

Bashir lowered his head, avoiding Paul's gaze. "Probably," he finally answered.

Paul was still staring at Bashir miserably when he became aware someone had come up. "Mom. Dad. I didn't know you were here today."

"Civilians usually get Saturdays off up here," his mother advised. "We were in the back. Let's go somewhere."

"I don't—"

"I'm sure you don't. Come on."

They sat in a small dining area, Paul staring at a bulkhead with an incongruous scene displayed of mountains and meadows and billowing white clouds. Finally his mother spoke again. "I wish there was something we could do."

Paul nodded. "I know. I wish there was something *I* could do."

His father shook his head. "I thought she did a good job on the witness stand, but she's really in a bind."

"The charges include murder?" his mother asked.

"Yes, Premeditated Murder."

"That's a—"

"Death-penalty offense. I know."

"What about character witnesses?"

"Captain Halis testified in favor of Jen's character! If they don't listen to Halis, why should they listen to anybody?"

"Is there anything else that can be done?"

Paul shook his head and picked at the food his mother had made him order. "No. Not now. Final arguments have been made. The members of the court will debate and discuss and vote, and when they're ready they'll announce the results."

"Monday morning?"

"If they're ready by then." He didn't say that he thought Carney had long since made up his mind and would push the others to reach a quick decision.

The conversation meandered for a while, Paul not really paying attention or trying to contribute. Finally his parents wished him goodbye and left to look up some old friends. He sat for a while longer, then called the brig to see when he could visit Jen. He couldn't. She'd be granted no more visitors until after the court-martial concluded.

Paul felt an odd sense of relief. He hadn't been looking forward to seeing her, even though he knew he had to if he could. *What can I say? There are no words of comfort possible, and damn little words of encouragement I could legitimately offer. Jen might just start throwing verbal punches at me again. Could I blame her? But I can't even offer her that diversion.*

He wandered down to Fogarty's and sat at a small corner table, nursing a drink. *If it couldn't have been an accident, and Jen didn't do it, then how'd it happen? How'd she happen to survive by such a narrow margin, reaching safety just in time? Why didn't that after power coupling show any signs of trouble that we could point to in support of Jen's story?*

Why do I keep circling back to the same points that the prosecution is using against Jen? Is there really no alternative here? Am I letting my love for Jen blind me to a very ugly reality? She's got a temper. She keeps a lot inside. Could she possibly...?

No. I have to hang on to that one certainty. There's nothing else left to hang on to.

As artificial afternoon began turning into artificial evening on the decks of Franklin, the number of people in the public areas started increasing. Paul knew many would recognize him, and that there was only one place he could avoid them.

The first class petty officer standing the quarterdeck watch on the *Michaelson* saluted Paul aboard. "The captain was wondering if I'd seen you, Mr. Sinclair."

"Is he aboard now?"

"No, sir. The captain left about, oh, forty-five minutes ago."

Paul sought solitude in one of the few places he might find it, heading for Combat. But when he got there, he saw Chief Imari already in the compartment with someone else. He turned to go, but Imari had seen him. "Mr. Sinclair?"

"Yeah, chief. I was just, uh, checking on the compartment."

"Sir, senior chief and I," Imari gestured toward Kowalski, who stood up so Paul could see him clearly, "were just talking about Lieutenant Shen. How's it look, sir, if you don't mind my asking?"

Paul came inside the compartment and shook his head slowly. "It doesn't look good. I don't know why, but it doesn't."

Kowalski frowned at Paul. "Sir, have they actually got evidence that Ms. Shen caused all that?"

"No. No, they don't. That's what's so frustrating."

"Then how...?"

Paul sat down, rubbing his forehead. "They had people, engineers, testify that it couldn't have been an accident."

Chief Imari looked skeptical. "How can you ever say something couldn't be an accident?"

"The equipment. They testified that the equipment couldn't fail that way."

"Even that new thing? Chief Meyer mentioned the *Maury* had some new thing installed."

"Yeah. Uh, SEERS. But the experts said that couldn't have done it because it was designed to prevent that kind of thing."

Senior Chief Kowalski snorted in derision. "I'm no snipe, Mr. Sinclair, but I never met a new piece of equipment that worked like it was designed to."

Imari nodded in agreement. "Right. Stuff's not that good."

Paul nodded as well, though wearily. "That's what I thought. But I've been over all the documentation on SEERS. There's nothing to indicate it might've been involved in what happened to the *Maury*. The experts said the thing was certified ready to install on the *Maury*. And on top of all the other safety features in an engineering system, they say they can absolutely rule out an accident like that."

Kowalski shrugged. "I never met an expert that knew as much as they thought they did, Mr. Sinclair."

Paul smiled bitterly. "I wish I could put you up there on the witness stand to refute Rear Admiral Hidalgo, senior chief."

"Well, sir, I'd do it, if'n I knew anything that could help. All I do know for sure is that nothing comes into the fleet working perfect. There's always problems to be worked out."

It was Paul's turn to shrug. "That's what I thought, senior chief.

But according to the SEERS documentation nothing like that turned up." He saw Kowalski and Imari exchange a quick look. "What?"

Kowalski frowned at the deck. "Uh, nothing, sir."

"Come on, senior chief. If it can possibly help Ms. Shen..."

"I don't think so, sir. It's just... well... you've heard of gun-decking, I'm sure."

"Yeah. Cooking the books to make things look better than they are."

"Well, sir, just maybe this SEERS—look, Mr. Sinclair. Sometimes folks decide something's so important they've gotta ignore the rules. And they tell other people to ignore the rules."

Paul nodded wearily. "I know, senior chief. I've heard about that kind of thing. But somebody would've written *something*, wouldn't they? And there's nothing."

Chief Imari snorted. "Maybe they left it out. Didn't give you the stuff about the problems."

I'd like to believe that. God, how I'd like to believe that. Paul grasped desperately at the thread of hope, even as he knew he couldn't accept it. *Commander Carr told Lieutenant Bashir that he'd gotten everything on SEERS. She wouldn't lie about that. Total paradox. In order for this to be a conspiracy to blame Jen, Carr would have to be part of it, but Carr wouldn't be part of something like that.* "I'm sorry, but the people we're dealing with, like the trial counsel, are honorable, or I'm no judge of character at all. They wouldn't do that. I know that as surely as I know Ms. Shen didn't sabotage the *Maury.*"

The two senior enlisted looked at each other silently for a moment, then Senior Chief Kowalski sighed. "Helluva thing, sir. What'll happen to her?"

"Ms. Shen?" Paul hadn't wanted to go there. Still didn't want to go there. "I don't know. If she's convicted, there's a... range of penalties."

Chief Imari and Senior Chief Kowalski fell silent again. Paul understood. *What else can they say?* He stood up and nodded to them. "Well, I need to get going." He left, wondering if the rest of his life would consist of people watching him and not knowing what to say.

"Hey, Sheriff."

"Mr. Sinclair." Sharpe blew out his cheeks in an exasperated gesture. "Nothing?"

"No. The members of the court are deliberating."

"Don't look good, does it?"

"No." Paul slumped against the nearest bulkhead. "I just don't get it. Okay, let's say it wasn't an accident. That means somebody else did it. Or knows who or what did it. And they're letting Jen take the blame."

Sharpe scratched his head. "I guess that's the only theory that fits right now, sir."

"But why? If it was some weird kind of suicide thing, why take so many of their shipmates with them? And how'd they manage it without being detected? Even the prosecution hasn't been able to explain how Jen supposedly blew up all the engineering stuff at once. They just say she's so good she could've figured out a way."

"Maybe the chief engineer did it, sir. And maybe he sent Ms. Jen to safety 'cause he liked her or something?"

Paul shook his head. "No. Lieutenant Bashir and I went over that. No evidence to support it at all. It's bizarre. We can't accuse a dead guy of doing it because there's no evidence but they can accuse a live person of doing it without any evidence except for the fact that she lived through it." Paul heard himself laughing in disbelief. "How's that for irony, Sheriff? If Jen'd died in the explosions, she wouldn't have to worry about being executed for causing them. But she lived so now maybe she'll die."

"Sir." Paul could see the worry on Sharpe's face. "Sir. You need some rest. You're worn out and strung out."

"I'm exhausted, Sheriff. Completely exhausted. You're a cop. Why can't we find the pieces that'll let us tie this whole mess up into one neat package?"

Sharpe visibly hesitated. "There's conspiracies, sir."

"That big? Involving people I *know* are decent human beings? Why would people on fleet staff, just to give one example, take part in such a conspiracy? Why wouldn't at least one of them tell the truth?"

"I don't know, sir."

"I can't put the package together because I can't find all the pieces. Why can't I find the pieces?"

Sharpe looked down for a moment, then unexpectedly smiled slightly. "I just remembered a time I couldn't put it together, either, sir. Drove me nuts."

"What happened?"

"Oh, we had a problem with some druggies running stuff through an area, and we also had a lot of burglaries and other thefts going on. We kept trying to tie the thefts to the druggies and kept running into blind alleys." Sharpe shook his head. "We finally figured out the druggies and the thieves were two separate gangs. Wasted a lot of time trying to make them one big problem, though."

Paul listened a moment longer, but Sharpe's story was done. Paul shrugged. "I don't see how that helps, Sheriff."

"Uh, no, I guess it doesn't. I just thought of it, is all."

"Yeah." Paul blinked as his vision fuzzed. "I'm so exhausted."

"Do you need help getting back to your stateroom, sir?"

"No. I can make it. Thanks, Sheriff."

He made it back, rolling into his bunk, thankful for a moment that he was so used to his surroundings by now that he automatically ducked low enough to avoid the tangle of cables, pipes and supports than ran along the overhead just above his bunk. Paul fell asleep almost instantly, his mind filled with absurd images of Commander Carr and the fleet commander jointly plotting to destroy ships.

He popped back awake several hours later, staring up at the overhead. Something had jolted his subconscious. What? Something somebody said. Something more than one person said.

Senior Chief Kowalski, saying he'd never known any new equipment to work as designed. *Senior chief's not an engineer, but he's been in the Navy forever. He probably helped Noah sweep up after the animals. But if there is some big problem with SEERS, or any problem with SEERS, the Navy has to know it, and that would mean people I know are honorable were lying in the most horrible way I can imagine.*

Or would it? The thing Sharpe talked about. Two problems instead of one. Is that what I'm missing? I keep trying to tie it all together. Jen's being court-martialed because... because of some grand conspiracy that doesn't make sense because of the people who'd have to be involved. What if that's not the case? What if the people I think are honorable are being honorable? What if they don't have any reason to think they're wrong about stuff like SEERS? But maybe there is something wrong, anyway.

What did Colleen tell me the other night? Even a lie has to agree with what people expect if they're going to believe it. Something like that. Well, everybody who's looked at this SEERS data has said they're surprised at the lack of problems during development. They don't really believe it. They just can't find anything that proves it's wrong and none of the people going after Jen have credible reasons to hide stuff that'd prove there were problems. But maybe they're not hiding it because they don't know, either.

It wouldn't be a matter of the left hand and the right hand working together. Or even a right hand and a left hand at all. It'd be two separate things entirely. And Jen getting stuck between them purely by chance. And no one able to see it because we're all trying to make sense of one big picture that isn't one big picture, and trying to see a reason for something, Jen surviving, that didn't have any reason.

Paul sat up so abruptly he rapped his head against the overhead. *Ow! Blast it! What time is it? Zero six thirty. How'd I miss reveille? Because it's Sunday. Who can I ask about SEERS on a Sunday? Who'd be able to answer questions about something new being built under contract?*

Oh. Duh.

"Mom, I really need some help."

She blinked blearily back at him. "Why do kids always really need help early on Sunday morning?"

"I need you. Jen needs you."

"What about?"

"Contractor stuff. Have you heard of SEERS?"

"Yes. That engineering system thing. Big contract. I haven't worked it, though. Different corporate entity."

"I need to know..." Paul's voice trailed off. *What do I need to know?* "If somebody was trying to hide something about SEERS, what would they do?"

His mother blinked a couple more times, her hands fumbling around outside of Paul's vision. "Coffee. I need coffee. Hide something? Hide what?"

"Uh, design features?"

"That's all protected. Industrial secrets and confidentiality. And then the Navy wanting to keep ship performance capabilities secret.

None of it's going to be sitting out on any public site."

"What about problems?"

His mother had finally found a coffee container and drank half of it before answering. "What kind of problems?"

"I don't know. Reliability? Test results?"

"Hmmmm. What is it you're looking for exactly?"

"I'm looking for something no one's found yet."

"That helps a lot."

"Something no one would *want* to be found. I mean, suppose there were problems with SEERS and no one wanted anyone to know that. And they hid that evidence from the fleet and from the investigators and the evidence gatherers after what happened on the *Maury*."

"That's a real big 'suppose.' Do you have reason to believe that's what happened?"

"No. Just a hunch."

His mother looked to one side. "I'll get your father. There's people we can talk to. Places we know to look. But you understand we're bound by confidentiality agreements for our work with contractors."

"I don't know exactly what that means."

"It means there's limits on what we can do." She took a good look at him. "You look awful."

"Thanks, Mom."

"Get some breakfast. I'll see what we can do. How urgent is this?"

"Life and death."

Her eyebrows shot up, then she nodded. "I should've realized that without asking. Oh-kay. Get something to eat. I'll call back as soon as I can."

Paul tried to clean himself up, then went to grab a quick meal. Kris Denaldo, obviously coming off the quarterdeck watch, spotted him. "Paul! Is..." Her voice ran down as she saw his face. "What can I do?"

"How are you at miracles?"

She made a helpless gesture. "Not much." Coming closer, Kris put a hand on Paul's arm. "You know whatever I can do, I will."

"I know, but there doesn't seem to be anything."

"Ahem!" Lieutenant Isakov squeezed by them, favoring Paul and Kris with an arch look that implied volumes.

Kris pulled her hand away and Paul glared after Isakov as she entered the wardroom. "You can keep *her* away from me."

"Like I told you, she's a bit of a psycho, Paul."

"I'd already figured that out. Didn't you guys warn Randy Diego about her already?"

Kris shrugged. "Randy's been a pain and he never wants to listen."

"No, he doesn't, but letting her run him around... geez."

"Okay, okay. I take it you've already talked to Randy?"

"Yeah. He didn't want to hear it."

"What a shock. If he's determined to be Isakov's lapdog, there's not much we can do about it, Paul."

"I know." Paul looked upward. "But it's something I can make a difference at. I hope. It's nice to know there's something I can still say that about."

"You'll make a difference with Jen. There's nothing happening today?"

"No. Final arguments happened yesterday. Today's a day off but also a day for the members of the court to make up their minds. The court-martial reconvenes Monday morning."

"Do you think they'll have a decision then?"

"I'm afraid they will."

She nodded helplessly and Paul went back to his stateroom, staring every once in a while at the outside phone connection while he pretended he was working on administrative tasks.

The phone finally rang. "Hi, Paul. Care to meet us for lunch?"

"Does that mean you found something, Mom?"

His mother made a slight shushing motion. "How's that place we ate at yesterday sound?"

"Fine."

"We'll see you as soon as you can get there, then."

His mother was drinking coffee again when Paul got to the restaurant. His father winked and gave him a thumbs-up.

"Did you find something?"

His mother sighed, lowering her coffee cup. "Now, Paul, I told you we probably couldn't help because of confidentiality agreements."

"I..."

"But I did find that other thing."

He looked at her blankly. "What other thing?"

"You know." She slid an actual piece of paper toward Paul's father, who glanced at it, nodded, then slid it over to Paul.

Paul examined the paper. Blank on one side, the other held a long web site address hand printed on it. "Do you think—"

"I don't know. But, if there's anything like that, it should be there if it's anywhere. Various... indicators... point that way. Unfortunately, we couldn't get into it. You probably can't, either. But good luck."

"Thanks. I hope you don't mind if I eat and run." Paul folded the paper carefully and went in search of Sheriff Sharpe.

Half an hour later, Sharpe eyed Paul dubiously. "Sir, what are you suggesting doing with that?"

"Try to break in."

"No, sir. No way. I'm an officer of the law."

"Meaning?"

"You know what it means, sir." Sharpe pointed at the address Paul held. "I only get to conduct searches with a warrant. If I search without a warrant, any evidence I find gets thrown out."

"Oh, yeah." Paul looked at the address bitterly. *So close. Maybe. But I can't get into a web site myself. My skills don't run that way.*

Sharpe seemed angry. "I can't believe you'd suggest that, Mr. Sinclair. I can't believe you'd come to me knowing that only Warrant Officer Bob Rose might be able to break into a site like that and I couldn't possibly provide any assistance or involvement in the matter. Don't even ask me!"

"Okay, Sheriff. Sorry—"

"Don't even ask me if Rose's contact information is in the ship's data base. I don't want to tell you."

"Uh, okay—"

"And even if Rose could maybe try to break into that site because part of his job involves testing government-related sites for security flaws, I wouldn't tell you, sir! Not a word. I am not involved, sir. Is that clear?"

"Yeah, Sheriff."

"So don't talk to me about it. Don't say anything else. I'm an officer of the law. Just because someone like you or Bob Rose isn't an officer of the law and anything you find without a warrant would be admissible in court doesn't mean I would in any way suggest or sanction such a thing in a way that would taint it in the eyes of any court!"

"Right, Sheriff." Paul put away the paper. "What was I thinking?"

"About what, sir?"

"Uh... nothing. Excuse me. I've got to make a phone call. After I look up some contact information."

Warrant Officer Rose couldn't get away to meet Paul until early evening. He heard Paul out, looked at the site address, and seemed to be thinking about it all. Paul tried to look as earnest and convincing as he possibly could. "Can you try this for me, warrant?"

Rose squinched up his face a bit. "It's a little shaky. I mean, yes, I'm supposed to check sites for security effectiveness, but this site isn't really anything I have any reason to go poking around in."

"I just need to see what's there."

Rose sighed. "Okay. Just hold on. Sit over there somewhere and let me work. If I do get access we might have only a very brief chance to look, so don't wander off."

"Yes, warrant. I owe you big time for this."

"I haven't done anything, yet. Did Sharpe tell you I could help you?"

"Uh, no. Petty Officer Sharpe is an officer of the law. He couldn't even suggest such a thing to me."

"Good. Wouldn't want to break any rules." Rose wriggled his fingers over the keyboard. "Now, let's see what kind of defenses this place has."

Paul had to sit a fair ways back, out of Rose's line of sight, so as not to distract him, but that also left Paul unable to see what Rose was doing. He just had to wait, hearing occasional words or sounds from the warrant which he strained to interpret.

He was actually dozing in and out sometime later when Rose's voice brought him fully alert. "We're in! Hurry!"

Paul scrambled over, peering at the display. "What is it?"

"Some kind of memo."

Paul scanned, his eyes skipping rapidly across the surface of the document and picking out a word here and there. He raised his gaze to the top again to actually read the document when the screen blanked. "What happened?"

Rose shrugged. "They kicked us out. Real nice security on that site. Did you see anything?"

"Yes. Did you?"

"A couple of things."

"Wh—Wait." Paul thought for a moment. "Could you write down anything you saw? I'll do the same and see if we saw the same sort of things."

"Good idea."

Paul hastily wrote down the scattered words he'd picked out. "Here's my list. I saw a name on the memo header. McNamara."

Rose nodded and pointed to his own writing. "I saw something like that. Sounds right."

"I saw SEERS in the subject line."

"Concur."

"And I saw the words 'further testing required.'"

"I just thought I saw 'testing required.' That's close enough."

"And 'failure.'"

"Not just 'failure.' I know I saw 'catastrophic' in there."

It was Paul's turn to nod. "I did, too." There were several other fragmentary phrases and words which didn't match on their lists. "But those are enough. Is there any chance you can get back into that site?"

"I doubt it. They're probably sealing the backdoor I just used. And they'll be watching for me."

"Then this'll have to do. Thanks, warrant. If any lawyers call you, will you confirm this?"

"Navy lawyers, you mean."

"Right."

"Sure. Where are you going now?"

"To see a lawyer."

Lieutenant Bashir answered the door to his living quarters, listening skeptically. He examined Paul's list of words. "You're sure? I mean, this isn't definitive."

"Isn't there a way to get into the site and know for sure?"

"Yeah, with a court order. Do you have any idea how hard that'd be to come up with at this stage in the trial?"

"No, I don't."

Bashir actually laughed for a moment at Paul's reply. "You can't be more honest than that. Listen, Paul, there's only one way we've got a chance of getting a court order in time to make a difference. We need another lawyer to help us."

"Who?"

"Commander Carr."

Carr was at home, too, in casual clothing. Paul found himself noticing how nice her legs looked in shorts and jerked his eyes away guiltily.

Carr eyed them both, then invited Bashir and Paul in. "Sit down. What's this about? If it's a plea bargain at this late point, Ahmed, then Mr. Sinclair shouldn't be here."

"Not a plea bargain." Bashir gestured to Paul. "Explain the situation, please."

When Paul was done, Carr shook her head. "That's a very thin reed. Some memo, maybe, at some web site you shouldn't have been accessing, with a few words which, if interpreted very liberally, might be worth looking at. Or maybe not."

"Ma'am." Paul pointed to his list of words. "It was a memo. I'm sure of that. I saw the subject line. And even though I didn't have time to read it in detail I did have time to skim it for an impression. And that impression was unquestionably that it was talking about unresolved problems with SEERS."

"As of when?"

"Sometime late last year. I didn't catch the exact date."

"How did you find this site?"

"Uh, I'd rather not disclose my sources."

Commander Carr looked away. "Can you at least tell me who this memo was addressed to?"

Paul nodded. "McNamara. Some guy named McNamara. I couldn't get his title in the time I had to read."

Carr's eyes locked back on Paul. "McNamara?"

"Yes. W. McNamara. I'm sure of it. I don't know what the W. stands for."

"William."

Lieutenant Bashir raised his eyebrows. "You know him, commander?"

"I know of him." Commander Carr looked unhappy as she massaged her forehead with one hand. "Deputy assistant undersecretary of defense for acquisition and development. I know that because his office provided the background material on the *Maury*'s new engineering equipment."

"But obviously that material didn't include any memos talking about catastrophic failures."

"No, it didn't. Not that I recall." Carr pulled out her data pad and typed rapidly. "Let's do a search of the evidence archive. Zero hits.

Those words didn't appear in anything I saw, in any context." Carr
leaned close to Paul, her eyes boring into his. "Paul, I know how
badly you want Lieutenant Shen to be acquitted. I know how badly
you want to find proof she didn't cause the disaster on the *Maury*.
Are you willing to swear to me that you actually saw those words on
a memo addressed to Undersecretary McNamara?"

Paul nodded, keeping his eyes on Commander Carr's. "Yes,
ma'am. I don't pretend to know the entire contents of that memo,
but I do know what I've told you."

"You're aware of the penalty for perjury?"

Bashir almost jumped up from his chair. "Commander! That's—"

Paul gestured him back. "It's okay. Yes, ma'am. I'm aware of
it. I'm not lying. I'm not engaging in wishful thinking. I saw that
much of the memo. I had independent confirmation those words
were there."

"And who is this other source who can confirm that information?"

"A warrant officer, ma'am. Not a cop. Someone who works in
computer support."

"How fortunate your warrant officer's not a cop." Carr leaned back
again. "If it's true..." She stared grimly at nothing for a moment.
"What do you want to do, Lieutenant Bashir?"

"Reopen discovery. Get a court order to access that web site. A
sealed order so we don't have to worry about the site being purged
before we can get to it."

"Judge McMasters isn't going to take kindly to the idea of
reopening discovery. We've had final arguments. The members of
the court are working on their decisions."

"The judge'll agree to it if the trial counsel supports the motion."

"I represent the government, not Ms. Shen."

Paul spread his hands, his face pleading. "You represent justice, ma'am. Don't you? If this evidence disproves the government's case—"

"That's a very big 'if' right now, Mr. Sinclair."

"You promised me if I found any evidence that might exonerate Jen that you'd give it a fair evaluation."

Commander Carr visibly winced. "Me and my big mouth. A lawyer should know better than to make promises. Paul, it's not my job to help exonerate Lieutenant Shen."

"Is it your job to convict someone by ignoring evidence which might prove her innocence?"

Carr's face reddened and hardened. "I don't like being accused of misconduct."

Paul dropped his gaze, took a quick breath, then looked back up at her. "My sincere apologies, ma'am. I didn't mean to imply misconduct. I know you wouldn't... I just... dammit, ma'am, I really admire you."

Her expression softened, though still plainly aggravated. "And you think I'm letting you down. Or letting down Lieutenant Shen."

"Lieutenant Shen is the most important thing in the world to me, ma'am."

"Oh, for..." Carr covered her eyes with one hand. "That's a low blow, Mr. Sinclair. Throwing young love at me. It *doesn't* conquer all, you know." She dropped her hand and gave Paul a rueful look. "But it does conquer my better legal judgment in this case. As far as moral judgment goes, I don't mind telling you I've hated every moment of this case. Sorry, Paul, I've seen it as necessary in light of the evidence. But I haven't enjoyed it. All right. We'll go to the judge and see what we can do."

"First thing in the morning?" Bashir asked, clearly elated.

"No. Right now. Stand by while I get back into uniform. We need to get the wheels turning on this, and authorization to crack that site, as soon as possible." They all stood, but Commander Carr leveled a finger at Paul. "Not you, young lover. This is for professionals. Go home. Or to your ship or whatever. And *don't* breathe a word of this to Lieutenant Shen or anybody else. Not a word. If anything gets out prematurely it could cause the judge to rule against this and let Lieutenant Shen stand or fall on what defense she's been able to present thus far. Understand?"

"Yes, ma'am. Thank you, ma'am."

"Don't thank me. I'm also doing this for myself. I really don't want to convict an innocent person. Lawyers have souls, too."

"Or so it is rumored," Bashir murmured.

"As if you have room to talk. Let's go get Judge McMasters and probably get our ears pinned back. Remember, Sinclair, not a word."

"Yes, ma'am."

"And be prepared to find out this site doesn't hold anything that makes a difference. Or it might hold something that hurts Lieutenant Shen, if you missed a word like 'impossible' anywhere in there."

"Yes, ma'am." *But it's not like I have a lot to lose at this point.* Bashir gestured Paul out, giving him a confident thumbs-up as Paul left. *Now all I have to do is wander around until Monday morning, not talking to anybody about this, trying to get some sleep despite everything, trying to not think about it. What was that old Eskimo spell for changing rocks into gold? All you had to do was stare at the rocks for an entire day and never think of walrus.*

In the morning, Paul tried to make it look as if he had indeed slept the night before, but his efforts didn't really convince even himself. *I've looked better than this after a night of partying.* He started for the courtroom, but almost immediately stopped as his data pad beeped urgently. *High-priority message. Let's see. Court proceedings postponed for twenty-four hours. Is that good or bad?*

He dialed Lieutenant Bashir's number, but only got the answering machine. The official court number provided no elaboration on the brief message. Court would resume the next day. Assuming it wasn't rescheduled again.

Frustrated, Paul walked to Bashir's offices, but he was told the lieutenant was unavailable. Same for Commander Carr.

If only I knew whether this meant good news or bad news. Or just the postponement of the inevitable.

Judge McMasters looked around the courtroom. "This proceeding will come to order. I wish to apologize first to all concerned for the postponement of these proceedings. Matters came to my attention that had to be dealt with prior to the members of the court rendering a verdict."

Paul studied the faces of the members, but he saw nothing there but the same uninformed interest most of the rest of the people in the courtroom were displaying. Jen hadn't looked at Paul since she'd been brought in by her guards, sitting perfectly erect in the posture of someone awaiting the impact of bullets from a firing squad. Lieutenant Bashir hadn't looked at Paul, either, concentrating on something on his data pad and ignoring Paul's attempts to get his attention.

"At the request of both trial counsel and counsel for the defense, discovery in this case was reopened and a warrant issued to access a site believed to contain evidence pertaining to these proceedings which had not previously been disclosed. Lieutenant Bashir?"

Bashir rose. "Your Honor. The web site in question was accessed in the early morning hours yesterday. Based on initial review of the material therein, court proceedings were postponed twenty-four hours to allow Commander Carr and myself to study the documents in detail and confirm their authenticity."

"It's my understanding that the documents were indeed authentic?"

"Yes, Your Honor."

Commander Carr, until now silent, rose briefly as well. "The trial counsel agrees that at this point in time the documents appear authentic, Your Honor."

Lieutenant Bashir walked out from behind the defense table, holding his data pad. "I would like the documents from that site to be entered into the official record of this proceeding."

McMasters eyed Carr again. "Trial counsel?"

"The trial counsel has no objection."

"Then it is so ordered."

Lieutenant Bashir turned to face toward the members of the court. "If I may, I'd like to ensure the members understand a critical point regarding evidence in a criminal proceeding. All evidence that is 'reasonably available' must be shared with the defendant in order to ensure an effective defense against any charges. That standard is set by the Uniform Code of Military Justice. Failure to provide the defendant with evidence which would serve to rebut criminal charges is a very serious matter."

McMasters looked from Bashir to Carr. "I assume this means the documents uncovered do indeed pertain to the issues before this proceeding?"

"Yes, Your Honor," Bashir replied. "They most certainly do. The site contained a number of memorandums, some with attachments, written over the course of the past year by individuals dealing with the office of the assistant undersecretary of defense for acquisition and development. All dealt with the status of the Ship's Efficiency Engineering Regulatory Systems, or SEERS. As previously established during this proceeding, SEERS is the new equipment which was installed on the USS *Maury* prior to her last underway period."

Bashir raised the data pad, no longer looking at it himself. "All of those memorandums were warnings from personnel involved in the development and testing of SEERS. Warnings that the system had not successfully passed all of its tests. Warnings that, contrary to the information presented during this trial, SEERS itself posed a threat of causing serious damage to a ship. Warnings to those responsible for overseeing the program that it was not ready to be installed on ships such as the *Maury*."

He lowered the data pad so he could read from it. "I'd like to quote from one memorandum in particular. Quote. Though designed to compensate for system-wide power fluctuations by dampening feedback cycles, test results show a real possibility that SEERS may enter its own rapid destructive feedback loop. Since SEERS controls all," Bashir stopped speaking and looked around. "I'd like to emphasize that. Quote. Since SEERS controls *all* safety interlocks in a system in order to regulate power loads effectively, this creates a situation in which SEERS could very rapidly mismanage power loads and with little or no warning cause near-simultaneous—" Bashir paused again, and looked around before resuming speaking. "Near-simultaneous destructive failure of multiple engineering components. Unquote."

Paul realized he was smiling like an idiot but couldn't stop. At the members' table, the officers were staring at Bashir with mingled expressions of astonishment and disbelief.

"Let me cite one other sentence a few lines down," Bashir continued. "Quote. Tests indicate the only warning that these power fluctuations will soon reach uncontrollable levels is likely to be when remote elements of the system grid begin reporting widely varying power load states at short intervals. Unquote." Bashir gazed at the trial counsel's table. "May I stipulate for the record that the after power coupling on the USS *Maury* is a remote element in its engineering system?"

Carr said nothing, but Captain Carney leaned forward. "What would be the basis for stating that?"

"The engineering systems manual for the *Maury*, captain."

"Oh." Carney sat back again.

Judge McMasters, his face looking angrier with every word Bashir spoke, nodded. "Let the record show the after power coupling on the USS *Maury* is a remote element of its engineering system."

Lieutenant Bashir pointed at Jen, whose own expression could only be described as stunned. "The essential basis for the charges against Lieutenant Shen is that *there was no other possible explanation* for what happened to the engineering system on the USS *Maury*. No *possible way* the system could have *accidentally* suffered from near-simultaneous catastrophic overloads of its equipment. But that is *not* true. The documents just now uncovered reveal beyond a shadow of a doubt that SEERS *could* cause such an accident. And that this was known to some officials in the government via official correspondence warning that SEERS was *not* ready to install on ships of the United States Navy. Further, in gross violation of the rules of evidence, these documents were *not* provided to Lieutenant Shen to aid in her defense."

Bashir turned toward Judge McMasters. "Your Honor, in light of the facts I have just described, the defense moves that all charges against Lieutenant Shen be dismissed."

The judge's jaw moved back and forth for a few moments before he answered Bashir. McMaster's eyes were angry slits as he nailed Commander Carr with his gaze.

"Commander Carr. Was the government aware of the existence of these documents prior to this?"

She stood and faced him, standing at attention. "No, Your Honor." To Paul's surprise, Carr's own voice seemed on the verge of shaking with anger. "They were not revealed to me, to my office, or to the best of my knowledge to my immediate superiors."

"Are you aware of how serious this transgression is?"

"I am fully aware of it, Your Honor. I assure you, I intend on finding out why this evidence was withheld."

"Oh, I'll help you with that, commander." McMaster's face wasn't a pretty sight. "Somebody's going to get nailed for this. If it were not for the high respect which your reputation commands I'd be sanctioning you for contempt right now. But I believe your assertion. Defense counsel has moved that all charges against Lieutenant Shen be dismissed. I want to know what you have to say about that."

Carr's face reddened. "If I may have a few hours to consult—"

"*Now*, commander. The government has had more than adequate time to compile this case. If the trial counsel wishes to register an objection, I want it *now*."

Carr looked downward. Paul couldn't read her expression but he could tell her body was rigid. Then Carr slowly raised her head to look back at the judge. "The trial counsel has no objection."

"Let me be certain what the record reflects, commander. Is the trial counsel agreeing these charges were brought in error?"

Commander Carr looked directly at Jen. "Your Honor, I did not personally bring these charges, but had the trial counsel been aware of these documents, I would have refused to prosecute this case."

The courtroom erupted in a whispers and murmurs. The bailiff and Judge McMasters glared around with sufficient menace to quiet the noise almost as soon as it began. The judge raised his gavel. "Then it is the judgment of this court that all charges against Lieutenant Junior Grade Jenevieve Diana Shen are dismissed with prejudice, such judgment to take effect immediately." McMasters pointed a rigid index finger at the masters-at-arms standing at the back of the courtroom. "The court further directs that Lieutenant Junior Grade Shen be released from custody *immediately*. This proceeding is closed. Trial counsel, I want to see you in my chambers in fifteen minutes."

McMasters left so quickly the bailiff barely had time to bring the people in the courtroom to their feet. The room erupted into a buzz of conversation, the neat lines of spectators dissolving into small clumps excitedly discussing what had just happened.

Jen seemed to be in shock, staring at Lieutenant Bashir, who was laughing quietly. Paul pushed forward. "What exactly does this mean? I can't remember what 'dismissed with prejudice' means but it sounds bad."

"Bad? Hell, no. Not for us." Bashir sobered enough to smile widely at Jen and Paul. "It means the government can't charge Ms. Shen with those offenses again. Ever."

"But she couldn't be tried twice for the same offense anyway."

"Uh-uh." Bashir shook his head. "This trial was never finished. Unless a verdict had been rendered, technically Jen wouldn't have been tried before. They could've brought the same charges later. I know that sounds screwy, so just accept that the judge's ruling means Jen is free and clear of this nightmare from this point forward."

The masters-at-arms who'd escorted Jen into court that morning appeared, looking ill at ease. One bent to remove the ankle restraint on Jen while the other looked into another corner of the courtroom. Jen glared at both until the first had finished removing her bond. "Get away from me," she ground out between clenched teeth.

Paul remembered what Sharpe had told him. *There's things guards can do to prisoners.* He stepped forward, commanding the attention of both of the masters-at-arms. "Remember this. They're not always guilty."

The guards exchanged glances, then the senior one answered without visible emotion. "Yes, sir."

Jen turned away so she couldn't see the guards. "Get out of here."

Another exchange of glances, then the guards walked toward the door of the courtroom.

Jen started to say something else, but her face went pale. Paul turned and saw Commander Carr standing close by, her own expression tightly controlled. Carr took a long breath before speaking. "Lieutenant Shen, I wish to offer my strongest and most sincere apologies for what you went through. I want to assure you that I would never have proceeded with this case had I known vital evidence had been withheld from me and from you. I *will* find out who was responsible and do everything I can to bring them to account."

Jen stared back at her, saying nothing.

"I wouldn't blame you if you refused to accept my apology for what could've been a gross miscarriage of justice. But I do want to ensure you know that duty or not I would not have done this knowingly, and that this man of yours," she pointed at Paul, "deserves every credit for this outcome." Jen nodded. Commander Carr waited a moment longer, watching Jen's unyielding face, then smiled tightly. "For what it's worth, I don't know that I'd accept an apology myself if our situations were reversed."

Paul watched Jen, trying to will her to respond graciously before Carr turned away. *C'mon, Jen. She did the right thing when the chips were down.*

Jen's expression didn't change, but she slowly nodded again. Then she extended her hand. Carr eyed it with surprise, then reached to shake it. However, when Commander Carr's hand was just about to grasp hers, Jen yanked her own up and back, grinning fiercely. "Psych. Ma'am."

Carr returned the grin and the fierceness. "Want to try again, Ms. Shen?"

"Sure. If you do." This time the two women shook hands.

Paul looked from Jen to Commander Carr and mentally shook his head. He could see their hands quivering from the pressure they were exerting. He couldn't tell if they were also digging their nails into each other's hands as they shook, but he wouldn't have been surprised. *Man, if you ever locked those two into a room together they'd either kill each other or come out as fast friends.*

The two women broke their grip. Commander Carr took a step back. "Thank you, too, Paul, for uncovering that withheld evidence." Jen's eyes widened and she stared at Paul. "You didn't hear that, yet, Lieutenant Shen? Yes. At almost literally the last minute, your lover here found that site full of material I never saw, and talked your lawyer and I into getting the court to force it open. I'd hang on to him if I was you." Carr inclined her head toward the back of the courtroom. "I have to leave for a command performance with Judge McMasters. Good luck, Ms. Shen."

Jen massaged her hand as she watched Carr walk away. "She works out."

Paul nodded. "She's got a chin-up bar installed in her office."

"I could tell. I need to get one, too." She looked over at Bashir. "Thanks, lieutenant. Now what?"

He waved toward the courtroom door, smiling broadly. "You're free. Charges are dropped. You can go anywhere and do anything you damn well please."

"Does that mean I report back to the *Maury*?"

Bashir looked surprised, then nodded. "Well, yes."

"Just like I've been on temporary duty and am checking back in, huh? 'Hi, guys. I'm back.' 'So, Jen, how was the brig?' 'It sucked.' 'Really?'" Jen shook her head and looked at Paul. "I can't believe I'm already joking about this."

"It's a coping mechanism."

"You've been talking to that chaplain, haven't you?" Jen grinned and raised her arms. "I'm *free*. Damn it feels good. C'mon, Paul, let's take a walk, just you and me and no guards or surveillance systems. Thanks, Lieutenant Bashir."

"Hey, it's my job." Bashir smiled even wider. "I beat Alex Carr! I've got to tell everybody at the office. Excuse me!" He rushed off.

Jen took a few tentative steps toward the door, then paused as someone else approached. Lieutenant Kalin's face reflected distress. "Lieutenant Shen, I wanted to apologize."

"You, too?" Jen managed another smile.

"I'm sorry? I just mean... we would've voted to convict. I know we would've. There just..." Kalin gestured helplessly. "I would've done the very best I could and I still would've done the wrong thing and I'm so very sorry I came so close to doing that."

Paul looked at Jen again, but this time she seemed unable to muster a response. "Lieutenant, I'm sure Ms. Shen appreciates that." Jen nodded mutely.

"Thank you." Lieutenant Kalin looked back to where Captain Carney and the other members of the court were standing and arguing with each other. "I'd better get back."

Jen closed her eyes for a moment, then started walking again. "I thought she'd vote for me," Jen whispered just loudly enough for Paul to hear.

Me, too. I bet Captain Carney's kissing goodbye those rear admiral stars he's been dreaming about.

"It's funny," Jen continued. "You always think, if I was accused of something I didn't do, I'd just show everyone I didn't do it and everything'd be fine. But it's not that way. It's a lot harder."

Paul nodded. "I never really thought about it this way before. I guess there's a reason it's been made hard to convict people."

"Not hard enough. And I never thought I'd say that. Maybe I'll change my mind again, some day. But it'll take a while. A long while." They cleared the door of the courtroom, Jen looking around, her expression gradually brightening. "Oh, this feels good. You never know how important it is to be able to walk out a door until you're not allowed to do it. But I'm free again."

Paul nodded, smiling. *I can't tell her yet about all the news coverage of the charges against her. She's been through so much and deserves not to have this moment ruined. The media spent weeks going over the awful things she supposedly did. How much time will the news media spend telling everybody she was innocent?*

Jen glanced at him, her expression suddenly rueful. "Okay. Say it."

"Say what?"

"I was a horrible bitch. I yelled and screamed at you and told you to shut up and go away while you were literally saving me."

Paul shrugged. "It's not like you weren't under a lot of stress."

"Are you trying to say you weren't bothered by it?"

"Uh, no. It bothered me. Truth to tell, it hurt. A lot."

Jen looked at him, her eyes searching his. "I'll make it up to you. I swear."

"I don't want—"

"That blasted sweet little lawyer of yours is right."

"Commander Carr? About what? And she's not—"

"I need to hang on to you. You deserve your answer by now. You deserved it a long time ago."

"My answer? To what?"

Jen buried her face in her hands. "He's forgotten. Marriage? *Remember?*"

"Oh, I, uh, Jen, I..."

"Never mind."

"But, Jen!"

She dropped her hands and peered at him. "I must really be crazy. Yes."

"Yes?" Paul hesitated, not entirely certain if he'd heard right, or what question it now applied to.

"I'll spell it phonetically for you, sailor." Jen leaned close, her eyes looking directly into Paul's. "Yankee. Echo. Sierra. Yes. I want to marry you. I've wanted to marry you for a long time."

"Jen, I... I..."

"You're so articulate at times like this." She glanced to either side, then risked a quick kiss. "I don't care if we're in uniform. Technically, I'm not, since I need to get my ribbons and all back. I take it you're happy?"

"Incredibly happy." Paul imagined he had a big, goofy smile on his face, but didn't particularly care.

"Good. That makes two of us. Did you arrange for Herdez to be there on Friday, too?"

"Not really. I did ask her to let you know she supported you."

"So she came as a favor to you. It was still a nice gesture."

"No, Jen, she came because she wanted to show she supported *you*."

Jen laughed. "Herdez? Uh-huh. Right. She was probably thinking 'that no-load Shen is just one problem after another.'"

"Herdez thinks you're a good officer!"

"She thinks *you're* a good officer. Not that it matters all that much right now. I'll even invite her to the wedding if you want."

Paul grinned. *The wedding*. Then something occurred to him. *Herdez wants me to go back on ship duty after a year on shore. But now I know I'm going to be married to Jen. Well, I'll just have to explain that to Herdez.*

"What're you thinking about?"

"Planning. For the future."

"Oh, yeah. A big family get-together. Did you ever try to tell my father about the charges against me?"

"No. You told me not to."

"Yeah." She sighed and looked outward as if she could somehow see her father's ship. "The *Mahan* probably heard anyway. Somehow. I'll need to send him an update and tell him he won't have to worry about visiting hours at Leavenworth. And I'm telling him that I'm marrying you whether he likes it or not."

Captain Shen's probably going to have a hard time deciding which is worse, having Jen sent to Leavenworth or having her marry me.

"What about your parents?" Jen continued. "I haven't had much opportunity to get to know them. Are you sure they'll be all that thrilled about this?"

"Positive." Paul stopped at a public phone and punched in a number. His mother's face appeared. "That stuff you didn't give me? It worked. Jen's free."

Julia Sinclair smiled brightly. "That was fast."

"It had to be. SEERS was installed on the *Maury* even though it hadn't passed its tests. Why would anyone have allowed that, Mom? Have something sent on to ships when they knew it might literally blow up someday?" She looked down and shook her head. "It does happen. This certainly isn't the first time. No one gets a reward for stopping a program in its tracks, Paul. No one in government gets thanked for killing a program, and no one in industry gets bonuses for finding big problems with something that's already over-budget and behind schedule. They try to bury the evidence and wave the program through and cross their fingers. I'd never do it. Your father wouldn't. But there are sometimes people who will. I'm afraid the sailors on the *Maury* aren't the first victims of that sort of thing, and they won't be the last. Buyer beware, Paul. It applies to the military, too."

"I won't forget that."

"Is Jen with you?"

"Yes. Uh, you remember that thing you asked me about earlier, Mom?"

"What thing?"

"The are-you-already-engaged thing."

"Oh. That thing."

"Yes, um..."

As Paul hesitated, Jen pushed her way in front of the phone. "I said yes. We're engaged, ma'am. Surprise!"

Paul's mother's smile got a little brighter. "I'm not all that surprised. Welcome to the family." Julia Sinclair paused for just a moment. "And no more ma'am, please. From now on, just call me 'commander'." She laughed. "I've waited so long to say that to a daughter-in-law!"

"I'm going to out-rank you someday, commander."

"Oh, no, you won't! Seniority will stay firmly with me, young lady. In perpetuity. The governing instruction for mothers-in-law lays it out very clearly."

"I've never seen that instruction."

"You won't need it for a while. Paul, I'll let your father know the good news."

Paul looked at Jen after he'd broken the connection. "And they lived happily ever after." He wasn't sure himself how much he was joking.

She laughed. "Oh, yeah. That sounds just like you and me. Right now, all we have to do is find out a time when your and my father's ships are both inport, I'm here as well, your parents can make it up to Franklin again, and anyone else we really want to have at the wedding also can be here."

Paul exhaled. "Maybe if we put that problem to the fleet scheduling mainframes they can come up with a solution. Eventually."

"It'll probably take a while." Jen checked her data unit, biting her lower lip in concentration. "As long as we can find a four-hour-long window where everybody's available, I say we go for it."

"Yeah. I guess that'll be the hardest part of setting up the wedding."

Jen stared at him for a moment. "No," she finally stated. "Not even close. Think of it as a military exercise, Paul. A big one. With lots of things to set up and coordinate."

"Oh." Paul grinned. "Maybe we ought to give it a code name, then. How about Operation Wedded Bliss?"

"Gag."

"Operation Hazardous Endeavor?"

"Eh."

"Operation Come Hell or High Water?"

Jen smiled. "Perfect. But there's something else I have to do right now. Is the *Maury*'s crew still billeted in the barracks near the shipyard?"

He nodded. "Are you going now?"

"I need to report for duty, Paul. Back to my command."

"Remember, they didn't go after you, Jen."

"Except for Taber."

"Except for Taber. But you've just had murder charges against you thrown out. We don't want to go through another court-martial."

"Nah. Taber's not worth it."

"The *Maury*'s crew supported you. Captain Halis stood by you."

"I know. But, heck, if even I started having doubts—" She gave him a demanding look. "I didn't say that."

"I already knew, Jen."

"How?"

"I wasn't the only person who believed in you. Some of them gave me good advice."

"I *will* get the details of that out of you, Mr. Sinclair." Jen grinned again. "Hey, want to come along with me and see the faces of my shipmates when I waltz in?"

"That'd be fun. I'd better check with my department head, though." Paul made another call.

Commander Garcia looked out of sorts, though for what particular reason this time, if any, Paul couldn't tell. "We heard. Sure. Take the rest of the day off. It's not like there's any *work* that needs done." Garcia looked slightly to the side. "There's a meeting at 1500 you need to be at. Be back on the *Michaelson* by then. You can take off until... no. There's a contractor coming aboard at 1400 and you have to be there. Until... no. The XO wants a training records review and I need *your* input. You'd better get back by 1300 to take care of that." His eyes shifted. "Glad to hear about Shen."

"Thank you, sir." Paul looked over at Jen. "I have the rest of the day off. Until 1300."

"Wow. A day off that's an hour and a half long. You guys on the *Michaelson* have it easy."

"Hey, we're space warfare officers." She began walking toward the dock area and Paul paced her. "Jen. There's something I've wondered."

"What's that?"

"It's very personal."

She gave him a wry grin. "I'd say you've earned the right to ask me a very personal question."

"Do you ever cry?"

Jen walked on silently for a moment before answering. "The last time I cried was the day my mother died."

Paul nodded. "I understand."

"Satisfied that I'm human?"

"Yes. Of course." *You just never want to show it. I saw the wall Jen's built around herself crack while she was in the brig. Am I going to be able to handle it if and when it breaks?*

Oblivious to his thoughts, Jen smiled again. "Then pick up the pace, Mr. Sinclair. We've both got a lot of work to do."

ACKNOWLEDGMENTS

I am indebted to my editor, Anne Sowards, for her valuable support and editing, and to my agent, Joshua Bilmes, for his inspired suggestions and assistance.

ABOUT THE AUTHOR

John G. Hemry is a retired US Navy officer and the author, under the pen name Jack Campbell, of the *New York Times* national bestselling *The Lost Fleet* series (*Dauntless, Fearless, Courageous, Valiant, Relentless,* and *Victorious*). Next up are two new follow-on series. *The Lost Fleet: Beyond the Frontier* continues to follow Geary and his companions. The other series, *Lost Stars*, is set on a former enemy world in that universe. Under his own name, John is also the author of the *JAG in Space* series and the *Stark's War* series. His short fiction has appeared in places as varied as the last Chicks in Chainmail anthology (*Turn the Other Chick*) and *Analog* magazine (which published his Nebula Award-nominated story 'Small Moments in Time' as well as most recently 'The Rift' in the October 2010 issue). His humorous short story 'As You Know, Bob' was selected for *Year's Best SF 13*. John's nonfiction has appeared in *Analog* and *Artemis* magazines as well as BenBella books on *Charmed, Star Wars,* and *Superman*, and in the *Legion of Superheroes* anthology *Teenagers from the Future*.

John had the opportunity to live on Midway Island for a while during the 1960s, graduated from high school in Lyons, Kansas, then later attended the US Naval Academy. He served in a variety of jobs including gunnery officer and navigator on a destroyer, with an amphibious squadron, and at the Navy's anti-terrorism centre. After retiring from the US Navy and settling in Maryland, John began writing. He lives with his long-suffering wife (the incomparable S) and three great kids. His daughter and two sons are diagnosed on the autistic spectrum.

BURDEN OF PROOF
JACK CAMPBELL
(writing as John G. Hemry)

THE SECOND VOLUME IN THE ABSORBING
JAG IN SPACE SERIES

After a suspicious explosion onboard the USS *Michaelson* costs an officer his life, Paul Sinclair risks everything to expose a cover-up—and prosecute the son of a powerful vice-admiral.

"First-rate military SF. Another absorbing novel. Hemry's series continues to offer outstanding suspense, realism and characterization, and this book, no less than its predecessor, only ratchets up readers' appetites for more."
BOOKLIST

"*Burden of Proof*, like each of Hemry's books to date, is a must for any military SF fan."
SF SITE

"An engrossing, addictive reading experience."
RAMBLES

TITANBOOKS.COM

AGAINST ALL ENEMIES
JACK CAMPBELL
(writing as John G. Hemry)

THE GRIPPING FINAL CASE FOR LIEUTENANT PAUL SINCLAIR

Someone onboard the USS *Michaelson* is selling secrets, and to uncover the traitor, legal officer Lieutenant Paul Sinclair must walk the dangerous line between duty and honor.

"Hemry's real-world experience gives the investigation and subsequent courtroom scenes a convincing feel. If you crave a legalistic space-*Hornblower*, you'll enjoy this one and you'll look forward to what he gets into next."
ANALOG

"Hemry concludes an exceptionally thoughtful and intelligent series on a strong note."
SF REVIEWS

TITANBOOKS.COM

THE STARK'S WAR SERIES
JACK CAMPBELL
(writing as John G. Hemry)

STARK'S WAR
STARK'S COMMAND
STARK'S CRUSADE

The USA reigns over Earth as the last surviving superpower. To build a society free of American influence, foreign countries have inhabited the moon. Now the US military have been ordered to wrest control of the moon.

Sergeant Ethan Stark must train his squadron to fight a desperate enemy in an airless atmosphere at one-sixth of normal gravity. Ensuring his team's survival means choosing which orders to obey and which to ignore…

"Gripping. Sergeant Stark is an unforgettable character. *Stark's War* reads as if Hemry has been there."
JACK MCDEVITT

"When it comes to combat, Hemry delivers."
WILLIAM C. DIETZ

TITANBOOKS.COM